READER REVIEW

Compelling!

> *"I was tied to the book. I could not put it down. A great read. Would make a great movie."*

Incredible talent!

> *"Fatal Absolution is a novel that invites us to look at human imperfections that so often render our lives tragically damaged and yet somehow renewed by faith. Overlapping the lives of a compelling cast of characters, Paul Mast's incredible talent for capturing real human interaction in a suspenseful, tightly woven plot will keep the reader engaged from beginning to end, and then have them begging for more! This is a novel that will hold you by the throat and make you stare down what may be the most primal sorrow in the human repertoire."*

Gift of storytelling!

> *Sharing his gift of storytelling Fr. Paul Mast has not shied away from the sad and shameful tragedy of the clergy sex abuse crisis now haunting the Catholic Church. Instead he has offered up a storied sacrifice where, yes – sin abounds, but grace and beauty abound all the more. And throughout it all he reminds us that true redemption is possible only when the lust for power and prestige finally succumbs and surrenders to the humble demands of faithfulness and love.*

> *Fr. Patrick Bergquist, author of "The Long Dark Winter's Night: Reflections of a Priest in a Time of Pain and Privilege (Liturgical Press). Recipient of the 2012 Voices of the Faithful "Priest of Intergrity Award."*

∾ Acknowledgments ∾

A n author rarely has a short list of people to thank for helping to bring a novel to birth. During the writing of this work of fiction, the birthing circle widened as the following people relieved some of the birth pains with their ideas, inspiration and professional help.

First, Brighton Publishing believed in this story by offering me a contract. Their editorial staff sharpened the plot and polished the characters with their expert eyes and professional editing.

Second, as trusted readers, Jennifer Krisp, Sister Catherine Higley, OSB and Virginia Brust provided constructive input that helped nuance details in the plot which I missed.

Third, my friends Diane Dee and Marlene Rosenberg, both of New York City, were generous in serving as my fashion experts so that all the characters were wearing the right clothes. I enjoyed window shopping with them along Fifth Avenue for people who only existed in my imagination.

Fourth, Warren Hensley, a friend and former private detective, made bearable the pains of getting the right guns in the hands of the right characters. And I am glad he did that without asking me to fire them.

Fifth, Tom Higley, a friend and licensed architect, offered valuable input in describing pictures of unique buildings and homes so as to make them appear authentic.

Sixth, Rob Pacheco, a good friend and gourmet chef, created menus and drinks so that the characters were dining on the right food and beverage for the proper occasion.

Seventh, my friends Tom and Donna Gaffney offered me a quiet space in their Florida home while the novel was being conceived and I was experiencing beginner's sickness writing the first few chapters.

Eighth, Alex Marthaler, a friend and aspiring composer, gave the lyrics to "You're the One," the kind of heartbeat that suspends a song into a tender humming long after the music ends.

Ninth, to the many victims of the clergy sex abuse scandal – far too many – I still reverence your stories and I hope my novel inspires you to find your voice for becoming a survivor, and to use it to promote healing.

Finally, to you the reader, clergy sex abuse is not a pleasant subject to write about even as fiction. Never catalogue it as a sad chapter in our church's history. Rather, include it as one of many issues in our pro-life ethic. May this story empower you to speak out collectively on behalf of all victims, for when we do then like the prophets of old we use our voices to enhance the quality of life in this time of our testament and witness.

Chapter One

Rock Creek Park—Washington, D.C.

October 30, 1990

When alive, you're a person; when dead, you're a corpse. Because of that, she couldn't speak her name.

What was known about the victim would now fit on a 3x5 index card attached to one of her big toes. Until her body was claimed, she would be known as the 395th homicide victim in the District of Columbia that year—not exactly a statistic people live for. Without identification, she was now Jane Doe, a name that fits every woman whose life ends being a victim of a murderer's violent rage.

They found her lying face down in a heap of wet autumn leaves in Washington's most fashionable jogging park. The presence of her corpse was as unusual in Rock Creek Park as a registered Democrat voting for a Republican in this city.

While the chief medical examiner studied her body to determine the cause and time of death, two crime scene investigators combed and mapped the area for evidence with the eyes of two hawks searching for prey. They were lucky enough to find the remnants of a cigar, which they carefully bagged and labeled.

Dr. Julianna Sabine, the medical examiner who advanced her theories about homicide victims by talking to corpses, said, "You look poor and Spanish my dear. What are you doing in Rock Creek Park?"

Translated, that meant the corpse didn't belong there. She was out of place, like a reformed alcoholic at a party with an open bar.

The victim's plain, Hispanic features and common dress bespoke her status as a domestic worker. These clues alone indicated that someone had probably lured her to this high-end real-estate section of Rock Creek Park. She may have lived in the area, but as a domestic worker, not a homeowner.

"Liver temperature makes the estimated time of death about eight hours ago," ME Sabine reported to Homicide Detective Joe

1

Sanders. "That would put her murder about ten p.m. A jogger discovered the body at six this morning.

"Her neck was broken. There are 206 bones in the human body, and just one important broken bone ended her life." Handling the body with a feminine tenderness, she added, "And these ligatures indicate her neck was twisted. There are no signs of strangulation."

Then, softening her tone, Dr. Sabine said, "I'm sorry, my dear, that your life had to end this tragically."

She never spoke coldly about—or to—the dead. Dr. Sabine was a typical forensic pathologist; she had a gentle way with murder victims. She believed they were still human, even if they were cold. But there was nothing cold about the way she interacted with the dead. She talked to them before autopsies, and she asked them to give her clues that would help find their killers. More often than not, the corpse revealed valuable evidence that was instrumental in tracking down a killer and bringing him to justice, giving the deceased final peace.

Practicing her trademark sensitivity paid off with this victim— Dr. Sabine hit a home run. Jane Doe told her three important things: first, her name, Elena Garza, was printed on a name tag sewn into the neckline of her blouse; second, she was six weeks pregnant; third, the words "Vatican Nunciature" were stamped on her right hand. Dr. Sabine found this third clue only with the help of infrared imaging. The pregnancy was a giveaway; Dr. Sabine always concluded that a victim in the first trimester meant an unexpected child, which pointed to a father who had other expectations as a murder suspect.

Dr. Sabine relayed this information to veteran D.C. detective Sanders and his partner, Al Mulchahy. They decided the best way to get answers was to visit the Nunciature, which was located on D.C.'s famed Embassy Row. Both detectives were devout, practicing Catholics, but neither had ever been inside the hallowed grounds of the little Vatican City. Whenever they passed the neo-Renaissance structure on Massachusetts Avenue, they always referred to it as a "prime piece of real estate where evil spirits no doubt wrestled with holy spirits." They weren't referring to the liquor cabinets.

The Vatican Nunciature—Washington, D.C.

They were greeted at the door by a nun who looked like a saint. She had a smile that looked like it had been carved by Michelangelo and a glow that must have been powered by an inner Duracell battery. The only thing missing from her saintly visage was a halo. Her cherubic presence could have lit up the Sistine Chapel.

"Sister, I'm Detective Sanders, and this is Detective Al Mulchahy. We have an appointment with Monsignor Albertini."

"Please come in. The Monsignor is expecting you," she said in a voice that sounded like Italian silk. She introduced herself as Sister Angelica.

As she escorted them down a short corridor lined with paintings and portraits of former popes and ambassadors, the detectives thought that if there were any ghosts or demons living there, they would surely be scared away by the morose faces in the paintings. Each wore an expression like those of the couple in the painting *American Gothic.*

The sister led them to a parlor the size of Detective Mulchahy's entire apartment. The only things missing were a TV, empty beer cans, and piles of dirty laundry and dishes.

Shortly after they were seated, Sister Angelica returned with a tray of coffee and cookies. On her heels was a figure that cast a long shadow. Monsignor Paolo Albertini, looking urbane and diplomatic, entered and cordially introduced himself. As that protocol was playing out, Sister Angelica exited the parlor as quietly as she'd entered.

Detective Sanders cleared his throat before saying, "Monsignor, we're here on official business. Do you know Elena Garza?"

Without missing a beat, the Monsignor responded, "Yes." There was a noticeable pause, as if Sanders were expecting a question or further comment, but the veteran clerical diplomat had answered the question diplomatically.

Like Sergeant Joe Friday of *Dragnet,* the Monsignor was a consummate practitioner of "just the facts"—he offered no commentary or words beyond a simple answer to a simple question.

"How do you know her?" Sanders decided to change his style of questions.

3

"She is a domestic worker here. Is she in some sort of trouble?"

"I'm sorry to tell you that she was found murdered in Rock Creek Park earlier this morning."

Controlling his calm demeanor and unflappable voice, Monsignor Albertini replied, "Then I take it by 'official business,' you mean your visit is part of a murder investigation."

"Yes," Sanders shot back with no further comment, thinking that *two could play the diplomacy game.*

"How may I be of help?" the Monsignor asked in tone that implied he was schooled in asking the right questions at awkward moments like this.

"Any information you can share would be helpful in solving her murder."

"If you'll excuse me for a moment, I'll retrieve her personnel file."

When Monsignor Albertini returned, he shared valuable information that would help the investigation, most notably family contacts in D.C. and Mexico.

Before their departure, Msgr. Albertini asked, "How did you know Elena worked here?"

Sanders officiously intoned, "That's information we can't disclose at this time." The detectives rose from their seats to leave. The Monsignor diplomat-priest escorted them to the door, frustrated that he did not get an answer, but pleased that he did not reveal that emotion to them.

Eventually, after several months, the trail went cold and the case went into the catacombs of police headquarters, relegated to a shelf that held the files of hundreds of other cold cases. By then, Elena Garza was no longer in the headlines or anyone's memory—except that of her killer. Even the killer did not know how the police had connected her murder to the Vatican Embassy and other evidence they had, if and when the killer was captured.

Holy Cross Cathedral—Boston, Massachusetts

June 27, 2006

"Bless me, Father, for I have sinned." Nora Owens had spoken that line so often in her life that the words were now without meaning. She said it as if she were on cruise control.

"Well, I haven't got all day," the priest said, agitated. Father Michael Mulgrew had turned into a grumpy old man for being only fifty-eight years of age.

Nora responded with her own brand of sarcasm. "That's right, Father, you don't."

"And what's that supposed to mean?" the priest said in a tone that turned the sanctity of the confessional box into the coldness of a refrigerator.

"It means I'd better get on with my confession." Retrieving her emotions with the skill of a psychotherapist, Nora slowed her breathing so it was in sync with her focus. "I am going to commit murder once today," she said with the calmness of a 911 operator.

"Is that a joke?" Father Mulgrew asked condescendingly.

"If it is, Father, the joke's on you." Before the priest could take another breath, Nora removed a handgun with a silencer from her handbag and smiled to herself as she placed it to the screen and fired. Mulgrew was dead faster than he could blink his eyes. Her kill zone shot was accurate.

"Your penance, Father, for molesting me and my sister thirty years ago is to spend your eternity burning in hell." She added cynically, "And may God absolve you, because I won't." Then she whispered vengefully, "You were right, Father. You didn't have all day."

She calmly placed a business card on the confessional ledge, adjusted the mantilla on her head to camouflage her face, opened the confessional door, and exited the giant, neo-Gothic cathedral as anonymously as she'd entered it. She walked briskly and confidently down Union Park Street, chanting to herself, "Nan, that's one down and three to go. Happy birthday!"

Nora Owens

I'm not who you think I am. Is anybody?

On the outside, I'm like most people; I put on makeup to hide a dark side, I wear fake smiles, I engage in mindless conversation peppered with platitudes. I'm easily bored to death with the empty conventions of the plastic lives expected of most people. I pretend to be nice even when it irks the crap out of me. I speak scripted lines to say what people want to hear. I play the game of life by the rules set by others, even though I consider them screwed up. Some call this normal; I call it part of the recipe for plotting revenge.

It's the game of life I play to take back lives stolen by others, particularly Irish priests who used me and my sister Nanette as sex toys in their youth. I write the rules of this game. Some live by them; others die by them. They're the ones who would call me a sweet, pleasant Irish girl. That's because underneath the eye shadow, make-up, and facial cream lurks a women fueled by contempt. It's the deception I use to lure my enemy. Without it, they'd know I'm a terrorist. Not the kind that blows up buildings and airplanes; I put sex-abusing priests out of their misery. It's a program I call "no priest-pedophile left behind."

On the inside I'm scarred from years of harboring grudges. During sleepless nights, I wrestle with demons; most of the time, they win. My mind replays, in my dreams, being sexually violated by evil men in Roman collars when I was a young girl, as well as having to watch my twin being raped and abused by a drunken, angry priest. It was the prelude to her suicide, and it is now the first of four movements in the requiem mass I'm composing as a killer of clergy child abusers.

These memories have turned me into a unique brand of terrorist. Rapists and pedophiles masquerading as priests are my enemies. I live to kill them. God forgive me for exacting the justice the justice system won't. It gives me an emotional high like nothing else does. Some people drink a gin and tonic to get intoxicated; for me, killing is tonic without the gin. I let the voices in my head that tell me, "*You go, girl*," live there rent-free. After all, I feel destined to rid the world of child sexual abusers. Like Anne Boleyn, I am the engine of my own destiny.

I never thought I would live this kind of life. I never harbored thoughts of becoming a wannabe bad girl like Emma Bovary; in my worst periods of denial, I dreamed of being an icon of female sexuality

6

like Anna Karenina. But those dreams for something more fulfilling collided with reality in 1956. That was the year I was born. Like good wine, it should have been a good year to be born, unless you were from Ireland and your Catholic mother was pregnant and unmarried. Then you were hidden away in Catholic institutions where shame, degradation, humiliation, and scorn were daily staples, like bread and potatoes.

It was a miserable existence. Life as a bitch-child in twentieth-century Ireland was as unpleasant as lives of slum children in a nineteenth-century Dickens novel. Angry women hiding behind nuns' habits inflicted their anger on us. No wonder my habits never improved with age.

In Holy Comforter Orphanage in Centre City Dublin, I schooled myself in temper management, social graces, and patience. I conflated the latter three and abbreviated them as BYT—"bite your tongue." I needed them for survival; I also needed them for my life as a homicidal stalker, which is what I became after nineteen years at Holy Comforter. That place was an emotional toxic-waste site before the age of environmental awareness. I learned enough painful lessons there to know that the rest of my life would not be wasted.

In the eighteen years I spent there, I was raped by four priests. My twin sister, Nanette, was raped by three priests before she took her life at fifteen. That was the crucible from which I emerged a woman with a dark destiny. One of those priests, Father Sean, was particularly sinister, a monster with a split personality. Another, Father Dennis, was a sexual terrorist long before "terrorism" became part of the vocabulary of life after the new millennium. He was what I called a double abuser—sexual and emotional. He made me feel like I was a gift from God only when he forced himself on me. I was determined to find him and give him the gift of a bullet.

It took me twenty-six years to hunt down the first priest. Thanks to the incompetence and arrogance of the Catholic Bishops of America, the revelation of the church's sex-abuse scandal was the event I needed to bring my living nightmare to closure. I followed the unfolding crisis on the Internet when I was 3,000 miles across the Atlantic. It began with a news story in *The Boston Globe* on January 6, 2002. Almost four months to the day after 9/11, a new form of emotional fury was about to rupture the Roman Catholic Church. It was daily headlines in the media.

Fueling my grudges became as regular as drinking tea and eating biscuits; my long awaited plan was about to unfold.

Thanks to a hawkish American press, the crisis was front-page news. It didn't take long for the name of Father Michael Mulgrew to pop up on a list of priests from Ireland granted protection from a plethora of accusations of sexual misconduct by the Archbishop of Boston, Cardinal Hugh Fellaney. The Archbishop's surname was almost fitting; for someone who conspired in hiding and abetting priest-child abusers, the joke in Boston was that they have a felon for an archbishop.

A Boston pastor who chose not to remain anonymous quoted the nineteenth-century British Prime Minister Benjamin Disraeli in an interview with the Globe, saying, "He was distinguished for ignorance; for he only had one idea, and that was wrong."

Thanks to this clown pretending to be an archbishop, Fr. Michael Mulgrew was exposed, and my countdown began. I knew something he didn't—the exact day of his death.

Holy Cross Cathedral—Boston, Massachusetts

The crime scene investigators were canvassing the church like minesweepers. The coroner had determined that Fr. Mulgrew had died about an hour before his body was discovered by a church maintenance worker. While one CSI gathered evidence from around the body, another focused on the business card left in the penitent side of the confessional. Typed on the card was the message, "Vengeance is mine, sayeth—guess who?"

Detective Tony Saluccio took it delicately in his latex-gloved hands.

"This is a hit," he said in his trademark Boston twang colored with Italian ghetto. "The murderer has a history with Fr. Mulgrew. It's time to dig into his past and see just what that reveals. We just might end up asking the real Fr. Mulgrew to stand up."

It took the assistant district attorney less than twenty-four hours to get a subpoena for Fr. Mulgrew's personnel file, and it took less than five minutes to decode it. Fr. Mulgrew was a priest child abuser with a trail that crossed the Atlantic from Belfast to Boston. God only knows how many people had a grudge against him, and only God knew which of them weren't able to distinguish between justice and murder. With the number and names of priest pedophiles being disclosed in the media every day, Saluccio tried to suppress the thought that a serial killer of priests was on the loose.

✍ Chapter Two ✍

Nora Owens

I arrived back in Dublin by way of London less than forty-eight hours after my first kill. Controlling the paper trail is a life-management skill I developed as a single, abused woman on a mission. My ability to kill and escape without leaving a trail is a testimony to my vision of feminine survival, namely, the best single woman is one who is not dominated.

I am not in the habit of calling any one place home. No one in the world would miss me if I disappeared. If I died prematurely, very few people would read my obituary, and fewer still would grace my funeral.

My industrial-cleaning business takes me to four different countries. Ireland is my homeland, but no one place is my home. Thanks to a lot of my life getting lost at Holy Comforter, I have a house but feel homeless. Before becoming a victim of sexual abuse, I had a twin sister, Nanette, whom I was fond of. In those days I had dreams of falling in love, marrying my prince, having children, raising a family, and living in an Irish manor house with rock fences for property lines. But those dreams were obliterated by dark days in a dungeon with a sexual terrorist and many dark nights of the soul.

I am a professional wanderer without the lust, establishing businesses that have made me rich but not necessarily happy. But I am also a restless wonderer, obsessing about the day when I can inflict my brand of justice on abusive, pseudo-celibate men who hide behind the lie of a Roman collar.

During my years at Holy Comforter, I became an expert in domestic work. I cleaned the homes and did the dirty laundry of wealthy Irish people with such finesse that, after graduating from the orphanage, I decided to make it my profession. Four years later, I added a "nanny service" to my curriculum vitae. While I have expanded my legitimate employment services beyond Ireland to England, Scotland, and Wales, I am nothing like the professional hit men in the movies.

My payroll includes over 150 people. I can afford a well-appointed four-room flat in London, a modest apartment on the Upper

East Side of Manhattan, a cottage for decompressing on the southwest coast of Wales, and a suite at the Hotel Corneille in the shadows of the Tuileries gardens in Paris. I travel first class, shop at Harrods, and am shuttled to airports in limos. I have season tickets to the London Symphony and vacation every winter at St. Lucia in the Caribbean. I speak three languages, have acquired a half-dozen fake passports, and can weave a lie with the best of deluders. Living on the edge between security and risk energizes me. God, the thrill of it all!

The way I lure people into my web is no different than the way priest-pedophiles lured children into dark dungeons to perform the most despicable sexual torture. On the surface, I'm a formidable antagonist, bristling with latent masculine toughness. On the inside, however, I'm the black widow to their piranha. The only difference is gender. My rush, my high, is letting them know that a vagina is just as deadly as a penis— that, and a .22 caliber bullet.

My expert marksmanship is the result of having been taught by a master. Lena Collins, a fellow inmate at Holy Comforter, opened her own shooting range after her liberation. I mastered her defensive shooting course in record time, which now enables me to rid the world of a few unwanted sexual predators. The murder of Fr. Michael Mulgrew shortens my list to three. Thanks to the Internet and the revelation of clergy sex scandals in the United States, spreading faster than a cyber-virus, my mission impossible is now becoming mission accomplished.

I'm sure some people think that resorting to murder to vindicate my own and my sister's sexual violation is romanticizing the quest for singular justice, from what could be construed as a bankrupt life. My answer is that ever since our lives were stolen by sexual abuse, my life has straddled reality and fantasy. Now it's time for the fantasy to become real. People who have never been violated by pedophiliac clergy live in protected worlds, like the figures that inhabit a Christmas tree snow globe. There is nothing fake about being chosen against your will to be a sexual receptacle for a sick priest.

And besides, where were those people and why were they silent when all this abuse was going on? They were no different than the townspeople in Germany who professed denial of the death camps in their back yards. Judging the victims now is no antidote for living in denial back then.

Are you getting a clear picture of the real Nora Owens? If not, you will as I draw you into the intensely layered world of my inner prison, I hope you stay a while and examine your own conscience about the immorality of clergy sexual abuse and the injustice of the church hierarchy's deafening silence and immoral conspiracy.

Fr. Brian Manley—Boston

Reading *the Boston Globe's* story of Fr. Michael Mulgrew's murder in the confessional at Holy Cross Cathedral was like having spinal anesthesia—I began to feel numb all over. As if that paralysis was not enough, a voice inside began to speak in a tone that released fear and worry, gripping my attention so that my anxiety level rose higher than my heart rate. Those emotions awakened me to a well-buried secret. Michael and I have a common history. Well, we had a common history. With his death, that history is history for him. As for me, I'm beginning to panic. There's a serial killer who may be on a mission to rewrite my history, too.

My first flashback was to Michael's first assignment in the Diocese of Dublin; he was chaplain at Holy Comforter Orphanage. His predecessor, Fr. Sean, ten years his senior, had mentored Michael in the art of getting as much sex as he wanted from any of the girls. Sean believed that celibacy was for monks and virgins who lived behind monastic walls, or eunuchs who hid their lies behind silk robes in the halls of the Vatican. But for the secular clergy, intercourse with the opposite sex was far more fulfilling than masturbating in a dark cell. And since the girls were freely available, why fight abstinence when you could use that energy to get high on pure pleasure?

Sean taught Michael, and he in turn taught me, never to reveal our last names to the girls we used. For that reason, we were only addressed by our first names at the orphanage. Could Michael's murder be the result of his full name being released in the press as someone with a history of sexual abuse in Dublin? Or did his Facebook page do him in? And how long will it be before my full name is released and the same murderer comes hunting for me as their next target?

I decided to be proactive; I shut down my Facebook page, took a temporary leave of absence from the Archdiocese of Boston, and went far enough away to get lost. Someplace like Long Island. I have connections there. And since it's a very long island, I may be able to hide there to prevent a premature end to my life.

Fr. Timothy Cavanagh

I was born a Monday's child—fair of face. And in my case, the adage is true. My jet-black hair, Emerald Isle green eyes, square jaw with a modest cleft, and smile that could light a wickless candle would open doors to any modeling agency. I'm the perfect alpha male, but I was not destined for the glossy cover of *GQ*, rather for the world of classical music. When I'm sometimes called old-fashioned, I take it as a compliment. I was raised to be polite and respectful and to live for faith and family and not cameras. I don't gloat on my sublime looks and air of geniality. In spite of my Hollywood green eyes, I am basically a non-heroic person. I don't buff up in a gym because I don't see myself as a sexual threat.

I was born into a kind of Kennedy-esqe nobility—the Cavanaghs of Stony Brook, New York, were a similar dynasty. My grandfather, Dermot Cavanagh, Jr., was from the rich Irish stock of Rosslare in County Wexford, Ireland. Gifted with a mind for business, he immigrated to the United States in 1935 and capitalized on new opportunities that presented themselves during the Great Depression. Within five years, he had a real estate license. Following the end of World War II, the rise of suburbs catapulted his real estate business like a NASA shuttle shooting into space.

In 1945, when he was thirty years old, he married Aishling Jane Stafford at St. James Cathedral in Brooklyn. The Gaelic meaning of her name is "dream," and he always referred to her affectionately as his dream girl. Though she was ten years his junior, they'd quickly fallen in love and had the common goal of establishing the most reputable and trustworthy real estate agency on Long Island. By 1950 they'd made their first million.

By 1960 their business had become an empire—without either of them turning into troubled tycoons. They survived the climb from middle to upper class by working hard, keeping faith, staying humble, and rewarding their employees. Their work ethic was this: if you want to succeed in any venture, first befriend the people who work on the bottom floor.

My father, Dermot Cavanagh III, was born in 1946, ensuring the continued growth of the Cavanagh fortune. In 1968, he married Clare Ann Woods. Two years later, my brother Dermot Cavanagh IV was born, a pledge that the legacy would continue. Six years later I was born—a bicentennial baby. Tradition was broken by naming me Timothy Dermot Cavanagh. My grandmother advocated the change saying the family needed to stop using Roman numerals since we were not Roman. Two years later, my sister Rose Ann was born. She was a deconstructed feminist by the time she learned to walk; by the time she turned sixteen, she'd become someone dark and sinister.

Our family pictures remind me of the Romanovs—elegant, formal, and distinctly royal, with men dressed in designer suits and ties and woman in sophisticated dresses. My grandmother always wore a hat, making her look like the Irish version of the Queen Mother. And like that estimable woman, she had a fetish for gloves. On many a shopping trip, I would joke with her by saying, "Granny, it's gloves at first sight!"

The family pictures that were framed and hung in our homes were mostly formal. The lighter side of family life—picnics, vacations, and pool parties—were catalogued in albums and video boxes.

Whenever we sat for portraits, my sister and I would call Granny "Lady Jane of Long Island." It would broaden her smile, which could release a form of Tinker Bell's twinkling pixie dust. Everybody caught it, and the family spirit was always captured in just one sitting. I was the envy of all my peers, being born into such a loving and blessed family.

Aishling Jane Cavanagh

I am the glue that keeps the family together. I'm the matriarch who plans every birthday party, every First Communion luncheon, every St. Paddy's Day brunch, and every Easter egg roll at the family estate. In public I am the consummate hostess; in private, I am a humanitarian without microphones or paparazzi. Instead of sitting on the boards of hospitals, universities, and museums, I volunteer weekly at a clinic and homeless shelter in Islip. When my grandchildren came of age, I taught them the value of volunteering by exposing them to this side of life.

When not volunteering, I correspond with every applicant to the Cavanagh Foundation. I also juggle entertaining North Shore's high society one day and serving dinner and washing dishes at St. Cornelius Parish the next day. I put on an apron to wash dishes at the church as easily as I wear a Donna Karan evening gown to attend the opening of the New York Philharmonic.

I oversee a staff of eight at Rosslare Park, the sprawling, eighty-acre estate my husband and I purchased over forty years ago and developed as a family legacy. We resisted the temptation to relocate to snobbish, gated communities elsewhere on Long Island; Rosslare Park and Stony Brook are synonymous as hearth and home for us. Our roots on the North Shore are deep, and our network of friends and neighbors sustains us. After taking ownership, we quickly deeded forty acres to Stony Brook for development as a nature park and walking trails. It was a testimony to our ecofriendly values long before the word "ecology" became part of the American consciousness. I am esteemed by my employees by deferring to their wish to address me as Lady Aishling. It sounds a bit Victorian, but if it pleases them, it pleases me.

Timothy Cavanagh

Thanks to Granny, the course of my life was determined when I received a spinet piano for my fifth birthday. In three years, I was mastering Mozart sonatas and Liszt études. For my tenth birthday, Granny gave me a William Knabe baby grand piano; for my fourteenth birthday, I auditioned for Juilliard. When I graduated in 1994, at eighteen, I embarked on what I hoped would be a career as a concert pianist. During the next two years, I played at the cathedrals of classical music—Covent Garden in London, LaScala in Milan, the Volksbühne in Berlin, the Sydney Opera House. It was like riding a rocket: critics were writing great reviews, and fans wanted as many encores as they could get. One month before I was to perform with the New York Philharmonic in Avery Fisher Hall, it all came to an abrupt end. On the night of October 25, 1999, my parents were tragically killed when their car struck a herd of deer just three miles from the family estate. They died instantly.

My grandparents went into mourning, my older brother numbed himself with real estate contracts, my sister turned to drugs, and I spiraled in and out of depression. An inner voice told me that my life was about to undergo a major overhaul, and I was too numb and sad to quiet it. A year after their deaths, I still missed them, like winter misses autumn, like Easter misses calla lilies, like children miss being hugged by parents. Their absence was an ache that would never go away.

My grandfather and older brother rebounded first and returned to work a week after the funeral Mass. I couldn't tell if it was a form of occupational therapy or emotional escapism. In three weeks, my sister had to be checked into detox, while Granny kept her grief behind a shield of fortitude. On the outside, she seemed strong and noble, but I suspected that, on the inside, she was screaming her anguish like a child who was mute. She kept her composure to keep us bonded with her special brand of nurturing.

I turned to spiritual direction as a form of conversion therapy. I was intensely angry with God; for one year, I punished him by not playing the piano. My heart needed redirection toward understanding and inner healing.

I took a sabbatical from mourning and traveled the world as a tourist, not a pianist. In the spring of 2001, I surprised myself and returned to the piano, and I went on tour again from 2001 to 2002. But this time something was missing, and it was more than my parents. My playing lacked its previous passion and charisma; critics said my hands no longer talked magically through the piano. What once were ten fingers and eighty-eight keys—no problem—had become a big problem! Something was tugging at my soul. After a long retreat with the Jesuits, I felt a call to the priesthood.

Somewhat to my surprise, the one who objected most was Granny. She had two strong arguments; she was not shy about sharing them with me in order of importance. First, her investment and support in my career as a classical pianist had been the equivalent of nurturing a vocation; second, the exposure of the clergy-sex abuse scandal had cast a disparaging light on the priesthood that wasn't going away any time soon. She thought my decision ill-timed and ill-chosen.

I stood my ground, entered the seminary in the fall of 2002, and was ordained a Catholic priest on June 1, 2006—one week after my thirtieth birthday—by Bishop John Campbell. Two weeks later, I celebrated my first funeral Mass for my eighty-six-year-old grandfather.

He suffered a massive stroke ten days after the ordination and died at home in his bed, which, according to Granny, is how the Irish do it.

Bishop Campbell presided while I celebrated the Mass; the attendance was overwhelming. During the homily, I alluded to granddad's aversion to politics with a line he often quoted by the British-born but all-American Bob Hope: "Normally I don't go for political jokes—too many of them are getting elected." There was muffled laughter from the predominately Long Island Republican pseudo-noblesse.

I ended the homily with a solo rendition of Antonín Dvořák's "Songs My Mother Taught Me" on the Steinway grand in the sanctuary of the Italian Renaissance cathedral. The composer would have been wowed by the prayerful echo in the vaulted ceiling of the massive structure. The lyrics were a fitting tribute to a great humanitarian, a respected businessman, a faithful Hibernian, a cherished husband, and an adoring grandfather.

Songs my mother taught me, In the days long vanished,

Seldom from her eyelids

Were the teardrops banished.

Now I teach my children, Each melodious measure.

Oft the tears are flowing, Oft they flow from my memory's treasure.

One haunting thought tugged at my heart as I played and sang with a weeping soul and tears filling my eyes. The Cavanaghs were catching up to the Kennedys in family deaths.

St. Sebastian Cathedral—Islip, NY

This cathedral would be Tim Cavanagh's first pastoral assignment. It was a good fit for a newly ordained priest who happened to be a concert pianist. The huge Roman Revival edifice with a capacity for 1,500 would become his concert hall. The large pediments over the entrances added nobility to the somewhat drab concrete exterior. Two massive bell towers gave the appearance of impregnable security, like an elevated battery offering protection to a dwarfed fort. The Roman arches inside give the feeling of an enclosed forum. The finishing touch was the decorative coffer system in the vaulted ceiling, hugged by six palladium stained glass windows. It was Long Island's version of the Pantheon.

As a newly ordained priest, Tim Cavanagh learned life-giving pastoral skills under the tutelage of the revered pastor, Msgr. Ambrose Quinn. Legendary for his gentle style and availability to all, he once dissuaded a vagrant brandishing a knife from robbing the poor box by insisting that he first attend daily Mass.

When the media asked to interview him, Msgr. Quinn demurred by saying, "The Sunday Breakfast Mission in Islip insists on people attending their service before getting a free lunch. In the spirit of Ecumenism, I insisted the robber attend Mass first before robbing the poor box." The miracle came later. After Mass, the robber repented, asked for forgiveness, and for his penance was given a full-time job. For the past ten years, Jim Hastings had served as the cathedral's gardener and handyman.

When the press asked him about the would-be robber's unexpected contrition, Msgr. Quinn, in a rare moment of self-flattery, responded in his lilting Irish brogue, "Ah, 'twas me accent, no doubt, that changed his heart."

Msgr. Quinn encouraged Tim Cavanagh to play the piano for liturgies, children's Masses, homilies, weddings, baptisms, and other events. He was shrewd enough to know that a priest who is also a concert pianist was an imaginative way to market priesthood as a both/and career, rather than an either/or.

During these years Tim Cavanagh wove a rhythm of piano and priesthood into what Msgr. Quinn called, "A tapestry for making both God and people happy," adding, "and to do that as a son of Ireland is a double blessing."

Those years were a prelude to Tim Cavanagh's being assigned chaplain to the Newman Center at the SUNY campus at Riverhead, on the east end of Long Island. This assignment was like a second movement in the symphony of his life as a priest; the only sorrow was that it was a short movement lasting less than a year.

In June 2009, Bishop Campbell appointed Fr. Tim Cavanagh his private secretary. His attempts to decline were rebuffed with a reminder, harnessed to a rough northern Irish exterior, about obedience. The bishop's life was about to become more high-profile, and there was silent speculation that more doors to the Cavanagh fortune would open for him and the diocese.

Timothy Cavanagh's life was about to become less his own, and a new form of grief enveloped him. Serious misgivings about the path on which he was about to walk gnawed at him. This third movement had all the leitmotifs of a Puccini tragic opera.

Moving out of his quarters at the Newman Center in the rustic, rural surroundings of Riverhead and relocating back into the noisy, stressful environs of Central Islip was Tim Cavanagh's own version of the exodus. He compromised with the bishop, who agreed that Tim could live in the cathedral rectory rather than the bishop's residence next door. This was the closest he came to the Promised Land.

At the chancery, his office was next to the bishop's, but that was the only commonality. The difference was as glaring as the West Wing of the White House was from your standard telephone booth in Times Square. Tim had barely enough room to maneuver within dimensions resembling a toilet stall. The private elevator from the parking lot to the fifth-floor offices was about the same size as his office, though the elevator's wood grain paneling gave it the appearance of being a cut above his space.

Bishop Campbell had already had the chancery staff arrange Tim's personal pictures and academic degrees on the walls. This was Tim's introduction to working for a control freak. If he dared to move one thing, the bishop would comment with his special brand of northern Irish cynicism, in which he was as fluent as he was in Gaelic. On his first morning, before Tim could ask himself what he'd gotten into, His Excellency interrupted his uncharitable reverie.

"It's eight a.m., and time to get to work," Bishop Campbell said in a tone one would use when commanding a dog. "Msgr. Barnes, Fr. Cavanagh, we need to meet about the mail. Bring a yellow pad and pen with you into my office."

He said it in such an officious tone that Tim wanted to straighten his shoulders, click his heels, extend his arm, and yell, "Heil Hitler!" It

19

made him wonder if the top floor of the chancery office was the front for a new version of the Gestapo.

The mail was neatly ribboned on Tim's desk by the curial secretary, Leona Helmond. A no-nonsense twenty-two year veteran of the curial offices, she protected the fifth-floor turf—and its secrets. As the bishop's 6 foot 3 inch figure exited the doorway, Tim thought, *It's nice to see you, too. And thanks for cheering me up.*

❦ Chapter Three ❧

Theodore Barnes, the diocesan chancellor, was a highly respected priest gifted with a quick mind, subtle humor, and a disposition that could temper a hornet. Under his charming persona, however, was a consummate canonical lawyer with a fierce loyalty to "the Boss"—although Tim wasn't sure that was a term of endearment. It was only the first day on the job, and Tim didn't find the boss endearing.

The morning mail, as the bishop called it, was depressing, bordering on dysfunctional. Correspondence from the United States Bishops Conference, some of which sounded like it was from the Middle Ages. Mail from local bishops about regional matters and mail from wealthy benefactors about bequests. But the majority of it was hate mail about priests.

Tim began reading some of it aloud to the bishop. It began to resemble a litany of sorrows.

June 27, 2009

Dear Bishop Campbell,

Our pastor, Fr. Neal Rowes, needs some mentoring in how to endear himself to parishioners. Hardly a weekend goes by when he doesn't scold people who arrive late for Mass. But, when he is late for eight a.m. Mass himself three out of four weekends, God forbid that anyone should scold him. He is utterly clueless about the saying, "What goes around comes around." As a psychologist, I am qualified to say that good people skills are a necessary art in medicine today. I know doctors are often asked, "Why do doctors call what they do 'practice'?" Well, bedside manner and medicine go together, like respect for people and pastoring. At St. Irenaeus, the pastor needs help with people skills. This assessment is based on my observations from the pew. I would recommend a professional intervention before the parish closes for lack of people who can no longer tolerate his self-centered behavior and immature outbursts.

Sincerely,

Dr. Richard Williams

There was a noticeable pregnant pause before Bishop Campbell instructed Timothy to place the letter in Fr. Rowes's personnel file. In a controlled voice, Tim asked, "Do you wish me to draft a response to Dr. Williams for your signature?"

The bishop replied with no control in his voice, "I am not going to dignify that letter with a reply; to do so would be giving Dr. Williams cause to practice his brand of psychotherapy on me. Next letter."

Their eyes locked momentarily, the bishop's burning into Tim's like a laser beam. It was the closest he had come to a John Wayne stare without the television. Tim wondered if the gruff bishop saw the sorrow in his eyes as much as he saw contempt in the bishop's eyes. He moved on to the next letter, hoping to avoid becoming infected by the bishop's spiritual blindness.

Dear Bishop Campbell,

I don't mean to tattle on priests, but Father Miguel Santos at St. Constance Parish needs some help with hygiene. His long hair has resulted in bangs, which he pushes aside about fifty times before giving Holy Communion. People have complained that he pushes his hair back as they wait in line for the Eucharist. It might be more helpful if you say something to him. He is a good, holy priest, and I don't like it when people complain about this behavior of his.

Mrs. Winifred Dolan

The first words of the bishop were beginning to sound like a broken record. "Place the letter in Fr. Santos's file."

The next letter complained about a priest saying Mass in tennis sneakers, and then taking them off and using them as the focus of his homily. Another complained about the pastor drinking too much at a wedding reception and making a pass at the mother of the bride; the next reported a priest using his homily to market a Caribbean cruise without ever mentioning the scriptural lessons for people's hungry souls.

As Tim read these letters of complaint, he wondered if there were any such letters in his file. That thought was quickly dismissed by an inner voice that said, "Fool, you wouldn't be sitting in this inner circle if people complained about you."

Then something alarming happened that threw Tim off track like a derailed train. He began reading aloud a letter that released a toxic cloud in the office and changed the timbre of his voice like a truck shifting into low gear.

June 28, 2009

Dear Bishop Campbell,

Our 13-year-old son, Jason, told me and my wife that he was sexually abused by the pastor, Fr. Terry Engals, during a Confirmation retreat last weekend at the Holy Child retreat center. It was during an interview which he did with each student. He told Jason that boys had to be circumcised for Confirmation so he asked him to show his penis. Jason thought that was strange, but did as the pastor asked. Then he began performing oral sex with him. Jason wrestled with him to stop him, but the pastor's physical frame and weight overpowered his resistance. He endured this despicable horror until he ejaculated into the pastor's mouth. We believe his account of this story and now you need to believe that our son is traumatized by this ungodly episode and we are mad as hell. My wife and I demand an immediate meeting with you to discuss this matter. If I don't hear from you by this week, I will take legal action against you and the pastor.

Outraged Catholic parents,

Dr. Ben & Joan Lyne

There was a profoundly silent moment before the bishop grabbed the letter from his secretary's hands faster than a diving hawk could catch its prey.

"I'll attend to this!" Campbell said in a commanding tone.

"Do you want Fr. Tim to make an appointment for Fr. Engals to see you today?" Msgr. Barnes asked straightforwardly.

Thank God he spoke; Tim was anesthetized like a tooth drugged with Novocain.

"The policy is that Msgr. McInnes, the Vicar General, attends to these special matters," the bishop barked.

After recovering, Tim asked, "Does that include some outreach and care for the family and the scarred teenage boy?" He felt a courage that he didn't know he had.

23

The bishop replied with jackhammer speed, "Since this is your first day on the job, allow me to clarify some boundaries. As my secretary, you make appointments and give advice when I ask for it; second, you answer questions, you don't ask them; and finally, you must learn that in this office we are in the business of protecting the church from scandal, not investigating accusations or babysitting angry adults. Are we clear?"

"Crystal," Tim said in a serious tone of voice.

Bishop Campbell instructed Msgr. Barnes to familiarize Tim with the confidential procedures for advising Msgr. McInnes about letters of this nature. In a final rebuke, he asked Msgr. Barnes to make an appointment for Fr. Engals to see the Vicar General later that day, and instructed him to orient Tim to the workings of the inner circle of their three offices. Timothy took that to mean memorizing some book of the bishop's rules about how chancery office games are played and secrets protected.

After they exited the bishop's office, Msgr. Barnes displayed his trademark diplomacy and deferred to Tim about alerting the Vicar General to make the appointment with the pastor. Tim then returned to his office in a mood similar to a lead character in a Wagnerian opera—heavy, dark, and brooding. Conflict had just been introduced into his life, but he'd play this game the same way he played Wagner on the piano: with focus and with heart. As he sat at his desk pondering what had just happened, the musician in him thought it was beginning to resemble a symphony of bad news. And, as a former concert pianist, if he didn't like the direction the music took, he'd write the final movement himself—or at least a long coda.

24

ᏝᏀ Chapter Four ᏀᏝ

Bishop John Campbell

hese letters are ready for your signature," Leona Helmond
said in a professional voice.

"Just leave them and I'll sign them when I'm ready," Bishop
Campbell retorted moodily.

She stood her ground, saying, "Don't use that tone of voice with
me. I've been here longer than you and deserve more respect than that."

"Okay. Leave them and I'll sign them when I'm ready. Thank
you." That was the best he could do at civility; she knew it and left
abruptly.

John Campbell had turned into a grumpy old man, and everyone
knew it. He was hungry for power—a hunger so sustained that it had
turned into an addiction. For him, power was a form of wanderlust. He
learned about it growing up in the Catholic ghetto of Falls Road in
Belfast. When you were in the minority in a city where religious hatred
was a form of oxygen, you learned how to survive or die. He survived by
learning how to use a gun and master the art of psychic control. These
skills had come in handy when he left the depressing confines of the
ghetto to study at the university in Dublin.

Back then, a defiant John Campbell had walked along the banks
of the River Liffey in Dublin, promising God that he would not return to
Belfast without power and prestige.

Power came first; he welcomed it in the form of a degree in civil
law. Prestige followed when he began studying for the priesthood. After
his ordination in 1968 and a four-year assignment in the Diocese of
Dublin, he was sent off to Rome to study for a degree in canon law.
Power and prestige were then branded into him with an appointment to
the Vatican School for diplomats. He mastered the art of diplomacy
quickly.

His star began to rise in 1978 with an assignment as a secretary
to the Nuncio in Zambia. Three years later, he landed a brighter star at
the embassy in New Zealand; from there he went to the Nunciature in

England. Finally, in 1984, he climbed to the brightest star in the constellation of Vatican embassies—the United States.

He was chief canonist and counsel to Archbishop Domenico de Burgos, a no-nonsense Spaniard with an inquisitional style, who taught him everything he didn't know because he hadn't asked. It was like a course in field education indoors.

For de Burgos, diplomacy meant, "Evading the truth to protect Holy Mother Church"; it meant, "Dancing around issues until people's mindless questions tired them out."

In less than a year, John Campbell—civil lawyer, canon lawyer, and Vatican embassy counselor—was the first Belfast-born mercenary-priest-diplomat who turned that wisdom into an art form.

When the first chapter of the clergy sex abuse scandal erupted publicly in a southern diocese in 1984, Archbishop de Burgos asked Msgr. Campbell to take charge of damage control. The media soon learned how he could mask a lie as truth and placate them with enough bullshit to throw them off. He had fun throwing out filtered tidbits of truth, like masters throw treats to their dogs—and the media was dumb enough to swallow them.

His reward was a call to the episcopacy. On the tenth anniversary of his diplomatic assignment to D.C. and his fifty-fourth birthday, John Campbell was appointed a bishop. The regular vetting process was waived—no screening, no background check, no time-consuming and banal discussions at a regional bishops' meeting, no letters of recommendation that would be labeled confidential before being shredded. In a word, he was exempt from the ordinary headaches that shadow any other candidate who is not a secretary for a Vatican ambassador. Such prestige had its privileges.

He liked being called Your Excellency. Who but Bishop John Campbell would have thought that a Catholic Belfast street fighter could rise to such prominence in the church? Cardinal de Burgos, now head of the Congregation for the Causes of Saints at the Vatican, did the honors and ordained him. It was the greatest gift for his 54th birthday, certainly better than cake and ice cream.

For five years he served as auxiliary bishop to the Cardinal Archbishop of New York, which was his apprenticeship for an appointment as the third bishop of Islip, New York, only four months after the terrorist attacks on 9/11. His installation was celebrated on the feast day of St. Sebastian, in the cathedral of that name, on Jan 20, 2002. He had thirty-three years of an unimpeachable service to Holy Mother Church.

The motto on his coat of arms, "For the glory of Jesus Christ," was an undisputable message of how he would handle the sex abuse scandal that was about to erupt on a national scale. Since he had been there, done that, Campbell was prepared to take control of the situation in Islip with abandon and diligence. The unwritten motto on his conscience was, "Evade the truth to protect Holy Mother Church," and this one was far more important than the ceremonial one. Practicing it was the next step on the path to becoming a cardinal, with all the new power and prestige that came with that honor.

At fifty-nine, he'd acquired more bad habits than good, like sarcasm that would be as priceless as a family heirloom, a style for Irish cursing that would make members of the IRA look like saints, a supply of impatience that could fuel a hurricane, a thirst for Irish whiskey, and smoking too many imported cigars.

"Get Msgr. McInnes on the phone for me, please," he asked Leona Helmond with his trademark "all business, no pleasure" tone of voice. Less than sixty seconds later, his request was granted.

"Joe, we have a matter filed under S that needs attention," he said pointedly.

"I understand," the Vicar General McInnes replied without needing the meaning of the cryptic letter "S" decoded. It stood for scandal and, with the vicar general involved, it meant clergy sexual indiscretion with a minor that had the potential for scandal and ugly media attention written all over it. McInnes hung up immediately.

Once the call had been made, words were wasted; time was at a premium. Msgr. McInnes knew what he had to do. He called Msgr. Barnes on his cell phone to get the name of the pedophile priest and the family whose child had been sexually abused. By keeping the circle of contacts small, any adverse fallout could be contained, and the agenda was to keep the scandal from spreading to the media.

After he ended the call, Bishop Campbell smiled with relief. By delegating these matters to his vicar general, his hands would be clean if civil authorities got involved. He opened the Westminster humidor on his credenza, a birthday gift from Leona Helmond, and retrieved an Arturo Fuente Maduro cigar—Ernest Hemingway's brand. The bishop believed that feeding his habit was elevated to a level of distinction when held in common with a celebrity. Besides, he liked Hemingway's novels. They expressed much of his life: dark, brooding, and messy. And the Equisito brand was small enough for a quick smoke, which was all he had time for. He clumsily opened a window to ventilate his office, allowing a minimum of cigar scent to foul a smoke-free building.

Monsignor Joe McInnes

Joe McInnes was aware that some priests in the diocese referred to him as a general rather than a vicar, and "general" was not used as a term of endearment. Some priests would be quick-tempered about such an uncomplimentary description; McInnes endured it the way a soldier endured pain as the price for not revealing military secrets to the enemy.

The price the monsignor had paid for keeping secrets about the church's internal demons was making enemies of the priests who were the subjects of those secrets; they didn't relish being put in a stranglehold of obeisance by what he knew about them. McInnes comprised the entire clergy internal affairs department for the Diocese of Islip. The affairs he investigated mostly involved pedophile priests engaging in deviant sexual behavior, which bordered on criminal, with minors. Internally, his job was to keep everything well documented but well hidden. He guarded secrets like a CIA agent working undercover.

Wearing two hats—one as the pastor of St. Augustine Parish in wealthy, nouveau-riche Southampton, and the other as vicar general of the diocese—sometimes turned him into a modern-day Jekyll and Hyde. His Dr. Jekyll side was friendly, humble, pleasant, and a consummate giver who loved being needed and attending to everybody's needs except his own. His Hyde persona was aggressive, unpredictable, sinister, and ruthless in doing whatever had to be done to protect the church from scandal and covering up details that might fuel a leak to the media. The priest-pedophile scandal had unmasked a dark side of the priesthood.

28

McInnes was appointed the unofficial director of the unofficial office of covert affairs for the Diocese of Islip when it was drawn into it in 2002. Since then, he had spent half his time wearing the covert hat and cleaning up messes for Holy Mother Church. He picked up his phone.

"Monsignor McInnes calling for Fr. Engals."

Less than five seconds later, Terry Engals was on the line. "Joe, what a surprise to hear from you!"

"We need to talk—today. Meet me at the bishop's summer house at two p.m."

"I have an appointment at two p.m. Can we change the time?" Engals responded apologetically.

"The time is not negotiable; change your appointment. See you in three hours."

He hung up, leaving the timid pastor to sweat about the meeting. One of the few priests in his inner circle had informed McInnes that this form of torture was widely known among the diocesan priests as the V.G. virus, which left one in a state of emotional paralysis. For the Vicar General, it was just another way of feeding an inner demon.

Nora Owens

It's a good thing I'm computer literate. During a single week, I searched twelve U.S. dioceses via Google, beginning in the northeast. Then I got a hit. Under the Diocese of Islip, New York, I clicked on the clergy link and scanned the faces of priests. When I got to Fr. Dennis Flaherty, my eyes locked onto his. Victims can identify their rapists by the eyes; "By their eyes you shall know them." It is how their identity is frozen in your consciousness. Their eyes convey control, torture, domination.

The picture was digital and the imaging was unclear, so I took a chance on Facebook. In a nanosecond, I was looking at a clearer picture of one of my rapists staring me in the face.

His chiseled dimples and generous freckles were a dead giveaway, despite his attempt at camouflage using longer and curlier red hair. But it was the scar on his left cheek that made him a marked man. I put it there when I clawed at him with my fingernails the second time he raped me. That's when he became ugly and more violent.

He took me to a torture chamber in the basement and tied me to a pipe. After raping me until he could no longer sustain an erection, he put a candle in my vagina and threatened to light the wick if I didn't lick his wounded face, and then perform oral sex on him.

On that day, Fr. Dennis Flaherty the rapist became Fr. Dennis Flaherty the terrorist; he was the most physically abusive of the four priests. Although I capitulated to his sick, evil desires, little did he know that he was teaching me how I would one day terrorize him before I killed him. When it came to plotting revenge, I passed his course with flying colors.

Next I went to the Diocese of Islip webpage and found that Dennis Flaherty, the rapist hiding behind a Roman collar, was pastor at St. Bartholomew's Church in Mattituck, N.Y. I began planning a return trip to the United States, as well as how I would exact revenge. I began to imagine how he would handle the terrorism I'd inflict on him.

The Bishop's Summer House

Fr. Engals arrived fifteen minutes late for his appointment, unaware of what lay ahead. The summer house of the Bishop of Islip is a misnomer. Affectionately called Solitude, it was anything but. Gracing the northern crest of Flanders Bay, the three-story, well-proportioned house was really part of an estate. Located on six acres of prime real estate, it comprised eight bedrooms with private baths, a dining room table that seated twenty, a butler's pantry, a wine cellar, a parlor with a hidden Moller pipe organ as a centerpiece, a screened porch on the back, a tennis court, a swimming pool, a gazebo, and a four-car garage.

The summer house was a gift to Bishop Martin Muller, now deceased. The benefactor, Isidore Levine, was a wealthy jeweler from the East Side of New York City and a friend of the bishop. Following the death of his beloved wife, Levine had deeded the estate in perpetuity to the diocese; five years later, Bishop Muller had died prematurely of a massive stroke. When Levine heard that Muller's successor, Bishop John Campbell, had converted the mahogany-paneled library into a smoking room, he deeply regretted his decision.

The rare book collection gracing the shelves included signed first editions of many famous books, including the 1975 edition of Norman Rockwell's visual lore, *America*. The thought of these icons of literature and art coated by smoke and choked by Cuban cigar fumes made his Jewish blood boil. He was sure the illiterate Irish thug posing as a bishop had no idea of the value of the books surrounding him. His reading was probably limited to the comics in the New York Times.

Isidore Levine never visited again because John Campbell had as little time for Jews as he did for non–Irish Catholics.

The late Bishop Muller had spent his summers at Solitude entertaining neighbors, taking some rest and relaxation, and hosting ecumenical gatherings, which sharpened his intellectual and pastoral acumen with interfaith dialogues and theological reflections on current church issues. Conversely, Bishop Campbell wined and dined cardinals, Vatican bureaucrats, and any other persons of prestige who would open wider doors that would lead to a higher satisfaction of his lust for power.

Campbell had no time for his neighbors. In fact, if someone quoted to him the parable of the Good Samaritan and asked Campbell who his neighbor was, instead of answering with Luke 10:37, "The one who showed mercy," Campbell would say, "I don't have any neighbors by the name of Mercy!" That would be accurate, since he didn't have a drop of Good Samaritan blood.

Joe McInnes's blood pressure was beginning to rise when he heard the wall clock in the entrance sounding quarter past the hour. As the last chime echoed into silence, the doorbell rang. He welcomed Fr. Terry Engals with a scolding for his tardiness and escorted him into the cavernous parlor, adorned with modern summerhouse furniture and an eclectic display of memorabilia, most of it from the days of Bishop Muller.

The furniture was arranged in small circles of seating. The vicar general waited for the anxious pastor to unwittingly choose his chair of execution, sat opposite him, and then handed him a copy of the letter of accusation with instructions to read it carefully. He watched the priest's expression turn from uneasiness to horror as beads of sweat began forming on his forehead. His color changed from warmth to cold; from healthy to sick. There was a prolonged silence as Terry Engals recalibrated his breathing and stumbled for words.

"I don't know what to make of this," he stammered.

"It seems pretty clear to me," the vicar general countered sarcastically. "You're being accused of raping a teenage boy." Then with a sense of drama he added, "Again."

"What do you mean by that?"

"What kind of question is that? You know damn well what I mean. This is the third accusation against you," McInnes said with a touch of arrogance. Then he added, "And don't give me any crap about his word against yours. We both know what's in your personnel file. We covered your ass the last two times—paid off the accusers and reassigned you. But not this time, Terry. Considering the climate for priest sexual abusers today, your timing is disastrous."

Intimidated by the officiousness of the vicar general, Engals asked, "What must I do to make this right?"

Handing him an official document, the vicar general said, "You're going to sign this letter of resignation as pastor of St. Malachy's. As of today, you're suspended pending an investigation.

"When you return to the rectory, Fr. Tim Cavanagh will be there to oversee your packing and departure. He will drive you to LaGuardia to catch a plane to the Sacred Ground Therapy Center in the Blue Ridge Mountains for treatment. While you're there, you'd better pray we can negotiate with the victim's family. If we can't, you'll be canonically removed from the priesthood. And in case you don't follow where this is going, you will never return to the Diocese of Islip again. And be glad the bishop isn't turning this case over to the district attorney."

Delivered with jackhammer speed, uninterrupted, the vicar general finished his delivery by asking, "Is there any part of this you do not understand?" Then he condescendingly added, "Speak now, for they may be your last words to me."

Holding his head in his hands, Terry Engals, forty-nine years old, a priest of the diocese for twenty-four years and pastor of St.

Malachy's for six, wept bitterly. "I am so ashamed," he gasped between desperate sobs.

"You should have thought about that before you raped a thirteen-year-old boy," Msgr. McInnes said as a stinging rebuke. "And we're beyond shame now, so pull yourself together and face the consequences of your actions."

The uncompassionate vicar general then gave the wounded priest time to compose himself without words that would inflict further guilt, shame, and anger.

After a silence that seemed like eternity, McInnes picked up his cell phone and dialed. There was no need to identify the person being called, since the cryptic message said it all. "Fr. Engals and I have finished our business. He is on his way back to St. Malachy's. The matter is now in your hands." He then walked the shattered priest to the door, opened it, and said, "I hope you find some peace this time, Terry."

What the priest wanted was a handshake or a hug or a civil goodbye; what he got was a door closing quietly behind him. He sat in his car a long time, pondering his sins, as an inner cloud cast a dark shadow over his soul. As he drove away, he wondered how this inner storm would end. He only knew the dark voices inside were screaming leaving him in fear and panic.

McInnes walked into the kitchen and poured a glass of Merlot to calm himself, and then he wrote the details of his meeting with Terry Engals on a yellow pad. Five minutes later, his eyes were drawn to the expansive bay window overlooking the cove as he pondered how much he disliked this love/hate piece of serving as the cleanup man for the diocese. The nakedness of the autumn trees echoed his inner nakedness. But for the sake of protecting the church from scandal of dysfunctional priests, he would put on the mantle of chief diocesan police and clean up another mess. Like his boss, he was infected with the virus of power and prestige; once again, he denied that what he was really protecting was his own welfare and his unconverted sense of moral righteousness.

After enjoying the last drop of wine, he made his way to a circular staircase squeezed into the northwest edge of the kitchen. The stairs spiraled from the second floor to the basement in a twenty-first-century version of the nineteenth-century Upstairs, Downstairs back stairwell for the domestic help that worked at the house during the summer months.

He slowly descended to the bottom, where he flipped a switch, illuminating a long hallway with a vaulted brick ceiling that resembled a modern-day stone pizza kitchen. The echoes of his steps bounced off the walls as he proceeded to the wine cellar. He unlocked an access door connected to a security partition made of wrought iron, and then stepped into the room. He flipped another switch that revealed layers of wine bottles whose price tags would qualify them to be auctioned at Sotheby's. Some were dusty, indicating that the current occupant preferred Guinness to the products of the vineyards of Beaujolais and Pouilly-Fuissé. He reached up to the highest shelf and removed a bottle of Cuvee Dom Perignon Champagne, vintage 1992, worth at least $1,000. Behind it was a switch he pushed upward. A section of the wine casing swung inward, revealing itself as a camouflaged door. It pivoted on a track system, visible only from the inside room, embedded into the concrete floor.

He flipped another light switch illuminating a small, windowless room containing three metal filing cabinets, a desk with an overhead ceiling light, and a copier/fax machine. He made his way to one of the cabinets and retrieved Engals's file. He then reviewed what he already knew about the predator priest from formal documents containing pertinent information about the three accusations of child sexual abuse in twelve years—all substantiated. Engals had received no treatment; instead, he'd just been reassigned to other parishes where the abusive behavior continued unabated.

McInnes placed the copy of the letter of resignation, the letter of accusation from the parishioners at St. Malachy's, and the synopsis of their meeting in the front of the file, replaced it in the drawer, closed it, and switched off the light. He again flipped the switch and waited while the wine casing door shut, then he returned the Champagne bottle to its berth, locked the outer security door, and returned to the kitchen upstairs. He had just enough time to wash his hands and face before the doorbell rang.

ꙮ Chapter Five ꙮ

St. Malachy's Rectory—Islip

Fr. Timothy Cavanagh had been waiting about twenty minutes for Fr. Engals to arrive. The parish secretary had escorted him to the pastor's quarters on the second floor of the Tudor-style rectory. He couldn't help but notice the expensive decorations adorning the living room of the vast, three-room suite. Mementos from trips abroad were labeled like pieces in an art gallery. Against an inner wall was a glass case filled with genuine Waterford crystal from Ireland, and the furniture was impeccably appointed. The one thing missing was family pictures. The few that rested on Engals's desk and a small end table featured a smiling Fr. Engals with his arms around teenage boys.

As he scanned the room like someone doing a media shoot, Tim Cavanagh realized that the room revealed the split personality of the occupant. There was so much order and neatness with tangible things, but disorder and messiness with the intangible things of his inner life. After reading the letter of accusation, he felt only sadness about Engals's double life.

Engals had acquired some precious things, making Tim wonder how someone could do so on a salary of $2,670 a month. When Tim had inherited a portion of his parent's lucrative estate, he had given half to charity. With the other half, he had established a foundation for gifted teen musicians called Be-Sharp. Being humanitarian was more important to Tim than acquiring museum pieces. Standing in the middle of this mini-temple to art and treasure, he was humbled by the truth that, as the grandson of a multimillionaire, his life was Spartan compared to Terry Engals, whose life of Impressionist luxury made Tim's look like Amish plain style. Engals's objects of multicultural tourism spoke of wealthy possessions owned by a morally bankrupt man. Tim was reminded of the wisdom of St. Augustine: "Woe to you who cling to passing things. One day you will pass with them." His reverie stirred pity. Had Engals been able to engage in healthy relationships with adults, he could have been freed from the inner demons that enslaved him to pedophilia. Tim felt sad that Engals used celibacy to hide his sickness and rob young boys of their innocence, and that church leaders were in denial about connecting the dots between clerical celibacy and the loneliness that many priests could not reconcile—a loneliness that fueled their pathology of sexual abuse. His contemplation was broken when Terry Engals appeared in the room, silent as a phantom.

"I'm sorry if I kept you waiting, Tim," Engals said in a contrite voice, both soft and sullen. Though he was startled, Tim recovered quickly.

"You don't need to be sorry, Terry. Just tell me what I can do to help."

"Spoken just like a Cavanagh—gracious and caring. I needed to hear that."

"What else do you need to hear?" "I wish I'd heard some kind words from the vicar general," Engals said in a tone that implied he had been shamed and rebuked at the bishop's summer house.

"Whatever words were spoken between you and Msgr. McInnes should be deleted like a nasty email. They probably won't be helpful here. So, let me ask again. How can I help?"

Sitting on the edge of the sofa, Engals put his head in his hands, sighed deeply, and began to weep. Tim moved to sit next to him. He threw his arm around Engals and held him while the man sobbed. Timothy Cavanagh trusted his instincts to be the compassionate priest Engals needed, and he allowed him to weep for a long time. As Tim held him in an embrace of comfort, he imagined that the great Hungarian priest-pianist Franz Liszt must have composed Libesträume for a moment like this. Tim had played it often with ease and emotion, but he had never performed it thinking of a scenario like this. This time he was playing it in his mind and heart while holding a wounded and broken man in his arms. Terry Engals was no doubt mourning the end of a life's search for true love, only to look into his life as into a grave, lined with false love staring back at him. That love was pictures of people with no faces. The shock of a grave filled with emptiness and not hope reflected in the faces of people he loved only erotically, and who never loved him back, was surely horrifying.

When his tears abated, Engals pulled away as if embarrassed. Tim released him gently, the way his parents had released him as a child, after a long hug had worked its magic and loved away his pain.

Engals walked to his desk and wrote some instructions on a yellow pad. He said unsteadily, "I'm writing a few requests and notes for you, including the name of a parishioner who owns a storage business. I'm sure he'll allow you to have my things packed and stored there temporarily."

He then read each item aloud, pausing intermittently to ask Tim if he understood and would attend to these personal matters. They included contacting his sister in Ireland, a lawyer in the parish, and two priest friends in neighboring dioceses.

"I give you my word they will be taken care of," Tim said when Engals handed him the paper.

"Your word is as good as you are, Tim," Engals replied sincerely. Tim thought fleetingly of how his grandmother had bristled whenever fellow clergy addressed him in by that name. She preferred the formal "Timothy," stating that he was not named or baptized after St. Tim. The brotherhood of priests, however, does not include standing on formality; being just Tim lifted him from the ranks of being artistic and wealthy and made him one of the boys. Tim and Engals talked quietly then, initially about banal things and not the stuff of headline news. Just two guys chatting about life, the messes made from mistakes, and how to learn and grow from them. After a momentary pause, Engals asked if Tim would hear his confession.

"It would be my honor," Tim responded in a tone that conveyed gentleness and care.

He made the sign of the cross on Engals's forehead and invited him to see this desire for intimacy with God as the same source of God's desire for intimacy with him.

Engals took a deep breath and then began, not with the opening line of the ritual, but with the line from Luke 18:13, "God, be merciful to me a sinner." Like the publican in the gospel parable, he kept his eyes lowered while his heart seemed to beat with contrition.

"I have grievously sinned against you and your people by stealing the innocence of some youth through sexual abuse. I have dehumanized others by out-of-control lust."

Tim reverenced the sacred pauses as Engals calibrated his words with a penitent heart.

"I have mocked the priesthood by living a lie. I have shortened my own life and contaminated the lives of others by empowering false voices to turn me into a false person. I kept the real me hidden from others because I was afraid they would not like the real me. I am sorry for choosing fear over trust.

"Finally, I have wasted your gifts, O God, on hurting people in a way that satisfied my sexual pleasures. For choosing my demons over your grace, I am very, very sorry."

When Engals paused, Tim sensed that his heart needed to say more, and so he refrained from speaking.

"Please, O God, free me from this guilt and shame with your forgiveness. I no longer wish to carry this inner baggage."

"Terry," Tim said in tone that implied someone whose dignity was about to be restored, "forgiveness was yours the moment you desired it; the fullness of this sacrament is to celebrate that truth with a thankful heart. For your penance I want you to contemplate the image of the happy and contented father in the parable of the prodigal son, with arms wide open, welcoming you home to his embrace and his bosom. Hold that in your heart for as long as it takes for you to see a God who is happy that, by finding your way home, the two of you can fall in love with each other again."

Facing him with tear-filled eyes, Tim asked, "Can you do that, Terry? Can you focus that deeply on God as a forgiving parent?"

Engals nodded as confirmation. This was not a time for words, but silence as his heart clicked on a kind of inner Map Quest search for a God who wanted to free this broken priest of all the dark places in his soul that had blocked the light of hope and healing from getting in. Engals took a long, deep breath as Tim laid his hands on the penitent's head and spoke the words of absolution.

They sat in silence for several minutes before Engals said, "Thanks for being so caring. I should have done this a long time ago." Then he added, "How much time before we have to leave?"

"You have a seven-forty flight this evening from LaGuardia to Charlotte," Tim answered. "Someone will meet you there and drive you to Sacred Ground. We'll need to leave for the airport shortly."

"I'm glad to have ended my time here at St. Malachy's with you," Engals commented, sounding relieved. Then he said, "I'll meet you downstairs in about fifteen minutes."

Tim nodded and headed for the staircase. Taking a seat at the kitchen table, he amused himself by reading *The New York Times*. He smiled, remembering his grandfather's quip about the Times. He was fond of saying its secondary use was wrapping dead fish, but only after the primary use of reading the comics. As Tim read one section after another, he became aware that more than fifteen minutes had passed. He returned to the upstairs suite.

Not wanting to violate Engals's privacy, he softly called his name. When he didn't get a reply a second time, his endorphins signaled trouble and his heartbeat kicked up into panic mode. He walked through the bedroom, noticing a partially packed suitcase on the bed; the bathroom door was closed, but he could hear water running in the sink. He knocked gently and quietly called Engals's name again, this time asking, "Are you okay?" The absence of a reply was deafening. Tim leaned his head against the door, needing a moment to collect himself.

He closed his eyes and breathed deeply, inhaling the strength to push against the door. At first it only opened a quarter of the way, and he saw that Terry's legs spread-eagle on the floor, were blocking the entrance. He reached in to move them inside and then opened the door. What he saw sent him into shock. Terry Engals lay in a spreading pool of blood. He had cut his throat with a razor blade, which was lying next to his right arm.

Tim knew that Engals was dead by the amount of blood on the tile floor. He also knew that he was plummeting into despair as he slid down the wall to the floor and sobbed. Terry's position was awkward, with his neck resting on the step of the opened shower door. Both arms were extended in an open position, giving the impression that as a victim, the only thing missing was a cross. His eyes spoke forgiveness while Tim's heart screamed mercy. Tim's semi-fetal position on the cold bathroom floor did not keep him from crying for Engals's tortured death and his own anguished soul. He wanted to hold Engals again, but Tim was so frozen in his own space that his brain could not connect with his heart.

Tim Cavanagh never imagined himself ever being in this position. A thousand thoughts passed through his mind to explain the meaning of this shocking moment. He swayed back and forth like a baby being rocked in a cradle, his tears co-mingling with Terry's blood on the cold floor.

All of a sudden he had a deep desire to be held by his mother. She would know what to say and do to take away the grief that was paralyzing him.

The music library in his head opened up. The pianist in him clicked on Samuel Barber's *Adagio for Strings.* Knowing it by memory, he instinctively began to hum its sound and rhythm, one of the saddest classical pieces ever composed. Tim needed it to nurse his own deep sadness at the moment. It drew him to a place inside his head that freed him from lashing out at Engals for the despair that fueled his poor choice of timing and death. Closing his eyes, Tim imagined playing the mournful chords on the piano as a dedication to Terry. The inserting, expanding, and ascending melody of the Adagio restored some rhythm to Tim's wrecked interior life on a cold bathroom floor. Eventually his desolation gave way to consolation, and then action. He reached for his cell phone and dialed 911.

He'd been grieving Terry Engals for almost an hour. It was not a holy hour; it was time that awakened him to another dimension of this scandal—that victims are created when God is absent from decisions that affect sick humans who prey on others.

Many bishops, especially John Campbell, were not schooled in how to reverence and practice a piece of behavioral wisdom needed in this crisis, namely, "Emotions are everywhere; be gentle." Tim's own emotions at this point defied any desire to call the bishop, which would only inflame his anger. Because Msgr. Barnes was not a volatile Irishman like Campbell, Tim called him and, with some restored composure in his voice, shared the painful story. The call ended with Ted Barnes's assurance he would be there as soon as possible to support Tim.

The Bishop's Summer House

Joe McInnes got to the door after the second ring of the doorbell. The Lynes stood before him.

"Dr. and Mrs. Lyne, I am Msgr. McInnes, the vicar general of the diocese," he introduced himself officiously. "Please come in."

He waited for the husband and wife to choose their seats before choosing his own. They sat in a love seat near a window overlooking Flanders Bay and held hands as they got comfortable. McInnes chose a Queen Anne chair just opposite them that afforded him clear visual contact.

"I appreciate your meeting me here on such short notice." He was about to say more before Dr. Lyne interrupted.

"Let me be very clear, Monsignor. This is no ordinary house call for me. As a doctor, I tend the sick and do my best to make them well. But this meeting is about a sickness for which there is no prescription or antidote. Our son has been emotionally scarred by one of your priests. We're here to talk about what you and the diocese are going to do to aid Jason's healing, not how to protect Fr. Engals. Is there any part of that I need to clarify?"

The usually volatile Irish priest gave Dr. Lyne the benefit of the doubt that he held all the cards, and so contained his Irish temper that ordinarily would have exploded had this been a priest. It is not his Irish DNA to give people license to address him in such a condescending tone of voice. But because of the delicacy of the subject matter, he responded with a sense of decorum.

"What can I do to help your son?"

"You can do three things and do them quickly," Dr. Lyne responded. "First, you can assure my wife and me that Fr. Engals will be permanently removed as pastor of St. Malachy's so that nothing like this happens to any minor in the parish again.

"Second, you can arrange payment for our son to get therapeutic help.

"Third, the diocese can compensate us for this reprehensible emotional stress in the amount of $150,000. We will put half of that in a trust for Jason's education."

Dr. Lyne delivered his demands in the same jackhammer style McInnes had used on Terry Engals earlier; the tables had been turned. McInnes chose his words carefully, not wanting to ratchet Dr. Lyne's aggravation to a higher level.

"First, I can assure you, as we speak, that Fr. Engals has already been removed. Second, the diocese is prepared to pay all expenses for your son's counseling—"Before he could continue, Joan Lyne interrupted. "Our son has a name. It's Jason. Please afford him the dignity of referring to him by name. He's not just another victim on your list of youth abused by pedophile priests; he is a teenage boy who has been traumatized by this experience." She took a short pause and stared directly at him before continuing her scripted lines.

"Do you have any idea what life has been like for Jason since returning from the retreat? He can't eat, and he's losing weight rapidly. He hasn't been able to return to school because he can't focus on his studies. He no longer communicates with friends because he's ashamed. He's haunted by the thought that he might be gay and lives with the trauma that he may engage in abusive sexual behavior himself someday.

"Moreover, he no longer practices the flute or rehearses with the marching band. He doesn't smile or laugh or engage in family chats; he lives in his room like a prisoner, wondering when he'll be free to dream and feel safe again.

Mrs. Lyne took a deep breath before continuing. "He doesn't go to church anymore because it's been contaminated by a priest who betrayed his trust. In fact, he doesn't pray anymore because he thinks God is deaf and heartless. He lives as if he is the only fish in a fishbowl.

"This is not our son—lifeless, unfocused, feeling like a caged animal. This is a victim created by a monster masquerading as a priest. And if we find out Terry Engals has a list of other victims, you're looking at far more than a $150,000 settlement. My husband's expectations are non-negotiable. If you think otherwise, you do not understand how far parents will go to protect their children."

Listening to her razor-sharp words and watching the anger play over her face was like being stung by a hive of bees. It nearly triggered Joe McInnes's Irish temper, but he willed the monster inside to stay calm, took a measured breath of his own, and responded,

"I am prepared to assure you that your first two expectations can be met. As for the third, I will need to speak to Bishop Campbell. He will have the final say about any monetary settlement. Whatever it is, you will be required to sign an agreement, drafted by the diocesan attorney, keeping the terms of settlement confidential. That is for the purpose of protecting your son—excuse me, Jason—while he undergoes counseling. Is this clear?"

"We will not sign any agreement that may be legally binding without our attorney present," Dr. Lyne answered firmly. "Is this clear?"

His patience wearing thin, the vicar general chose to ignore that question. "The first thing for me to do is confer with Bishop Campbell. I will get back to you shortly and we can go from there." He stood as a cue that the meeting was over. Escorting them to the door, he opened it and bade them goodbye.

As Joan Lyne stepped out on the porch, she turned, planted one foot in the doorway, and asked sarcastically, "What do you think it means, Monsignor, that you never asked about Jason?"

Caught off guard by her question, he responded, "Please let him know that I am praying for him."

"Since he no longer prays, I doubt your prayers will comfort him," she said unapologetically. "This tragedy in our church doesn't need prayer; it needs leadership. Prayer is no excuse for inaction. On that issue we suffer a great impoverishment." With that she locked arms with her husband, and together they walked slowly down the steps to their car.

McInnes closed the front door delicately, betraying a desire to slam it. His final impression of Joan Lyne was diametrically opposed to his first impression: the quiet, genteel mother had turned into a shrew. *I will have to program myself to tolerate her,* he thought begrudgingly. Celibacy had its virtues, and one of them was not being married to a woman with the scornful temperament of Joan Lyne.

He returned to the kitchen, poured another glass of Merlot, and wondered how he would approach Bishop Campbell about the settlement figure. It was far outside the normal range of $10,000 to $15,000. Knowing him, he thought, he'll be transformed into Bishop Cauchon who, in the fifteenth century, ordered Joan of Arc to be burned at the stake. McInnes knew it would take all his pastoral skills to avert the bishop's rage. He needed prayer now more than Jason Lyne. God help him!

◦✐ Chapter Six ✐◦

St. Malachy's Rectory

The first to arrive on the scene were Detective Sergeant Sam Bannion and Detective Lou Perkins, both veterans of the Islip police force. Bannion interviewed the parish secretary, who was still in shock about the suicide. Perkins made his way upstairs to survey the crime scene; what he found left him speechless.

Father Tim Cavanagh sat curled in a semi-fetal position, leaning against the bathroom wall with one hand supporting his head and the other locked with the right hand of the deceased. Perkins did a quick visual sweep of the bathroom. Traces of blood were on Tim Cavanagh's sleeve, as well as the hand intertwined with the victim's. He wondered how long he'd been in this position. The door was still only half open, but he could tell Cavanagh was oblivious to his presence. He squatted down to make eye contact with him.

"Fr. Cavanagh, I'm Detective Perkins of the Islip police. I have to ask you to let go of Fr. Engals's hand and step out of the bathroom, please." The detective mustered as much sensitivity as a Flatbush native could. He was greeted with silence; it was like talking to a mannequin. He debated whether to touch the priest's shoulder. Thinking the shaken man might overreact and disturb the crime scene, Perkins decided to wait for his partner.

After about ten minutes, Bannion entered the bedroom suite with the forensic team from the police department. Perkins brought his partner up to speed, particularly about the apparent state of trauma that gripped the priest sitting on the floor.

"Is this Father Cavanagh related to the Cavanagh real estate family?" Bannion asked.

"One and the same," Perkins replied.

"Then we have to tread lightly here," Bannion remarked. "This is not only a potential first witness to a suicide, but the grandson of the benefactress of Suffolk County."

The two police officials stood looking at the bathroom, waiting for someone to break the silence and make a move. Bannion walked to the doorway, sat next to Tim, and waited for him to become aware of her presence. She watched his eyes blink between shock and reality. When he slowly tilted his head to face her, she spoke to him in a gentle, caring, feminine voice.

"Father Cavanagh, I'm Detective Sergeant Samantha Bannion from the Islip police. I'm going to help you let go of Fr. Engals's hand. We can take our time, but let's do it together."

Tim nodded and complied without resistance.

"Now I'm going to ask you to take several deep breaths," Bannion said. She waited for him to breathe as instructed. "Now stand up with me. When you feel up to it, step out into the bedroom."

When they'd exited the bathroom, the forensic team took over, and the detectives escorted Tim to the living room. Before they sat, Bannion asked Cavanagh to remove his jacket so it could be tagged and bagged as evidence, and he did so quickly. Then she began asking questions while her partner took notes. They did not allow their body language to reveal their shock and horror as they listened to his story. As he recounted the last two hours of Terry Engals's life, he became agitated that he hadn't connected the dots between the confession and what Terry had said about his last day at St. Malachy's.

Sam Bannion recorded her own mental notes about the suicide while hiding her distraction with this famous native son. His speech was polished, his gestures deliberate but not distracting.

His fingers were like trophies—ten digits like the ivory they touched on a piano. His emotions were unfiltered, revealing a man comfortable with being fragile and transparent. But his eyes were his most attractive feature. As they darted between the two detectives while answering her questions, they looked like green jade. He was thoroughbred Irish, distinctly handsome, with a caring demeanor and a noble carriage that was genuinely demurring. And he was a man totally oblivious to his celebrity status, his pedigree that would stir hot flashes in many women—and probably some men. She wondered if the labels inside his clothes said, "Made to fit great but humble men."

She'd always had a secret wish to meet the famous pianist-priest, but never imagined these circumstances. Nor did she think she'd find him so endearing, especially after the trauma of the day. Through it all, he never lost his dignity, no doubt attributable to his Cavanagh DNA. The Cavanaghs were not a family scorned; many lives of those in Suffolk County had been touched by the Cavanagh generosity—some publicly, most privately—but all were grateful. It was a testimony to their legacy that wealth and good fortune existed to help others hope. Sam Bannion's reverie broke when she realized that she must now help him find hope again.

Satisfied with his account of Fr. Engals's death, she said, "Fr. Cavanagh, you've been through an extraordinary ordeal today, and I want to thank for your cooperation. You've shown great resilience under the circumstances." Pausing, she added, "Is there someone we can call to come and get you? Or can I drive you somewhere?"

With his composure restored, Tim, forgetting about his call to Ted Barnes, asked, "Are you implying that in my current state I shouldn't drive?" "I'm saying that I care about you, and I'd like you to care enough about yourself to let someone make it easy for you to get home." Touched by her sensitive words, he replied, "Since you sound like my grandmother, would it be too much trouble for you to drive me to Rosslare Park?"

"It would be my pleasure," Sam Bannion stated professionally, hiding any hint of delight with his request. "My partner will remain here to complete the crime scene investigation."

Detective Perkins nodded and winked, beaming a conspiratorial smile at his partner.

As she drove north, the silence in the car was monastic. Sam didn't want to intrude on Tim Cavanagh's conflicted thoughts; she guessed he was on the edge of acute traumatic stress. During the drive to Stony Brook, she noticed the occasional head turn when a driver noticed the famous native son in a Roman collar riding in an unmarked police cruiser with a female driver.

During the drive, Sam contained her anticipation about seeing Rosslare Park. The neighbors along Harbor Road in Stony Brook refer to it simply as the Cavanagh home, making them neighbors in the true sense of the word. It was a place you could go to borrow a cup of flour as well as attend a garden party, an Easter egg roll, or the annual twelve days of Christmas celebration. There were no keep-out signs on their property. When the Most Valuable Player at a Super Bowl Game was asked, "What are you going to do now," his answer was always, "I'm going to Disney World," but on this part of Long Island, people said, "I'm going to Rosslare Park."

As they turned west through St. James, the sun began to set. Fr. Cavanagh looked into the sunset, warming his jaundiced features in its auburn and goldenrod glow. Then he gave clear directions for the last two miles.

The two-lane concrete driveway was landscaped on both sides like a golf course. No doubt much wildlife made its home in the thick underbrush and with the blessings of unfettered protection. The lane gradually opened to a wide, circular driveway. Nestled in the center was a massive structure with a breathtaking view of Smithtown Bay as a backdrop.

The sun, bidding its farewell on the horizon, had turned the water to gold. With no waves or whitecaps, the undisturbed Bay looked like a gold necklace reserved for the royalty whose elegant homes hugged the shoreline.

The house had all the features of a traditional Irish manor house. Its lines were simple yet graceful. Interior lights were sparkling in a way that gave the edifice the impression of being a life-sized doll house.

Sam parked under the canopy and walked Fr. Cavanagh up the steps. Before she could ring the bell, the great cedar door swung open. The next scene took her breath away with grandmother and grandson locked in a loving embrace and Aishling Cavanagh patting his back, as mothers do with frightened children, as if to say, "You are safe, all will be well." They spoke in tears and not in words. They shared their vulnerability with tender dignity. Sam felt like she was intruding on a sacred ritual not meant for her eyes.

As she quietly turned and began walking to her car, a feminine voice, with the texture of silk but a tone of commanding authority said, "Officer, I am Jane Cavanagh. Thank you for bringing my grandson home safely. You've had a long drive. Can I offer you a cup of coffee or tea?"

A moment that seemed like a freeze-framed scene in a movie turned a usually motor-mouth cop into someone speechless. Everything Sam had heard about Jane Cavanagh had just been validated. She not only had a heart full of love for her grandson, she also had the capacity to put her own pain aside and make room to care for a stranger.

Before she could reply, the lady of the house said, "Please come in so we can comfort each other with a pot of tea and shortbreads."

A voice inside Sam's head said, "Leave, leave." A voice inside her heart said, "Stay, stay." The next sound she heard was the great door closing behind her as she entered the home.

Nora Owens—East Side Apartment

The long flight from Paris to New York was smooth. No turbulence and the comforts of flying first class afforded me an environment to plot a strategy for bringing my unique brand of Irish retribution to Dennis Flaherty. I mused about whether he would find my form of retro-terrorism a cut above his. As I mapped out details in my mind, I made several mental notes of items I needed for the kill. After settling into my apartment, I would research mid-town cutlery stores on the Internet. To make sure there was no paper trail, all purchases would be cash only. I would also need to play my Phantom role and create several disguises. That meant using the hidden chamber in my apartment that stored the many hidden faces and aliases of Nora Owens.

Insisting the taxi cab stop three blocks from my apartment building, I used the ruse of needing to buy food items at a local produce market. I paid in cash, and a generous tip brought a broad smile to the driver's face. Once out of view, I pivoted on my heel and headed in the direction of my apartment building at East 78th Street and 2nd Avenue.

Like the rest of New York, my neighborhood was a United Nations ghetto. Varied cultures and languages came together like a quilt whose patches were stitched by the hands of every ethnic group that called West Yorkville home. Blending together like the different ingredients poured into a Margarita, the final product was a salty, tangy, sweet blend of different faces, languages, customs, behaviors, and lifestyles that made the neighborhood, like the drink, worthy of wanting more.

I had always thought that the most outstanding quality of all New Yorkers was the value and practice of privacy as if it were a constitutional amendment. Our smiles were body language for "Thank you for not violating my space." Our silence on subway platforms, in the trains, on the streets, in the elevators was the result of a non-scripted indoctrination that says, "Your space is sacred." And if any attempts were made to violate it, there would be hell to pay.

My neighborhood was a place where I could be duplicitous and still remain anonymous. I might be the only serial killer living in a fashionable Upper East Side building wearing designer clothing, but I surely wasn't the only one living a double life or hiding behind lies with the cover of cosmetics or fake smiles. My plan was to keep it that way at least until I retired from the practice of fine tuning the science of revenge.

Warren, the doorman at my building, opened the door as I approached. He was like a robot coated with flesh: his instincts superior, his demeanor approachable, his attitude considerate, his radar well developed, and his discretion invaluable. Doormen were a necessary part of the human mechanisms that kept Manhattan grinding. Every person living on this concrete island had a relationship with a doorman that was equal to co-dependency. I was no exception. Though my presence was infrequent, the relationship was frequently renewed.

"Welcome home, Ms. O'Neill," Warren said, like the professional doorman he was.

"Thank you Warren. I hope you, Maggie, and your son, Jonathan, are all well."

"Well indeed, and thank you for asking."

"It's good to be back in New York."

As he handed me a recent copy of the Manhattan telephone directory encased in plastic, I informed him that I would be home for several months. It was information I volunteered since he would practice the art of discretion and never inquire into such personal matters. "Don't ask, don't tell" was practiced by doormen in New York City long before it became a failed policy toward gays in the military.

"I will need some things sent to the dry cleaners tomorrow, and will you please call Liza and set up a schedule for her to clean the apartment?" I said in a manner intended to renew my familiarity with someone who had been a stranger for at least three months.

"I will make it so," Warren replied, evoking a warm smile on my face which he repaid with one of his own.

With these protocols complete, I made my way to an elevator. During the ride up I programmed myself to take on the role of Clare O'Neill, my New York alias. My apartment was on the 16th floor of an 18-floor building. The small patio off my bedroom offered a view of the eastern edges of Central Park. And anywhere in the apartment, the cacophony of police sirens, emergency vehicles, and horns from taxis and delivery trucks was music to any New Yorker's ears.

I loved the rhythm of this city. There was a pulse to it that never vacillated. It beat as if it were a life support machine keeping eight million people alive. New York was a city that knew how to breathe and live and, most of all, keep secrets. Its resiliency after 9/11 was a testimony to the DNA of the inhabitants. This was my city, and I would get lost in it for as long as needed to erase another name or two off my hit list.

For now I composed a list of things I needed. Once completed, I turned on my desktop computer and Googled cutlery shops in Manhattan. I noted the addresses of several I would visit tomorrow. I intended to be selective, for I was looking for a special piece for a not-so-special person in my life.

With another Google search, I typed in St. Bartholomew's Church. After carefully reviewing all the links, I copied only the information pertinent to my plan. Molding a curious smile on my face, I decided it was time to play the Catholic game again. I used my land line to reserve a rental car for Sunday. Tomorrow would be a good day to take a long drive to Long Island and attend Mass in Mattituck. No dark confessionals this time. This kill required exposure and cunning. I would set the trap in three days and then spring it when I was ready.

After drawing a warm bath and spoiling myself with a salt treatment, I stretched across my queen-sized bed. In an instant I was in dreamland, my imagination in full swing. When I awoke, the plan would be complete. Then I would need only time and patience to convert my dream into reality.

ᥴᏚᎯ Chapter Seven ᏗᎯᎦ

Fr. Dennis Flaherty

My life has been running low on grace for more years than I can count. I have been a failure at life and a fraud as a priest. Ordained in 1973 for the Archdiocese of Dublin, I quickly worshipped at the altar of lust. The oils of ordination did not spare me from that temptation. In the words of a seminary professor with a cryptic sense of humor, "Lead me not into temptation, thank you I can find it myself."

My first assignment as chaplain at Holy Comforter Orphanage was the sacred ground I contaminated by feeding that demon. Too many girls were available and willing to satisfy my sexual needs. I slept with so many of them that I turned into a tramp. That led to drinking and mood swings and violent behavior. Less than one year after ordination, my sexual lifestyle would have made the Marquis de Sade blush.

Some of the girls were willing toys, while others had to be molded into submission. A set of twins, Nora and Nan Owens, were so defiant that I took on the personality of a monster. Nora was especially combative. With her I liked using the sex chamber I created in the basement of the chaplain's residence.

Mimicking the style of the evil emperor in the Star Wars movies, I mocked her by saying, "I can feel your anger Nora, and it energizes me."

"Sorry to hear that," she bellowed back, "since it is meant to insult you, you ignorant fascist pig."

Enraged by her boldness, I slapped her face, leaving a palm print. She countered by scratching the left side of my face with nails as sharp as a paring knife. When I felt the blood trickle down my cheek, I lost all control and began hitting her so violently that she passed out. When she regained consciousness, my face was still bleeding. I forced her to lick the blood.

I felt so high by this display of hardcore violence that I immediately had sex with her again, even though she lay there like a mannequin. Proud of my manhood and letting her know who was in charge, I threw a towel at her so she could clean herself up as she groaned back to life. During my tenure, the little orphan Nannie twin committed suicide. I stayed in the land of denial long enough to preside at her funeral with plenty of false composure. Her sister Nora never shed a tear. Instead her eyes riveted through me like a laser beam. To make sure she would never blow my cover, I taught her the meaning of sacred silence in that basement torture chamber. In the end she was transformed into an obedient sex slave, giving me pleasures not included in any seminary curriculum.

My predecessor at Holy Comforter was Fr. Sean. He was a great mentor in how to live the double life. It has taken so much energy to maintain that lifestyle that I have grown old beyond my years. Thanks to Sean's intervention, I crossed the pond in 1986 and came to America.

For some it was a personal exodus that ended in the land of opportunity. For me it was a new feeding ground. Young virgin American girls were exactly what my Irish sex drive needed to be jump-started like a dead car battery. After ten years in four dioceses, I had left a trail of sexual abuse that would qualify for honorable mention in a Rand-McNally road Atlas. But the paper trail inside confidential files would be the cause for many of my sleepless nights. Add to that the aggravation of stomach ulcers, anxiety attacks, obesity, and a suppressed addiction to "the drink" as the Irish call it, and an unrestrained Irish temper, and what you have is a prescription for a priest with so many hidden emotional scars that defining me would baffle a psychotherapist.

After being on the run for eleven years, I finally found a new home in Islip, N.Y. Thanks to the welcome of Bishop John Campbell, my stressed-out life began to settle down and assume a more normal rhythm. With only one incident of sexual abuse in the diocese on record, and well contained by His Excellency, within five years I was appointed pastor of St. Bartholomew's Parish in Mattituck.

I was installed on the parish feast day, August 24, 2002. The bishop warned me that any further accusations would merit my complete banishment from the diocese. The famous "Dallas Charter" in effect only two months before my appointment meant that the next time I would face the district attorney and possible criminal charges. That threat was enough for me to take a vow to give celibacy a chance. I didn't know who the patron saint of child sexual abusers was, but I knew that abstinence and prayer were more preferable than jail.

My reverie was broken by the buzz of the telephone.

"Fr. Flaherty, have you forgotten you have children's confessions before First Friday Mass?" the secretary asked, as if she were speaking to someone with dementia.

"I am on my way," I said. The thought of being in the reconciliation room with all those pretty seventh-grade girls put a smile back on my forlorn face.

Bishop John Campbell—Rosslare Park

I bristled at the thought that I had to call the Dowager Matriarch Jane Cavanagh to be screened before meeting with my own priest secretary. She had taken his cell phone away, making her the clearing house for visitors during his recovery. I would be sure to clarify that Tim Cavanagh's recovery from the trauma of Terry Engals's suicide could be handled just as well at the cathedral rectory in Central Islip.

Though I rarely crossed paths with the widow multi-millionaire, I would surely assert my authority in this matter. After all, Tim Cavanagh was a son of the church as much as a grandson to Jane Cavanagh. As I drove to the family estate in Stony Brook I recalled my first unpleasant encounter with her.

It was April 2002, the first Easter after my installation as Bishop of Islip. I accepted an invitation to the annual Easter Egg Roll at Rosslare Park. Insensitive to her status as a widow I addressed her as "Aishling."

Without missing a beat, she corrected me by saying, "You may call me Jane. Only my husband called me Aishling. It was a term of endearment."

I gave in to the demon of resentment and replied, "Thank you for that clarification Jane. You may call me Bishop."

Without missing a beat she countered, "That isn't a name. It's a title. Let's keep the playing field even, John."

Since the Cavanagh fortune greased the wheels of the Diocese of Islip—keeping schools open, food pantries stocked, scholarships plentiful, social services available, and God only knows what else—I smiled while hiding my contempt for her Irish boldness. She, on the other hand, smiled in a way that hid her relish at cutting my Belfast ego down to size. Jane Cavanagh had left no doubt that she was my equal and not my minion.

This second visit to Rosslare Park was more official than pleasant. While I gave the impression I had come to check on the health of my secretary, it was a pastoral visit with a hidden agenda.

I wanted to know what Tim Cavanagh knew about the suicide that I didn't know. I was furious about not having access to the police report and the diocesan attorney's inability to acquire one. Such an unfortunate incident would have to be reported to the Nuncio in Washington, D.C., and as the bishop, I wanted to get all the facts before fabricating my version of the story in a way that ultimately made me look good.

No emotionally unstable priest, and a pedophile at that, was going to sabotage my career in going higher up the hierarchical ladder. I would make sure the report would elicit praise from the Nuncio for the sensitive and pastoral way I handled it. The only one who could jeopardize that goal was Tim Cavanagh; thus the need to interrogate him under the ruse of compassion. I would insist on confidentiality if his grandmother insisted on being present during the visit. She was the fox that I needed to out-fox.

As it turned out, my anxieties were premature. The day I came to Rosslare Park, Jane Cavanagh was volunteering at St. Cornelius food pantry. This news provoked delight, for now I could probe Tim Cavanagh without matriarchal interference.

My attempts to be compassionate toward my secretary were as spurious as a lion pretending to be a lamb.

"I am sorry you had to go through this ordeal with Fr. Engals," I said in a tone of false care. "But, I need to hear the details from you so I can write a report for the Nuncio in Washington. I'll take notes as you talk."

I suppose Tim Cavanagh was perceptive enough to catch the fact that I expressed neither care nor mention of his needs. He knew me well enough to take meaning from what I did not speak, perhaps correctly concluding that my visit was more about protocol and my eventual, inevitable promotion to a larger diocese—one with greater exposure to those who feed the hunger demons of lust for the power to rule rather than the call to serve.

My secretary, with trademark Cavanagh composure, began recounting his version of his visit to Terry Engals that ended with the shock of the suicide. He spoke in rapid-fire fashion, hoping I'm sure that the quicker he finished the more quickly I would leave. In my position, I am feared, not one whose company is sought or relished.

After about twenty minutes of listening to his story, spoken through slurred lips as if he was drunk, I closed my notepad. I reassured Tim that he would be well cared for at my home in Islip.

Tim Cavanagh said, in a non-committal tone of voice, "Thank you. That's nice to know." He nodded as a gesture of deference, with a meager attempt at a genuine smile masking how he really felt. He had as much evasiveness about him as his grandmother. As I left the house and walked to my car, I began having second thoughts about my selection of a priest secretary.

Fr. Tim Cavanagh—Rosslare Park

Tim Cavanagh opened the shutters on his bedroom window to watch the bishop leave. As John Campbell drove down the driveway, Tim wondered what it meant that an ordained bishop never prayed with him, never mentioned the name of Jesus Christ in a comforting way, and never thought enough about his traumatized secretary to bring the healing presence of the Eucharist to him. It was a sad commentary on a man who is so full of himself that there was little room inside him even for God.

A half-hour later, Jane Cavanagh knocked on her grandson's bedroom door.

"The password is come in," he called.

"Meals on Heels," she replied. Wearing a pair of three-inch Gucci heels, she carried a tray into his room. "It's tea time, and, since we're having it on the second floor, I guess you could say we're having 'high tea.'" They both laughed at her Irish brand of humor.

Tim always found his grandmother's happy spirit infectious. She was a far better antidote for his recovery than the anti-depressant drugs the doctor had prescribed for his trauma.

This was his only reason for staying at Rosslare. It was where he found recovery through her nursing, her care, her laughter, and her energy for loving him back to health with an affection that only a-one-of-a-kind grandmother could give.

Being in her presence felt like getting high on hope, and he drank as much of it as a thirsty camel refuels on water at a well. Also, playing the grand piano in the salon was a form of therapy he practiced every day. He didn't know that she had it tuned for that very purpose.

As she recounted her day at the parish food pantry, he could envision hope on the faces of the people she had served with bags of food. At that moment he knew she was feeding them with the intangible food of hope. In this role she was a different kind of bag lady: one who remained humble in great wealth. She was putting a modern-day face on the gospel story of the multiplication of loaves and fishes. And she did so without bringing any attention to herself, for she knew that her own soul was being fed by the God who was revealed in the faces and hearts of the hungry whom she served. Her spiritual life had matured as she aged, and Tim knew that her inner life was able to make those connections.

When it seemed she had avoided the question as long as possible, Jane Cavanagh finally asked, in a rather dismal tone of voice, "And how was your visit with John Campbell? Was it worth talking about or not?"

"The latter... not worth talking about."

"Well then, let's talk about something more life-giving. I have asked Molly to fix your favorite meal tonight, Irish stew, and I instructed her to add extra brandy!"

Before he could reply, she added, "Oh, I almost forgot. You have mail... the real kind, not the computer kind."

She handed him a greeting card envelope. "You will recognize the return name as I did. How nice of Detective Bannion to send you a card. I hope it's a Hallmark—the kind you send 'when you care enough to send the very best.'"

56

As he opened it with a sense of camouflaged delight, she gathered up the dishes, placed them on the tray, and headed for the door. Her parting words were, "And don't forget to be a good Cavanagh and send a thank you. I wouldn't want you to embarrass me when she comes to lunch on Saturday without your thank-you… to her of course, and not me."

Noticing the stunned look on his face, she said, "As for me, a short prayer to the Almighty would suffice for the blessing of having a meddlesome grandmother."

With "speechless" written all over his face, she added,

"Dinner at seven as usual, dress is casual, smiles always expected, and laughter in place of salt with the pepper. After all, you and laughter are the spice of my life."

Before she closed the door she mirrored the same grin she saw on his face. What he didn't see was the giant smile inside that evoked delight in her. She had every intention of making it a lunch the three of them would remember.

For Jane Cavanagh, her grandson's trauma of witnessing one priest's suicide was enough. Though she enjoyed sharing his company for the week and nursing him back to health, she was now more determined than ever to plot a plan to free Timothy from further nightmares associated with the growing scandal that tainted the very fabric of the Catholic priesthood. She knew how deeply her grandson cared and wanted to be a spiritual healer for the faithful, but she also knew that if he remained in this vocation, he would never achieve the respect he had earned and so greatly deserved.

She was ready to solicit, voluntarily or involuntarily, the assistance of anyone who could help in that goal. Detective Sergeant Samantha Bannion leaped to the top of her list.

Nora Owens

"Thank God for Google," I thought to myself as I searched for cutlery shops on the Upper East Side. My eyes widened and my eyebrows arched as I noted the location of "A Cut Above" just a few blocks away. I was in the mood for exercise, so I dressed for a power walk to find the right blade for the right cutting.

✺ Chapter Eight ✺

Detective Sam Bannion—Rosslare Park

It had been five days since I had walked the grounds of Rosslare Park. That first time was at sunset, and with the fading light I couldn't get a real sense of the eye-catching beauty of the vast estate. But as I retraced my path on the driveway on this clear, day, I surveyed what I had missed earlier in the week, with eyes like an architect looking to be wowed by a classical manor house on the north shore of Long Island.

What I saw did not disappoint. There was a simple grace to the landscaping, with colors as alluring as the flowers in a Monet painting. An abundant supply of white and pink Dogwood trees were glistening like the smiling faces of actors in a silent film. Daffodils and tulips sparkled in such an array of colors that the endless rows looked like complimentary rainbows on both sides of the driveway.

Several people were jogging on the foot path parallel to the driveway, while others were walking with their children, no doubt breathing in the aroma of the spring flowers and admiring their beauty. The flowers were so enchanting that I could imagine some people talking to them. The scene reminded me of the friendly atmosphere typical of Andy Griffith's Mayberry. The only thing missing was the whistling theme, with everyone saying, "Have a very Mayberry day!"

The manor house revealed breathtaking grandeur in the full light of day. I had already done my homework online and researched the elegant house I was about to enter as a lunch guest. It was a typical English Tudor manor house. The depth of the windows on the three different levels designated public areas from private areas. Four arched fascias in the front acted as facades from the third story, hiding vented chimneys protruding through the slate roof. An elegant porte-cochère extended from the main entrance. It was wide enough for any size automobile and offered protection for guests during inclement weather. An L-shaped extension protruded from the left side of the house, leading to a four-car garage. The enclosed connector-walkway was designed to give that addition a monastic look, with its vaulted archways.

Though it was no Tara, I could tell high-powered people lived here, but not the kind who were arrogant or who lived behind a mask of false pride. It was well known that the Cavanagh house was a giant welcome mat, and everyone, including people who were nobodies, was received with one-standard-fits-all, namely, you're welcome! FedEx and UPS delivery men were addressed by their first names. Children from the neighborhood could ride their bikes on the property and their parents could do power walks on the driveway without permission.

Rosslare Park was a private home with public access. There were no electronically operated gates, keeping the patricians in and the plebeians out. Rather there was just a long, alluring driveway. In place of family secrets, there were unobstructed pathways, open doors and hearts.

Jane Cavanagh's personal wealth would put her in the same league as TV celebrities and superstars. But her lifestyle and accessibility gave her the impression of being everybody's neighbor.

As she had when I drove her grandson to the estate five days earlier, Jane Cavanagh was waiting to greet me on the spacious landing of the granite steps. Standing next to her was Tim. As I slowed the car and put it into park, my anxiety level increased.

An unknown voice within said, "Venus to Earth: this is only lunch and not Operation Fall in Love." Buoyed by that reminder, I alighted from the car and walked up the steps with a smile that was mirrored on their faces.

"Welcome back, Detective Bannion," Jane Cavanagh said with no pretentiousness in her voice. She met me with a gracious hug. "Timothy and I are so glad you could join us for lunch."

The alert detective in me downloaded the way she called her grandson by his full given name. Although initially I had been wondering why I was there, all my apprehensions melted when I heard his name. My heart increased its rhythm with each step I took. I willed it back to a normal rhythm.

As my eyes locked onto his, they seemed to change each time he blinked, from one shade of green to another, each with an enchanting sparkle. I was once again caught by them, like an insect in a spider's web. They were eyes I would love to be looked at someday as more than a visitor.

I snapped out of my romantic reverie and said, "Father Cavanagh, it's good to see you again and looking so much better." That was the best I could do for a canned line. The truth was that someone with his sculptured features would look good no matter what trauma he had endured.

"It's nice of you to notice how much better I am doing," he said. His voice exuded a sense of sexual energy, and his touch felt like a minor shock when he grasped my hand to shake it.

Jane Cavanagh then placed her arm in mine and escorted me through the great door into the house. As we walked a few steps she seemed to clarify some protocols that caught me by surprise.

"Do you mind if I call you Samantha?"

"I've been called Sam for so long that I sometimes forget what my real name is," I said, choosing my words carefully.

"I'll take that as a yes. Please call me Jane, and I prefer you to call my grandson Timothy rather than Tim. I dislike the American tradition of shortening names," she said in a comical tone of voice that was non-abrasive.

"I am not sure my parents would approve of that. Even though they are both deceased, they raised me a good Catholic so—"

She seemed to have anticipated what I was going to say next and finished my sentence without being rude. "I know what you're about to say. It's not typical for you to call a priest by his first name."

Nodding in agreement, she continued, "But you know, Samantha, my grandson was Timothy before he was Father Cavanagh, and besides this is not a business luncheon, if you know what I mean. There is never any need to be formal in this house."

Jane Cavanagh had a way of making her point with her brand of Irish diplomacy and deference. I turned to face her grandson, who was walking on my right. With raised eyebrows, his expression read, "Don't argue with an Irish grandmother."

I was hoping he noticed my long, red hair feathered in a sassy shag, the black mock turtleneck I was wearing with a denim jacket, my formfitting jeans, and modest heels. At 5'10" I didn't want to stand above his 6' height. Rather, I wanted to stand eye to eye with him, to drink in as

61

much of his enchanting eyes as possible. And I wanted the spell they would cast upon me to last as long as possible, like forever, although I would settle for a two-hour lunch.

The detective in me scanned his casual attire. His grey, button-down shirt had such a tactile finish that it seemed to contain a story. The front was open from the neck to the second button, revealing a well-trimmed endowment of chest hair. Hidden underneath had to be a disciplined six-pack that would make any woman swoon. Neatly pressed Dockers jeans with a woven leather belt highlighted his trim waistline. Polished penny loafers were well chosen for someone who walked like royalty even in sandals. A newsboy cap would have completed his Great Gatsby American look. I stilled my heart in quiet approval of how this apparel elevated his image and status far more than a bland black suit and a Roman collar.

Sensing that his radar was catching the lust in my eyes, I turned my gaze to the interior of the great manor house, as if curious about its contents.

I contained my first impressions by suppressing banal oohs and aahs. My expectation of being treated to a grand tour was not met. Instead of receiving me like two docents in a museum, they made me feel at home. I soon realized that I was the focus of their attention and not their house.

We slowly walked down a hallway wide enough to hold a city bus. My new shoes glistened as they connected with a well-polished parquet hardwood floor. If it could talk it would say, "Walk proudly on me, for I give the house an upscale appearance." It had a finish that looked like honey and smelled as sweet as the people who lived there.

As my ears attended to Jane Cavanagh's conversation, my ever alert eyes caught brief glimpses of framed posters hanging on the walls. They were wisdom sayings of famous people. It quickly dawned on me that these tastefully framed posters were more than just wall decorations. They were the philosophy that articulated the Cavanaghs' outlook toward life. They conveyed far deeper morals and values than million-dollar paintings by Dutch and French master artists that were meant only to be seen and envied. Walking down this hallway was like being schooled in a class titled, "Attitude toward life 101."

We turned into a room where the environment was arranged not around a television but a baby grand piano. If I were in a Jane Austen novel, this room would be a conservatory. But I was in a twenty-first century Long Island manor house. The room was peppered with a collage of photos on every table. The smiles and happy expressions seemed to say family at first sight.

Similar framed wisdom sayings adorned these walls. The messages fit the musical focus of the room. "I have found that if you love life, life will love you back," said a quote by the world famous pianist Arthur Rubenstein. Another, by celebrated soprano Beverly Sills, said, "I've always tried to go a step past wherever people expected me to end up." They were testimonies to the priest-grandson whose life as a famous pianist was fashioned by such ordinary wisdom. It was obvious to anyone that this was the Timothy Cavanagh room.

Two enormous vases of cut calla lilies added color, beauty, and a fresh scent that wafted throughout the entire room. This, no doubt, was where stories were told and memories cherished. It smelled of love and welcome, like the alluring scent of freshly cut grass during a new spring. Jane Cavanagh gestured for me to sit on a sofa upholstered with exquisite fabric.

The lady of the manor chose a Queen Anne chair. Her erect but graceful posture announced, "I am a very strong woman." The brilliant light piercing through the clear glass of the French doors enhanced her regal features. Her hairdo, though modest, spoke a preference for a natural look over something colored. It embellished her features as a thoroughly modern woman and was a clear statement that there was nothing artificial about her. If anything, it highlighted her creamy-skinned looks. Her appearance spoke the truth that this is what a really cool grandmother looks like. She would turn heads if she wore a T-shirt that said, "I am really 39—it's the shirt that's old!"

Her capital with me had soared the day I brought her traumatized grandson to Rosslare for TLC. In a week she had worked a miracle. Sparkle had returned to his signature eyes, warmth to his voice, and laughter to his spirit. If I dared, I would have given her a hug. But instead I commanded that voice to be quiet. I knew all about boundaries. One day, I hoped, I would give myself permission to fall into Tim's arms and let him hold me for the rest of the day. For a moment I cursed the inner voice that said, "That will always be a fantasy."

To my surprise, the man of the hour sat next to me with ease and confidence. His closeness sent out a wave of energy that turned me on like a light switch. Though this was not part of my fantasy, I enjoyed the surprise of him changing it. After all, fantasies are better when real people are in them.

As I played with this fantasy, a middle-aged lady brought in a tray of appetizers. Jane Cavanagh, the consummate hostess, introduced her as Molly Malone and added, "She is a member of our extended family."

Once again she revealed her classiness by introducing an employee not by a title but by a term of endearment.

Jane asked about my choice of drink. Not wanting to appear a fool by implying that my beverage of choice was in an aluminum can, I calmly replied, "What's on the menu?"

"Well, in your honor Molly has prepared some Irish cocktails. You may choose an Irish Julep or an Irish Rickey or both."

Since I had never tasted either drink before, I quietly played a game of eeny, meeny, miny, moe before placing my order. I was hoping the alcohol content was low enough that I wouldn't say something that would haunt me later.

Molly then served hors d'oeuvres. Her culinary radar sensed my low appetizer IQ, and she came to my rescue by naming them. First were asparagus bundles wrapped in bacon, Long Island Oysters on the half-shell, and red bliss potato cups with Crème fraiche.

The most touching feature were the linen napkins. I masked the truth that my napkin etiquette was limited to paper products. The only time I had used linen was at the reception for my brother's wedding. Using them with the Cavanaghs made me feel very special. The conversation kept clear of Timothy's trauma, centering instead on details of the annual Easter egg hunt at Rosslare Park just two weeks earlier. When the lady of the manor told stories about the children—when she talked about others—it created a brighter glow around her.

As Molly served lunch, she again anticipated my low culinary IQ and named the dishes. First, there was cream of turnip soup with Wheaton bread. Next was a dandelion green salad, followed by the main entrée: roasted salmon on top of colcannon.

So much for anticipating Irish stew served with a slice of bread. I had never before eaten so elegantly. The mystery that captivated me was that this was a meal fit for the dining room of the Pierre Hotel but enjoyed by three down-to-earth people bound together by the intangible food of storytelling, laughter, and delight. It was served with a continuous flow of Stony Brook Sauvignon Blanc.

"We support the local winery," Jane said in a congenial manner.

Timothy surprised me with a toast: "May your life always be good again whenever you come to visit." I willed myself not to melt at the tenderness of his words. All that I remembered was the part about "whenever you come to visit."

As we clicked glasses, I said, "I'll drink to that!" What I really wanted to say was, "If you have a vacancy, I can move in today."

Following the long, leisurely lunch, I anticipated some ritual of closure and farewell. Instead, to my surprise Molly re-appeared as if on cue with clean napkins and fresh drinks. We each hugged a warm mug of Irish coffee before she served strawberry rhubarb crumble with Baileys whipped cream for dessert. I savored every bite like a child tasting samples in a pastry shop.

Since returning to the parlor, my detective's eyes watched the concert pianist move his fingers on the arm of the sofa as if he were playing a piano with no sound, except the one in his head. It gave the appearance of his inner child doing what it naturally did best.

When Molly reappeared to collect the dishes and refill the coffee, on her heels was a beautiful dog mimicking the trademark Cavanagh erect posture. Once inside the room, it bolted toward Timothy like horses shooting out of the gate at the races. He opened his arms, inviting the dog to fill that empty space. At that moment, for the first time, I envied the four-legged animal.

"Hey Bach," he said in a tone that reminded me of a child playing with a pet. After the two embraced he said, "We have company, would you like to meet her?" The dog, as if understanding English perfectly, tilted its head and instinctively turned toward me. In a formal tone of voice, Tim introduced us.

"Bach, this is Samantha. And Samantha, this is Bach."

The dog quickly came to me and licked my hand. I found the dog's welcome and friendliness endearing and shook one of its paws as if to say, "Nice to meet you, Bach."

"What kind of dog is this?" I asked, trying to cover my stupidity with an inquisitive tone of curiosity.

"He is an Airedale and has been part of our family for nearly ten years," Jane Cavanagh said with pure pride in her voice. Then she continued in the style of a storyteller. "After the grandchildren were born, I thought their visits to our home would be more enjoyable with a dog. My husband disagreed. He disliked dogs shedding their hair. So we compromised by getting a dog that does not shed.

"Bach is our third Airedale and has filled a lot of emptiness in the house since my husband died four years ago."

Her words triggered a moment of silent reverence before she continued. "Like everyone else here at Rosslare Park, Bach is part of the extended family and is Timothy's shadow whenever he visits. Having him here the past week has sent Bach on a doggy-high. He has been good medicine for my grandson's recovery." At that point the dog gravitated back to its master like a magnet draws metal.

Having opened the door, my curiosity about the name prompted me to ask, "Is he named after the famous classical composer?"

"Which one?" Timothy volleyed with his own question.

"You mean there is more than one Bach?"

"There are three," he replied with lightness in his voice. "Johann, Sebastian, and Offenbach."

When Jane Cavanagh emitted a hearty laugh, I knew the classical pianist was playing with my sense of humor as delicately as he no doubt played the piano.

I garnered the timing and countered, "And will Bach and I be entertained before my leaving with your playing any of the three Bach's on the grand piano?"

I glanced toward Jane Cavanagh quickly enough to see a grin of approval on her face.

Without missing a beat, the classical pianist replied, "I take requests. Do you have a particular Bach piece in mind?"

Feigning a smile to cover my panic, I said, "I am sure any piece of Bach you play would please him and me."

"Are you talking about the dog or the composer?"

"Okay, I am sure any piece of Bach you play would please them, him, and me."

"I am sure Timothy would oblige your request, and I speak for the dog too," said Jane Cavanagh with a lyrical tone of delight.

"No matter where he is in the house, whenever the piano is being played, he invites himself in, takes his place near the piano bench, and behaves like a civilized audience. In place of applause he barks his approval. Since my grandson is here rent free, I am sure I can talk him into compensation with a solo performance after dessert."

With those reassuring words, I was sure neither of them missed the smile on my face. After all, it was the width of Long Island.

As we continued to sip Irish coffee, to my surprise Jane Cavanagh opened a door with questions about my family. I wasn't sure if she was snooping for information or genuinely interested in knowing more about me. I trusted my inner radar and played along.

I shared in the style of "once upon a time" that I have a sibling, an older divorced brother who was an alcoholic, without giving away the secret that my family tree had some twisted roots. One of those secrets was my younger brother, Kurt, who was sexually molested by a priest. Eventually he turned to drugs, couldn't kick the habit, and died of an overdose at twenty. After his death, I discovered a journal in which he wrote about the sexual abuse. That solidified my decision to go into law enforcement and become part of a Special Victims Unit to help various kinds of victims find their voices and the courage to seek justice.

"And what about your parents?" Jane asked in a caring tone.

"My parents were married thirty-five years before my mother died of cancer in 1999 and my dad died of complications from diabetes in 2002. My mom was the manager of a local doctor's office. My dad was a decorated police officer with the Queens Borough Police Department." Nodding toward Timothy, I added, "I got my calling from him."

Encouraged by his smile of affirmation I continued, "I miss them both very much. They sacrificed a lot for us. They loved us equally, though they kept their disappointment about my brother to themselves."

"And are you a charming aunt to any nieces or nephews?" she asked.

"Actually I am the crazy aunt they adore, and am I paying a high price for that! My nephew wants to be captain of a Quidditch team someday, and my niece wants to go to Hogwarts. I think I pushed them too far when I got them hooked on Harry Potter. Who knew it would lead to Potter-mania?" I paused long enough to replenish my oxygen.

"My brother has a kind of love-hate relationship with his two children, fueled mostly by contempt for his ex-wife," I explained. "But I am the aunt who spoils them and tries to make up for his distance. I enjoy going to their sporting events, taking them out to dinner for their birthdays, and spoiling them at Christmas."

My family engine was revved up, so I decided to continue sharing more. "I was married for two years to a fellow police officer in Vice. He was killed in a drug raid just three months after my dad died. I was six weeks pregnant at the time and had a miscarriage. It was a season of losses for me. I took a leave of absence from the police force to clear my head and heal my heart. There were two hidden blessings in the sabbatical. One was that I moved here to Long Island and took a position with the Islip police force."

At this point Jane Cavanagh reached across and held my hand in a way that spoke sympathy.

"I share the heartbreak of being a widow with you," she said in comforting tone. My smile spoke acceptance of her care.

Before I could glance to the other side, Timothy Cavanagh carbon-copied his grandmother and reached for my other hand. No words were spoken. They both had a way with silence that turned the moment into such reverence that words would have spoiled it. The hopeful glow on their faces began to warm my face.

He broke the trance of the moment by saying, "You said there were two blessings. What was the second one?"

"Oh," I said, hiding the surprise I was feeling that he had listened that deeply. "The second blessing was a decision never to marry a police officer again."

Without missing a beat, Jane Cavanagh said, "So, you plan to marry again."

"Well, I don't have any immediate plans since I am not dating anyone, but I am open to being surprised."

"It's nice to know you like surprises," she replied with a hint of mischief in her voice.

☙ Chapter Nine ❧

Detective Sam Bannion—Rosslare Park

My vulnerability gave Jane Cavanagh permission to share details about the deaths of her son and daughter-in-law, the spiraling of her granddaughter into the dark world of drugs and cybersex, and the stability of Timothy, her older grandson on whom she relied as an advisor and confidante.

With her face firmly locked onto her priest grandson, she added, "I love them all, but my love for Timothy is special."

Tim moved from his chair to the piano. "To keep this from turning into a Kleenex moment, let me bring Mr. Bach into the room," he said. He opened the keyboard and let it nestle in a cavity hewn for the cover only. What looked like a piece of Oriental silk was draped elegantly over the chest of the piano. A wooden framed needlepoint that said "Piano Whisperer" rested in a small wooden tripod. Tim adjusted the piano bench to his liking. During this ritual the dog laid instinctively on the edge of an oriental rug behind the pianist.

Tim dropped his hands softly into his lap, closed his eyes, and briefly assumed the attitude of prayer before placing his hands on the keyboard. Once he began playing, it was as if Jane Cavanagh and Bach and I were not even in the room.

He was so wedded to the instrument that they appeared to be making love more than music. I didn't have to be an authority on J. S. Bach to guess that they were so entwined that they knew each other's rhythms and passions, like lovers moving in sync with the pulses and energy of passionate lovemaking.

I reflected on my own memories of Todd, my deceased husband, and knew instinctively that what I was both hearing and seeing was exactly what had brought me sexual fulfillment with him. The only thing missing in those memories was the music of Bach in the background of our bedroom or living room or any other room where our hot urges gave way to the fireworks of foreplay, as two bodies became one in love making and the long embrace that followed.

Watching the vulnerable priest being transformed into a passionate pianist was a miracle before my very own eyes. The electrical charge that was released in the room expanded my admiration for the gifted musician who was different when not wearing a Roman collar. All at once I so desperately wanted to hear a few revelations about this one man with two callings. And I wondered if he worshipped at the altar of God with the same intensity as he was now worshipping at the shrine of this marvelous piano.

I knew that the sounds coming from inside of it were only possible because of the musical passion he was releasing for our private pleasure.

For a good five minutes, the room became a shrine to Bach's music and Timothy Cavanagh's artistic skills. Silence was reverenced like the consecration during Mass. I felt like I was on holy ground. Words were useless. All that was needed was attentiveness to the heart being lured into God's world, Bach's genius, and Timothy's hypnotic playing.

When he finished, the silence held in the room like the echo of one's voice in the Grand Canyon. Jane Cavanagh and I applauded in unison while the dog barked approvingly. The celebrity pianist took a modest bow.

I got up my courage to ask a question. "Since I didn't major in music appreciation in college, may I ask what piece you just played?"

"That was the first movement of Carl Philippe Emanuel Bach's Prussian Sonata in C-minor."

"How about one more, Timothy, perhaps something by Beethoven," Jane Cavanagh said, dropping the great composer's name as if he were family and would soon step into the room unannounced.

"One encore accepted," he said, turning back to the keyboard and repeating the same ritual as before of getting prayerfully centered.

For the next ten minutes, he played a sonata that moved quickly through startling changes in tone and dynamics. The economic use of his fingers revealed a dexterity that showcased the highest quality of his training. The piece ended in a long, deep, dark tone.

Out of the corner of my eye I noticed a look on Jane Cavanagh's face that expressed both pride and sadness: pride in his musical genius and sadness that he gave it up for a Roman collar.

Two of the audience clapped while the third again barked its excited approval.

Anticipating my student-level question, Tim said, "That was the first movement of Beethoven's piano sonata #23, called the *Appassionato*. It was composed in 1803 and is written with a brilliant display of emotion because that was the year Beethoven came to grips with the irreversibility of his deteriorating deafness."

"Too bad hearing aids were not available back then," I said.

"True, but he didn't let that handicap keep him from composing."

"How about closing your program with Beethoven's *Moonlight Sonata*," Jane Cavanagh asked delicately.

"She's teasing because she knows I only play that piece when there is moonlight."

Before I could speak my line, Jane said, "We'll have to pay attention to weather reports and make sure your next visit has moonlight in it." She sounded like a devious Jewish matchmaker. "That sonata is my favorite, and Timothy's rendition gives me much pleasure. It is pleasure I would like to share with you one day, Samantha."

I could feel myself blushing, which is something I hadn't done since my first crush in high school. But it felt good to know I could blush as a thirty-year old. I turned toward Timothy unashamed, hoping he had noticed. His flushed cheeks were the sign I was looking for. After today I would elevate the exercise of reading daily weather reports to an art form.

I basked in their company for another hour before signaling my departure. The tangible food of Irish drinks and entrees that filled my stomach coupled with the intangible food of their friendship, delighted my soul and left me feeling like a butterfly newly released from the cocoon and full of hope that I would feast on both again in this grand house with these special and humble people.

Grandmother and grandson, with Bach the Airedale in tow, escorted me through the great canopy doors to the driveway. Jane Cavanagh hugged me as if I were a granddaughter. Timothy hugged me as if I were someone who had cared for him when he most needed it. I would replay it in my mind during the drive back to East Islip and, yes, all night long in my dreams.

I don't have contempt for all priests, just one. Msgr. Joshua Carruthers, who molested my younger brother, was a monster. Fr. Timothy Cavanagh was cut from another cloth. I read him as someone who could partner with me in helping to connect with clergy abuse victims and lead them toward healing. And if some of that healing rubbed off on me, I would welcome it as collateral grace.

Nora Owens

Thank God for GPS. I drove the rental car from Manhattan to the far edges of the eastern tip of Long Island, where it splits into two sections. The great Peconic Bay opening out into Long Island Sound gives the north and south portions of the island a resemblance to the mouth of a giant whale opening its jaws to consume its prey.

After driving through the dead zones of farm country and potato fields for what seemed an eternity, I was relieved to enter a small town that had the appearance of being used in a Norman Rockwell painting. A welcome sign reminded travelers about the annual Strawberry Festival. Sails from one- and two-masted boats anchored in the cove could be seen above tree lines. I consciously reduced my speed to avoid a traffic ticket. I allowed myself to grin about this irony. People like me, who killed others for justice, honored traffic laws with a different standard than we used for honoring human life. Child sexual abusers were expendable in my mind, whereas a twenty-five-MPH speed limit needed to be obeyed. Keeping them in tandem allowed me to continue my mission as a serial killer unabated.

The electronic mapping device directed me to the front doors of St. Bartholomew's Church on Main Street. The small, Gothic structure with an appealing grey brick exterior seemed out of place in such a rural setting. Three narrow, pointed arched windows above a covered entry porch no doubt encased stained glass windows whose beauty would be revealed on the inside. A bell tower on the right side of the main entrance contained louvers for echoing the sound of bells hidden within it. If this church could talk, it would have said "I am the presence of God in stone."

I slowed down to pull into the narrow parking lot thirty minutes before the eleven am Mass. The additional time would allow me to scan the territory like sonar scans for enemy submarines. I inhaled a long, deep breath of fresh air before exiting the car. Then I suppressed the hateful thought about facing another abuser from my past and walked toward the church with a surge of defiance and determination.

Thanks to Facebook, I already had an advantage over Fr. Dennis Flaherty. He, on the other hand, would never recognize me. I had blunted the aging process by camouflaging my appearance like an expert make-up artist. This was not the first time I had changed faces for work. The two hundred dollar color job would fool even a professional cosmetologist. My make-up was soft and eye-catching without drawing attention to myself. I dressed down, in order to blend in with the rural culture of Mattituck.

Today Dennis and I were two actors in the sacred drama that would unfold inside the church during the next sixty minutes. A victim of sexual abuse and my priest sexual abuser would worship under the same roof. The absence of any naiveté dismissed the thought that this sad scenario was limited to this church. I was mature enough to believe that every church, synagogue, and mosque was full of hypocrites. And some of the most well-oiled practitioners wore Roman collars. I would perform my role today with military precision. Though my face would be strange to all the regulars, I would make all the right gestures and genuflections in order to blend in. There would be no slip-ups and certainly no mistakes. I was beyond that, since my experiences had elevated me to teaching the art of serial killing on a master's level.

I entered the church with an air of confidence, knowing well that I had stepped into a time machine and reversed my life by thirty years. I dipped my hand in the holy water font, made the sign of the cross like a well-cloned Catholic, genuflected in the aisle, and selected the pew that would give me a commanding view of the star leading actor.

I wanted to study his every move, his cadence of speech, his gestures, and his tics— indeed, everything I knew to be the false self he

74

revealed to everyone as his true self. I was probably the only one in this church who knew the real Dennis Flaherty.

The three hundred seat church was full by the time Mass began. The beautifully stained wooden floor and vaulted ceiling with wooden cross beams enhanced the level of echo with the singing and praying.

The Mass lasted for one hour, with all the smells and bells associated with my Catholic youth. The priest, exhibiting a dominant character flaw at the beginning, scolded some people for not turning off their cell phones. Some in the assembly played along by shaming these sinners with angry faces. After that the Mass continued uninterrupted with a cadence that was typical of Catholic sacred drama.

I blended in with the crowd as they exited through the main doors. The pastor—the child abuser in a white dress and vestments—was greeting people with the joviality of a Santa Claus engaging people at Christmas.

He picked me out and commented, "I always like to welcome visitors. Where do you hail from?"

"From Manhattan," I replied without divulging any further information.

I thought that was the end of the encounter, but he pursued me like a prosecutor questioning a witness.

"And what brings a city girl to rural Long Island?" he asked abruptly.

"It seemed like a perfect day for a drive in the country," I replied. "Wouldn't you agree?"

"I would," he answered quickly, then to my surprise added, "Do you need a tour guide? My services are free."

My inner radar, detecting he had grown bolder with the years, inspired me to say, "Thanks, but this is as far as I am going today." I left him to decipher the double entendre of my words.

"Well, when you come again, call me." As he handed me a business card, he added, "I will be happy to help you explore the remaining portion of this part of Long Island. Shelter Island is particularly enchanting."

"Thanks, I may do that."

"I'll take that as a promise."

"Are you this friendly with all visitors?" I asked, like an adult playing a game of hide and seek with someone I knew to be a predator and therefore someone who never respected boundaries.

"Just practicing our special brand of hospitality on this end of the island," he answered with a subtle smile.

"Well, thank you for your welcome. I am sure I'll be back for more," I replied, while at the same time turning toward the parking lot. I walked stalwartly toward my car, sensing that his eyes were riveted on me. I willed myself not to turn around.

As I replayed the conversation, it was like unabridged Morse code. I had sent him enough signals today and did not want to engage in any further web spinning through body language.

❧ Chapter Ten ❧

Funeral Mass for Fr. Terry Engals

Bishop John Campbell broke all diocesan protocol and scheduled the funeral Mass for Terry Engals at St. Sebastian Cathedral. Many in the clergy ranks who were privy to his history of child abuse thought such a display of attention was fuel for the media. They were right. Every local TV station covered the event. For the bishop the issue was exercising his authority over pressure to put the deceased priest to rest without fanfare, like the funeral for poet Edgar Allan Poe in 1849. He had been buried quickly, before anyone knew he died.

In his funeral instructions, Terry Engals had requested Fr. Timothy Cavanagh to preach. Two things worked in Tim's favor to prepare during his convalescence at Rosslare Park. First was the extra time the sister of Fr. Engals needed to travel from Ireland, and second, the body was not released by the coroner until four days after his suicide.

As Tim preached, his delivery was soft. His style of weaving stories into the scripture readings was tantamount to medieval artists weaving tapestries that would outlive them. He began with a story from Eastern wisdom literature. A wise teacher answered a pupil's question about life after death by saying, "Have you ever wondered about those people who don't know what to do with this life, but they want another one that will last forever?"

"But is there life after death or not?" asked the pupil.

The teacher responded, "Is there life before death? That is the question."

He then linked this story to the Old Testament reading from Lamentations and the gospel text from St. John. By using the scriptures and stories, he tactfully avoided turning the homily into a commentary on the life of a priest pedophile.

In the end his message was received by the meager assembly in the cathedral as a call to access God as the answer to both questions: is there life before death and after death? He segued from the homily to the piano and concluded the ten-minute sermon with a prayerful rendition of

Frederic Chopin's Piano Sonata #2 in B-flat, Opus 35, affectionately called, "The Funeral March."

The only one not expressing any warmth with this co-mingling of liturgy and classical music was Bishop John Campbell. But, he never warmed to anything when he wasn't the focus of attention. The coat of arms hanging over his Episcopal throne contained the words "All for the glory of Jesus Christ." Every priest in the cathedral that day who knew the true side of the bishop knew that the letters J.C. really stood for John Campbell.

The eulogy, usually given by a member of the family, was instead delivered by Bishop Campbell. It was a ten-minute canonization of Terry Engals. He conveniently omitted any history of child abuse and chose instead to extol only the public priestly qualities of a man who lived a double life. Most of the clergy sat in abject boredom, knowing that it was pure unfiltered bull. If their thoughts ever became public through blogging, each of them would be unmasked as secretly nurturing a hope that John Campbell would not be around to contaminate their funerals with his phony brand of Irish blabber. He was about as transparent as a fox hiding in a lair.

At the end of the funeral, Tim Cavanagh was pleased with his re-entry into ministry after a week of quiet and rest at Rosslare Park. But as the day waned, an unwelcomed cloud of sadness was unleashed within him. It was a reminder that he would return to his office tomorrow. Just the thought of it sapped the remaining sunlight of the day from his cheerful countenance. It was like a power outage at mid-day. He willed himself back into happiness if for no other reason than to rebuke an evil voice that threatened to infect him with the virus called John Campbell. Once he regained his focus, he uttered a quiet prayer of thanks for deliverance.

The Chancery—Morning Mail

After six months in an office routine, Tim Cavanagh had learned how to balance being a caged animal with maintaining his own identity. Unlike other Chancery officials who were treated like slaves, Tim Cavanagh's pedigree, popularity, and personal fortune gained him leverage that forced Bishop Campbell to walk a tightrope with his priest secretary between pure envy and masked aloofness.

Bishop Campbell was not a fair player when it came to the game of turning the other cheek. Abdicating control to a younger, albeit wealthy priest had limits for him. He wanted greater access to the Cavanagh Trust, since for him money meant knocking on more doors in the Vatican and having them opened like the doors to the Wizard's palace in the Land of Oz That meant promotion to a more prestigious See. In the American hierarchy, it wasn't who you knew but how much you contributed to who you knew that mattered. Money talked more than greedy celibate mouths.

John Campbell was a master at the church Mafia game that influenced Episcopal appointments. He was also frustrated that his handpicked secretary could not be manipulated like the other minions who did his bidding. He would have to re-calibrate his strategy toward the multi-millionaire ex-pianist without compromising the staunchly greedy principles that fueled his unconverted ego. He was not about to be a puppy. Other people cleaned up his messes and not vice versa.

This was Tim Cavanagh's first day back since the trauma of Terry Engals's suicide. John Campbell couldn't understand what all the drama was about. Engals wasn't the first priest to take his own life, so get on with it. And after the account of Msgr. McInnes's meeting with Dr. and Mrs. Lyne, including their insulting demands, he was not in the mood to coddle anyone who needed to have their hand held.

All of these thoughts collided in the bishop's head as he prepared for the first staff meeting in over two weeks. He would take charge and regain his authority after a week of being kicked around like a soccer ball. As he flushed out the remains of a half-smoked Cuban cigar and reached to close the opened window behind his desk, there was a knock at his door.

"Come in," he said like the Commander-in-Chief he pretended to be.

Three priests—Msgr. Joe McInnes, Msgr. Ted Barnes, and Fr. Tim Cavanagh—marched into his office in hierarchical order. They each exchanged deferential greetings with their boss then seated themselves around a circular table. Its woodwork shone as if brand new, polished that morning by the undocumented immigrants who worked for the cleaning service. A wide tiffany lamp with a tinted globe hung directly over the center of the table.

Swallowing a dose of false pride, Bishop Campbell began by saying, "It's been a stressful week, and I want to welcome everyone back. Thank you for everything you did to get us through the sadness of Terry's death and funeral, and..." stretching out his words with a noticeable pause, "I am happy to see how Tim has rebounded. I am hoping that getting back into the rhythm of work will be good therapy for all of us."

Fr. Cavanagh, with a slight bow of his head, acknowledged the bishop's words without comment before proceeding with the morning mail.

April 27, 2009

Dear Bishop Campbell,

Fr. Terry Engals's death means one less priest child molester in the diocese. If you think his passing has changed our requests for compensation for our son Jason, let me be clear. It hasn't.

We have retained an attorney, Mr. Ellis Longsworth. You will be hearing from his office shortly. We are not in any mood and you are not in any position to negotiate. If his history of child abuse ever comes to light, every word you spoke at his funeral will unmask you as a liar.

Dr. Ben Lyne, M.D.

To everyone's surprise, Bishop Campbell remained calmed and unaffected. Msgr. McInnes seized the moment first.

"My advice is to consent to their demands, have them sign the Confidentiality clause, and put this matter to rest in the filing cabinet."

Msgr. Barnes added, "We've been in the press enough this week with Terry's funeral and some suspicious innuendos surrounding his suicide. I agree with Joe. We need to bury this case as we buried Terry. God knows we don't need more headlines."

The bishop moved his eyes back and forth between the two priests like he was watching a tennis match. In between them sat his secretary. A silence as thick as steam from a hot tub hung over them as they waited for Tim Cavanagh to speak.

Ted Barnes, sensing that the young priest's emotions about the suicide were still raw, broke the silence. "Tim, is there anything you want to say?"

Tim shook his head and turned his attention to a yellow pad he was using to make notes. His body language had spoken volumes.

The bishop snapped out of his reverie like a soldier snapping to attention.

"Joe, meet with them and their attorney and bring this matter to closure. Put it in the appropriate file." Then he barked to Tim Cavanagh, "Next letter."

April 29, 2009

Dear Bishop Campbell,

Two months ago my mother, Sally Wills, a devoted parishioner at St. Ireneaus Church, died of cancer. Two days before her death we called the pastor, Fr. Neal Rowes, and asked him to come and give her the Sacrament of Anointing. He said he would, but he never came. The hospice nurse called the next day. Again he promised to come, but did not show up. My mother died without the Last Rites. We buried her privately without a funeral Mass.

My father is deeply hurt by this negligence. But, we have forgiven the pastor for his lack of compassion. It has been helpful in our grieving so we can move on, living in hope and being a source of comfort to our dad.

Sincerely,

Sharon & Carl Wills

Three of them sat shaking their heads in disgust. The fourth and youngest priest at the table, Tim, was braced for more absence of accountability. Neal Rowes had a documented trail of shame and embarrassment that would keep a paper shredder busy for a month. It had become part of his abusive behavior because he had only had his fingers slapped like the nuns did to kids in grade school, rather than being forced into therapy like other pathological liars who turned scarring people into an art form.

Msgr. Barnes, speaking like a canon lawyer, said in a professorial tone, "Canonically there isn't anything we can do since Tom still has four years left on his tenure as pastor. But that doesn't mean he shouldn't be confronted about this."

"Joe," the bishop said, "Speak to Neal Rowes and read him the riot act. Copy this letter and let him read it. Maybe their forgiveness will touch his heart, though I doubt it. Tell him that I said I want him to apologize to this family with you present."

Tim Cavanagh sat emotionless in his chair, pondering the multiple layers of victims created by an institution that had not grasped the meaning of the wisdom saying, "What you focus on determines what you miss."

He broke out of his reverie and read a letter from the chairman of Region V about pastoral health care. He had a fleeting thought about whether or not it would include a chapter on the health of some dysfunctional clergy. Tim moved on to another letter.

April 30, 2009

Dear Bishop Campbell,

I am asking for your help in trying to locate Msgr. Randall Blaine. Before my mother, Sophie Cahill, died of cancer last year, she told me that Msgr. Blaine is my real father. I always thought my father died before I was born. But my mother came clean before her death and told me they had an affair for over fifteen years.

They met when he was appointed the pastor of St. Constance Parish in 1975 and my mother was the Director of Religious Education. He supported us through a trust fund which paid for my education at the parochial school and enabled me to get a college degree at St. John's University. He retired in 1997 and relocated somewhere in Arizona. According to my calculations he would be around 80 years old now.

Please have someone call me with information about how I might contact him. I am happily married with three children and living in Rhode Island, but I have a desire to meet him and close this chapter of my life before it's too late.

Thank you for your help in this matter.

Sincerely,

Robyn Donohoe

"Is there any credibility to this letter?" Bishop Campbell asked, like a lawyer deposing a witness.

"I am afraid so," Msgr. McInnes said bluntly, then added, "There is documentation in his file. There is also a copy of the daughter's birth certificate sent by her mother about a year after her birth. I confronted Randy and he admitted to the affair and the child being his. It triggered his premature retirement at age sixty."

"Did the diocese contribute any money to this trust fund for the child's care?" asked the bishop pointedly.

"No!" Msgr. McInnes replied unequivocally.

"Thank God for that. We don't need a money trail with this mess, considering all our other headaches today."

"Do you know how to contact him, Joe?" the bishop asked with little emotion.

"Yes."

"Then do so and ask him what he wants us to do with this woman's request."

Tim Cavanagh was pretending to take notes. It deflected his true inner thoughts, like why no one paid any dignity to the woman by addressing her by name and also why her request for information never made it into the conversation. He refrained from shaking his head in disgust. Instead he wondered what it meant that four men in black were hiding their inner aliens by being in denial about the true issues here.

It became clear how he was going to take these matters into his own hands by reaching out to them and other victims who had been further victimized by silence and neglect.

The meeting ended after about an hour. Msgr. Barnes and Tim Cavanagh returned to their offices, while Msgr. McInnes remained with Bishop Campbell for another thirty minutes.

The bishop hid his displeasure when Tim told him he would be staying the night at Rosslare Park. What Tim didn't tell him was that he would be the first one in the office tomorrow. He wanted to retrieve the letters of complaint from the laity, write down their names and addresses, and practice his own brand of outreach and apology for the hurts an uncompassionate church had inflicted on them. And he wanted to do it in a way that would heal them without bringing any attention to him. It was risky, but he believed that any healing was worth any risk taking.

ᥱ᠍᠍ᎁ Chapter Eleven ᥱᎁᎁ

Bishop Campbell & Msgr. McInnes

The pretender Commander-in-Chief and his General of Covert Operations for the Diocese of Islip remained at the conference table in the bishop's office.

"I want you to settle the matter with the Lynes, and do it without a paper trail. Make sure they sign the confidentiality agreement not to disclose anything related to Terry Engals. And do it quickly."

"I'll get it on after I leave," Msgr. McInnes said with clear assurance in his voice.

Then, changing the subject, the bishop made the following observation. "Tim was noticeably quiet today. I'll give him some leverage regarding his preference for support at Rosslare Park, but if that hasn't changed by the end of the week, I will put a stop to it and Jane Cavanagh be damned," John Campbell said scornfully.

"Be gentle with him, he is fragile right now," Joe McInnes said pleadingly. "And we can't afford to isolate Jane Cavanagh."

"Her wealth is not going to dictate how I run this diocese."

"And it shouldn't," Msgr. McInnes said, "but she will always be in our corner as long as we handle her grandson with velvet gloves."

"I'm from Northern Ireland. I grew up wearing boxing gloves, not velvet gloves."

"Well, since I am used to gloves, let me handle him for the both of us."

The bishop pondered those words, and then said, "Keep me up to date on Msgr. Blaine."

After a pregnant pause, he added, "Christ, I wish these screwed-up priests could keep their penises in their goddamn pants. Their unchecked hormones are not good for my blood pressure."

Msgr. McInnes left the office contemplating a strategy for practicing a subtle form of care giving with Fr. Tim Cavanagh.

Fr. Tim Cavanagh

I had a restless night. But in spite of losing sleep, I awoke early, showered, and left Rosslare Park before dawn for the Chancery Office. Being slightly ahead of the rush hour traffic, I soon arrived. I accessed the elevator with my keycard and was on the fifth floor by 6:20 a.m. Leona Helmond, the hawkish protectress of the Curial Offices, would arrive at seven. She was as punctual as the Swiss rail system.

I left my briefcase in the office and walked toward the filing cabinet room behind Leona's office. Unlocking the cabinet labeled PERSONNEL, I pulled the file for "Engals, Terry." To my surprise the letter of April 27, 2009, from Dr. and Mrs. Lyne was not there. Nor was the letter of March 30, 2009, which detailed the rape of their son. I looked elsewhere, but there was only one file for Terry.

I moved on to the file labeled "Rowes, Neal." Once again surprise was the morning special as the letter of April 29, 2009, from Carl and Sharon Wills was not there. Also missing was the letter of March 27, 2009, from Dr. Richard Williams. My brain deleted surprise and replaced it with suspicion.

After closing that drawer, I opened the bottom one labeled "Inactive Clergy" and pulled the file labeled "Blaine, Randall." The letter dated April 30, 2009, from Robyn Donohoe was not there. Suspicion gave way to the thought of a cover-up. If the letters were not here, than where were they? Questions swirled in my head, like what happened to them, especially the ones discussed just yesterday? Was there another filing cabinet for correspondence about clergy of a scandalous nature? And if so, then where was it?

I didn't have time to ponder these questions. Instead, I turned off the light and walked briskly back to my office. I had fifteen minutes to return to the car and then drive somewhere for coffee and return thirty minutes later without raising any suspicions in the ever-covert mind of Leona Helmond.

Driving to the nearest Dunkin' Donuts, I began to imagine how I was going to add detective to my resume.

Was there an online course or information on Google I could access? Were there tricks I could acquire purely by instinct? What were the risks I hadn't yet pondered? These and other questions swirled in my mind as I soothed my nerves with a large Mocha Frappe and a blueberry muffin. I was hoping they would comfort me in a way that the last fifteen minutes had not.

Nora Owens

Memorial Day weekend was forecast to be ideal for a second trip to Mattituck. I decided to make a hotel reservation for an overnight in case this would be my last trip. I had done my shopping and was ready for another kill if it was meant to be. That decision was not entirely mine, so I was prepared for a Plan B if the pedophile priest ruined Plan A.

After arriving, and during Mass, I noted that Fr. Dennis Flaherty seemed moody. While everyone else was prayerful and the choir inspiring, the priest was restless. His preaching was un-focused, and he appeared agitated about something. Was this just a typical mood swing from an unhappy celibate? No, I thought, make that an unhappy ordained rapist, or did his hormones kick in when he scanned the congregation and noticed me seated just a few pews from the sanctuary? I would put that on my analysis list if our paths crossed, I thought as I left the church.

"Welcome back to our little heaven," Dennis Flaherty said with a broad smile as I walked through the narrow, vaulted doorway. It was obvious to me the melancholic priest who had just said Mass had morphed into a cheerful one.

"When did I miss the news that Mattituck is now little heaven?" I asked like a woman with seduction on her mind.

"It's a term of endearment, my way of helping strangers see this area the way I see it."

"Well, this time I plan to stay longer and see more of heaven, as you put it."

"I'm happy for you but sad for me, since I can't play host today. I have to lead a retreat for our youth."

I stayed composed and was about to respond when he added, "But I can treat you to dinner later. The best restaurant in the area is the

North Fork Table & Inn in Southold. The food is good, and I would enjoy hearing your story of conversion after your meanderings around heaven today. It's on Route twenty-five. As soon as you enter Southold you can't miss it."

"I accept the invitation. What time should we have dinner?"

"How about six?

"I hope you don't stand me up," I said like a woman who was scorned once, then added, "There's nothing worse than eating out alone. Don't you agree?"

"Well, I eat alone so much it's like second nature to me now."

"Then you can count on me to rescue you tonight. See you at six."

I gracefully walked down the sidewalk to the parking lot while denying the urge to look back to see his eyes riveted on me.

Fr. Brian Manley

It has been too long since I have heard from Dennis Flaherty. We are still priest friends from our days in Dublin. Like bosom buddies. Since moving to the Diocese of Islip we have kept in touch, though the geographical distance between us is almost sixty miles. Like me, Dennis has kept a low profile since the murder of Michael Mulgrew in Boston. It's one thing to stay under the radar of a serial killer and another thing not to know where the radar is. That frightens the crap out of me.

I was a child rapist in my early days as a priest. I was a master at playing the fear game with young girls. The power it released in me was addictive. Even though there wasn't any love involved in the sex, the objective was control and not climax. Ejaculation was simply an added thrill. Sometimes I was so horny I forgot to wear a condom and got a poor girl pregnant. On those few occasions I recovered from those guilt trips quickly by taking pride in assuring future chaplains at the orphanage of the abundance of new young girls for their use.

One of my offspring was a boy. In that case he may have made a future gay chaplain very happy.

Since being on the run and hiding after the murder of Michael Mulgrew, I have grown old. More grey hair, a larger girth, a bulbous nose, darker circles around my eyes, a louder cough from smoking, and a forehead resembling a Klingon has turned me into a middle-aged fugitive with a Roman collar. The truth is, I don't wear it that much, since priests are not high on people's respect list these days. It has taught me to control my eyes even when my hormones are racing out of control.

It has been months since I have been laid. The last time was with a prostitute in Manhattan. I loved her rough ways, but hated having to pay her $250. While it was just business for her, it was pure pleasure for me, and it comes at a high price today. Masturbation doesn't hold a candle to intercourse. And I have held my share of candles. No comparison!

There was a time when I got sex for free. The prices these days for celibates to have sex with escorts is causing me to dip into the collections. An inner voice has begun to tell me that an old addiction is creating a new addiction, namely, embezzlement. I decide to ignore it by calling Dennis Flaherty on his cell phone.

Dennis answered on the second ring. He said, "Brian, me boy, are you calling to tell me good news or bad news," he said using his old Irish inflections.

"Both," I said, parroting Dennis's brogue.

"In that case let me hear the good news first."

"I got laid last week, and it was nine on a scale of ten."

"And the bad news?"

"It cost me $250 dollars."

"Ah, yes, nothing is cheap these days, not even good sex. Remember the days in Dublin when it was free and the harems always plentiful."

"Yeah, I remember them well, but getting those days back is pure fantasy."

"Maybe not, Brian me boy," he said with an inflection that sounded intriguing.

"What do you mean?"

"I mean I have met someone who has excited my sex juices."

"Does she have a sister?"

"I don't know since I really don't know much about her. I know her name is Clare and she lives in Manhattan. She has visited Mattituck twice, including today. We're having dinner this evening in Southold. I'll know more then. But, there's something about her, just a feeling, like I've known her and she has re-entered my life. That's the suspicious me talking, which is why I am looking forward to dinner. I'm no Hercule Poirot, but I can play along to an extent that she will reveal some things to me. And whatever it is, I hope it leads someday to getting in bed with her."

We chatted about some mundane things before Dennis had to begin a youth retreat.

"We've got some teenage girls in the Confirmation class I would like to give a sex education class with, but as the bishop has reminded us, they're off limits. We can't abuse his trust, can we?" I asked sarcastically.

"No, we can't, even though there's more fun abusing the girls than abusing trust. Call me later with the scoop!"

After we hung up, I replayed pieces of the conversation and was haunted by Dennis's words about feeling like he might have some history with this woman. I hoped he trusted his instincts. After all, trust is a two-way street. One way it nurtures a relationship. Another way it could kill it, especially if used as a weapon for a prelude to murder. I hoped Dennis used his brain more than his hormones. Better to be smart and stay alive than seduced and end up dead.

⚜ Chapter Twelve ⚜

Detective Sam Bannion

Even though Fr. Terry Engals's suicide investigation was officially closed, my detective's instincts had an urge to discuss the matter with Timothy Cavanagh. What I really wanted was to know more about the world of priest child abusers. Convinced that I could learn more from a priest over a cup of coffee than from some expert psychologist in a lecture hall, I was more interested in having a conversation at a café than taking notes at a desk in a police precinct. Since we had already exchanged cell phone numbers, I called him. To my surprise, he answered on the second ring.

"What can I do for Miss Marple of Islip today?" he said as if reading from a script.

"You sound like one of those customer service reps who answers, 'How can I make banking easy for you today?'"

"Okay, how I can make being a detective easy for you today?" He was quick with rebound lines, which always evoked a grin on my face. Just another personality trait to check on his "most endearing quality" category list.

"You can join me for a cup of coffee when you have some free time."

"And the purpose of this meeting over a cup of coffee is…"

"Can I tell you that when we meet?"

"In that case can we meet soon, since I am already intrigued?"

"Are you this impetuous with all women, or are you not good at handling mystery?"

"If that is a double question, then the answer is, yes and yes! How about Coffee & Company on Euclid Street in half an hour?"

"See you then," I said with a smile that only he could paint.

I hung up and wondered if his smile was as animated as mine and if it was so contagious that Bach the Airedale picked up the scent thirty miles away. I had just enough time to grab my purse, which doubled as a small backpack and portable office, before heading to my car. I secretly hoped nobody noticed that I was skipping to the beat of a new drum after that phone call.

When I arrived, the impeccably dressed priest-pianist was waiting at a table in a far corner and signaled with his hand. I would have known where he was sitting just by following the trail of the sparkle left by his eyes. I was wearing the typical female cop dress-down attire. My denim blouse was open just enough to trigger wonderment about the hidden cleavage. My jeans were sporty and neatly pressed, a habit I inherited from the mother who spoiled me by ironing my jeans. My red hair was pulled back in a phony tail, a preference that goes with the territory as a female cop. Less hair in the way means less getting in the way of practicing the art of chasing and arresting criminals.

He spoke first. "You didn't indicate if this was official, so I dressed down. I left my collar at the office," he said as the corners of his mouth creased upwards, revealing a smile. If it was intended to leave me smitten, it worked.

"Well since I don't wear a veil, I dress down most of the time, except when I have lunch with Bach on the piano as background music."

"I'm afraid you'll have to have coffee without Bach today."

"And what makes you think I wasn't listening to Bach on the CD player in my car while driving here?"

His face mirrored my impish grin.

"Classical culture through CDs is the next best thing to being in a recital hall," he said, sounding like a Juilliard graduate. Ever the gentleman, he went to the counter, placed our orders, and returned to the table.

"Okay, enough suspense. What's the mystery behind our meeting?"

Like Superman in a telephone booth, I was instantly transformed into a detective. I calculated my words like a CPA doing an audit. I wanted to probe, but without revealing anything about my brother, Kurt. "I want to talk with you about priest pedophiles."

Instantly I noticed a similar change in his features. His face took on a serious demeanor, transforming him into the likeness of a monk. His voice softened as he asked, "It's not a very pleasant topic, so what exactly do you want to talk about?"

"Well, let's start with Fr. Terry Engals."

"Is this off the record?" he asked, like a witness being interviewed by a reporter.

"Yes, I'm not here on police business. I just want to learn more about it so I can handle it better in the future."

"Do you have reason to believe there's going to be another Terry Engals suicide?"

His questions were dead center, revealing a heart that always listened carefully and a mind that sometimes thought like a detective. I found the latter quality dangerous.

I could tell by his body language that he was getting defensive, so I changed my strategy. "Let me start over. So delete all the above. Tim, I don't know much about priest pedophiles. What can you teach me that would be helpful to me as a detective?"

"Well, speaking from experience, you certainly know how to handle a priest who witnessed the suicide of one." He paused as if to choose his words carefully. "To be perfectly honest, I don't know much about them either."

He paused again and I gave him space so as not to interfere with his train of thought.

"I heard rumors in my childhood days and as a student at Juilliard. Once, when I was on tour, I had a priest flirt with me at a bar in a London hotel where I was staying, but I chalked that up to his spiraling to the other side of drunk. What I know about the science of clergy child sex abusers you could fit in any crack between the keys on a piano."

"Okay do you suspect there are other priest pedophiles in the diocese?"

Without taking his eyes off me, Tim assumed a reflective mood while pondering his words. His answer was brief but to the point. "I don't suspect, I know!" "What do you think we can do about that?"

93

"What do you mean?"

"I mean, how can the police assist the diocese in this matter?" What he said next stunned me like being hit with a Taser gun. "First, I am not the one you should be asking that question of. And second, the one you should be asking isn't going to give you the answer you may want. In his own words, 'He asks questions, he doesn't answer them.' You don't have to be a brain surgeon to figure out who I'm talking about."

"Yes, Bishop Campbell is not on anybody's people-friendly awards list," I said. "In fact he works overtime getting poor ratings from everyone he meets. Everybody knows he holds his cards close to the chest, especially when those cards are about protecting sick clergy."

"I've worked with him long enough to know that's his first agenda," Tim agreed. "It's his way of getting Rome's attention. He was raised wearing combat boots in the Falls Road section of Belfast. Behind his Episcopal title is a warrior that will do anything to defend the secrets of the church, including protecting clergy who are criminals. So don't cross him because he can inflict his own kind of crosses on people— especially women, whom he holds in lower esteem than priest child abusers. I am beginning to wonder if his attitude toward the opposite sex or any sex is hidden behind a suspicion that he is castrated."

"How have you managed not to cross him?" I asked with point-blank intensity.

"Who said I haven't crossed him?" He hesitated and deflected his attention to people peering in the coffee shop window, squinting their eyes to see the menu board hanging on the window facing them. Satisfied they weren't spying or lip-reading, he continued.

"Because of my name and money, he pushes far enough to make his point without me pushing back. That's because it isn't me he fears but my grandmother. Though they're not exactly bosom buddies, it's the money he wants more than my allegiance. But, back to the priests. I'm struggling with not only the scandal, but a possible cover-up."

My inner radar caused my eyes to narrow on him, signaling surprise, before I said, "What do you mean—a possible cover-up?" Once again he paused without losing eye contact. That pleased me more than taking time to choose his words.

"I mean, there may be hidden filing cabinets I don't know about."

I had problems computing what I was hearing, but I didn't show any alarm. Instead, I said with clear composure in my voice, "If there are documents missing or being shredded, then this is serious. It is a matter for the district attorney."

There was a long silence between us as the conversation became more focused and intense. He placed both hands together like a steeple and brought them to rest on his cleft chin. He had taken risks, and because of such trust with me, his capital soared. But alarm bells were also sounding inside me—maybe he was planning to take some actions that might backfire. Call it police instinct, but I was truly concerned about him. So I repaid his trust with some of my own.

"What can I do to help?" sounded much better than, "Don't do anything stupid." Tim Cavanagh was many things, but stupid was not one of them.

"Well, we can begin with my calling on you as a consultant whenever I need it."

"I'll take that as a compliment and say, please do."

He cracked a smile that said, "Thanks."

For the next few minutes we talked about the Mets winning streak and their mutual hopes for a championship season. Then he surprised me with an invitation.

"My grandmother is taking the children of the Rosslare staff to the Mets–Phillies game on Sunday. Would you care to join us? You can come as my guest."

With a muted sigh, I replied, "I would love to, but I am entertaining my niece and nephew on Sunday."

"Bring them along. She has plenty of tickets and believe me, the seats are to die for."

"Well, dying for a certain baseball game seat at Shea Stadium isn't on the top of my bucket list, so I accept on behalf of the two people in my family fan club," I said. I hoped my shocked enthusiasm didn't show on my face. A whole afternoon in his company sounded great, kids or no kids. "I'll bring restraining jackets so they don't embarrass me."

That evoked a hearty laugh. "Meet us at the stadium at 12:30 at the Players entrance. Now I have to get back to the office before somebody sends out Gollum to find me." He winked at me.

"Who's Gollum?" I asked with a hint of curiosity, though I knew full well who the JRR Tolkien character was. "Who is Gollum? We'll we have to do something about your Hollywood illiteracy." He laughed again.

"What do you recommend?"

"I'll think about it and let you know. It's a no-brainer, so don't lose any sleep over it."

As he left the café, I wondered if he read the expression on my face that said, "How do you know I have been losing sleep lately?"

Nora Owens

I checked out the rating of the North Fork & Inn at Southold on my iPhone. It was four stars. I couldn't figure out if the priest pedophile I was having dinner with had gotten cultured since relocating across the Pond or whether he wanted to impress me as a prelude to getting me in bed. Since this was his territory, I would play by his rules until I grew weary and changed them to suit myself.

I arrived first, gave my name, and was surprised that he had made a reservation.

"Father Flaherty has a usual table, so please follow me," the hostess said, like someone whose familiarity with him did not include being on a first-name basis. When she asked about ordering a drink, I deferred, choosing to wait for my dinner guest to arrive.

He was ten minutes late. I wasn't annoyed since that was a nanosecond wait compared to the last 30 years. If anything this was only a prelude to a murder, and since he is paying for it, I would milk it for all it was worth. It would be the first and last time he would keep me waiting. My role was simply to perform like someone whose wait for revenge with another priest sexual abuser was about to come to an end. I was in no hurry to get someplace, so I'd sit back and enjoy the show. It might be worth a Tony nomination.

He arrived sporting a well-starched pinstriped shirt, an expensive ascot, and a double-breasted blue blazer, which gave him the appearance of being a Long Island snob. If I hadn't known his true identity, I would have guessed he was dressed for a date with someone arranged using an online dating service. The only thing missing was a mask, and I was the only one who knew he wore that on the inside.

"Sorry to keep you waiting," he said with detectable insincerity.

"I'm just glad you kept your promise and didn't stand me up."

"Not to worry. The cooking here is best when shared with someone."

He ordered a bottle of wine and shared stories crafted in lies and innuendos over our appetizers. During dinner I camouflaged being bored with details about a Dennis Flaherty I knew never existed. I pretended to be impressed with information that fed an ego the size of the prime rib he was devouring like a street canine. At the same time I was thrilled with my Tony nomination performance hidden behind perfect American English and a wit that could charm a self-absorbed Irishman like him into believing he was entertaining me for the first time.

We both waived dessert in favor of Irish coffee. He walked me to the car and said, "There are other restaurants worth exploring the next time you come to heaven."

"Are you inviting me on another date?" I asked, like an innocent high school sophomore infatuated with the senior football quarterback.

"Was this a date or dinner?"

"I hope it was both—and yes, I would like to do it again. But next time let me pick the place, the restaurant, and the tab."

"I graciously accept your invitation. Here is my cell phone number. Call me when you're ready to dine out again."

"It's a date. Oops, make that 'it's a dinner date,'" I said in a feigned tone of voice and wearing a girlish smile.

As I drove back to the Hilton Hotel at MacArthur Airport, I replayed every line spoken, every innuendo uttered, every eyebrow raised, every tic observed, every lie revealed, and decoded it like a master spy. It was all helpful in laying the trap that would bring this chapter to closure.

Detective Timothy Cavanagh

I pretended to be busy at my desk in the Chancery Office. The fifth floor was cryptically referred to by the clergy as the Power Dome. Little did they know all the power resides in just one office, while the rest of his minions pump ongoing supplies of oxygen because it is constantly depleted by the distasteful aroma of toxic Cuban cigars. The thought entered my mind that we would be doubly blessed, both ecologically and spiritually, if the smoker would die prematurely of lung cancer and spend his eternity in the smoke-free crypt of St. Sebastian Cathedral. Knowing I was not the only worker in the building who entertained such a thought, my conscience quickly recalibrated from the momentary thought of guilt back to the matter of missing files.

I found myself in a no-option situation. On the one hand, if I said anything to Msgr. Ted Barnes about the missing letters, I would be drawing attention to myself. On the other hand, if I asked Leona Helmond about them, she would ask questions that would eventually get back to the Fuehrer. The Sherlock Holmes in me began to unravel the mystery through the art of deduction.

Fact number one was, there were no files at the Chancery Office. I had done a mine sweep of every room, nook, and corner. Fact number two was, if they were not placed in the Chancery Office files, then they must either be in Msgr. McInnes's rectory or in the bishop's summer house. Getting into either one of them would be like trying to steal the crown jewels from the Tower of London. Since that had already been done in fiction, why couldn't I do it as the real thing? After all, I was not without connections, and if I designed an air-tight plan it could work.

With my novice detective imagination, I decided to start with the bishop's summer house first. I just had to remain calm, be methodical, and think like a master detective and not a priest unskilled in the art of breaking and entering. I would begin with "casing the joint" this weekend. Bishop Campbell would be traveling and celebrating confirmations, so his absence would mean less sweat. Once the surveillance phase was complete, I would have an entire week to illegally enter and search with the bishop away for the annual summer meeting of the National Conference of Catholic Bishops in three weeks.

Bishop Campbell never entertained visiting hierarchy at Solitude until the fourth of July through mid-September. With the national bishops' summer meeting scheduled for the latter part of June, I would have unfettered access before a cleaning crew readied the house for the season.

I had been at Solitude several times as a guest with my grandmother. I was already familiar with the floor plan. The only roadblock was the security system. I was sure that information was stored in a file in the Chancery Office. Retrieving that info was my first order of business. The rest of the plan for breaking and entering would be in place by then.

ᴄ♪ Chapter Thirteen ᴄ♪

Lock Down Security Systems

L ock Down Security Systems, this is Debbie speaking. How may I help you?"

"This is Father Timothy Cavanagh, is Mel there?"

"He's on a job, but I can send a text message so he can call you back soon," she said, the sound of bubble gum clicking in her mouth.

"Please do that, here is my cell number," Tim said, hiding the amusement in his voice.

Mel Staudameyer was affectionately called "the doorkeeper" at Rosslare Park by Jane Cavanagh. He had changed enough locks at the manor house to elevate him to the rank of St. Peter, since he allowed people to enter and leave the pearly gates of the Cavanagh residence at Stony Brook.

Tim would need Mel's expertise to pick the lock at Solitude. Once inside, Tim would disarm the security system, pay Mel a generous tip for his silence, and put on his Sherlock Holmes deerstalker cap. Just a ruse, he thought, as he told his conscience that he was stalking information for the sake of victims who had never had justice.

He would then have to locate the key box, hopefully finding a spare key so he could regain access during the week. He began to implore St. Anthony (patron saint of lost things) to help him seek and find the key box quickly.

With all the pieces of his plan falling into place, Tim Cavanagh chose the date for his first criminal activity. Something he didn't anticipate was the surge of energy that aroused his metabolism. The adventurer in him was being released. Once again he convinced himself that this battle was not about winning or losing but about justice for people victimized by the unjust practices of the institutional church and some of its leaders. Leaders like John Campbell, whose style was to stigmatize sexual abuse victims by inflicting on them the added abuse of neglect, shame, and humiliation.

Nora Owens

During my debriefing drive from Mattituck to MacArthur Airport, I gained certainty that this charade with one of my former priest molesters was already becoming old for me. It was Pentecost Sunday, and I decided to use this new fire of insight to put the finishing touches on my mission.

Once I got home to east Manhattan, I would take an inventory of all the details needed to scratch the name of another sexual priest rapist off my sexual abuser list.

I had already purchased the murder weapon of choice. I brought with me from Europe a print of a renowned painting that my victim could meditate on before his death.

My plan to gain access to Dennis Flaherty's rectory would include gourmet food from an exquisite mid-town deli for dinner in his home, top of the line wine to subdue and weaken his resistance, valium to drug his system so his state of delirium would muffle the torture of the final moments, and the Bad Boy rope to tie him up into submission.

As an afterthought, I made a mental note to bring candles to accentuate the prop used by a figure in the painting of the martyrdom of St. Bartholomew. After all, I wanted to replicate the death scene in the painting to the smallest detail. My career as a murderer of priest sexual abusers had an artistic flare. I was no homeless street killer. I was as deliberate and methodical in my revenge as my abusers were in their sodomy and rape. It was my way of putting a face on the idiom, "Getting a taste of your own medicine."

Flipping open my cell phone, I accessed the calendar app. August 24 was exactly nine weeks away. I would have to make sure Dennis Flaherty would be home for his death. To put that piece of the puzzle in place, I needed some bait.

By the time I returned to my apartment later that day, I knew exactly where to get it. And it wasn't at a fishing store.

The Break-in

Tim Cavanagh wasted no time planning his break-in at Solitude. He drove Bishop Campbell to Kennedy Airport for his morning flight to Denver to attend the national bishops' conference summer meeting. Following a terse good-bye at curbside, Tim activated his Bluetooth and placed a phone call to Mel Staudameyer.

After the second ring, a voice said, "This is Mel. I do break-ins, not break ups. Talk to me." He was a man of few words, Tim thought as he broke into a wide grin upon hearing Mel's subtle and ear-catching marketing line.

"Mel, this is Tim Cavanagh."

Preferring to communicate informally through the familiar first names, Mel replied in a raspy voice,

"Father Tim, what a nice surprise. I got the text yesterday that you would call. What's up?"

"I need a favor, Mel. I have lost my key to the front door at Solitude, and I need to get in today and see what has to be done to get the house ready for the summer."

"Well," he said confidently, "knowing yourself how many doors I have broken into at your grandmother's home, I welcome the chance to break into a bishop's house. Give me the address and the time you want to meet me."

They agreed to meet at the Flanders Bay summer house after lunch.

Tim arrived five minutes before the locksmith. It had been a long time since the two crossed paths. As a young boy growing up at Rosslare Park, Tim had always stopped what he was doing to watch the meticulous locksmith ply his trade on one of the many locked doors at the family house when keys were lost. Now he watched Mel's Toyota van chugging slowly up the driveway to Solitude. It was painted the most brilliant shade of orange, so eye-catching that it would be the first vehicle picked out anywhere on the Long Island Expressway by traffic helicopters. It probably contained material that made it glow in the dark so that Mel could advertise on the road twenty-four hours a day.

On both sides was stenciled the message, "Mel the Locksmith. Call when you need a break-in, not a break-up." That line alone earned him the reputation as the most popular locksmith on the east end of Long Island.

Mel once told Jane Cavanagh that some of his break-ins were preludes to break-ups. He was even subpoenaed to testify at several divorce hearings for couples looking for dirt on a cheating spouse inside a locked getaway home. He always managed to maneuver his way through the minefield of contentious break-ups by pleading what he called "the fifty-fifth amendment." For him that was telling the truth that his fingers did all the looking and feeling and not his eyes. He always convinced a judge that he closed his eyes and opened his ears for aligning the tumblers in a locked door and therefore saw nothing that would be helpful to the case. Jane always told her grandson that Mel Staudameyer was a master artist without a master's degree. Tim was about to see that played out once again.

Though they had not seen each other in a long time, Tim couldn't contain the thought that Mel had turned into a double for Danny DeVito. His Brooklyn accent was a dead giveaway.

"Fr. Tim, what a pleasure to see you again," Mel said with sincerity.

As they shook hands, Tim said, "I appreciate your help. As the Irish Mafia are fond of saying, 'I owe you a favor for this favor.'"

Mel diplomatically chose to deflect a response to the line and asked in a caring voice, "How is your grandmother?"

"As meddlesome as ever," Tim said with a hint of sarcasm.

"Glad to hear it," Mel said with a chuckle. "Please give her my regards."

Then as an afterthought Mel added, "It's been a while since I was called to Rosslare Park. Maybe you should talk her into getting some new doors!" He winked, knowing Tim would appreciate his sense of humor.

As Mel walked up to the front door, he studied it momentarily, like a sculptor studies a piece of stone selected for his next masterpiece.

"What we have here is a BMW door with a Volkswagen lock. It's your lucky day, Fr. Tim, since I am an expert in matching wits with foreign locks."

Balancing one instrument in his left hand and the other in his right, Mel began a delicate dance of moving them together while pinning his ear to the door knob.

In less than two minutes, there was a click. Mel turned and faced Tim with a grin that was contagious. He then duplicated the procedure on the dead bolt.

"It's all in the hands, Fr. Tim. Whether you're playing a piano concerto or opening a locked door, it's all in the hands. Wouldn't you agree?"

I couldn't express it better myself," Tim Cavanagh said with an affirming nod. Tim stepped inside the entrance and instinctively headed toward the security alarm system hidden behind the staircase. After two attempts the system was disarmed.

After completing his tasks, Mel closed his instrument case. Tim offered him a $100 bill, Mel shook his head.

"I have been paid by your grandmother many times over. This is a small way to repay her for her generous kindness."

Before Tim could object, Mel continued in a serious tone of voice, "She helped me get my business started many years ago. She referred people to me who are still clients. She co-signed the loan for my van and even suggested the color orange and the one-liner. She said it would bring more business than a telephone book ad." Mel laughed. "She was right. I get more calls from people who notice the van and the one-liner. Instead of money, say some prayers for me, especially to the patron saint of people with arthritis. It's beginning to make my work difficult and turning me into someone who curses a lot. So, tell God, if he wants me to stop taking his name in vain, then he better speed up a miracle for arthritis."

"I'll say a prayer for you," Tim agreed. "And thank you."

"Glad to be of help, Fr. Tim," Mel said as he extended his hand. Tim shook it and added a smile that was endearing. He waved goodbye as Mel drove the classic orange van back down the driveway.

Tim Cavanagh then stepped into the entrance to the summer house for the first time in a long time. The sound of silence echoed through halls and over the polished parquet floors and the fabric-covered walls, reminding Tim that solitude was more than a word.

He decided to scout the house one floor at a time, beginning with the basement, hoping to find a key box, either behind a stairwell or in a closet that would hide a spare key, allowing him to gain access until he had his own key. Once he gained familiarity with the layout, he would return each day this week and uncover whatever secrets it was hiding about missing files.

Thirty minutes later, after finding the key box on the wall at the bottom of the circular staircase, he surfaced from the basement level. He returned to the entrance and did a last-minute pirouette with his body as a sign that he was pleased with what he had accomplished in less than one hour.

"By the end of the week we will be friends," he said, realizing he was talking to a house. Fully aware that he was not hallucinating, Tim Cavanagh coached an inner voice to reassure himself. What he was doing for the sake of justice for victims would help him transcend any fear about ending this caper, because it had danger written all over it.

As a concert pianist, he lived dangerously every time he pushed himself to the edge with a new piano concerto. He would approach this venture, like a concerto, one movement at a time even if he didn't know the climax.

His pianist artistic brain could already hum themes of the first movement. It contained features of the Allegro con spiritu – the alluring first movement of Tchaikovsky's Piano Concerto #1 in B-flat minor. Tim Cavanagh felt buoyed as he stepped off the porch of the summer house. As he opened the car door he surveyed the house one last time, as if it were eye candy. *Tomorrow,* he mused, *I will see what secrets you may be hiding.*

After he saluted the three-story structure, he veered down the driveway and headed toward the Southern Parkway. The not-ready-for-primetime-detective felt pleased with what he had accomplished in just a few hours. His return tomorrow would make this adventure a series labeled, "To be continued."

ᴄᴨ Chapter Fourteen ᴅᴧ

Detective Sam Bannion

Detective Lou Perkins knew me well and he could always tell when I had issues. Every time I hit my desk with both ends of a metal pen, he knew my insecurities were fueling my behavior.

"Do you want to talk about it?" he said cautiously.

"Talk about what?" I countered, looking dumbfounded.

"Whatever it is that's bugging you."

"What makes you think something's bugging me?"

"That thing you do with your pen. It's always the giveaway when something's bugging you."

I dropped the pen when I realized my partner had connected the dots between some unresolved inner itch and the behavioral tic I unconsciously practiced to process it.

"I didn't know I was being spied on. Are you studying people for a new reality TV show?" I said with a practiced fluency in sarcasm.

"Come on, Sam, you know me better than that. Besides, I don't watch reality TV. My life as a detective is reality enough."

I pondered his words while eying him with a serious look. "I am still haunted by the suicide of Fr. Terry Engals." I paused to calibrate my words.

"I can't shake the feeling that it's just the tip of a volcano, and not knowing when it might erupt again leaves me feeling uneasy. We're a small police force within the boundaries of a vast geographical Catholic diocese. My instincts tell me it's a minefield, and I am not confident about when and how we might have to walk through it again."

"All we can do is to learn something from each experience," Lou said with a shrug.

"And that, my dear partner, is what's bugging me. Not knowing how many more experiences we might have to face."

We both got quiet. Lou went back to completing paperwork. I went back in my mind to the scene of Fr. Tim Cavanagh in the rectory bathroom at St. Malachy's. I hoped it would never be replayed again.

Fr. Tim Cavanagh

I couldn't have picked a worse day to play Sherlock Holmes at Solitude. By 10 AM the temperature had turned the day into a Turkish sauna. The waters in Flanders Bay were as motionless as a picture of a still pond in a real estate ad. I dressed casually, knowing that I couldn't risk using the air-conditioning since the house would not be re-opened for the summer season for two more weeks.

Using the new key I had made from the spare key, I stepped inside the house. The level of humidity hit me like walking into a steam room, and the temperature felt like I was in the Sahara desert. In seconds beads of sweat were dripping from my forehead and my METS T-shirt was sticking to my torso. I slowly made my way to the kitchen then down the spiral staircase to return the spare key to the box. In a nanosecond my body temperature dropped in the coolness of the basement. I decided to begin my search there, partly out of location and partly out of common sense. The basement was the closest thing to natural air-conditioning. I flipped on a light switch and pivoted toward the wine cabinets.

The wrought iron gate protecting the high-priced bottles of imported wines lying reverently on their bank of shelves was locked. I walked back to the cabinet, surveyed the key guide with my index finger, and pulled key #24 from the hook. The squeaky sound of my sneakers echoing off the brick floor in the vaulted basement was a muffled difference to the dress shoes I had worn just yesterday. It was enough that I was breaking and entering a house. I didn't want to be distracted with sound effects that had me looking over my shoulder like someone being followed in a Stephen King horror movie.

The gate door swung open without a squeak. Stepping into the area with an attitude of standing on holy ground, I flipped a switch to the right, and a track of lighting from a ceiling fixture illuminated the wine cellar gradually, like singular paintings being narrowly highlighted in an art gallery.

In spite of the muted lighting, I guessed the wine cellar was about 24 feet wide by 20 feet deep. Three sections of shelves protruded out from the north wall, leaving a walking aisle about 3 feet wide.

Holding a small flashlight the way a CSI would use it to comb a crime scene for evidence, I began checking out the wine labels on the bottles. It was obvious the first section of shelves contained all white wine: Bianco delle Venezie at $40.00 a bottle, Spain's coolest Rueda, and shelves of Baileyana Chardonnay from California's Edna Valley. The entire bottom shelf was reserved for German Reisling, some with price labels of $100.00 a bottle. The second casing was all red wines, while the third casing housed aperitifs, crème liqueurs, and enough Baileys to create a miniature Flanders Bay in the back yard. Perched high on the top shelf were bottles of champagne. Curious to see the labels, I reached up to retrieve one. "Curvee Dom Perignon, vintage 1982" evoked an impressed smile on my face. As I was about to replace the bottle, my 6' stature was all the height I needed to notice a switch. I raised the flashlight to get a clearer view. The switch was recessed into the wall in such a way that the bottle of champagne was meant to camouflage it without changing its alignment on the shelf.

I flipped the switch and then stood in frozen suspense as I watched the entire casing slowly pivot on a track embedded in the concrete floor. In less than a minute it locked itself in place. I blinked slowly to make sure that what I was seeing was not a mirage. The opening had revealed an inner, hidden concrete room that looked like a bunker.

Cautious about what I might be stepping into, I reached for the inside wall and felt a light switch. Flipping it on revealed an interior room no larger than 12' by 10'. I breathed a sigh of relief that I hadn't stepped inside unaware and fallen down the kind of caved tunnel typical of a thrilling ride in an Indiana Jones movie. The room was windowless and without ventilation, emitting a dank and moldy smell. The concrete walls made it look cold and depressing, the kind of room where interrogation secrets were stored. Three filing cabinets rested against an inner wall. I noticed the locks were in the open position and concluded that the hidden room was all the security needed to hide whatever secrets were in the files.

I surveyed the room with Hercule Poirot eyes and catalogued its Spartan furnishings: a 20th-century straight-backed wooden chair; a 19th-

century, single-bulb desk light; and a small wooden table holding a photocopier. That piece of office equipment spoke volumes. I took two steps and one deep breath before opening one of the filing cabinets.

Detective Sergeant Samantha Bannion

I had been staring at the mound of paperwork on my desk for over thirty minutes. As much as I wished it, it wouldn't go away or self-destruct. After ten years in police work I hadn't reconciled myself to writing reports, transcribing interviews, and all the other endless categories of paperwork that strangled my morale. In spite of honors, promotions, and increased respect in the public safety sector, I was first and always a person of action. I preferred being on the beat to sitting at a desk. I hungered to hunt down criminals more than interview suspects. I thrived on solving crimes rather than sitting through meetings and furnishing updates.

My partner was out of town for two days attending his niece's college graduation. And without him I was getting itchy. He was the closest thing to having a man in my life, and we were a good team.

So my thoughts were steering toward another man who was beginning to occupy a larger role in my life, including my dreams and fantasies. Tim Cavanagh had become my brilliant, baby-faced, born rich, humble-of-heart obsession. I loved it that he lived beyond the edge of a fake tycoon's existence. What I couldn't get enough of was the poignancy of his wanting to make everyone happy. That was what made him so appealing to me and was fueling a desperate need for his company.

So, my brain said to my arm, reach for your cell and call him. And my arm offered no resistance. After six rings the voice mail kicked in. I hesitated then decided to leave a message.

"Tim, it's Sam. When you get this message, please call me." I hung up while my imagination started to perk. That impulse, when combined with hot flashes, always triggered a light blinking inside, like a neon sign flashing the message DANGER. A plot began to take shape in the form of an idea to return the favor for the fun day at the Mets ballgame. But my idea was thoroughly downsized and did not include a grandmother, employees' children, my niece and nephew, a cold concrete stadium, and 30,000 fans. I was thinking of something more quiet and intimate, like dinner for two, good wine, and unique vocal entertainment. I was hoping the last feature would convince a concert pianist not to say no.

Fr. Tim Cavanagh

I opened the top drawer of the first filing cabinet and found the names of the clergy listed in alphabetical order. I noticed that some had red dots stuck to the labels. I interpreted that as a red flag. The first one I pulled so marked was *Lyle Aiken.* I spread it open on the table and began scanning it with X-ray eyes.

A personnel profile was placed inside the left pocket of the file. It recorded his birth date, family history, academic records, etc. He was a priest of the diocese from 1940 to 1972.

The material nestled inside the right pocket of the file was personal letters. At the top of the pile were complaints about sexual abuse of boys in as many as six different parishes. Bishop Robert Morrissey retired Fr. Aiken at age fifty seven in 1970 following a strong letter of complaint by Msgr. Stan Carlisle, pastor of St. Victor's in East Islip. The letter contained documentation of Fr. Aiken taking certain altar boys on trips to the beach, entertaining them in his rooms, and subduing them with alcohol before raping them. Six of those resigned as altar boys within several months of Fr. Aiken's sexual overtures or abuse. Three of their parents withdrew them from the parochial school. Their letters of complaint were filed along with Fr. Aiken's death certificate. A letter from Bishop Morrissey, outlining payment of $5,000 each as a settlement for his sexual abuse of three boys, contained a strong reminder about CONFIDENTIALITY. The absence of any apology from the bishop was glaring.

The next file in alphabetical order was Msgr. Maurice Brownloe. His personnel profile form revealed his long tenure from 1955–1983 as pastor of St. Veronica's Parish in Quogue. After that was one letter of complaint from parents at St. Giles Parish, where he served as assistant pastor from 1952 to 1955. Next were two letters from two different sets of parents expressing strong complaints about his alleged sexual abuse of their teenage daughters during his assignment at St. Veronica's Parish.

Next was a similar form letter signed by Bishop Morrissey with a reminder about CONFIDENTIALITY regarding the settlement of $15,000 plus counseling for the two abused girls. Next was a strongly worded letter from both sets of parents about the bishop's decision not to remove Msgr. Brownloe from St. Veronica's after their complaint about his propensity for sexual abuse.

Underneath that correspondence was an equally strong letter from Bishop Morrissey rebuking them for their presumption to tell him how to do his job and a veiled reminder about their signing the CONFIDENTIALITY clause as part of the settlement agreement.

After reading just two personnel files, I began doing the math and concluded that the possibility of a cover-up went back as far as the mid-1950s. My eyes locked onto the photocopier so I flipped on the switch while my brain began computing a plan for justice for these victims, which no doubt had trouble written all over it for me. As I waited for the machine to warm up, I pulled another file.

The label read "Msgr. Joshua Carruthers." My eyes widened as I read *Judicial Vicar from 1965 to 1990* on his personnel file. I spiraled into shock reading fourteen letters of complaints from parents about his sexual abuse of boys. His access to money came from the fact that he was a priest-son of the wealthy Carruthers Plumbing Company. According to the letters he endeared himself to young boys with gifts and trips to the Carruthers's family cabin in the Catskill Mountains, where he lured them into his sick cauldron of sexual abuse. The letters were explicit about his techniques for pumping the boys full of alcohol before raping and torturing them.

As I read the details of his anal sex without protection I started to tremble and had to sit down. A nauseous feeling enveloped me, and I thought I was going to vomit. To regain my composure I stepped outside the room momentarily to breathe some fresh air.

Recovering from what felt like hyperventilating, I continued reading the contents of the file. A letter from Bishop Martin Muller was adamant about putting a stop to the abuse. In his letter dated March 6, 1988, he stated that Msgr. Carruthers was sent for psychological evaluation at a center in New Mexico. He stayed for just six weeks before moving to Belize, where he lived a life of luxury using his own personal fortune. He avoided extradition and prosecution by paying off Belize authorities who harbored him from the U.S. justice system. His death certificate specified he died of natural causes in Belize on April 22, 1998. His body was cremated, the ashes buried at sea.

The next file was Fr. Larry Chilcott. According to the personnel profile, he had six accusations against him for sexual abuse of boys. He never stayed longer than two years in a parish. He held eight assignments in sixteen years before being named pastor of Visitation Parish in Middle Island. I found four letters accusing him of sexual abuse of five boys in the parish school. Two were twins. One of them attempted suicide at age fourteen.

There was significant correspondence between Fr. Chilcott and Bishop Morrissey. The latter only scolded him for what the bishop called "the problem" and then sent him to another parish without any treatment or supervision. Finally, Bishop Muller took the strong advice of Msgr. Maurice Fenton, Larry Chilcott's pastor at Holy Savior Parish, and sent him for treatment. The bill was $75,000.

Upon his return six months later, Chilcott was assigned as pastor of Visitation Parish. It didn't take long for his demons to return. The first letter of complaint was dated ten months later. I shook my head in disgust, thinking, *what a waste of money.* Even the insurance company would agree. And the bill for gaining the silence of the victims' parents was $110,000. Realizing that Larry Chilcott was becoming an expensive liability to the diocese, Bishop Muller retired him at age 69 in 1994 and banished him to a monastery.

Once again I shook my head in disgust, realizing that pay-offs, as the motivation for termination, trumped immoral and criminal behavior.

I pulled more files with red dots and read while totally oblivious of time passing. Most of the names I was unfamiliar with: Msgr. Fred Clennan, Fr. Austin Cooney, Fr. Mario Corona, Fr. Derek Cummings. They had a total of 24 credible accusations against them. The next name turned on light bulbs since it had become a media case.

Fr. Nikko Sardis became a poster priest for the diocese in the '90s. He was a rakish looking priest with Mediterranean features. His GQ looks would have left most women salivating and some men envious. Hidden behind the Adonis smile and the dark Greek eyes, however, was a sinister sexual predator. The letters revealed he had raped and tortured 14 teenage boys in his first two parishes. His letter of

113

resignation, four years after ordination, indicated he would pursue a career in counseling. I shook my head in disgust, wondering if the greater sin was the denial of brain cells that blocked his making connections between his sexual deviancy and the profession of counseling—or Bishop Morrissey's lack of conscience about releasing a sexual predator into the world with impunity.

Two more files with red dots, Fr. Gary Dayton and Fr. Romero DiMedio, raised the number of victims in the diocese to 70 that were sexually abused from 1955–1985. I started to sweat, the result of a combination of rising humidity in the "secret" room and rising anger in me. I didn't know how much more my stomach could tolerate. My head was spinning and the room was beginning to feel suffocating. I began copying selective material from each of the ten files before rearranging the contents in perfect order and replacing them back in alphabetical order in the drawers.

Then I counted the number of pages copied and made a mental note to replace the same number of pieces of paper tomorrow when I returned.

After turning off both the copier and the light, I exited the inner room, flipped the switch above the wine shelf, and waited while the casing pivoted back in place. Then I replaced the vintage champagne bottle, locked the iron security door, put the key back in the box, and made my way up the spiral staircase to the first floor.

After locking the front door, I faced the hot, humid outdoors. I retrieved my bike from the side of the house, and at the end of the driveway I craned my neck to look back at the front of the Summer House. Because of what I knew was hidden inside, I looked at it for the first time as a house of horrors.

I looked at the sign "Solitude" neatly anchored in a manicured lawn with new eyes and saw it as a lie. The ugly secrets hidden inside would qualify for a name change.

I cycled a mile to where I had left my car in the parking lot of a 7-11. It took a while for the car's AC to cool down my body temperature. I needed a shower at St. Sebastian Rectory to cool down my emotional temperature, and only God knew what I needed to refresh my soul from what I had just experienced in that dungeon of woes.

As I drove back to the cathedral rectory, I checked my cell phone for messages. The only one that ignited an inner spark was the voice of Sam Bannion. I didn't need to save the message, for I already knew her cell number by heart.

✍ Chapter Fifteen ✍

Tim & Sam

When I saw the name "Tim Cavanagh" on my cell phone I lit up inside like a Christmas tree. I decided to bypass formalities and go directly to fun.

"Miss Marple," I answered with a fake British accent.

"Hercule Poirot," he countered with a fake Belgian accent. "Did you call because you need someone with a waxed moustache to help you solve a crime?"

"That sounds so sexist."

"It's a little early in the day to be thinking about sex, isn't it?"

"I guess that depends on your hormone level."

"Is it me, or is this conversation beginning to sound like a reality TV show?"

"I don't know, what does a reality TV show sound like? Police detectives don't have time for reality TV, since that's our work environment most of the time."

"So you called to elicit my sympathy."

"No, I called to ask if you would like to have dinner at a first class restaurant with waiters who will charm you off your feet." I then began biting my lip waiting for him to say yes.

"Okay, I'll say yes because I am intrigued by waiters who will charm me off my feet." He cleared his throat. "Considering where I live and in spite of the breakthroughs of the women's liberation movement, it might be in my best interest if I pick you up. So what's the day and time?"

We agreed on Thursday night at 6 PM. We also agreed on casual dress. What we didn't agree on were the mutual smiles on our faces when we ended the call. Mine reflected delight at taking a risk that didn't backfire. As I felt pleased, I was hoping he felt amused. Something he had said during lunch at Rosslare Park made me smile once more: *"May your life be good again."*

Fr. Tim Cavanagh

When I alerted Leona Helmond that I would be out of the office each morning this week for at least for three days, she pressed for details, but I evaded her. She could be pushy. She seemed to forget she was a secretary, not a biographer.

I quickened my pace on this second day at Solitude because, after yesterday, I knew the routine.

The name on the next file, Fr. Terry Engals, gave me pause. Flashbacks of his suicide increased my heart rate. I took several deep breaths before sitting at the desk and opening the file.

Six letters revealed Terry had been accused of three instances of sexual abuse against teenage boys. The letter from Dr. and Mrs. Ben Lyne was at the top of the pile. My familiarity with their letter solved the riddle about its absence in Terry's file at the Chancery Office. I speculated that either Ted Barnes or Joe McInnes knew of this "panic room" and had access to these secret files. I guessed the vicar general would fit the role of diocesan policeman better than Ted Barnes, who didn't have a duplicitous bone in his body. The former suffered from duplicity like bone cancer.

Under the letter was Terry's resignation, typed on Chancery stationery and dated June 28, 2009. Below that was a yellow piece of paper with notations and the initials "JM." The same date indicated a meeting with the parents at Solitude to discuss monetary compensation for their son's rape and emotional damage. The vicar general's initials just validated my intuition.

The total number of credible cases of sex abuse of minors by clergy was now 63 from files A to E. My emotions told me to stop for today, but my brain engaged my arm and pulled the next file with a red dot. The name on the label was Flaherty, Dennis.

He was born in 1947, ordained in 1973, and assigned as chaplain at a girl's orphanage from 1973 to 1977 in Dublin. He came to the U.S. in 1986, was incardinated into the Diocese of Islip in 1997, and appointed pastor, by Bishop Campbell, of St. Bartholomew's in Mattituck in 2003.

A letter from my boss to Fr. Flaherty dated 6-12-2002, alluding to a priestly friendship in Ireland, triggered my inner radar. It referred to a mutual assignment they shared at Holy Comforter Orphanage in Dublin in the early '70s. I made a mental note, like a tickler, to file this in my memory bank.

I pulled more files: Msgr. Fred Gardner, Msgr. Joe Halladay, Fr. Jay Hudson, Fr. Lyle Keach, Fr. Nate Keenan, Msgr. Adrian Kerr, Fr. Will Krepki, Fr. Steve Logan. I updated the math—the total abuse victims in my research stood at 165. I emitted a deep sigh; I was only at the letter "M." I decided to read just one more. The name on the label was "Manley, Brian."

Initially I began reading the material quickly then slowed down when I did a double take. A similar letter from Bishop Campbell referring to their acquaintance during an assignment at Holy Comforter Orphanage in Dublin sounded an alarm. My heartbeat quickened as I pulled Dennis Flaherty's file again and connected the dots. These three had a history, and the bishop's reference to their fondness for girls made it an unpleasant history. I smelled collusion, protection, and cover-up.

My watch reminded me that I had spent over two hours in the chamber of horrors. I retraced my routine of copying papers, locking up, and heading back to the cathedral rectory for a long, cold shower. Hopefully it would wake me out of the nightmares I had just experienced. I promised myself I would speed up the process tomorrow as time was running out, my morale was running on empty, and my inner life desperately needed recharging.

On Wednesday I finished reading the remaining files with red dots. I copied what I discerned was the most pertinent material, replaced the paper I had used, closed the last file drawer, and sat down at the desk to calculate the results. Sweat beads began to form on my forehead. I needed some fresh air.

In three days I had read 78 files out of a total of 210 priests in the Diocese of Islip. Those 78 priests had victimized 281 children. God only knows how many more are unnamed and unfiled. I rested my head in my hands in a prayerful bow, as if I were standing on holy ground. This room, like the space where Anne Frank wrote her diary while hiding from the Nazis, ought to be turned into a victims' shrine.

Before leaving I pulled three files labeled Msgr. Lou Mursden, Fr. Jake Tunney, and Fr. Craig Walker. I was curious why they had green dots stuck to their labels. The answer was revealed in the first file. Each had embezzled from his parish. Three more criminals guilty of three new crimes. Total loss to the diocese was over $900,000.

Glaringly absent from all three files were any reports to the civil authorities. No accountability for their mismanagement of the people's money. No punishment for their greed. Was this the new scandal that would uncover a new, hidden face of the church, namely, fiscal fraud?

I looked at the two color codes. They seemed misplaced—the green should have been for the sexual abusers, since after their repetitive crimes their hands were slapped, giving them the green light to abuse again. And the red dots should have been stuck on the embezzlers, since all three left their parishes in the red following their theft of parish funds. What organization other than the Catholic Church handled its employees with such a laissez-faire attitude? No wonder the pool of vocations was eroding.

I turned to look at the filing cabinets one last time, with sadness. So many lies were hidden here, so many lives ruined by priests' sexual abuse and embezzlement. So many people betrayed by duplicitous bishops and their lackeys. So much fraud veiled as religion, and so much hurt left unhealed by big pay-offs. My best calculation was over four million dollars in forty years. And the people of the diocese were never asked if that was okay.

Questions I had never asked before raced through my mind. Whatever happened to leaders with a conscience? Whatever happened to the morality of integrity? When did moral theology taught in seminaries get lost in translation into criminal lifestyles masquerading behind ordained ministry? When did bishops begin to abdicate their authority to lawyers? When did prophetic leadership lose out to hidden rooms and confidential deals? When did settlements become preferable to healing of victims? And where in sacred scripture could any of the above be substantiated?

As I scanned the room for the last time, I was overcome by the sad truth that it revealed a church with two faces. Two sets of filing cabinets—one here and one in the Chancery—only fueled a pathology of the two faces of certain priests. Hidden in these files were victims whose voices were silenced by pay-offs and confidentiality agreements. They would never get any justice because they never got the chance to ask the question: Will the real Father So-and-So please stand up?

No wonder the leadership was so dysfunctional. The energy it took to hide one face from the other left little energy for a face that was happy, hopeful, and most of all, transparent. Two uncomfortable questions erupted in my gut. Would the real Catholic Church please stand up? And how much longer would I serve an institution that I was beginning to see was a lie?

I performed my detective routine at Solitude for the last time. Placing the copied papers in a shoulder valise, I took a final look at the summer house. I knew I would never return there. I pondered the "Solitude" sign at the end of the driveway—what a misnomer. "Wilderness" seemed a more apt title. I had come face to face with many ugly beasts hidden in secret files in the basement of this house. After four days this had become a house built on sand, and I would not be around for its collapse.

As I pedaled back to my car, I wondered what to do with the copied material. I had enough files to shake the very foundations of the Diocese of Islip. Maybe the CIA headquarters would be the safest place to hide them. Or a missile silo. *Enough sarcasm*, my conscience said. *Just settle for a safe-deposit box.* Then I debated whether I should get one large enough to hide myself if my caper was ever uncovered. For my own safety, I might need to come up with a follow-up plan.

I was on sadness overload as details of the files played through my memory bank like an uninterrupted horror film. I had to shake it off—this was a Thursday I had lived for all week. I found myself chuckling as I remembered a car bumper sticker that read "S.H.I.T. *So happy it's Thursday.*" My sentiments exactly, after all the garbage I had read in secret files this week. I needed some release from the depression in the catacombs. I was grateful the antidote was an evening with a redheaded detective and not a bottle of valium. At least a redhead could talk back to me.

Naturally, my grandmother detected a different beat to my step as I came down the grand staircase at Rosslare Park two stairs at a time. She stood at the bottom with a grin on her face as dirty as the gardening clothes she was wearing. Even before she spoke, I knew her intentions were cunningly wicked.

"Well, since you're not in clergy clothes and since your boss doesn't stir that kind of happy behavior in you, I can only guess you're meeting someone who does," Jane Cavanagh said with a seasoned twist in her voice—like lime in a vodka and tonic.

"So, you approve of my having dinner with an Irish female police detective with red hair?"

"I would approve even if she wasn't Irish. And where are you taking her to dinner, if I may ask?"

"Actually, she's taking me to dinner, someplace, as she put it, where the waiters will charm me off my feet. So, the Cavanagh curiosity was hooked. What could I say except yes?"

"And what can I say, except may that three-letter word be the appetizer for much laughter and happiness tonight."

"Spoken like Emily Dickinson," I quipped as I kissed her cheek.

I hadn't been on a date since my final year at Juilliard—dinner with a charming violinist who was now the first chair in the Seattle symphony. We reunited for drinks nine years ago when I performed a piece by Brahms in Seattle. My rendition of his "stormy scherzo" was a fitting conclusion to our stormy relationship. By that time she was married and mothering her first child. I stayed married to a concert grand piano for ten more months before my departure from the stage and my engagement to the Catholic Church, which culminated in my ordination in 2006.

Thanks to Sam Bannion, my desires for the intimate company of a woman had been reawakened. I liked the risks she took. I had grown fond of her blazing red hair that swayed as she walked, her sparkling blue eyes dancing over my face like a laser, the fragrance of her body wash, like the gardenias in my grandmother's green house, and how she would bite her lower right lip as a way of holding an issue in tension until she got an answer. I liked how she had introduced me to female musicians I'd never heard of, like Sarah McLachlan and Norah Jones. Taking a line from Henry Higgins, I'd grown accustomed to her face.

As I waited on the porch for her to answer her door, I felt a flash of guilt that I hadn't brought flowers. *Maybe next time.* Then I chuckled softly. *What makes you think there will be a next time?*

As she opened the door, my heart leaped, taking in her flaming red hair wound up into a flashy red scarf and her low-cut, gypsy-style black dress. I took a step backward and said, "Whoa. I thought you said casual dress. You look like Carmen."

"Who's Carmen?" she asked, like she was answering a question on *Jeopardy.*

"A character in Bizet's opera, a temptress, a seductive gypsy woman whose goal in life is to arouse the passions of every man she meets," I said. I was an authority on opera characters.

"Well, I like her already and I've never met her."

"Are we going to dinner or to a costume party?"

"Why to dinner and," she said, stretching it into a pause, "be a nice Don José to my Carmen and escort me to the car."

It was banter like this that turned my smile into a shit eating grin. She had done her homework and knew her lines perfectly. We hadn't even left the porch and already she was playing the role of Carmen. She had turned into a vixen with a hypnotic charm. I was smitten and she knew it by the way she wrapped her arm in mine. With the smile of a temptress, she charmed me off her porch and down the steps, heading for some unknown restaurant where the waiters would charm me off my feet. As I gently steered her toward my car, she steered me back toward the driveway.

"Since I invited you, I'll drive," she said, sounding like it wasn't an option.

"No argument there since I don't know where we're going."

"It's a surprise," she said, staring at me with eyes full of Carmen intrigue. We got into her car, and she popped in a CD.

"I thought we would listen to a little John Mayer going east, then some Brahms on the way back."

"Sounds fair; something for you and something for me."

The music began as our banter continued. Our conversation was a healing diversion from the emotionally distressing files I had read so recently. I had willed myself to close them out of my brain as I closed the drawers in the secret room. After 40 minutes of chatting, she pulled up next to a charming restaurant nestled between a curio shop and what appeared to be former warehouses converted into upscale lofts. Four faux gas lights hung from a rectangular pediment above the main door, highlighting two café windows with muted effect. A sign between the two windows read, "La Casa Nostra." The mafia? I was with the police; I felt safe.

The interior looked like it was decorated for a mobster movie: dim lighting, candles stuck in empty vintage wine bottles with wax melting for visual effects, ceiling fans spinning slowly above, waiters in white aprons tied in front with their menus and order pads stuffed into deep pockets, and Italian music playing softly. Our host seated us in a booth toward the rear but away from the main path to the kitchen. The high backs muffled the noise, giving us privacy and quiet. I wondered if Sam had connections or if she had won the booth in a Thursday night lottery.

"Don't be fooled by the modest ambience," she said, adjusting the flashy red scarf in her equally flashy red hair. "It's upscale, so don't let the menu prices affect your selection."

I nodded while surveying the customers. Was anyone else dressed for a role in an opera? Not a one—my companion was unique. I asked if she wanted me to order for both of us.

"Thanks, but since this is my treat and my fantasy, I can do that."

She was Carmen *and* Susan B. Anthony! Feigning surprise I retorted, "So, when did having dinner with me become a fantasy?" I was curious to know how she would answer.

"Since you said yes to my invitation," she said, scanning the menu nonchalantly.

"In the words of Shelley, have I said yes to a night *'of hopes and fears and twilight fantasies'*?"

"No fancy poetry please, or you'll spoil the mood of a simple dinner at a Brooklyn restaurant with a soon-to-be-revealed surprise." She scrutinized the wine menu.

"And what else is in your fantasy that I should know about before I say yes again?"

"Answering that would spoil the surprise," she said, this time with a touch of the seductive Carmen in her voice.

She ordered what sounded like an expensive bottle of wine. The wine steward uncorked a bottle of Pouilly-Fume vintage 2000 and poured two glasses of wine. The waitress served bread and salads. Then the music track changed. Our waitress took a step back from the table, the lights dimmed, and a single track light above the booth spotlighted her. On cue she began to sing the aria "L'amour est un oiseau rebelle" from the first act of *Carmen*.

I sat in stunned silence listening to her pure and passionate rendition of this lively aria. As I occasionally glanced toward Sam, her eyes danced between me and the waitress, like the scheming gypsy she was dressed to play. If this was Sam's surprise, then it released in me a glee that, when added to the tantalizing aroma of the wine, turned me into a Thursday night Don José.

The waitress's area evoked applause from the dinner guests; mine was loudest. Her French was flawless, her vocal range as smooth as a glassblower forming a crystal vase, and the level of seductive emotion in her musical interpretation was palpable. She bowed like a professional, and then disappeared into the kitchen.

I raised my wine glass in a gesture of salute to my dinner partner. "My compliments," I said with a smile.

As we touched glasses she said, "Is the compliment for the wine or the surprise?"

"Both."

"In that case drink slowly, because there is more of both to come," she said, speaking more with her eyes than her voice.

"Then it's a good thing I have a designated driver tonight."

"Yes, I will see you get home safely." Then with the eyes of Carmen the temptress she added, "Maybe not sober, but safe."

"I'll drink to that comforting thought," I said. "By the way, where did you hear about these singing operatic waiters?"

"I Googled singing waiters, and La Casa Nostra appeared. After reading their website I knew you would want me to bring you here, especially since they are students at your alma mater, Juilliard."

Raising my glass a second time, I said, "To Juilliard!"

For the next two hours we savored the wine, along with ravioli stuffed with seafood and delicious spinach lasagna. We sampled each other's entrées as we kept the chatter light and occasionally morphed into reverent quiet to savor the singing waiters at other tables. Our waitress, Carla, entertained us with three more arias. While we ate, she sang the silky "O mio bambino caro," from Puccini's *Gianni Schicchi*. After she cleared the table she sang for us "Un bel di," from Puccini's *Madame Butterfly*. During dessert she performed her encore, "Lascia ch'io pianga," from Handel's *Rinaldo*.

With my eyes closed to capture the mood of the imprisoned Almeinda's plea to be left alone with her anguish, her sorrow, and her tears for her lover Rinaldo, I was so caught up in the moment that I didn't realize I was playing musical conductor. Sam noticed the swaying of my right hand as I kept tempo with a subtle bobbing of my head. It took me several seconds after the song to return from my imaginary lure to seventeenth century Jerusalem of the opera back to twenty-first century Brooklyn. I slowly opened my eyes.

"I take it you have been charmed off your feet," Sam said, sounding like she was pleased with her scheming escapade.

"I can't wait to see what you plan as an encore."

"Well, speaking of encores, I have a favor to ask," she said, shifting into a serious tone of voice. Clearing her throat and looking me square in the eyes, she said, "Every year the Long Island Police and Public Safety League has a fund-raiser for a scholarship to help children whose parents were killed in action or wounded. I was wondering if you would perform with the Long Island Symphony for this year's program."

I paused, filtering her words through my consciousness, which was seriously destabilized by two bottles of wine and a Baileys Irish Crème.

"What do you mean by perform?" I asked, baiting her.

125

"I mean sit at a grand piano on the stage of the performing arts center and play a piano concerto with the symphony."

I gulped down a generous cup of coffee to quicken my state of comprehension. Then I waited a few seconds. I had already decided how to answer, but I wanted to heighten her anxiety a bit.

"I haven't performed in public in a long time, but… it sounds like a good cause. And," I added with a generous portion of Don Jose wickedness in my voice, "You're a good temptress."

"Is that a yes or a maybe?"

"I know I am somewhere between clarity and drunkenness, but I seem to remember that line as, is that a yes or a no."

"I'll settle for maybe, since I don't think Carmen ever took no for an answer."

"If you wanted to ask me this favor, Sam, you didn't need to pump me full of Puilly-Fume and Puccini. Although after tonight I must admit they're a wonderful combination."

"So, you'll think about it?" she asked like a seductive Carmen, using her trademark tic of biting her lower right lip.

"Let me sleep on it first, then ask me again when I wake up two days from now. Then give me another day to recover from what it going to be a classic hangover." I took the momentary pause in our conversation to ask,

By the way, did I reveal any secrets tonight as I took in too much wine?"

"What do you mean?" she asked pensively. We were walking to her car, and the night air felt good.

"There's an old Babylonian proverb, *'In came wine, out went a secret.'"*

"So that was the language you were speaking." As her lips tightened to form a devious smile she added, "You're in luck. I don't understand Babylonian."

She slid into the driver's seat and popped in a Mendelsohn CD. A minute later I was sound asleep in her car. I don't remember what time we arrived back at her house; I was zoned out and unclear about which opera I was still living in. I was thankful she put a pot of coffee on, since I needed a little time and another dose of caffeine to clear my head so I could safely drive back to the rectory. An hour later, after more light but warm conversation, I was in my car. With my eyes glued on the roads I missed seeing Sam in the rearview mirror, shadowing me for my own safety.

In bed that night, I fell asleep quickly, but not before replaying the memorable scenes of this drama in four acts and recapturing the many faces of the Carmen of East Islip, whose company, wit, charm, and mystique I would dream about tonight.

◞ Chapter Sixteen ◟

Fr. Tim Cavanagh

The Chancery

Following a week of playing detective in the chamber of secrets at the Summer House, I wasn't looking forward to the return of Lord Voldemort from the bishops' meeting. His absence for five days had made my heart grow fonder for a certain police detective. The Thursday night dinner date, with all the special effects she attended to just to please me, was still fueling my new reservoir of happiness like rods fueling water in a nuclear reactor.

I grabbed the pile of mail Leona Helmond had placed on my desk and walked into the bishop's office for the Monday staff meeting, carefully masking my unhappiness with my boss and my workplace. I was getting better at playing the game, "This is the last place I want to be," but I did so without giving any clues that I wouldn't play the game much longer.

Bishop Campbell talked on and on, seldom coming up for air, about the annual summer bishops' conference meeting in Denver. Joe McInnes mumbled an occasional grunt and expressed an intermittent fake laugh while bobbing his head in agreement with his boss, looking like one of those celebrity bobble-head toys. Ted Barnes and I sat stoically quiet, as if we were mannequins wearing plastic, counterfeit faces that occasionally broke into counterfeit smiles.

"The issue that generated the highest-octane discussion was the conference statement soon to be released regarding the presidential election," the bishop said. He sounded like he was reading from a teleprompter. "We can't let a pro-choice black American set the country's agenda for four years."

I bristled at the intended slap at identifying Senator Obama by his color rather than his name. I bit my tongue hard and decided not to dignify the stupidity of a Belfast bloke's adolescent comment with a reply. After what I had read in priests' personnel files last week, I failed to see the difference between a pro-choice president running the country and a pro-choice bishop running a diocese. The bishop chose to protect criminal priests over shepherding innocent victims of child abuse. It was pro-choice no matter how you cut it. But the depth of pastoral care in the heart of this pretender-to-a-higher-throne would not see the comparison, since his heart lacked the kind of compassion to connect the dots.

So, like many of his bishop brothers, this one lived geographically in the state of New York while living emotionally in the state of denial about his own criminal complicity in a fraudulent, criminal, covert affair. Any lay corporation would have fired them. But, like the dysfunctional corporation they worked for, they practiced among themselves what they practiced with abusive priests, namely protection. After all, victims of clergy rape and molestation were far more expendable than priests.

My unhealthy reverie was interrupted by the bishop.

"Let's get on with mail, can we?" The first letter I read evoked a glazed look on everybody's face, except mine.

Dear Bishop Campbell,

I am sick and tired of Fr. Neal Rowes using the church pulpit as a platform to expound his political agenda. Since he can't preach a decent sermon he's now shaming us for how we may have voted in the recent elections. When did the good news of salvation get reduced to extolling the Republican platform? For your information and his, pro-life is not the only issue Catholics are concerned about. When is he going to wake up and learn that his issues are not everybody's issues? I don't know what you're going to do about it, but here's what I'm going to do about it. Beginning this week I am going to start recording his homilies then mailing them to the I.R.S. requesting they investigate the non-profit status of a church that is crossing the political line regarding our tax-exempt status.

Do I have your attention?

Sincerely,

Steve Carrington, Attorney

Bishop Campbell, with a fiery look on his face, pounded the conference table with a heavy fist. "Jesus Christ, Who does this son of a bitch think he is, sending me a threatening letter like this? And the fact that he is a damn attorney doesn't scare me at all."

Msgr. Ted Barnes, ever the consummate, calm diplomat, spoke in a synchronous and logical tone. "There might be some wisdom in paying attention to his letter. This could snowball to other parishes, and I would not want to see our pastors get entangled in a legal mess with the I.R.S. It could inadvertently get us into a canonical mess with the Vatican Nuncio."

This statement got sharp attention from the bishop. Pausing briefly, Msg. Barnes continued. "Correct me if I'm wrong, Bishop, but I don't believe this is the intent of the conference statement soon to be released to U.S. Catholics. Those statements are not crafted to teach Catholics, but to please Rome. Even the papacy has become addicted to political correctness."

Silence hung over the office like a storm cloud. We waited to see if it would pass or if another bolt of lightning would strike from His Excellency. He assumed a state of deep pondering, no doubt focusing on the impact of the chancellor's words about the relationship of the diocese to the Vatican Nuncio in Washington.

"It's probably best to lean toward the side of prudence," he said sullenly.

"Ted, issue a statement to all the clergy to keep election year politics out of the pulpit. And the first one I hear about who ignores it will find himself unemployed by the diocese. Next letter."

When I heard his last command, I thought to myself, *Chalk one up to hypocrisy. Who's issuing threatening letters now?* I read on.

Dear Bishop,

My husband and I are from the Diocese of Alexandria, VA. For the past five years we have vacationed every June at Hampton Bays. It has always been a quiet and peaceful break until two years ago. That is when Fr. Lou Corrigan was named the pastor of Our Lady of the Harbor Parish. This is the second year we have had to endure his heretical preaching. He can't get through a homily without mentioning some movie star or celebrity. Just last week he mentioned Oprah Winfrey ten times. While we respect her for her humanitarian causes, she is also an advocate for abortion and for that reason her name doesn't belong in a Sunday homily. And he is also critical of the Holy Father.

130

It bothers us when he doesn't use a chasuble in the summer saying it causes him to sweat too much. We are also annoyed when he tampers with the prayers and spends too much time welcoming people for their vacations. We don't go to Mass to be welcomed. We go to pray and to be sanctified by the Holy Eucharist. This man is disrespectful in many ways when saying Mass.

We hope bringing these infractions to your attention will prompt you to help him change his ways. We find his style very distracting, especially how he turns the Mass into a circus.

Respectfully,

Carl & Eleanor Sheffield

"As if I didn't have enough to worry about, these medieval Alexandria Catholics spend more time policing clergy than they do celebrating the presence of God in the sacraments," the bishop said with patent sarcasm. "Not one of them knows the difference between religion and faith. Matthew 15:7–9 fits them like a glove—their vain hearts are far from God. Every bishop in the country knows Alexandria is the birthplace of the new Phariseeism in the Catholic Church. They're putting a new face on the words of Jesus in Matthew's gospel 24: 24-29. Christ how I wish they would just stay home and spare me and other bishops from being infected by their misery with their self-righteous attitude about correcting the liturgical infringements of every priest outside their diocese."

Taking a long pause to breathe deeply, he added, "The best antidote for this kind of juvenile Catholic who pretends to be an adult is to completely ignore them. Throw the letter away. There are more life and death issues to deal with than chasubles and liturgical infractions."

As I discarded the letter, I couldn't help but think how sad that adult Catholics who wrote poison pen letters about clergy who didn't meet their expectations would never use their voice to speak out about the clergy sexual abuse of children and the hierarchical conspiracy to cover it up. What had the church come to, when priests not wearing chasubles had become more important than clergy raping children?

And when would these Catholics wake up and realize that someday they would give an account to a higher authority than a bishop about their deafening silence during the crucifixion of these victims?

131

I turned to the next letter.

Dear Bishop Campbell,

I am the director of Religious Education at St. Sophia's Parish in Calverton. We have a seminarian assigned here for a pastoral year. Based on some conversations I have had with him, I have reason to believe he frequents child pornography sites on the computer. I am alarmed by some of the inappropriate things he says about children. He is planning an outing with the altar servers next month, and I fear for their safety.

Also, his cavalier attitude toward his vocation gives the impression he is better than everyone else on the staff. He has only been here one month and has managed to alienate many people. He needs some guidance about how his style is not healthy for the current climate in a post-scandal church. I discussed this with Fr. Petrie, the pastor, but he doesn't seem at all alarmed. I am copying this letter to Fr. Nick Johannson, the vocations director. Please have someone get in touch with me before I take this matter to the police for an investigation. And yes, this issue is too important for me to care about whether I keep my job or not.

Desperate for some help, I am,

Sincerely,

Julianna Heller

I looked up to see horror on everybody's faces. Everyone but the bishop.

"Joe, you're excused. Get on this right away. Talk with Nick and waste no time investigating this," the bishop said flatly, as if speaking a memorized line. "Call this woman and tell her I received the letter and delegated you to attend to this matter quickly. I'll be damned if I let a puny seminarian get me into hot water with the Nuncio by tabloid headlines if this can be substantiated."

As Bishop Campbell interacted with Joe McInnes I felt sorry for the Director of Religious Education who had already been de-humanized by referring to her by her gender and not by her name. I wanted to stand up and shout, "You go girl," but I thought it might mean more if I told her that myself, rather than make a fool of myself by saying it in the company of male celibates who would not get the meaning.

Bishop Campbell's phone buzzed. He walked to his desk to answer it. Covering the mouthpiece with his right hand, he said, "You are excused. This is an important call I must take."

As the three of us made our way out of the office, I noticed Msgr. McInnes was already on his cell phone. No doubt he was trying to reach Julianna Heller so he could quickly plot a strategy to thwart an unwelcome scandal.

Before I stepped out of the office, Bishop Campbell said rather officiously, "Tim, I would like to meet with you after I finish with this call." I nodded before closing the door, wondering about his summons to a private conference.

Nora Owens

I decided to plan one more trip to Mattituck before I ended another priest abuser's life. I stepped into the walk-in closet in my bedroom and pushed back a row of clothes hanging from the center of a metal rod. Behind that I moved a piece of paneling out of sequence from the next panel and stepped into a small secret room. It contained a table of make-up, a variety of wigs, eyelashes, facial creams, eyeliners, a laptop computer, a .22 magnum revolver, gun cleaning fluid, a silencer, and some lethal cutlery. This was my chamber of secrets; my own private make-up salon where Nora Owens morphed into the serial killer Claire O'Neill. D-day was just six weeks away. I was beginning to feast on the energy of killing Fr. Dennis Flaherty on the feast day of St. Bartholomew. Short of turning the sexually abusive pastor into a martyr, when I was finished with him he would rail against the night.

This Sunday would be the visit that would put all the pieces together. After August 24th, I would never again set foot in Mattituck, N.Y. What Dennis Flaherty called "Long Island Heaven," I called "Long Island Hades." Every time I was in the company of a priest rapist, I always felt like I was transported back to the hell of Holy Comforter Orphanage.

There would be no heaven on earth for me until I purified it of four priests who had violated my human dignity, and my twin sister, with their sexual perversions.

For me Dennis Flaherty was just a small man whose name was on a short list. I would relish the media coverage of his murder and bask in knowing I had unmasked another priest sexual abuser. My tolerance level for his company was waning. His impending death put me closer to the goal of four lives for eighteen years of sexual abuse, followed by thirty years of nightmares about Nanette's suicide; thirty years of waiting for justice which they had avoided; thirty years of practicing predator skills while remaining above suspicion; thirty years of seeking, hunting, plotting, and exacting revenge.

As I selected my facial makeup for playing the role of Tosca to his Scarpia, I glanced toward a picture stuck in the frame of the vanity mirror. It was the Martyrdom of St. Bartholomew. Soon, I would duplicate this piece of Italian art in Mattituck, N.Y. The masterpiece death would have my signature, though it would be a stunning copy of the Venetian artist Tiepolo.

ᶜᵛᵖ Chapter Seventeen ᵉᵛᵏ

Fr. Tim Cavanagh

I had no sooner returned to my office and sat down at my desk when the bishop buzzed my intercom.

"Okay Tim, can I see you for a few minutes, please?"

My ears perked up, alerted by suspicion. "Please" was not a common word in John Campbell's vocabulary, so using it in a tone of civility raised my eyebrows. "Yes," I answered simply.

When I returned to his office, he remained sitting behind his desk like a CEO who uses that position to intimidate people. I decided to sit in a chair to the left of his desk, closing the gap between us and thus making the playing field more even.

"I have some good news for you," he said in a manner of speaking that seemed like a foreign language to me. "I have decided to name some monsignors, and your name is on the list." He delivered his line like someone playing Santa Claus in July.

My mind quickly flashed back to the files in the secret room at Solitude and those priest abusers with the title "monsignor" who had dishonored the priesthood. Also, I did not want to be included in the same league as Joe McInnes, whose name was initialed to confidentiality agreements and spurious correspondence connected with a clergy sex abuse cover-up. Since I could not divulge what I had discovered in the secret room at Solitude, I would have to decline on integrity alone.

Bishop Campbell mistook my reverie as unexpected delight. I dug deep into my inner well for courage and replied, "I am flattered, but I decline."

Instantly, his fake northern Irish composure melted, transforming him into a sadistic Mr. Hyde. Vaulting from his chair, he slammed his fist on the desk and said, "Excuse me, but you don't have the option of declining."

"Excuse me, but I do have that option and I am declining," I countered with calmness.

"And may I ask why?"

"Certainly! First," I said with the color of honesty in my words, "I didn't become a priest to earn the title of monsignor." Pausing only to catch my breath, I added, "Second, there are more-seasoned priests who have earned that honor than me. And, third, that title is so Pre-Vatican II. It is from a chapter of church history that is part of the past, not the future. And rather than going backward, I believe we should be moving forward. A better fit today would be to offer two priests a sabbatical every year for professional updating with travels to broaden their cultural horizons. It seems to me that would bring benefits to the diocese in the ways we minister to multi-cultural Catholics, rather than some priests getting titles. Or instead of giving a priest an honorary title, while not honor the parish? Forgive their debt or give them a loan for a new ministry?"

Deflecting attention away from himself while trying desperately to regain some composure, he countered, "And what do you think your grandmother would say about your declining the honor?" His insecurity masqueraded as a way of making others feel guilty when they didn't meet his expectations.

"I would hope she would be proud of my integrity. After all, that is how she raised me. And integrity, rather than false honors, is the real issue for me."

"What do you mean by false honors?"

"I don't think that needs any commentary."

He ignored my challenging remark. After a momentary pause he decided to change his strategy and tighten the vice that would change my mind. "I have already processed the names with Rome, and the clergy bios are being readied for the diocesan media. What do you suggest I do?"

"Since you initiated this matter without any consultation with me, I don't see how that is my problem."

His features turned him into a volcano about to erupt, but he stayed silent.

"Is there anything else on your mind," I asked, hoping he would get the hint and excuse me or possibly throw me out physically.

"I am seriously displeased with you," he barked. "A bishop's priest-secretary should have the honorary title of monsignor."

"In that case I can suggest not a few priests who would be glad to take my place. Some of them consider getting such a title a full-time job."

"Get out. Get the hell out of here."

"Do you wish for me to return with my resignation?" I asked submissively.

"Get out. Get out," was the trail of words he spit out like someone chewing on anger as I closed the door to his office. I could imagine that the next website he visited would be "pissed off.com"

Fr. Brian Manley

I located Dennis Flaherty's phone number in my cell phone's contact list and dialed it.

"Ah, Brian me boy, tell me something that will cheer up a lonely, unhappy celibate," he said, sounding as if he wanted to be set free of an inner prison.

"How about I come to the parish for your feast day and treat you to dinner?"

"How about the day after? August 24th is already spoken for."

"Let me guess. Is your date on August 24th with a certain lady friend from Manhattan?" I asked, already knowing the answer.

"It is. I thought we would begin with dessert first in my bed, and when we've had enough of that, maybe dinner, also in my bedroom," he said with a riotous laugh.

"Then why don't I come out the day after, and you can tell me all the juicy details about your feast day dinner and dessert, though I must confess, Father, that I would be more interested in the dessert," I said with my own brand of Irish wit.

"Sounds like a plan. Why not come out early in the morning, and we'll do breakfast after my nine a.m. Mass? Then we can play a round of golf."

"I am so damn jealous," I said.

"Well, Brian, I am sure you don't need me to tell you how to convert that jealousy into a more productive sexual energy."

"If you're referring to adult porn there is just so much to watch and then it becomes like faded reruns. I mean, eventually, you yearn to be in the movie rather than watching it."

"There's nothing wrong with mixing a little jacking with yearning. I've got to run. See you on the 25th."

When the call ended, I was haunted by two conflicting feelings: happiness and fear for Dennis. I quickly leapfrogged to hope that he knew what he was doing.

Nora Owens

As I drove the last few miles to Mattituck, I realized I had never celebrated a feast day before. Besides my birthday, the only annual event I remembered and ritualized with quiet pondering was the anniversary of Nan's suicide. Twins are so tightly joined physically and psychologically that pieces of each other are forever ensconced in memories. My dominant memory of Nan was the face of sadness and despair she was wearing when I found her hanging from a beam in the basement of Holy Comforter Orphanage. Her lifeless body and her glazed eyes sucked out the energy of life in me as I held her in my arms, weeping until I ran out of tears. Then just as quickly the energy of revenge was released in me. In the course of an hour in that dark, dank space, I had felt an inconsolable loss, but I also had found a new motive for living for us both.

I had stored that energy in a hidden inner room for days just like this. Dennis Flaherty was an hour away from finding out a few new things about me and St. Bartholomew. There was a kind of power surge in me, knowing how he was going to die.

I followed his instructions and parked my car in the driveway behind the rectory, then closed the vinyl gate. With no neighbors on the block, privacy was assured. Then I called his private number using a disposable cell phone. It was rule #2 which I practiced as Clare O'Neill:

no evidence left behind that could be traced. At 7:30 p.m., the sun was beginning to set.

When he answered, he sounded confused by the unfamiliar phone number. "Hello," he said with obvious caution.

"I hope I am in time for the feast day fun," I said, feeling like a black widow spinning a web.

"Indeed you are."

He met me at the back door with mischief written all over his face. "And now that you are here, let the fun begin."

I had brought several containers of Chinese food and two bottles of wine, one laced with a slow-activating depressant. Instead of commenting on the food, what he noticed was the extra-large shoulder bag hanging over my right shoulder.

"I hope you have your toothbrush in that bag."

"That and a few other surprises," I said without skipping a beat.

"Good, I like surprises, especially in the bedroom."

"Then why don't we pass on the food, pop the wine, and begin the feasting with some role playing in the bedroom?"

"God, how I love a woman who has a plan."

"Then show me the way so I can execute it," I said.

"Follow me," he said, and I could tell his testosterone level broke the chart.

The bedroom at the top of the staircase was huge and tastefully appointed with Tiffany lamps, polished hardwood floors, and a queen-sized bed as the centerpiece. Oddly enough the bed was not flush with a wall, but positioned in the middle of the room. I refrained from comment once I noticed the two thick, sturdy posts at both ends of the headboard. They would serve as good anchors.

After shutting the door, he immediately made a pass at me. I steeled myself for his sloppy sexual advances. Dennis Flaherty was about as romantic as a gorilla in heat. I tolerated about two minutes of his clumsy attempts at arousal before I broke out of my passive role and took the lead.

"Why don't we drink a little wine then do some role-play to juice things up?" I asked seductively.

"What roles do you have in mind?"

"Why don't you play St. Bartholomew and I'll play myself?"

"Okay," he agreed a bit uncertainly, "as long as we play in the nude."

I uncorked both bottles of wine and poured him a glass from the tainted bottle. He would need about two glasses before the drug kicked in. I pulled a piece of clothing from my shoulder bag, handed it to him and said, "You get naked then put on this tunic and lie on the bed while I go into the bathroom and put on something sexy."

"Can you do that in less than thirty seconds? I'm getting horny."

"Dennis, let's not watch the clock tonight, it will spoil the fun."

"Okay, but make it quick."

"After tonight you will learn a new meaning for a quickie. I'll be back to put the finishing touches on your erection."

Two minutes later, I returned wearing a bright red teddy and a pair of red silk panties. I handed him his wine glass and did a salute while we both emptied our glasses. Then I poured him a third glass. From my shoulder bag I retrieved a length of rope and a small candle.

"What are those for," he asked curiously.

"These are the final touches to our role playing," I said. As I sat beside him, I softly stroked his borderline obese torso, peppered with graying chest hair, and coached him to relax. He gradually became erect.

I began stroking him delicately with my fingers. His ooh's and aah's sickened me. Then I whispered in his ear, "Tying you up will make the climax more enjoyable." Reaching over, I stretched out his left arm and with the extra strength Island Bay rope used for making hammocks I began tying it to the bedpost. Then I walked around the bed, stretched out his right arm and tied it to the other bedpost. I repeated the ritual with the right foot then the left.

"Where did you learn to tie knots like that," he asked with latent curiosity.

"It's called a Clove Hitch and I learned it in Girl Scouts. Little did I know it would come in handy," I said, then in tone of ridicule I added, "get my meaning…..hand-y?"

"I didn't take you for hard-core sex," he said approvingly with his speech slightly slurred.

"This is the first of many surprises awaiting you," I said like a bondage expert.

Then I struck a match, lit the candle and turned out the lights. I retrieved a piece of extra thick masking tape from my shoulder bag and before he took another breathe I shielded it across his mouth. His eyes widened with panic like someone asleep who is awakened by the unexpected presence of an intruder, or rapist or worse yet, a murderer. I stroked his chest to slow down his panting heart beating with fear. When I sensed a calmness returning to his rhythm of breathing and the effects of the drugged wine on his consciousness, I reached into the shoulder bag and pulled out a flaying knife neatly fitted in a leather holster.

"Since St. Bartholomew was flayed alive I thought I would make our role playing as real as possible," I said like a torturer who was once tortured. Then I laid the cold knife on top of his erection.

"Shall I begin cutting here," then slowly dragged it up his torso. His body stiffened as he felt the sharpness of the blade against his tender skin. "Or here," I mused as I crossed from one nipple to the other. Then I smiled in a way that left him wondering whether it was real or fake.

"It's story time Dennis," I said while slowly moving the blade over his body now caste in pure fright while his eyes flashed between horror and heaviness.

"Once upon a time two twin sisters, Nanette and Nora found themselves at the mercy of an evil priest at Holy Comforter Orphanage in Dublin. He mentally tortured and physically raped them until Nanette took her life."

As he heard the details of his contemptible past his eyes began to freeze like a panicked animal trapped with no way to escape. His vocal groaning's behind the tape sounded like mercy; like someone sentenced to die begging for a reprieve.

"Yes," I said sarcastically, "I groaned like that too along with my sister. I groaned for you to stop raping us and abusing us like sex toys.

141

But, did you listen; did you have a change of heart?" I left the question hanging like a musical chord in a coda.

As I tightened my grip on the knife his body stiffened while he succumbed to feeling delirious and losing his strength to resist physically.

"I have waited a long time for this moment. This is better than what I imagined it to be like. Seeing your panic and feeling your fear. I wanted you to experience what they were like for me and my sister in that cold, dark dungeon at Holy Comforter. This is not about revenge Dennis, this is about justice."

As I spoke my next line I stuck the blade deep into his abdomen. "For all the injustices you did against me and Nan," then I stuck the blade into his chest cavity, "and for all the injustices against the Roman Catholic Church that shielded and protected you from your evil lifestyle that allowed you to continue harming innocent people. May you know what it's like to bleed to death as Nan and I bled inside every time you raped and tortured us."

I looked into his eyes and said with coldness in mine, "May God forgive you Dennis Flaherty, because I don't."

As he jerked violently trying to free himself from the tethered ropes, I perched myself against the back of the headboard and with a wide stroke of the knife cut his throat. Blood splattered everywhere except on me. In a second his struggling ceased and his head dropped leaving him motionless. In less than fifteen seconds his heart stopped.

Standing beside his bed and surveying his lifeless, blood stained body for the last time now soaked in blood stained sheets, I relished the thought that no one will come to grieve over this demon of a man.

After completing the ritual of purging the murder scene of any evidence, I stuffed everything back into my shoulder bag. Before blowing out the candle, I placed a holy card of the martyrdom of St. Bartholomew in the dead priest's left hand. In his right hand I placed a business card with the phrase, "Vengeance is mine, sayeth guess who? (Romans 12:18)."

Wearing surgical shoe covers and vinyl surgical gloves, I collected the food on the kitchen table before exiting through the back door. I opened and closed the driveway gate as quietly as a church mouse and waited until I got to the end of Canal Street before turning on the car headlights. The dashboard digital clock blinked 9:15 p.m. I had accomplished my mission in less than 90 minutes. As I drove back to Manhattan I feasted on the justice I had exacted tonight for Nan and for myself. The atonement would come later, and hopefully, not before the last two on my list. The score was now two down and two to go.

ᑲ Chapter Eighteen ᑳ

Fr. Brian Manley

As I drove the last five miles to Mattituck, I cracked my window to enjoy the sea breeze piercing the sticky humidity of the western portion of Long Island. Then I turned off the AC and opened the passenger window to thoroughly enjoy the fresh salt air. I pulled into the rectory driveway at 9 a.m. No doubt Dennis was just beginning Mass, but I knew where he kept the spare key so I let myself in the back door.

Gloria Stenson, the parish secretary, met me in the kitchen.

"Fr. Brian," she said, "I think something's wrong. Fr. Flaherty is not in church yet for 9:00 Mass. He never oversleeps. Would you please check on him?" I heard a mixture of panic and mystery in her voice.

"There's nothing worse than one Irishman trying to wake another Irishman after a feast day celebration, but I'll give it a try," I said, trying to add some levity to the moment.

I tip-toed up the stairs to the second floor and stopped in front of the room where I knew Dennis slept. The door sat slightly ajar. I opened it slowly, noticing the curtains were drawn. No lights were on inside, making the room appear too dark so early in the day.

"Peek-a-boo," I said in a tone of voice that sounded like plain chant. "Dennis, are you awake, or hung over, or can I make this a multiple choice question and ask if you're decent?"

When I didn't get a reply, I called his name again. Then I reached over and flipped on the light switch. What I saw next froze me in my tracks. I saw Dennis lying in bed, covered with blood. He had been tethered to the bed like a helpless victim. I couldn't bear to look any closer; I was quickly becoming nauseous and closed the door to keep from vomiting. I wasn't sure I could make it back downstairs. I began slowly walking back down the staircase, holding tight to the railing for support. I had to call for help, but I didn't want to panic Gloria.

Stepping into the office, I said, "Gloria, please call 911 and ask the police to come fast. There's been a break-in."

"I take it the news is not good, Fr. Brian?" she asked.

"No, but I can't talk right now. Please, let's wait for the police in the kitchen," I said. While she made the call, I returned to the kitchen and poured a glass of whiskey. I was hoping it would perform a miracle and delete from my memory every detail of the horror I just witnessed in Dennis's bedroom. I took a second gulp, as if it would wake me up from this nightmare.

It only took about five minutes for two squad cars to arrive. I escorted two officers upstairs, while others waited on the main floor. Before opening the door, I said, "I need to warn you both about the crime scene you are going to witness. I hope you don't mind going in alone as I can't go in again."

The officers entered Dennis's bedroom as I turned to retrace my steps down the stairs. I heard one of them exclaim, "Damn, Jesus Christ, we're going to need CSI and the medical examiner."

In less time than it takes to boil water, a phalanx of law enforcement personnel and vehicles surrounded St. Bartholomew's rectory, like an army besieging a castle. Next came the media vultures in their vans, with enough reporters with microphones and cameramen to fill the Suffolk County Arena. Ninety minutes later quiet, rural, picturesque Mattituck was making headline news. The last time there was a murder in this sleepy town was 30 years ago. And the last time the murder victim was a priest was never.

As I waited for the officer to take my statement, I reached for my cell phone and dialed Tim Cavanagh. He answered on the second ring.

"Hello," he said in his trademark calm voice.

"Tim, this is Brian Manley. Are you sitting down?"

"As a matter of fact I am."

"Listen, I am at St. Bart's in Mattituck, and I have some shocking news. Dennis has been murdered. I found him dead in his bed this morning. I am too nauseated and disoriented to give you details."

"Oh, dear God," was all Tim said.

"The police are here in large numbers, and the media are here in larger numbers. I think someone from the Chancery needs to get here

ASAP, as this is going to be everywhere very soon. Sorry the news isn't better, but I have to give a statement to the police. Please keep in touch."

The officer who took my statement was sympathetic and patient. I gave as many details as my frozen brain cells could recall, especially Dennis's plans to have dinner last evening with a lady friend from Manhattan. He only knew her by Clare, her first name.

The officer paced the procedure with an abundance of time-outs for tears and vocal adjustments. In the end I had lost all sense of time and was shocked when I noticed my watch register 11:45 a.m. When I signed the document testifying to the truthfulness of my account, I asked if I could leave. I needed to get out of Mattituck and drive for as long as it took to come out of this nightmare.

Fr. Tim Cavanagh

I had just ended my call with Fr. Manley, trying to absorb the horrible news about Dennis Flaherty, when my phone rang again. The name and number on the screen flashed Sam Bannion. I knew she had already heard the news. Police, like clergy, were in a pipeline of instant access to information before it hit the news stations. She said she was calling to ask if I wanted a ride to Mattituck.

"I'll get right back to you," I said. "First, I have to inform you-know-who."

I said goodbye, then I took a deep breath and buzzed the bishop from my desk phone.

"I hope this call is to tell me you have changed your mind about the honor of becoming a monsignor," he said. He seemed to be functioning with a one-track mind.

"I have something more serious on my mind, and I think you should hear it in person."

When I entered the bishop's office, I took a deep breath, and then spoke like I was reading an email.

"It saddens me to tell you, Bishop, that I just received a phone call from Fr. Brian Manley. He found Fr. Dennis Flaherty dead in St. Bart's rectory this morning."

"What?" The bishop stood, leaning heavily on his desk. "Did he give you any details?"

"Just one. He was murdered." Silence hung in the room. I added, "The police and the media have descended on the rectory. I think it is safe to assume that whatever is happening out there, it will be on the evening news."

"Then get the hell out to Mattituck and contain as much of the gory news as you can. And call me no matter what time it is."

"Someone from the Islip Police Department is picking me up shortly so I can get there faster."

"Not fast enough. Stay in touch." The bishop waved me out of his office and sat down heavily, turning his back to me.

I raced out of my office to the cathedral rectory next door. I dialed Sam's number on the way, asking her to pick me up as soon as she could. I took the rectory stairs two at a time, retrieved my files on Dennis Flaherty, and met Sam at the back door. Our timing was as accurate as a ground play called by a football quarterback. As we swung onto Mt. Vernon Avenue with the giant cathedral to our right, we passed a media vehicle heading toward the Chancery Office. Although the Diocesan communications director would handle all press releases, I had a sickening feeling that things would not go exactly as scripted.

I asked Sam to give me a few minutes of privacy during our drive to read the files. Ten minutes later, when I closed the folder, she gave me a rundown of details she was privy to as a detective. I listened in horror and began wondering if there was any connection between what I just read and what I had just heard. An unfamiliar voice awakened a frightening presence in me with the thought that the secrets well-hidden deep in the bowels of Solitude were about to show their ugly faces, like a venomous monster being released. My reverie was broken by a question from Sam.

"If you don't mind my asking, did you read anything that might be helpful in solving this case?"

Caught off guard, I lost my cool. "Christ, Sam, when did a murdered priest become a 'case'?"

"When someone broke the law, committed a capital crime, and killed him. If you need more details, he became a police case sometime after 9 p.m. last night according to the medical examiner."

Distracted with facing my own inner demons, I refrained from replying to her words. Instead I chose to survey the rural landscape as she increased her speed toward Mattituck.

Finally, she broke the interminable silence and said with genuine compassion, "This is not going to be easy for you, so what do you need from me to be helpful?"

"Can you tell me what the drill will be?"

For the next ten minutes she briefed me on police protocols and how they would affect me as an official representative of the diocese. She was also kind enough to coach me about how to handle the media.

"The cameras and lights will get hot for two reasons. First, the electrical wattage they draw and second, the celebrity wattage you will draw. Whether you like it or not, you are going to be on a different kind of center stage, so play your role as clergy spokesperson as calmly and professionally as you did as a concert pianist."

Those were the last words I remembered as we made the final turn onto Canal Street. The number of media mobile vans and police cars gave the appearance that this quiet, reclusive street had turned into a circus supported by an army of ancillary trailers and equipment vehicles.

Sam had to slow her speed to a snail's pace to keep from making contact with the media reporters who swarmed her car like wasps on the attack. When we finally arrived at the gate to the back driveway, I was relieved that a local policeman opened and closed it again, keeping the reporters at bay like a bouncer at a nightclub. I sighed with relief. I knew eventually I would have to face them, but that would be my timing and not theirs.

When we entered the rectory, I followed Sam's lead in connecting with the local authorities processing the crime scene. We were confined to the office space on the first floor. Fr. Brian Manley and the parish secretary had left earlier after giving their statements. I was introduced to Chief Hollowell of the Mattituck Police Department, who gave us a thorough briefing on the crime. As I listened in silence, I willed my stomach not to be sickened by details of Dennis's tortured death. I thanked God that Brian had already identified the body and spared me that unpleasant experience.

Sam and I sat in silence in the office as I tried to comprehend the magnitude of what I had just heard. I excused myself to step outside into the yard for fresh air and some private space to call the bishop. The beauty of the manicured gardens helped to calm me. I repeated to the bishop all that I had downloaded into my confused memory cells from the briefing. I withheld what I knew from the file and kept to myself the questions spinning in my brain about Bishop Campbell's connections with Dennis Flaherty and, possibly, this crime.

Nora Owens

After spending the night in a hotel near the airport, I returned my rental car and caught a noon commuter train to Manhattan. This way I would be seen by two different doormen on different days and at different hours. I had unmasked myself as Clare O'Neill at the hotel and buried the filleting knife in a grave in a nearby cemetery, where I had crashed a funeral after the mourners had left. I had asked for some privacy while faking grief before the coffin was lowered into the ground. The burial of a total stranger and my need to dispose of the murder weapon were perfectly timed. Before I left, I prayed quietly, "May you both rest in peace."

Later that night, I watched the local news account of the murder in the quiet, sleepy town of Mattituck. Words like "brutal," "horrible," and "avenging," were used to describe the crime. As I sipped a glass of wine, I thought about the double entendre of those words. They could also be used to describe Dennis Flaherty's crimes of rape and torture perpetrated on my sister and me, crimes that eventually led Nanette to commit suicide. Where were these voices when we needed them?

I was reaching over to refill my wine glass when the sound of a name perked my ears to attention. The newscaster reported that a Fr. Brian Manley had discovered the body at 9 a.m. They were supposed to have spent the day together following the celebration of St. Bartholomew's feast day. Noting that a Fr. Brian was on my hit list, I began to wonder about possible connections with Dennis Flaherty and Holy Comforter Orphanage. Only one way to find out.

I Googled his name and was directed to a website for St. Simon the Fisherman Parish in Bayport. I stopped reading his bio after the fourth line revealed that Fr. Brian Manley was once a priest in the diocese of Dublin, Ireland, and served three years at Holy Comforter Orphanage.

I couldn't believe my luck. The possibility of killing two priest-rapists back to back and in the same diocese released a rush in me.

Maybe this mission will end sooner than planned, I thought as I sipped more wine, now served with the garnish of a broadening smile blossoming on my face.

Fr. Tim Cavanagh

Bishop Campbell called an emergency clergy staff meeting at his office on Friday, August 28th, at 3:30 p.m. The delay allowed Ted Barnes to return from vacation. Unfortunately for me, that was the time I had allocated to practice the piano at Rosslare Park in preparation for the concert event I had committed myself to, thanks to Sam's evening of seduction at *La Casa Nostra.* But the business of Dennis's murder, press releases, and planning his funeral trumped Giuseppe Verdi.

I hadn't yet shared the news with Granny about my return to the stage. The concert was two months away, but I decided now was as good a time as any. I dialed her number on my cell phone.

"I've heard enough horrible news about Fr. Flaherty's murder, so I am only listening to good news," she said in a failed attempt to sound like a late-night comedian.

"Okay, here's some good news. How would you like to be the guest of Samantha Bannion and Giuseppe Verdi for a fund-raising concert in October?"

"Well, I can see enjoying Samantha's company, but how are you going to manage someone who has been dead for over a hundred years and lying in a tomb in Milan?"

"Quite simply—I am going to bring him to life by playing two pieces of his repertoire with the New Long Island Symphony."

"Aha! I asked for good news and got shockingly good news. Is there more? If so, I probably should sit down."

"Yes, there's more. I'm going to ask you to buy some complimentary tickets and give them to children whose parents have been killed in the line of duty as police, fire, and emergency rescue personnel. It's to support a scholarship fund for them."

"Leave that detail to me and Samantha. That way you are free to concentrate only on practicing the piano so Mr. Verdi can smile on you, while the rest of us applaud."

"I'll be at Rosslare later tonight so I can practice early in the morning. Got to run now, to what will be a depressing meeting about Dennis Flaherty's funeral."

I could sense when we hung up that she was recharged enough to restart a shutdown nuclear power plant.

I grabbed a note pad and, hiding a subdued manner with a fake disposition, I walked into the bishop's office for a meeting that I already knew would leave me with heartburn. Behind me was Msgr. Ted Barnes with a tan that had the tropics written all over it. The door closed with an empty hallway on one side and an office full of hidden fear and worry on the other side.

I brought everyone up to speed about details of the murder that Sam Bannion had shared with me. The medical examiner had released Dennis's body two days ago following a thorough autopsy. The final report indicated Dennis Flaherty died of exsanguination, literally drowning in his own blood from three mortal stab wounds.

"These are the kind of details scripted for a CSI TV series. Who would do something like this to a priest?" Ted Barnes asked with a mixture of innocence and shock in his voice.

There was a silence in the office that was so raw it would take a filleting knife to cut it. I looked at Bishop Campbell, who was looking squarely at Joe McInnes. Whatever they were communicating was meant for their eyes only. Little did they know that I could interpret what they were saying based on what I now knew about Dennis Flaherty from his secret personnel file.

"Let's move on to planning the funeral," the bishop said as a way to escape any talk about secrets that helped contribute to this death. His request only fueled greater suspicion about Dennis, thus feeding the Chancery culture of secrecy.

An hour later when the funeral plans were complete, I said, "I am wondering about the wisdom of meeting with the clergy sometime after the funeral and giving them an opportunity to ask questions and to grieve."

Ted Barnes nodded and started to speak, but Bishop Campbell interrupted him. "For Christ sake, the clergy aren't a group of weeping women at the tomb. Let them grieve their own way. We don't need more meetings following the funeral. Let's get it over with and bury this whole mess with him."

I leaned on fortitude and, with persistence in my voice, countered him by saying, "I mention this because several priests have asked for such a gathering, including Brian."

"I will take care of Brian," the bishop barked, then, sounding like an insecure dictator, he continued his rant. "Tell the others we're not going to hold their hands. After the funeral and all the press interest dies down, the best therapy is for everyone to put their hands back on the plow and get to work."

As an afterthought he added, "What you can do, Tim, is get an email to all the clergy clarifying that if they are approached by the media they are to refrain from making statements and refer them to the chancery. Make that clear. I'll see everyone on Monday at the funeral in Mattituck. This meeting is over."

Ted Barnes followed me to my office. "I admire the way you champion the brother priests," he said. "Don't let the bishop's reactions keep you from caring."

He patted me on the back like an athlete patting a fellow teammate whose attempts to score points always failed. I had a sinking feeling that not only were my days numbered in the Chancery Office, but perhaps my days in the priesthood as well.

I was rescued from drowning further into that pool of sadness by the thought that the team of Samantha Bannion and Giuseppe Verdi might restart my life in a different direction.

ᴄ✍ Chapter Nineteen ᴄꙨ

Detective Sam Bannion

The business card with the quote from Romans 12:18 found at the crime scene in St. Bartholomew's rectory caused me to send out a national alert to law enforcement agencies. In less than an hour I got a response. Detective Saluccio from the Boston Police Department called to give me details of a similar piece of evidence at the crime scene of a murdered priest at Holy Cross Cathedral. We both concluded a priest serial killer was on the loose. The objective now was to connect the dots between Fr. Michael Mulgrew and Fr. Dennis Flaherty. Those dots might lead to a suspect. Assistant District Attorney Judith Steiner already had a personnel file for Fr. Flaherty.

When I called for an appointment and shared the information I had learned, she cleared her calendar to meet with me two hours later. The D.A.'s office in the three-story federal building in Riverhead was a typical concrete fortress. It was built in the '60s in a style that was neo-intimidating. If the building could speak, it would only say one word: Power. The only extreme makeover improvement would be a wrecking ball.

Judith Steiner was a no-nonsense assistant D.A. I noted that she preferred a natural look, foregoing excess make-up and jewelry. I assumed it reinforced her work ethic that "what you see is what you get." Her hair, pulled back into a bun, elevated her persona with a shrewish Victorian look.

I had already done my homework and had Detective Saluccio fax me the file on Fr. Michael Mulgrew. That way we could easily compare similar MOs from the two cases.

Judith scanned the papers with practiced eyes. "Your conclusions?" she asked.

"I think we are dealing with a serial killer." Hanging that thought in the air for a moment, I added, "Make that a priest serial killer."

"The common denominator here seems to be Holy Comforter Orphanage in Dublin. What's your theory about that?" she asked dispassionately, but in a tone that wanted a brief answer to her brief question.

"The fact that both priests are in their late fifties and that thirty years have passed since their assignments at Holy Comforter, tells me whoever they sexually abused in the orphanage was young back in the '70s and spent half a lifetime planning their revenge."

She pondered my reply with eyes that looked like they were branding me, "What do we need to convert your theory into reality?"

"We need to have access to the files at Holy Comforter." I stopped there, allowing her to draw the conclusions that were as clear as the glass that shielded her academic degrees hanging on the wall behind her desk.

"How soon can you plan a trip to Dublin?" she asked.

"It will have to wait until after the annual fundraising concert, so, in about six weeks."

"Let's hope there are no more priest murder victims between now and then. Is there someone from the Diocese of Islip you trust as an insider who won't push any panic buttons or raise any caution flags?"

"As a matter of fact there is. Timothy Cavanagh is someone I have already had discussions with about clergy sexual abuse. I trust him."

"Is he by any chance related to Aishling Jane Cavanagh?" she asked, raising her eyebrows.

"Yes, he's her grandson."

"And you are on a first-name basis with him?" she asked, as if she wanted me to admire her listening skills. She had noticed how I spoke his name without using his title.

"We are."

"Then trust your trust and see what he can contribute to this investigation. You have my cell number, so keep in touch."

With that she stood, signaling an end to the meeting.

But my work was just beginning, especially the new issue of planning a trip to Dublin. Excitement began to mix with ingenuity as I pondered how to convince Tim that his traveling with me to Dublin might speed up the investigation. His title and Roman collar could open doors to a now shuttered orphanage and gain access to church authorities and records that might be denied to me. Not wanting to distract his piano practice for the concert with this issue, I decided his grandmother might be just the resource I need. I made a mental note to call her later.

Jane Cavanagh

After my cell phone conversation with Timothy, I am certain I wore a smile on my face as brilliant as the orchids, calla lilies, and gardenias I was gazing at in the greenhouse. Without a mirror I knew the inner glow I was emitting was as much a kaleidoscope of beauty as these floral gems. If it was possible to be contagious with their silent beauty and the scent of wonder, then I was truly infected. Savoring the moment for more than a moment, I made another call.

"What a nice surprise, Jane," Samantha Bannion said, sounding nothing but pleasant.

"Actually, it was I who was just surprised by a call from Timothy, inviting me to join you and Giuseppe Verdi at a fundraising concert."

"Who is Giuseppe Verdi?" she asked in a tone of childhood innocence.

"He is the composer of the two sacred pieces Timothy will play with the New Long Island Symphony."

"And will Mr. Verdi be attending the concert?"

"Hardly, he has been dead for over a hundred years."

With a contrite voice, she said, "Sorry about my classical music illiteracy. And what pieces of Verdi's music is Timothy going to play?"

"Why don't you ask him yourself? He's practicing here at Rosslare on Saturday for about three hours in the morning. Can you join us for lunch about noon?"

"I'm flattered, but I don't want to interrupt his practicing and his time with you."

"After three hours at the piano, you and Bach will be just the interruption he will need."

"In that case, would you mind if I came earlier to discuss something with you?"

"Not at all." Intrigued by her question, I couldn't resist some clever probing.

"Can you brief me now so I can ponder whatever it is between now and Saturday?"

"I have been asked by the assistant D.A. to travel to Dublin to investigate some details there linked with Fr. Dennis Flaherty's murder. I was wondering how to ask Timothy about joining me, since he might be of value in gaining access to the church authorities in Dublin."

It's a good thing we were not on Skype, or Samantha would have seen the ever-widening grin forming on my face. I was tempted to say, "Yes, there is a God," but composing myself, I settled for the line, "I will give that serious thought, and I am sure that after Saturday, when we put our heads together, we will make him a deal he can't refuse."

After ending the call, my brain began to spin in a hundred different directions. The grandmother in me gave way to the matchmaker in me. I had long ago given up that role after Timothy married first the grand piano, and later the Catholic Church.

But hope endures after all. I threw my greenhouse smock in the direction of the Bonsai trees and adjusted my straw hat. After dancing a few steps on the wooden pellets and humming a tune from *Fiddler on the Roof,* I opened the door and river-danced my way to the kitchen to tell Molly Malone about lunch on Saturday.

Nora Owens

I decided to delay my return trip to London so I could attend Mass on Sunday at St. Simon's Church in Bayport. The scent of autumn in late September was ushering in a welcome change in Manhattan, so a Sunday drive to a quaint Long Island town facing the Great South Bay might provide a change of climate along with a change of perspective. Dennis Flaherty's funeral was three weeks old and no longer a media story. Time to see how Brian Manley was coping and what, if anything, I could do to assist.

Knowing that Fr. Manley was privy to police info that a middle-aged woman named Clare from Manhattan was a prime suspect in the murder of Dennis Flaherty, I would need a radically different disguise to approach him. Perhaps a 70-year-old woman with gray hair and a cane would confuse his radar. Add a stutter and metal-rimmed glasses, and he wouldn't be able to resist my senior citizen charm.

There would be no wooing and seducing as with Dennis; no fine dining and clinking of wine glasses; no sexual innuendos or falling-into-temptation talk. I had never forgotten what Fr. Sean, the ominous first priest rapist, once said: "Lead me not into temptation for I can find it myself." Little did he know I would adapt his cruel humor as a legacy for my Coat of Arms.

Brian Manley would have to be the victim of a strategic strike: one Mass, one personal appointment, and then the kill. One, two, three, and then an escape to St. Lucia. There was no better place to hide in plain sight then with the laissez-faire people of the island. Their friendliness mixed with the warm sun and crystal clear waters of the Caribbean was the perfect cocktail to become myself again. Peace, love, and happy hour would be here sooner than later.

Fr. Tim Cavanagh

I slipped into the house at 8 a.m. and quietly made my way to the grand piano in the sitting room. I closed the door so Bach would not be a distraction. After adjusting and arranging the first piece of music on the lyre, my pianist habit kicked into play. I lowered my head and had a brief chat with the divine musician as the source of my gifts and passions. Then I had a brief chat with the composer. Giuseppe Verdi was someone whose music was the foundation of an enduring friendship.

I would play three selections with the kind of prayerful passion that would help the living remember and honor their deceased family and comrades so the mystery of loss could revive in them a passion for keeping their memory alive—how they lived their lives before death.

Finally I chatted with the Knabe baby grand piano that had graced this elegant family room for over twenty years. We had been friends that long. Talking quietly with the piano was my way of bonding with the instrument and letting it know that we needed each other to make great music that would leave people yearning for more.

My chatting with a musical instrument was the equivalent of Granny's talking to her flowers and potted plants in the greenhouse. If her whisperings could produce beautiful buds and eye-catching blooms, then the piano and I could produce equally beautiful music.

I invited the spirit of Verdi to join me at the bench. I played his music like a prayer for those first responders killed in action and who would be honored in the concert. I also played it praying for my own deliverance from a sadness that had entered my life, gradually eroding a happiness that I was hoping Verdi's musical genius would help me recover.

After the singular focus of practicing all three pieces like a trilogy of sighs, I was surprised to hear the grandfather's clock in the hallway strike 12. It was time for a break.

As I opened the doors to the sitting room, Bach stood up on all fours and barked his applause. I bent down to hug him. Then I heard the sound of feet echoing on the parquet floor. I was expecting Granny and Molly, so seeing the combination of Granny and Sam was a total surprise. My smile was as wide as a football field, and it was mirrored on Granny's face.

"The surprised look on your face means I have to apologize for forgetting to tell you about our lunch guest," Granny said as if she really meant it. The truth was that she relished different ways of plotting how to catch me off guard with Samantha.

Quick to recover, I said, "Well, it's a nice surprise." I changed my focus from one face to the other. "How long have you been here?"

"She's been here long enough for us to enjoy each other's company without looking at a clock," Granny said. "Can Giuseppe spare you long enough for some drinks and a Molly Malone lunch?"

"Since he's not around for me to ask, I'm all yours," I replied.

"Are you speaking to me or to Samantha?" Granny asked. Sam's face blushed with shades of red and pink like the flashes of a strobe light.

"To whomever wants my company," I said.

With Verdi's requiem music secured on the piano lyre stand in the family room, lunch would not be served with sadness and sighs, but with laughter, and the element of surprise. I loved the taste of those nouns when served with Molly's four-star cuisine and Sam's eclectic company.

ᴄ⤴ Chapter Twenty ᴄ⤵

Nora Owens

I decided to leave less of a trail with Brian Manley than I had with Dennis Flaherty. Instead of a rental car I took a bus from the Port Authority terminal to Fire Island, and then backtracked via the ferry across the Great South Bay to Bayport. I then hired a cab to drive me to St. Simon's Church. I arrived ten minutes before the 11 a.m. Sunday Mass.

I would be unrecognized as a stranger. Masquerading as one who walked slowly with a cane, I qualified for a seat in the pew reserved for senior citizens. I had remade myself from head to toe, including silk gloves to hide my much-too-young-looking hands. Once again my principle of "revenge with no mistakes" ruled the day.

The nave of the church was long, so it took the priest-rapist Fr. Brian Manley a long minute to pass by my pew. Although the reading glasses I was wearing slightly blurred my view of him, I confirmed my suspicions after a quick study. He had aged, but he was the one—my next victim.

He appeared somber, as if he were still thawing from the shock of discovering the bloody corpse of his murdered priest-friend. His voice fluctuated between clarity and dissonance, like a baritone struggling to find a consistent pitch. I could tell he was playing with the people's heartstrings, evoking sympathy for his unplanned role in a real-life tragedy.

Unlike St. Bartholomew's, there was no choir animating the congregation at St. Simon's. No flower arrangements adorned the sanctuary. No young faces served as lay ministers. The liturgy for this twenty-second week in Ordinary Time was as bland as a wine and cheese gathering without the wine. His homily, if you could call it that, was a rambling reflection on this summer of his life that he wanted to forget. He had hoped things would quiet down in Bayport now that September was in full swing, and the absence of summer churchgoers, along with the elimination of two extra Masses, enabled his regular flock to take back their parish.

My ears awakened when he mentioned a planned trip to Ireland in mid-October following a fundraising concert for police and firemen killed in the line of duty. He encouraged the congregation to attend the concert for two reasons: first, to support the cause, and second, to applaud Fr. Tim Cavanagh's return to the stage for his solo performances with the New Long Island Symphony. I made a mental note to Google that concert. It might determine the date of Fr. Brian Manley's death.

An hour later I made my way out of church with the slowness of the proverbial tortoise. I pretended to stumble on the step and reached over to grab the pastor's arm to recover my balance.

"Thank you, Father, for keeping me from falling," I said, using my best fake elderly voice. "I can't afford to fracture a second hip."

"I am happy to be in the right place at the right time," he answered with a quick wit.

"Father, I need a favor," I said. "Can someone call a taxi for me? I need to go to the ferry."

"The ferry port is close by, and I will be happy to drive you," he said caringly.

"I accept your offer. I live on a fixed income and welcome every chance to save pennies."

After he unvested from his robes and locked the church, he retrieved his car from the rectory next door and opened the passenger door for me. He would be shocked if he knew how clearly I remembered that this display of warm hospitality had been hidden from me the first eighteen years of my life.

During the ten-minute ride to the ferry port, I had just enough time to weave my lies into a story that would be the web to draw him in. I had come from Newburgh to visit my fictitious grandson on Fire Island. Part of the script was to share with him how troubled I was that my grandson was homosexual and living in sin with a male partner.

Brian Manley's silence in listening to the details was broken only with an occasional, "I see" or "I understand."

When we arrived at the ferry port parking lot, I reached over and touched his arm. "Father, I will be staying with my grandson for a month. Can I come back to St. Simon's and talk with you more about this?"

"I'll be happy to listen and offer you some guidance any way I can." He handed me a business card.

As he drove off, I stood in position with one hand on the cane while using the other to wave goodbye. My senior citizen alias had worked.

The only thing left on my agenda was to get information on the fundraising concert. Once I knew that, then I would balance my plans for his murder with plans for a much-needed vacation to St. Lucia. I wanted to be as far away as possible from media hype about another priest's murder. St. Lucia was far enough away that I could once again just be Nora Owens.

Fr. Tim Cavanagh

I had no sooner booted up my computer in the Chancery Office then my phone buzzed.

"I would like to see you in my office now," Bishop Campbell said in his dictator voice. I took one deep breath and steeled myself for an unpleasant encounter.

As I approached him, he threw a copy of yesterday's *Long Island Gazette* on the edge of the desk.

"What is this?" he asked.

My eyes locked onto the front-page story about my upcoming performance at the concert, but I decided to treat him to a taste of his sarcasm.

"It's a newspaper."

He winced. What I then saw was the face of a man whose eyes burned like someone had stoked a fire with butane. Slamming his fist on the desk, he growled, "Stop trying to be a late-night comedian with me. You know damn well I meant this article about you playing the piano for a fundraising concert."

"What about it?"

162

"When did we have a conversation about this, and when did I approve it?"

"I guess we're having the conversation now, and when did I need your approval to help raise money for the children of first-responder parents who have died in the line of duty? When did an issue about compassion for others become an issue about your authority?"

Choosing to ignore the question, he barked, "And do you intend to perform in a white tie and tails like this picture of you?"

"Yes, I do."

"And how will that improve the image of the priesthood in the Diocese of Islip?"

"Since I am not the cause of the image of the priesthood needing improvement in the diocese, I will defer that question to those who are responsible for that."

Once again his eyes tightened with rage. I thought I saw spittle forming at the corners of his mouth. During the standoff I knew that he knew he was teetering toward the edge of pushing himself too far with the grandson of Aishling Jane Cavanagh. Once again his unpolished Northern Irish hubris had created a tense, no-win situation, with him displaying more tension than me.

"And do you expect me to attend?" he said, barely keeping his anger in check.

"I believe the answer to your question is in you, not in me," I said, countering his arrogance with the wisdom to be non-defensive.

He dismissed me with, "That will be all."

Before I turned to leave, I said calmly, "While we're on the subject of the concert, I will be practicing the piano every Friday until then. Also, my grandmother will host a party at Rosslare Park the night before the concert. You can expect an invitation."

Then I made my way toward the office door, not caring to look back to see if my last line had placated him at all.

Bishop John Campbell

Once the multi-millionaire pianist-priest left, taking his one-of-a-kind boldness with him, I cracked a window and began puffing on a Cuban cigar. The nicotine quickly entered my system, becoming the miracle drug I needed to calm my frayed nerves. No other priest in the diocese took such liberties with me as Tim Cavanagh. If he had any other last name, he would be pastor of the parish in the last outpost in the diocese. "Out of sight, out of mind," as they say.

With a priest's death, Tim's challenging style, and an ominous cloud hanging over me about Dennis Flaherty's murder, I would need to call for reinforcements. I had kept that special phone number hidden in my memory for years, and I wouldn't be afraid to use it—if and when the time came.

Jane Cavanagh

Following my "girl time" with Samantha one week ago, I had plenty of time to put all the details in place. Faithful to my Saturday ritual, I spent the morning in the greenhouse relating to my hibiscus, amaryllis, and array of fall mums, which affect me like no other kind of therapy. Timothy and I would be having lunch alone following his concert practice. The plot was in place and my script was edited.

At 11:30 a.m., I made my way across the patio to the house for what I hoped would be lunch with surprises on the side.

"How was your practice session this morning?" I asked Timothy with genuine interest.

"Fine," Tim replied with a hint of reservation. "I am beginning to have second thoughts about an all-Verdi program. Most of those in attendance probably won't know who he is nor connect the musical selections to complement the purpose of the concert."

"The baseball fan in me wants to say, 'If you play Verdi, they will come.'"

A smile broke out on his face, signaling approval of my humor. During a brief pause, as we enjoyed Molly's signature Shrimp Fra Diavola with Linguine and a bottle of Italian Chianti, I captured the moment.

164

"I have a surprise for you."

"Your timing is good," he said. "I could use one right now."

"In that case, I hope you will be happy to know that I made plans for us to travel to Ireland after the concert. With a heavy cloud of stress hanging over you from Dennis Flaherty's murder and funeral and the piano practicing leading up to the concert, I thought a trip to the Emerald Isle would have relief and pleasure written all over it. Besides, it's been too long since we last visited the Cavanaghs and Staffords, and since I long to see the real Rosslare again, I wanted to do so with your company."

He raised his wine glass and said, "I'll drink to that." We saluted the travel plans with wide smiles.

"When do we leave?" he asked, his mood shifting to high excitement.

"A week after the concert—Sunday, Oct. 17. We have first-class tickets on the last Aer Lingus non-stop flight from JFK to Dublin. I thought we would spend a few days there, museum hopping and shopping, before heading down to Rosslare to visit family. Your aunts and uncle are delighted about our visit."

"Pardon the correction, but I think what you mean to say is, I will be museum hopping while you go shopping."

"'Tis true, Timothy, you certainly don't carry my gene for shopping, which means we will spend quality time together frequenting the Irish pubs and the theater."

"I will have to break this news to you-know-who quickly," Timothy said, without speaking John Campbell's name. "He has to have time to throw a temper tantrum before calming his nerves with a Havana cigar. I don't know how long he has been smoking them, but I am surprised he doesn't speak fluent Spanish by now with all that Cuban nicotine in him."

I chuckled at my grandson's humor. I knew the bishop would make some sarcastic remark about the Ireland trip, but in the end he would not interfere with my plans. He knew who the general underwriter was for crisis projects in the Diocese of Islip.

165

The lunch reminded me how much I missed Timothy's company, and I was not the only one. When he was here, Bach shadowed him around the house and not me. At the table Bach lay at his feet and not mine. He waited for Timothy outside the family room while practicing the piano, rather than being bored with me and my flowers in the greenhouse. They bonded together like male friends playing in the garden rather than taking naps in the house.

As I watched this twosome play in the yard after lunch, with the caring heart of a grandmother, I imagined another person in the picture. Though Bach was as fond of her as we were, he couldn't satisfy Tim's needs like Samantha.

Now that I knew Timothy was delighted about the Ireland trip in three weeks, it made it easier for me to spring the second surprise that she would be joining us. I would wait on that, however; maybe Providence would intervene and do it for me.

Fr. Tim Cavanagh

Buoyed by an A+ practice session and Granny's news over lunch about the Ireland trip, I decided to finish a perfect Saturday by calling Sam. Tomorrow was forecast to be a beautiful fall Sunday, so I decided to plan my own conspiracy with an invitation to lunch in Manhattan that would upstage her dinner conspiracy at La Casa Nostra.

I dialed her cell, and when she answered, I said, "HI, you've been chosen to have lunch tomorrow with Tim Cavanagh at Joe Green Square in the upper east side of Manhattan." I did my best imitation of a game show host announcing a prize.

"I would like to accept, but there's one problem," she said regretfully.

"And that is?" I said.

"There is no Joe Green Square in the upper east side of Manhattan."

"Trust me, there is," I assured her.

"You forget I am a Flushing girl who is a cop and knows every borough like a road atlas," she countered, like a school teacher trying to outsmart her pupil.

"Then you're in for a surprise."

"Maybe you're the one who will be surprised," she said.

"If I am, then I couldn't think of a nicer person to share the surprise with than you."

"Okay," she said unhesitatingly, "I'm hooked. What's the plan?"

"I have the first two Masses at the cathedral, and then I'll pick you up about 11 a.m. We can be in Manhattan by noon, enjoy an outdoor lunch, and be back here before your partner calls in a missing cop report."

"First of all, Lou Perkins doesn't know what I do with my life outside the precinct. And second, if filing a missing cop report is part of your plan, you should know that kidnapping a police officer is a capital crime."

She knew I was grinning from ear to ear with these unscripted, playful lines. And I knew the same grin was painted on her face. This was one of the many features that made her so damn attractive to me, so alluring, and yes, so sexy. She was one of a few people who knew how to make me blush. And worse yet, she knew that I knew, and that I was okay with her crossing that boundary.

"Until tomorrow, may all your dreams leave a smile on your face," I said.

"And what famous person are you quoting now?" she asked.

"Someone named Timothy Cavanagh. Have you ever heard of him?"

"I know a Tim Cavanagh. But he's a pianist and not a poet," she countered playfully.

"What can I say except he is one and the same?"

"In that case, check out my smile in the morning." Then, in a lilting, seductive voice, she said, "Good night, Tim McDreamy."

The phone went dead, but my pulse was off the charts.

❦ Chapter Twenty-One ❧

Nora Owens

The forecast for a clear, autumn Sunday inspired me to attend church again at St. Simon's. Another piece of the web would be spun, and in two weeks Fr. Brian Manley would be lured into it.

Since I was my own make-up artist, I arose early to transform myself into a senior citizen named Agnes Mullen. A thoroughly Irish woman gave my accent authenticity.

I replayed my travel routine from Manhattan to Fire Island to Bayport, arriving at the church ten minutes before Mass. I had a senior citizen pew all to myself. It was like asking for a pew for one.

Once again, Brian Manley appeared to still be in a funk. I had underestimated how Dennis Flaherty's murder affected him. I wondered who would be similarly affected by his murder. I released that thought as soon as I spoke the memorized words, "Lord have mercy."

Unlike Dennis Flaherty, who liked to hear himself talk, Brian Manley was a homilist gifted with brevity. "Be brief, be bright, and be gone" seemed to be his motto. That, along with basic music and no other thrills, resulted in a forty-five minute Mass. It was just the right amount of time for sitting on a hard church pew.

Once again, I was the last to reach the front door.

"Agnes, it's good to see you again," Fr. Manley said as if he really meant it. "Do you need a ride back to the ferry port?"

"It's kind of you to ask, and yes, I do," I said, sounding like a solicitous old woman. "But I was wondering if I could chat with you some more about my grandson Kevin before we leave."

"Just let me un-vest and lock up, then we can have a cup of tea in the rectory."

In less than ten minutes we were sitting at Fr. Manley's kitchen table waiting for the kettle to boil.

"I won't keep you, Father, because Sunday is a work day for you and you're due for a nap. I just need to talk about my grandson's homosexual lifestyle," I said. "He wasn't raised like that, and I am ashamed of him. And I can't understand how someone as young and handsome as he is could be in love with an older man. And surely they can't get any satisfaction out of sex without the possibility of conceiving children."

"I agree with you on that score, Agnes. Gay sex cannot be as fulfilling as heterosexual sex."

Little did he know that he was speaking with someone who found his sexual abuses totally unfulfilling. I mused over his duplicity and the lies hidden behind his pseudo-charming face.

"But times have changed Agnes," he continued, "and the whole gay culture, if you know what I mean by that, is open and carefree."

"What about his soul, Father. The Bible is very clear about this gay lifestyle being an abomination. I worry he is making God angry and won't get into heaven."

"You'll have to let Kevin and God work that out. That will free you to love him despite his choices."

We volleyed back and forth on the subject for a half hour while sipping our cups of tea. I was pleased that he never commented on my not removing the gloves in his house. He reminded me that the ferry schedule had changed and we should leave soon.

Before I got out of his car, I turned to him and said, "Father, next Sunday will be the last day of my visit. May I stay after Mass and go to confession?"

"Certainly. I will have a few minutes before leaving to attend a fundraising concert."

When he had dropped me off, I once again stood still, leaning on my cane while he exited the parking lot. I waved like Aunt Bea from Mayberry, but without the sincerity. Then I folded the cane and placed it in my purse. Walking briskly toward the ferry, with a stiff wind from the bay beating at my face, I began counting the days like a child counts down to Christmas. Seven days to honor another promise to my dead twin sister. Seven days until I scratched another name off my list. Seven days until Brian Manley, sexual abuser and priest-rapist, would rest in hell on the seventh day and, no doubt, not in peace.

170

Fr. Timothy Cavanagh

With a double dose of luck with traffic and lights, the three of us—Sam, Giuseppe Verdi's *Variazioni Per Piano in E-Minor* in the CD player, and I—arrived at 72nd Street between Broadway and Amsterdam at noon. As I pulled my car alongside the curb, Sam craned her neck to get a clear view of the statue that was the centerpiece of the square. I opened her door and escorted her to the front of the monument secured by a wrought iron fence. Then I made the introduction.

"Samantha Bannion, meet Joe Green, a.k.a. Giuseppe Verdi," I joked.

"Well, if you had given me his name in Italian, I would have solved the riddle," she said with a look of mischief in her eyes. "And where are we having lunch?"

"Over there," I said gesturing toward the concrete mall area resembling a park.

I opened the trunk, took out a picnic basket and two seat cushions from Granny's patio porch, and spread out a feast on a small, grassy area close to Amsterdam Avenue. Then I retrieved a CD player, popped in a CD of Verdi's most famous arias, and uncorked a bottle of Classico 2003 Bardolino.

"It's not *La Casa Nostra*," I said, "but at least the composer is in our company, along with four of his most famous characters." I pointed to the four statues of Verdi's most famous operatic characters: Falstaff, Leonora of *La forza del destino*, Aida, and Othello, resting at the base of the 1906 monument. Then I proposed a toast before we clinked glasses.

"Here's to life always being good again, whenever we're in the company of Joe Green."

Sam's smile gave way to words. "I'll drink to that."

"So, is this all about you trying to second best me?" she said, glancing toward the monument.

"Now, where did such a foolish thought like that come from?"

"Well, wherever it's from, I am surprised and touched."

"I'll drink to that," I said, with cunning written all over my face.

We talked about the pre-concert party next Saturday and the concert on Sunday. I limited myself to just one glass of wine, since I was the designated driver for this picnic. By the time Sam finished the bottle, I couldn't make out whether she was speaking English or Italian.

By 3 p.m. I was packing the car for a return trip while Sam was clearly not going to pass a sobriety test. A CD of Sarah McLachlan put my passenger to sleep with her head nestled on my shoulder. This romantic scene inspired me to take a more scenic route home via the Brooklyn Bridge. As I crossed it in fast-moving traffic, I recalled that Walt Whitman once wrote an ode to the bridge and Henry Miller likened it to a harp.

Heading east on the Long Island Expressway, I began counting the days to the next time Sam and I would be in each other's company. That would be the pre-concert party hosted by Granny at Rosslare Park. Six agonizing days.

With over 100 guests expected to attend the party, it wouldn't be as intimate as today. Maybe we could sneak away for a few minutes and have a private moment. I was beginning to feel like a troubadour, and claiming a moment of prayerfulness, I offered my thanks to God and Verdi for making this day possible.

Jane & Samantha on Fashion Row

Jane Cavanagh's fashion instincts suspected that Samantha needed a new wardrobe for the party and concert. Jane lured her to Rosslare Park, and then the two were driven in Jane's BMW to Fashion Row in Manhattan. During the drive, Jane made it clear that the shopping and lunch were her treat. She had called ahead to a prime fashion house for a private showing.

They arrived at 79th Street and 3rd Avenue at 10 a.m. and were greeted at the door. After they selected their premium lattés, they were escorted into a private salon, where they met with a well-known designer.

After several showings, Jane chose a leopard print skirt and brown leather 3" heels for the party. Sam's world of high fashion, up until this moment, had been limited to anchor stores in suburban malls. Her wardrobe expanded each time the designer presented a different fashion. She selected a knit tunic with a matching shawl and chocolate-colored slacks to complement her runway-model legs. Her copper sandals sported a 2" heel. A bronze metallic beaded evening bag was the finishing touch.

At another Madison Avenue fashion house, the two women selected formal evening wear for the Sunday concert. Jane chose a stunning black evening dress, while Samantha selected a gunmetal satin gown. Jane Cavanagh approved with a pleasant smile intended to say that her grandson would approve too.

During a final stop at Jane's favorite jewelry store, they found a pair of diamond earrings for Sam. She felt like she had stepped into a fairytale book.

The final fittings would take place at Rosslare Park on Friday. On that day, a Long Island detective would transform into a runway model.

As they drove to a restaurant on the west side for lunch, Sam was at a loss for words. She had promised Jane Cavanagh not to talk about price tags, which was easy because the designer clothes did not have price tags on them. In her silence, Sam calculated that the final tab for her outfits probably exceeded the full amount of her 401k.

Jane chatted endlessly over their salads and entrees. "One last thing, Sam—please join me at Rosslare Park on Saturday at 2:00 for a spa treatment and to have our hair styled. I am anxious to see what my stylist does with your hair."

Not giving Sam the opportunity to decline, she continued, "Timothy will arrive about 7:00 to dress in time for the receiving line at 8:00. And I am sure you will take his breath away."

Sam's smile hid her true fantasy of having some time alone with Tim on Saturday to take his breath away and give him some of hers, in what she hoped would be their first kiss.

Rosslare Park

It has been some time since Rosslare Park had been the venue for a pre-concert party. The Cavanaghs use to host parties whenever Timothy performed as a concert pianist in or around the greater New York City area. To celebrate this event, Aishling Jane Cavanagh pulled out all the stops.

The house at Stony Brook was lit up like a carnival tent. The lady of the manor and her grandson greeted guests personally at the great doors. Also standing in the receiving line was the youthful and colorful Sicilian-born conductor of the New Long Island Symphony, Carlo Renzi. An aura around him confirmed his delight at standing next to Timothy Cavanagh. For it was the conductor himself who had suggested Fr. Cavanagh for this concert and who had plotted with Samantha Bannion to pull it off.

Valets parked foreign-made cars all around the expansive property. Three open bars satisfied the liquid appetite of every guest, while an army of waiters wearing tuxedos served hors d'oeuvres. A string quartet played music that wafted throughout the house. Sam smiled as she heard them segue from Johannes Brahms to Tony Bennett like a seamless garment. And the floral arrangements looked like the finishing touches in a Monet painting.

Aishling Jane Cavanagh beamed like a lighthouse. Dressed in her designer outfit, she made her way through the labyrinth of halls and rooms, working the guests like a politician running for office. Always reserved, but overflowing with hospitality, she was the consummate hostess. Timothy stayed close to her side, assuming his place as someone who was familiar with all the details of a high-brow party at Rosslare Park. He had been in this role many times before and did not hide the delight written all over his face.

Tim had dressed less formally for the occasion, shunning the traditional black clericals for a navy Ralph Lauren notch lapel suit. He did not feel upstaged by Bishop John Campbell, who was parading around the Manor House in his Episcopal robes.

One guest whispered into Tim's ear, "Was the bishop the only one who didn't get the message that this is not a masquerade party?"

Tim gradually separated from his grandmother's side and went looking for a certain redheaded female guest. He felt like a teenage boy cruising a crowd for a secret admirer at a high school dance. They bumped into each other in the grand hallway, trying to practice crowd avoidance and find a quieter space.

Tim grabbed Samantha's hand and escorted her up the grand staircase. The noise level lowered when he closed his bedroom door behind them. He did not realize that Bishop Campbell, who was talking with a guest in a corner of the hallway, had watched every step they took up the staircase.

"Thanks for the rescue," Sam said while trying to catch her breath.

"It's not a rescue. I wanted to tell you how beautiful you look without 100 people overhearing me. I think I'm the only one here who knows you're working undercover tonight, dressed like a model and turning every head. Let me guess—you went shopping with Granny?"

She feigned surprise, but replied, "Does it look that obvious?"

"Only to me." He gently touched her hair with the tips of his fingers, as if he were playing a Brahms sonata. As he slowly pulled her closer, something Sam had wished for many times came true. He was looking at her with those mesmerizing green eyes that said he wanted and desired her. She would not resist.

"Would you mind being kissed by someone whose breath smells like a liquor cabinet?" he asked.

"Not if you don't mind kissing someone whose breath smells like a wine cooler," she countered with a grin.

With that he kissed her slowly at first, lips just touching and moistening, then, more deeply and passionately, as if he were diving from shallow into deeper waters. She enjoyed every movement of his lips, their passion intensifying like the last movement in a symphony neither of them wanted to end. When they finally came up for air Tim rested his head on her forehead.

"I love your kisses when they're laced with Cabernet," Tim said jokingly.

"And I love a mouth washed in whiskey rather than Listerine," she countered in her trademark wit.

Their eyes riveted on each other for several minutes. Sam locked onto Tim's eyes long enough to commit their green sparkle to her memory.

"We'd better return to the party before Granny sends out a missing persons report," Tim said with a soft laugh.

"I know all about that, but I wouldn't mind going missing with you again," Sam said.

"I'll remember that the next time I want to go missing," Tim said. "Can I have your phone number to call you so you can find me?"

"You already have my number, and please call anytime."

"It's a promise," Tim said. He kissed her tenderly while softly stroking her cheeks, treating them like ivory piano keys.

"Would you do that again, please?" she asked, wanted to extend the moment she knew must end.

"I was hoping you would ask," he said.

When they returned to the party, Jane Cavanagh met them. "I was just getting ready to send the police to look for you, but I can see, Timothy, that you're already in the company of the police."

With that she tipped her drink to them, spun on her heel, and walked down the grand hallway wearing a grin even larger than theirs.

⫷ Chapter Twenty-Two ⫸

After the party

After the last guest left Rosslare Park around midnight, grandmother and grandson decompressed in the family room. They slowly sipped the remnants of a bottle of Reisling and listening to the last crackles of the wood burning in the fireplace. Molly had released Bach from the greenhouse, and he was happily parked at Tim's feet.

The lady of the house finally broke the silence.

"When are we going to do this again?" she said, hinting that a certain concert pianist grandson shouldn't wait so long again between concerts. "The walls are still breathing with secrets even after everyone has gone. It's been a long time since the house has pulsed and laughed with life as it did tonight."

"I have to admit there was a high level of energy here that I could get used to again," he said. "Is that what you wanted to hear?"

"If that will make you happy, then I will be happy," Jane said, always the veteran diplomat.

"What will make me happy is to find my bed and get to sleep. I'll go out for a bike ride early to wake myself up." He kissed her on the forehead and said, "Aishling Cavanagh, you are the light of my life. I love you, Granny. Good night."

Usually the night before a concert, Tim would replay the score in his mind, having memorized every sharp and flat, every crescendo and recitative. But tonight he found his mind fixed on a certain redhead who was quickly becoming the light of his life. He wondered if she was thinking of him and if they shared the same smile before succumbing to a deep sleep with each other in their dreams.

The Concert

Tim woke at 7 a.m. and dressed warmly for a long bike ride. The autumn air was nippy as it whistled around his bike on this beautiful fall

Sunday. Cycling was part of his daily routine, even on the day of a major performance. It woke up his muscles and joints, expanded his lungs, and quickened his heartbeat. The faster he rode around Stony Brook, the more his brain and memory cells came to life.

He replayed all the vital specifics from the two exhausting rehearsals he had had earlier in the week with the New Long Island Symphony and the Suffolk County Chorale. Instead of listening to an iPod, he recalled his rehearsal interchanges with Maestro Renzi. He knew his music by heart, but he never stood on memory alone. Each concert was different, each concert hall was different; each concert audience was different. He psyched himself to adjust to all those differences and remember that the concert was not about him.

Today at 2:00 he would entertain 2,000 concert-goers who gathered at the Suffolk County Performing Arts Center to honor beloved heroes first and enjoy his musical talents second. Tim was not the kind of self-absorbed artist to get in the way of celebrating heroes. Instead, he and Verdi would draw the audience deeper into the experience of loss that would help turn collective hurt into redemptive suffering. Together with Maestro Renzi, an 80-piece orchestra, a 200-voice chorale, and two soloists, the artistry of God would comfort 2,000 hearts through the power of classical music.

As he biked up the driveway to Rosslare Park, he kept invoking his motto as a pianist: "I am only an instrument, I am only an instrument. Like the Steinway concert grand piano, I am only an instrument."

After a long, hot shower he dressed casually and hurried downstairs to the breakfast room, with Bach following close behind.

Molly set a plate before him. She had remembered that his menu for a concert day was meager.

"Molly Malone, you still cook the best poached eggs on Long Island," he said with a prolonged "Yum."

"I'm happy to make a small contribution to your performance today by keeping you well fed," she replied with a noticeable Irish lilt in her voice. "It will be a special pleasure to hear you perform again, Timothy."

"Did my grandmother coach you to say that?"

"No, she didn't," said Jane Cavanagh, entering the breakfast room from the kitchen. "And you know Molly is not alone in that sentiment."

Over breakfast they chatted about the 100 tickets Jane had purchased for the families of the fallen heroes, the 50 tickets she had purchased for clergy, and the $5,000 she had spent on flowers for the stage. She had invited Bishop Campbell to share her box, along with Maestro Renzi's wife, the executive of Suffolk County and her husband, and, of course, Sam.

After warming up at the piano for half an hour, Tim took Bach for a short walk. With one hand holding the leash and his other, the cell phone, he dialed Sam. When she answered, he decided to forego the conventional greetings.

"Let me guess, you're putting on make-up."

"I finished that about twenty minutes ago and was going to call to see if you needed help with yours," she countered without missing a beat.

"The make-up artist will do that in my dressing room at the Performing Arts Center. Would you like to watch?"

"Watching someone else apply make-up is the worst kind of punishment for a detective. I'll let you know if I approve after the concert." She laughed. "I understand the line 'break a leg' is traditional for the theatre, but what is appropriate for a concert?" she asked sincerely.

"Wish me luck."

"Okay. Wish me luck," she repeated with a giggle.

"Gotta go," he said, "but your luck is all I need."

Jane had arranged for a limousine to drive them to the Performing Arts Center in Central Islip. Bach obediently stayed behind with the staff while Jane, Molly, and Tim got comfortable in the limo for the forty-five minute ride to the next movement in this long-awaited day.

Fr. Tim Cavanagh and Fr. Brian Manley

Tim and his guests arrived at the stage door of the Performing Arts Center at the same time Fr. Manley was concluding the 11 a.m. Mass at St. Simon's Church.

Tim dressed in his white tie and tails, which Jane Cavanagh had arranged to have tailor-made for him at Bergdorf-Goodman especially for this concert.

At the same time, Fr. Brian Manley removed his liturgical robes.

Thirty minutes later, while Tim was seated at the Steinway grand piano, warming up with the orchestra and chorale, Fr. Manley and Agnes Mullen, a.k.a. Nora Owens, chatted in the confessional.

As the chorale ignited the chorus with the Latin words, *Libera Mea*, Agnes pleaded with Fr. Brian Manley for deliverance from her guilt over the harsh judgments about her grandson.

The chorale increased its volume with the words, *"Dies illa, dies irae, the day, the day of anger."* Agnes released her true anger toward another priest-rapist in the confessional, hiding it behind the false anger of having a gay grandson. The person she truly despised was on the other side of the confessional grille. The person who was the object of her bitterness was the confessor.

As the chorale sang the tearful lyrics, *"Requiem aeternam dona eis, Domine, Eternal rest grant unto them, O Lord,"* Nora Owens squeezed the trigger of her silenced handgun and sent another priest molester to face the judgment of God.

As the chorale ended with *"Lux perpetua luceat eis, let perpetual light shine upon them,"* Nora Owens exited the side door of St. Simon's Church and waited for the taxi she had prearranged to meet her. She felt warmed by the light of a beautiful Sunday. She turned directly to face it, to allow its rays to shine upon her. In four hours she would be on a one-stop flight to the island paradise of St. Lucia to bask in the warmth of its Caribbean waters.

Exactly two hours later, the concert ended with 2,000 attendees on their feet applauding an event that lifted grief and put everyone in suspended animation. As the concert hall grew quiet, a nine-year-old boy named Jarod Tully walked from stage left and joined Timothy Cavanagh, standing in the well of the concert grand piano. Two high-powered stage lights shone on the two artists as Timothy played and Jarod Tully sang Andrew Lloyd Webber's stirring solo, *Pie Jesu.*

The reverent silence in Jane Cavanagh's box was broken by the vibration of Sam Bannion's cell phone. Her partner, Detective Lou Perkins, had sent a four-word text message: "Fr. Brian Manley murdered."

Sam sat frozen in horror while everyone else jumped to their feet in jubilant applause for Tim, Jarod, and Andrew Lloyd Webber. Her mind raced to find words for the bishop sitting in front of her, for her hostess beaming like the grandmother of the year, and for Tim, who, after this remarkable return to the stage, would have to transition from a classical Requiem to a real one for another murdered priest.

While other guests left the box, Sam asked Bishop Campbell, Msgr. Barnes, and Jane Cavanagh to remain. She shared the tragic news as delicately as she could. Msgr. Barnes looked horrified, Bishop Campbell seemed stoic with eyes that looked like they had been replaced with enamel, and Jane Cavanagh looked lost. Jane was revisiting her earlier thought about divine Providence arranging for Sam to join her and Timothy on the trip to Dublin. This news was not what she had in mind. She and Sam agreed to withhold the tragedy from Tim until after the reception in the grand foyer.

For obvious reasons, Bishop Campbell and Msgr. Barnes asked Jane to convey their regrets to Tim for their absence.

During the reception, champagne flowed like water over Niagara Falls. Tim endured the hot camera lights and media interviews like a true celebrity. Once he began to mingle with the crowd, his eyes scanned the cavernous foyer for two familiar female faces. The first one he spotted was a redhead, coming toward him.

Making her way through the crowd, she inched up to him and said, "I came to rescue you from the paparazzi."

What Sam really wanted to say was, "You look stunning in that designer white tie and tails. Can I take you home with me?" She knew that every woman there had their eyes on Tim and that they were full of lust and sex. Sam would be the only one not getting in that line, because her name was the only one on his dance card.

"As always, your timing is perfect. Where would you like to whisk me off to?" he said romantically.

"How about the limo?" Sam replied with a serious look in her eyes.

"What do you have in mind?" he asked flirtatiously.

"I know what you're thinking," Sam said, "But I was thinking more like escorting your grandmother home. She looks tired."

"Okay, let me say some goodbyes, and then each of you can have a different arm getting to the car."

Twenty minutes later, Sam, Jane, and Tim got into the limo for the return trip to Rosslare Park. They let Tim chatter like a TV talk show host until he paused and said, "Okay, this is beginning to sound like late-night monologue, so I'm guessing you must already know about a poor review of the concert."

Jane nodded to Sam, and then clasped Tim's hand for maternal support.

"There's no nice way to tell you this," Sam began, "but around 1 p.m. today Fr. Brian Manley was murdered in a confessional in St. Simon's Church."

With color instantly drained from him, Tim felt like he was back at the Summer House, and he began reviewing in his mind the file he had copied on Brian. Sam continued to talk, but Tim's mind, moving with the quickness of a spy taking pictures of classified documents, zoned her out. He quickly connected the dots with Dennis Flaherty and Bishop Campbell.

"We have a priest serial killer on the loose, don't we Sam?" he said.

"Yes, we do."

"And they're all linked with a certain orphanage in Dublin, aren't they."

"I think so," she said while nodding in agreement. "Which is why the assistant D.A. wants me to accompany you and your grandmother on your trip to Dublin."

When Tim heard those words, he instantly lit up like the national Christmas tree. He felt resuscitated by the tender face of a woman who had delivered him from another moment of sadness. He basked in a vision of the two of them floating down the River Liffey while he held her hand and drank in the elixir of a love he could no longer deny.

While Sam and Jane reverenced his silence, Tim clasped his grandmother's hand tighter and placed his arm around Sam's shoulders. He quietly invited Sam to rest her head on his shoulder. Then he closed his eyes to upload the image clearly in his mind so that he could download it to his heart shortly after they touched down on the shores of Ireland. For him, that destination couldn't come soon enough.

Fr. Tim Cavanagh

Another emergency meeting on Monday to plan a second murdered priest's funeral played out like the rerun of an old movie for Tim Cavanagh. The autopsy report indicated Fr. Manley was shot at point-blank range. He had been found by the church sexton a little after 1 p.m. when he came by to lock the church. The chief medical examiner reported he had been dead about an hour.

A task force was mobilized, and the hunt was on for a female killer known for a variety of disguises and aliases. The FBI database linked the two Islip priests' murders with a murder in Boston with similar M.O.

The media turned the Chancery grounds into a scene that looked like a venue for a major sports event. The sport, unfortunately, was the murder of priests, and though it was drawing a small army of reporters and newscasters, no one was cheering.

Tim had heard that Bishop Campbell had spent a restless Sunday night at his cathedral residence. Rumor had it that the bishop had managed to access the private elevator from the parking lot to his office by stealth. He avoided the press like Republican and Democrat legislators avoided being in the same room with each other. Everyone in the meeting knew that when the bishop wasn't in complete control of a situation, his heart burn kicked in, and then he started kicking whoever got in the way. He particularly spurned the media because they looked for dirt to uncover in places where they shouldn't be looking. The bishop unaffectionately called them "the dirt squad."

The bishop cleared his throat and looked directly at Tim. "When this meeting is over, I want you to go out and placate the press with as little information as possible. Just do what you must do to get rid of them." The bishop's disdain came through his voice unfiltered.

"What if they start asking questions about possible links between the two murders?" Tim asked without sugar-coating the issue.

"What do you mean?" Bishop Campbell fired back.

"I mean the obvious. Dennis and Brian are both from Dublin. They both were assigned to the same orphanage there. They both came to the U.S. around the same time, with Brian being welcomed in our diocese two years ago, shortly after the murder in Boston.

"You don't have to be a brain surgeon to connect the dots and conclude that someone from the Dublin orphanage is out for revenge. My guess is that sexual abuse is the motivation, and if I skirt that with the press, they will dig until they uncover it themselves."

"And if you make such a suggestion, then you are giving them a shovel. I forbid it," John Campbell commanded with blood vessels pulsing in his neck with anger. "We are not going to smear the names of two dead priests with food for the media's appetite for dirt."

After reading the files on these two dead priests, Tim knew their reputations in death couldn't be smeared any more than their reputations when alive. He was certain that the bishop's refusal to be transparent only fueled silent speculation in the room that he was in a state of denial. By continuing to lead like an ostrich with its head stuck in the sand, he was avoiding a cancerous lesion on the diocesan presbyterate that would eventually metastasize into terminal despair.

Joe McInnes spoke up. "Since you are just coming off a very successful concert yesterday, Tim, and since I knew both Dennis and Brian longer, perhaps I could handle the press and give you some breathing space," he said sympathetically.

"Splendid idea," Bishop Campbell agreed without hesitation. "That frees you up, Tim, to plan the funeral Mass. I hope we can close the page on that chapter before the end of the week," he said firmly.

"I share that hope with you," Tim said, "since I am accompanying my grandmother on a two-week trip to Ireland beginning next Sunday evening."

He let that news hang in the air and watched the bishop inhale it. Instantly all color was sucked out of him, his face changing from warm flushed redness to cold, icy paleness. The bishop's eyes locked onto Tim like a steelworker drilling rivets into a bridge.

"And how long have you been planning this trip?" he asked.

"You'll have to ask my grandmother that question, since I just found out about it a week ago."

"And will you be spending much time in Dublin?" he persisted, like someone itching to know a secret.

"Once again, you'll have to ask my grandmother. The itinerary is a surprise, if I may use her word."

Tim could see Joe McInnes shift in his chair. Ted Barnes looked totally lost and innocently said, "You've earned a break, Tim, and I'm happy your grandmother is treating you to one. Let's plan the funeral so we can move on."

"Well, while Joe is manipulating the press, why don't you and Tim do the funeral planning," Bishop Campbell said, sounding like someone who had other things on his mind.

With that the group exited the office, each with different facial expressions and different questions haunting them like demons on the prowl.

After getting a jump start on the funeral liturgy in his office, Tim felt tempted to call Sam about the police investigation. He decided it was better to wait until he was in a more secure space. He had always suspected the Chancery walls had ears.

☙ Chapter Twenty-Three ❧

Bishop Campbell

A s soon as the clergy staff left, I cracked a window and inhaled deeply on a Havana cigar. A nicotine fix was what I needed to calm my nerves and lower my blood pressure after a double dose of bad news. Tim Cavanagh's quantum leap in linking Dennis and Brian with Dublin and Islip seemed more than just an educated guess. And sexual abuse at Holy Comforter Orphanage as the motivation for their murders either qualified him as a contestant on *Jeopardy,* or he and that redheaded detective had been spending too much time together. The personnel records on Dennis and Brian were hidden deep in the wine cellar of the Summer House. So what was I missing?

Whatever it was, I had to catch it fast. It was only six days and counting before the Steinway piano boy and his grandmother left for Dublin. I wouldn't put it past him to go snooping for information. Rather than sabotage his plans, I would have to formulate my own. I didn't care how much money he was worth, I couldn't afford to have him uncover records three thousand miles away that could put my own career in jeopardy. Besides, no Belfast survivor was going to be outfoxed by a County Wexford novice.

I wasn't without resources; it was time to use them.

I would need an international calling card, which I would have Leona Helmond purchase so it couldn't be traced back to me.

Then I would have to wear a disguise and mix with the steerage class by using the New York City transit to find a pay phone in Brooklyn, so the call couldn't be traced to me either.

I hadn't made such a call in over thirty years, but I knew the number was still current and the password unchanged.

I would wait until the funeral was over on Friday to make the contact. While Timothy and his dowager grandmother were making their plans and packing their luggage, I would plan my own surprise. Saturday night would be a good time to make the call and put the plan in action. When they arrived in Dublin on Monday, a welcoming committee of one would be there to shadow them and to make sure Timothy's attempts to gain access to church records were thwarted.

My half-smoked Cuban cigar was working its magical effects. I was beginning to relax again. I exhaled several circles in the air as if I were sending thank-you smoke signals to Fidel Castro.

Detective Sam Bannion

In cooperation with the Bayport Ferry Port authorities, Lou Perkins and I viewed the cameras on board both ferries that had operated last Sunday. The 12:30 p.m. ferry had one elderly woman passenger traveling alone, but her physical condition seemed to eliminate her as a suspect. I was ready to let that slide until she was captured again boarding a bus to the Port Authority. Her wide brimmed hat blocked out any facial recognition, but it was the gloves that caught my attention. It was not cold enough for gloves yet, so that was a flag for possibly hiding younger hands. That meant her elderly features were a disguise.

Another camera outside the Port Authority Bus Terminal exit caught her getting into a cab. The clarity of the picture caught the cab number. I made a call, and Lou and I were on our way to interview the driver and check the log record.

Our excitement defused when we found out she exited at East 51st St. to catch the Lexington Ave. subway. With the help of the NYPD technology center, we established a grid and started viewing tapes from last Sunday beginning when she was photographed entering the taxi. Less than an hour later, we saw her leaving the 86th St. subway station.

Once again her attempts to hide her face seemed futile. The wide-brimmed beach hat was a dead giveaway. It was like a flare lit before sundown.

The grid was now downsized to the Yorkville area of the Upper East Side.

Lou and I arranged to return tomorrow and begin viewing surveillance tapes from an area about two square miles wide. That sounded daunting, but it would go faster with each of us viewing different tapes.

Part of me was pumped up that maybe we were closing in our killer, while part of me was watching the clock and counting three days left before my flight to Ireland.

Which reminded me—I needed to call Jane Cavanagh to ask about her plans to tell Tim that I would be joining them in first class for the flight to Dublin. After that, it was anybody's guess what surprises she had in store when we touched down on the Emerald Isle.

By mid-week, Lou Perkins and I had followed dead-end leads at over 20 apartment buildings in the Yorkville section. We finally decided to skip the rest of the surveillance tapes and limit our conversations with doormen to just one question: Does anyone in your building live here seasonally and speak with an Irish accent?

By late Thursday we got a hit. A doorman at Liffey House said that a middle-aged lady had come and gone occasionally, from Europe.

"I'm pretty sure she is single, since she is always alone," the doorman said hesitatingly.

"Is she at home right now?" I asked, looking him square in the eye.

"No," he answered without volunteering any other information.

"Is she traveling again?" I asked, trying to respect his boundaries.

"Yes," he answered.

"When did she leave?"

Checking a log book behind his reception desk, he said, "Sunday evening."

"Did she say where she was going or when she would return?"

"No and no," he answered.

My next question was risky. "What is her name and apartment number?"

"I would have to check with the manager before divulging that information."

Lou piped up with a threatening statement. "We could arrest you for obstruction of justice."

"I've been doing this job as long as you have been a cop," he retorted without intimidation, "and I know the boundaries about confidentiality."

I decided to intervene and try to mediate. "While you check that out with your manager, we have other leads we need to follow, so my partner will be back tomorrow with a search warrant. Thanks for your help."

As we walked toward 2nd Ave., Lou released some steam by saying, "How come I'm working alone tomorrow?"

"Because I have some last-minute things I must do before leaving for Dublin Sunday night. At the top of my list is to buy some luggage before I can pack anything. Besides, I trust you to be diplomatic tomorrow and make us look like smart cops by the way you get the information." I winked at him as a sign of affirmation.

He managed a smile, his way of saying, "Okay."

We talked about setting up a surveillance team outside Liffey House, at least until I returned from Ireland. We agreed to send daily emails to keep each other up to speed while 3,000 miles apart.

Tomorrow I would attend the funeral Mass for Fr. Brian Manley in Bayport. I wouldn't be looking for suspects, just making sure Tim was safe and, like me counting down the days when priests' murders, autopsies, and funerals were replaced with Irish pubs, Guinness beer, and kissing the Blarney Stone, which I was sure wouldn't be as exciting as kissing the lips of someone who was not full of Blarney.

Nora Owens

The flights from Newark Airport to Atlanta and then on to St. Lucia were smooth and seamless. The comforts of first class, with plenty of wine and liquor, had a calming effect on my frazzled spirits. I arrived in St. Lucia in the early afternoon. The ground shuttle from the airport to the Jade Mountain Resort lasted an hour, just the right amount of time to breathe in the balmy Caribbean air and to allow it to melt away the tensions of the past several weeks. Before I checked in, my stressed body clock had adjusted to island time.

The world-class Jade Mountain Resort served as a good place to hide after committing two murders. The cantilevered structure, built in the side of the mountain, was called "the Sanctuary." It was just the refuge I was seeking.

The amenities included everything I could possibly want for the next two weeks. I had reserved a guestroom with an ocean view and a private pool. The luxurious bedding would help me sleep like a kitten. After the heaviness of the past month, I needed to feel light as a feather. I would take advantage of some leisurely recreational options, like yoga and snorkeling.

After I had unpacked and placed all my clothing in the walk-in closet, I connected to the wireless Internet. As I waited for it to come on line, I dialed room service and ordered some wine and appetizers. Then I dressed in a white linen caftan and traded my shoes for sandals.

Back at my laptop, I watched the funeral of Fr. Manley from St. Simon's Church on YouTube. During the procession of the body, I was impressed with Fr. Timothy Cavanagh's rendition of a Celtic lament on a baby grand piano. It was the bishop's features, however, that caught my eye and left me wondering if I had seen them before.

All of a sudden, conflict entered my room, and like an unwelcomed guest it released a cloud of suspicion that turned my getaway paradise into a possible U-turn to Dante's Inferno.

Bishop Campbell

While Tim Cavanagh was celebrating the Saturday 5 p.m. Vigil Mass at the cathedral, I caught a C train heading toward Brooklyn. I made sure my car was parked off Rockaway Avenue in an area with no surveillance cameras and within walking distance to the subway.

I substituted my pectoral cross and Episcopal ring for street clothes that helped me blend in with the plebeians who used the subway for transportation. In place of my skullcap, I donned a Yankee's cap that made me look like part of a local baseball flock.

I exited the train at Jay Street and walked south toward St. James Cathedral. I continued walking until I entered the revolving doors of the Marriott Hotel. I made my way down a carpeted circular staircase to find a bank of pay phones. Since the cell phone explosion they had become dinosaurs and hard to locate.

From memory I dialed the international code for Ireland, then the ten-digit number. Then I entered the numbers from the phone card Leona Helmond had purchased. After the third ring, the other party picked up.

I said, "I need something fixed." It was the code for contracting a highly paid covert job.

"You're in luck," the heavily accented Belfast voice said. "I still fix things."

"Are the Swiss bank account and protocols still the same?" I asked, already knowing the answer to my question.

"That's right."

"I'll transfer the money on Monday. The clock starts ticking then," I added, meaning the job would get clocked in.

I gave information on the contract, the Aer Lingus arrival flight from JFK, names, and strict instructions to shadow grandmother and grandson but do no harm.

"Message received. Goodbye."

With that the phone went dead and I began retracing my steps back to Islip and a world that seemed further away than just half the length of an island.

Fr. Tim Cavanagh

"When did you decide to invite Molly?" I asked with genuine curiosity. We stood in line, waiting for the call for first class to board the Aer Lingus flight.

"When I knew I needed someone to help with my shopping bags while you were playing Brother Cadfael to Samantha's Miss Marple," Granny countered, as if reading her line from a script.

During our banter, Sam was on her cell phone talking with Lou Perkins. She ended the call when the gate agent invited first class passengers to board. Sam and I sat together, with Granny and Molly seated across the aisle.

Not long after the food service, Sam snuggled in her seat for sleep, her head against my shoulder. I watched a movie, although I can't remember which one, since my eyes were mostly occupied watching Sam sleep. She breathed lightly and slept without movement, like a child stilled by a nap. I wondered what it would be like to watch her sleeping without so many other people looking on.

The airplane touched down at Dublin Airport on time. During the six-hour flight Granny got some sleep while Molly was immersed in a paperback romance novel, her favorite pastime.

We cleared customs, retrieved our luggage, and walked toward the receiving hall for international passengers. Molly spotted a waiting driver holding a sign that read, "A. J. Cavanagh." As we walked toward him, he closed the distance and greeted us with: *"Cead Mile Failte."* It was Gaelic for "Welcome to Ireland."

Thirty minutes later we were checking in at the Merrion Park Hotel. It comprised four Georgian Houses webbed together to form a quintessential Dublin venue. It also had the advantage of being off the heavily traveled business and shopping center on the north side of the River Liffey.

"As soon as me feet touched the ground in Ireland, all stress left me body," Molly said, sounding like someone giving testimony at a trial.

"And that calls for a pot of tea and biscuits," Granny added while ringing for room service.

While Molly and Granny shared a suite, Sam and I were assigned to rooms that connected with a single inner door. I tapped for Sam to open it.

"Sorry, I don't know Morse code," she said in her playful tone, "and if you're trying to break and enter, I have to warn you—I am a police officer."

"In that case, this is room service."

"And what exactly are you serving?"

"It's a surprise."

"You're in luck," she said and unlocked the door. "I like surprises."

With that I pulled her into my arms and kissed her long and deep. It seemed that only seconds passed before Granny rang my phone to announce tea time.

We couldn't disguise the smiles on our faces, which said that even in Ireland, we couldn't escape from a woman who was both grandmother and chaperon.

The Fixer

He never used a name, just the title "Mr." or "Sir." If he was pushed for more, he added, "Mr. Fix." It was more a label than a name, expressing what he did and not who he was. He had been in the fixing business for thirty years, since the days when the IRA recruited agents to "fix things" that would not go well for the occupying British forces in Northern Ireland.

With the Good Friday Peace Accord of 1998, business had fallen off, which explained why he was delighted with the phone call Saturday and the deposit of $150,000 in a Swiss bank account that very morning. The fee was scaled depending on terms of the contract. If things escalated beyond surveillance, weapons were needed, and his safe zones compromised, then it tripled.

As far as covert agents went, the Fixer didn't have the youthful features or physical agility of Jason Bourne. He was more in the class of an aging Harry Callahan. But in the aging process he has acquired a steadiness of will and computerized mind that gave him an edge in high-speed chases and close encounters of the regrettable kind, an edge that helped him avoid mistakes and, so far, capture.

The Fixer preferred to sleuth rather than assassinate. He could, however, switch roles as easily as identical twins could switch their identities—and with deadly consequences.

Today he would hone his radar skills in spying on Fr. Timothy Cavanagh. The odds were in his favor. Tracking a priest whose singular focus was getting access to files on a shuttered orphanage should be as easy as babysitting an unsupervised adult. Practicing his uber-private persona, he would stay in the shadows and follow the priest like a fox whose stealth was its best weapon.

His dress was not meant to turn heads. Wearing a gray T-shirt with a blue hoodie, wrinkled jeans, and a pair of Adidas sneakers helped him blend in. His thinning, strawberry-blond hair, tousled and not combed, gave him the appearance of someone who had weathered well with age.

But underneath his grunge clothing was a body toned and hardened by discipline, sit-ups, and cycling. To run into him felt like hitting a battering ram.

Sitting at a window seat in Bewley's Café across from the Merrion Hotel, he watched for his prey to exit the revolving door. Three cups of coffee later, his expression changed to surprise as Tim Cavanagh left the hotel holding hands with an attractive redhead.

Where the hell did she come from, an inner voice asked, *and how did this change the plan of action?* He placed two Euros on the table, stepped outside, and began walking in sync with them across the street, but always giving them some lead distance.

He wondered why his contact in New York City hadn't told him about the redhead. As his mind processed that question, the thought occurred to him that perhaps the contract assignee didn't know himself.

The couple stopped at the corner of Merrion Square West, waiting as a DART train approached. The Fixer had to run hard to catch it, leaving him out of breath. He used his arm to block the automatic door, opening it with just enough time for him to get on the third car.

Ten minutes later his targets exited at Bachelor's Walk, just short of O'Connell Street at the foot of the River Liffey. Next they turned onto Abbey Street and started window shopping in the boutiques and highbrow shops that adorned the strip. Whenever they stopped to browse, he did the same from across the street. The windows made for an easy reflection, giving the impression that he had eyes in the back of his head.

At the next block Tim Cavanagh entered Trinity Sweater Shop while the redhead walked on to College House Jewelers. Within half an hour, he walked out carrying a paper shopping bag with the store insignia on it. Then he joined the redhead in the jewelry shop.

The angle of the morning sun clipped by a canvas awning did not help his view of the interior of the shop. He pulled out his cell phone and pretended to place a call while leaning against a bus sign. It was a good diversion while he waited for them to exit.

It took them thirty minutes before reappearing on the street. They retraced their steps back to O'Connell, took a right onto Earl, then the first left onto Marlborough. One block later they stood in front of St. Mary's Catholic Cathedral.

By the time he caught up with them inside, Tim Cavanagh was talking with a female usher at the foot of the sanctuary. The Fixer did a complete scan of the neo-Greek interior, but the redhead was nowhere in sight. When he came back full circle, in complete wonderment about her disappearance, he saw the priest being ushered through a door to the right of the altar. He didn't know the redhead's eyes were tracking him from behind a heavy, red drape inside a confessional less than 50 feet away.

☙ Chapter Twenty-Four ❧

Fr. Tim Cavanagh

The usher led me through the sacristy, then down a circular staircase squeezed in a corner that led to a tunnel. About ten yards in length, the drab, concrete enclosure ended at an elevator. The usher pushed a button and the mechanism kicked in.

The clanking noise evoked a look on my face that prompted the usher to say, "I can tell what you're thinking, but don't let the sound effects scare you."

I smiled a little, indicating my appreciation for her reassurance. The elevator moved slowly to our level. We rode two flights to the second story of the Dublin Archdiocesan Curial Offices.

I showed my credentials to a receptionist inside a small kiosk from the Diocese of Islip Chancery Office and a letter I had typed on chancery stationery with John Campbell's forged signature and the diocesan seal embossed on it. After scanning my driver's license, the receptionist buzzed me through the door and escorted me down the hallway.

The floor plan resembled a rectangular-shaped building with an enclosed inner courtyard capped by a pointed skylight. The offices were on the outside of the hallway, while the inside revealed signs of Mother Nature adding some quiet beauty to this otherwise Draconian-looking building, with lush ivy, greenery, and flower baskets hanging from the inside hallway windows.

Halfway around the building, we came to a room on the left. He opened the door to a miniature library. The walls were covered with elegant mahogany wood panels with crown molding. Shelves of record books were arranged like stacks in a college library. A wooden ladder attached to a track system leaned against the inside wall. A large, arched window supplied ample light.

Using an antiquated card filing system, the receptionist helped me retrieve the records for Holy Comforter Orphanage, which was shuttered in 1979. Once we found them, he left me sitting alone at a table.

Before I began scanning the records, I punched in Sam's number on my cell phone. It vibrated only once before she turned it off. That was the signal we had agreed to.

While Sam continued spying on the mystery man stalking us, I turned the pages, looking for familiar names. I started from the current dates in the back and quickly found Brian Manley's name. He had served as the last chaplain from 1975 to 1979, before the orphanage closed. Flipping the pages backward, I then found Dennis Flaherty's name. He had served as chaplain from 1973 to 1975.

Then I went back and scanned the names of girls who were listed under both their tenures. During Dennis's assignment, two names caught my eye: Nanette and Nora Owens. During Brian's tenure, only Nora's name appeared. When I flipped back to study both names again, someone had written a reference alongside Nanette's name. I put a paper marker in the page and flipped to the back of the book. A one-line entry took my breath away. It read: "Nanette Owens: Committed suicide on June 1, 1975." It was one of several entries listing girls who died at Holy Comforter Orphanage.

In a moment of inspiration, I flipped back earlier in the records. I was shocked to read the name Fr. Michael Mulgrew. He had preceded Dennis as chaplain from 1970 to 1973 and was the same priest murdered in Holy Cross Cathedral one year ago. I noted that both Owens sisters also were listed during his tenure.

Using my own brand of deduction, I sadly concluded that Nanette Owens took her own life while Dennis Flaherty was the chaplain. My brain computed just one motivation for doing so—sexual abuse. And that was the only motivation a twin sister would need for revenge.

As I contemplated the magnitude of this information, I lost my place and began flipping to earlier pages. As I tried to retrieve the last page, my eyes glanced at another name, and I froze like water turning to ice. A "Fr. Sean Campbell" had served as chaplain from 1968 to 1970. *Could it be,* I asked without speaking the words. Were Fr. Sean Campbell and Bishop John Campbell one and the same person? If so, why did he change his first name from Gaelic to English? And what other secrets was he hiding?

I took photos of the pertinent pages with my cell phone, returned the books to their proper shelves, and graciously thanked the receptionist for his help. I then asked to exit from the back door, which put me into an alley.

I walked toward Cathal Bruga St., and then quickly turned left toward O'Connell Street. I picked up my pace as I walked toward the Parnell Monument. There was a certain redhead shadowing me to the DART stop for a return train to the hotel. Our stalker was nowhere in sight, no doubt angered that he had lost our scent.

I exited the train on the west corner of the hotel. Sam remained aboard and exited on Hume Street three blocks away. Then she backtracked and entered the hotel from the rear doors facing Merrion Square South. This was a last-minute plan to further evade our stalker. Once we arrived safely at our rooms, I went through the connecting door into Sam's room.

"What kind of built-in radar do you have that locked on to that guy?" I asked. I really wanted to have that secret weapon.

"The first flag was his aggressive attempts to get on the train. Second, he got off at our stop. Third, while we were window shopping, he was stalking us using the reflection in the windows of the shops on the other side of the street. He didn't know I was doing the same. That's when I came up with the idea of having us separate into two stores. That gave me a chance to spy on him and formulate a plan. When I noticed his eyes flashing back and forth between both stores, I knew we were a target. The question is, why?"

"Why what?" I asked, completely dumbfounded.

"Why is someone having you followed?"

I retrieved my phone and navigated to the photos. I said, "Probably because of the pictures I took of the records from Holy Comforter Orphanage. What's in here is damaging, but it also provides answers to questions about three priests' murders."

"I'm listening," Sam said, inching herself forward in a chair. She looked very eager to hear what I'd found in the archives.

I shared about the three priests all being assigned as chaplains. Sam leaned forward when I mentioned the Owens twins and Nanette's suicide during Dennis Flaherty's watch. Her eyes widened when I told her about a certain Fr. Sean Campbell serving as chaplain just before the other three priests.

In a moment of suspended silence, we both did the math and came to the same conclusions without uttering a word. Fr. Sean Campbell and Bishop John Campbell were one and the same person. Our faces both said the same thing—this story was about to change, as the connection with the Dublin stalker was now set and matched.

Aishling Jane Cavanagh

While Tim and Sam freshened up after an unpredictable day, Jane and Molly returned to the hotel. Molly set the shopping bags on the beds, and Jane made dinner reservations for 7 p.m. The four met in Jane's suite for appetizers and drinks at 6.

"Tell us about your first D.I.D., so we can compare it with ours," Jane said while sipping on a gin and tonic.

"What's a D.I.D.?" Samantha asked.

"Day in Dublin," Jane answered like a United Nations translator. "I'm sure you can't best ours." She recounted the clothing and jewelry stores where she and Molly had shopped.

"We spent over an hour in Carroll's Gifts and Souvenirs alone. And then we browsed in all the shops along Talbot Street. It's wall-to-wall Celtic. But enough about us—how was your day?"

"We shopped on Abbey Street. I bought a sweater and Sam bought a necklace with a Celtic cross. We did a lot of window shopping, strolled along the River Liffey, visited St. Mary's Cathedral, and ended up at the Parnell Monument," Tim said without pausing to take a breath.

"And how did you find St. Mary's Cathedral?" Jane asked in a voice that made it sound like double entendre.

"With the help of a tourist map," Sam replied, and then added, "Police are experts at reading maps, you know."

"Well, how did you find it when you got there?" Jane spoke like someone who thought the hotel room was bugged.

"If you mean was I well received, the answer is yes. And if you mean was the mission successful, once again the answer is yes," Tim answered, an equal match for his grandmother's attempts at speaking in covert language as if the room was bugged.

Jane nodded, indicating she understood that he got all the information he needed on Holy Comforter Orphanage.

"Well, speaking of the cathedral, we're having dinner tonight at The Church," Jane announced. "It's a top tourist destination restaurant, and since I'm treating, there won't be a collection."

She rallied everyone to the elevator, then to a waiting cab under the hotel canopy. She tipped the driver well for maneuvering through the chaotic Dublin traffic, which enabled them to arrive on time.

They enjoyed pints of Guinness and an array of Irish entrees, which they all shared as if they were eating family style. Jane basked in the delight of being in their company. Like a battery, she was charged by the banter between Tim and Sam and how they had grown intimate with each other by their ability to risk trusting each other.

She hoped that would take a new turn when they arrived in Rosslare in two days and discovered the special surprise she had planned for them.

Sam Bannion

While Jane and Molly feasted on custard pudding for dessert, Tim and I excused ourselves to take a leisurely walk to work off the Irish stew and make room for some booze. It was time to experience the legendary social outing known as the Irish pub.

Tim had gotten a short list of Dublin's most famous pubs through Msgr. Ted Barnes, a Long Island authority on Guinness beer and Irish camaraderie.

We hopped a taxi and made our way to Grafton Street, where many of Dublin's famous pubs were, in the words of Msgr. Barnes, "in stumbling distance of one another."

According to Tim, most Dubliners would admit the pub was the Irish equivalent of America's chat rooms. In Dublin they not only served booze but also community. Tonight Tim and I wanted a social outing with the locals. Our first stop was the famous Temple Bar.

As we settled into a corner banquette, I saw pensioners nursing their pints, suit and tie professionals alongside street thugs, all of them occasionally glancing at the soccer and rugby matches on the flat-screen TVs. In the far corners, where it was dark, I spotted couples kissing by candlelight. The level of chatter and noise reminded me that, in a Dublin pub, the blarney still runs thick.

We shared our pints with two Irish dudes decompressing after a long day's work. They asked about the American president and, in a humorous moment, one of them commented that our leader should come to Ireland and reclaim the apostrophe in his name.

The warm welcome given in Dublin pubs have boundaries, so the local gents respected them and avoided questions about our professions, our relationship, and reasons for visiting Ireland.

Instead Tim and I managed to pepper them with a list of questions about life in Dublin, the different cultures in the one country, and the scope of Irish music and the legendary ballads.

After our fourth pint of the night we decided to call it quits.

"It's almost midnight, do you have to return before something turns into a pumpkin?" Tim whispered playfully.

"I don't think that fable applies in Ireland," I fired back like a prized debater.

Tim flagged down a taxi to return us to our hotel by way of Merrion Row. Stopping for a traffic light one block away, we heard the lilting sounds of Irish music wafting from a place called O'Donoghue's Pub, so we decided to explore a bit more. As we left the taxi, the driver commented, "It's the strongest traditional Irish music in town."

Ordering club soda for this last stop of the night, we sat at a table near two guitarists and one fiddle player with their pints sitting on an empty wooden beer keg. Their tempo and passion ignited clapping hands and stomping feet, charging the place with an electricity unique to O'Donoghue's.

After completing a musical set, the group took a break. Tim calmly walked to the spinet piano behind the stage platform, lifted the key cover, and began playing a running selection of Irish tunes, like "O Danny Boy" and "When Irish Eyes are Smiling." The level of noise turned to a whisper, chatter turned to wonder, and every eye in the pub watched Tim's masterful dexterity on a piano badly out of tune. But no one seemed to care as he and the piano cast a reverent spell in one of the best known pubs of Joycean Dublin. I knew that everyone there was thinking the same thing—this wasn't just a pianist; this was an artist.

Ten minutes later, Tim finished to a standing ovation and shouts for an encore. His professional training prompted him to oblige with a slight bow and a modest smile. Then, to everyone's surprise, the combination of ten fingers and 88 keys combined for a stirring rendition of "Love Me Tender." His playing lifted it to the level of sacred music, haunting and contemplative. All I knew was that Tim was looking at me while he played, with eyes that glowed like the Blarney stone on the summer solstice.

Then it was time to go. Tim grabbed my hand and we bounced out of the pub like a couple with a good supply of Irish music, laughter, and booze in our steps. It was a good thing we only had to cross the street. Entering the hotel from the back door, we took the elevator to the fourth floor.

After four pubs and plenty of pints, we weren't exactly as quiet as Irish mice in a church. Tim did manage to open my door without someone calling security.

Once inside, he kept the room dark, drew me close to him and said, "Can I taste the Guinness in your mouth?"

"I was hoping you would ask," I answered, giggling and teetering on the edge of being drunk.

"I don't want to take advantage of your condition," he said apologetically.

"If I don't mind, then why should you?"

In a flash, we had undressed each other. Then time seemed to stand still. Tim made love to me slowly, like the movements of a lush Brahms symphony. He had a tenderness, a touch, and a rhythm that elevated love-making to a level I had never known before.

Afterward, we held each other in a long embrace before beginning it all over again.

I had willingly chosen to ignore the fact that Tim was a priest, instead choosing to engage him as a man with passions and gifts. He had a heart with a capacity to make mine beat again, with the desire to be loved by the God who once took Todd from me and who now gave me Tim. No Catholic guilt trips over that.

When we were completely spent, we cuddled on the bed, speaking only with our eyes. Then Tim broke the silence in a voice soft as satin.

"So far I've counted 50 different smiles on your face and each of them sings a different song."

I replied with an equally soft kiss on both his cheeks. At this moment I felt I was in the arms of an angel who had reawakened in me a new desire to love myself and Tim in a way that shouted, *Life is good again*. My cluttered inner life had been mysteriously emptied of stress and junk in the past two hours by a man who filled up that emptiness with a new lust and passion for him and for the God of love who had arranged this encounter like a divine maestro.

It was after 2:00 a.m. when Tim collected his clothes and walked to the connecting door. He blew me a kiss, and that was the last thing I remembered before surrendering to a deep sleep and the hope that when I woke again, the past five hours would not be a fantasy.

ᴄᴀ Chapter Twenty-Five ᴄᴡ

Touring Dublin

All four Americans from Long Island dressed like tourists and got an early start, putting their feet to the ground to see how much of historical and cultural Dublin would rejuvenate their Irish souls.

It was a picture perfect, late October day. Molly defied the weather report and carried an umbrella. The streets were empty of school children and summer tourists, so maneuvering around the narrow labyrinth of Dublin streets proved an easy task.

They began with a two-hour tour of Dublin Castle, the fortress-like icon of Irish history. From there it was a short walk to Christ Church Cathedral, and then on to St. Patrick's Holy Well.

They ate a late lunch in the Epicurean Food Hall along Abbey Street. A walk around Trinity College campus and a leisurely visit to its most famous attraction, the Book of Kells, wrapped up their day of sightseeing.

Before exiting the campus Tim grabbed Molly's arm and escorted her to a monument perched in a square across the street from the college green. Jane and Sam followed, curious to see what Tim would do.

As they stood facing a bronze figure pushing a four wheeled cart, Tim said, sounding like a stand-up comic, "Molly Malone, meet Molly Malone." Then, growing serious, he told the story of the maid's namesake. Molly Malone was a legendary Irish woman of the 17th century. The song "Cockles and Mussels" told her story, the tale of a beautiful fishmonger who plied her trade on the streets of Dublin, but who died young, of a fever.

As Molly Malone of Stony Brook eyed the statue, hearing this story for the first time, Tim opened his arms and poured out the song. When he finished with a flourish, Jane, Sam, and several passersby applauded his dramatic moment with a woman who had served not as a maid but as a nanny to him when he had lost his own.

"Oh Tim," Molly said, her face scarlet. "I'm embarrassed."

"Okay, so I'm not one of the Irish Tenors," he apologized.

"Oh no," Molly interrupted. "It's not your singing, but the size of her breasts that causes me to blush. I don't care for the seventeenth-century dress and shoes, but I surely would like to have some of her cleavage."

With that the chorus of Tim, Jane, and Sam broke out in uncontrollable laughter. It didn't subside until they hopped aboard a DART train to make their way to the hotel.

The Fixer

When my prey returned to the lobby of their hotel, chatting about the sights and sounds of their day, the redhead and the priest never even noticed me. I was dressed as a banker and sitting in one of those high-backed chairs, pretending to read a newspaper. I noticed them, though, and I listened carefully.

"While you two take naps," the priest said, "Sam and I will make a fast trip to Connolly Station and get the train tickets for our trip to Rosslare tomorrow."

I decided not to follow them. Instead, I would buy my tickets tomorrow just before they boarded the train. And this time, I wouldn't lose the priest or the redhead.

Sam Bannion

The Mainline train to Rosslare was a scenic delight. Once it left the busy metropolis of Dublin, it headed south. Hugging the coast, it followed a meandering path in and out of story-book villages and underneath perfectly arched overpasses. I had only seen such sights in movies. That explained the look of wow on my face.

Viewing the quaint villages, with their gabled houses and narrow streets on one side of the tracks and the golden fields of barley and the Irish Sea on the other side, was like watching a tennis match in motion.

This scenery was not only delighting my eyes but also rejuvenating my soul.

Two hours into the ride, the train entered Wexford, the seat of the local county. The geography resembled San Francisco. The business center, parallel with the train tracks, was situated on a flat plateau aligned with the Irish Sea to the east. The cathedral, church spires, row houses and individual living units were perched high in the background along narrow and winding streets that could only be maneuvered like riding a roller coaster.

As the train slowed coming into the station, I bolted from my seat. I couldn't believe my eyes. A restaurant named "Springsteen's" was located in the middle of a shopping strand.

"Promise me we'll have dinner there before we leave," I pleaded with Tim.

With a wide smile that matched hers, he said, "If it will make you happy, it will make me happy having dinner with you and the Boss."

Surprised by his response, I quipped, "You know his kick name?"

"Actually it's a term of endearment, and yes, I do."

"I thought you only favored classical music."

"What can I say? I'm a classical guy who likes a lot of music, including rock classics."

"But you didn't grow up with Springsteen," I said. I had learned something new about Tim.

"True, he grew up on New Jersey, and I grew up on Long Island."

I punched him in jest. "You know what I mean."

"Yes, I do, but a trained classical musician should have an appreciation for all kinds of music. Isn't that what you find so irresistibly attractive about me?" he purred.

"Among other things, yes." I couldn't help but remember last night.

Ten minutes later, the train pulled into the station at Rosslare Euro-Port. Jane's relatives were waiting with two cars. Following the ritual of Irish hugs and kisses, we drove to the original Rosslare Park about twenty minutes away.

The Fixer

As the two cars pulled away from the rail station with four new passengers, I hailed the last taxi. I said I was going in the same directions as the car ahead. The driver followed at a close distance. About three miles outside the limits of Rosslare town, the two cars turned right through a wide gate. Fifty yards beyond the entrance was an elegant manor house. As we slowed to pass, I saw the sign on the gate read "Rosslare Park."

I decided to be diplomatic in my questions.

"Is this a bed and breakfast, or a private home?"

"It is the ancestral home of the Cavanagh family. They have lived there since the end of the 19th century," the driver answered like a tour guide. Then he asked, "Do you have an exact address where I am taking you?"

"Yes, I forgot to tell you I am staying at the Best Western Sea Side Hotel."

"In that case, we're going in the wrong direction. The hotel is back in the village." He spoke with a hint of Irish temper in his voice. Making a U-turn, he retraced the route and brought me to the hotel about ten minutes later. I tipped him generously, which cooled his temper like air-conditioning on a hot day.

As pre-arranged with my contract in the U.S., I made an international call at 3:00 local time.

"Are you fixing things okay?" the voice on the other side of the ocean asked in code.

"It would go easier if I only had to deal with one person and not two. Redheads make life complicated."

"I understand," was all the response I needed to know that he was unaware of that piece of information.

Communicating through a phone line 3,000 miles apart kept me from studying the shocked expression on his face. His next words were calculated to be an FYI for me.

"Redheads are like police. They cause you to be on guard."

I de-coded his line with the comment: "Thanks for that insight."

"Was your Dublin visit successful?" he asked.

"Not for me," I answered, trying not to sound like a disappointed loser.

We agreed on another day and time for the next call. He told me to return to Dublin, check in at the Clarence Hotel, and wait for a Fed Ex package containing instructions for hunting down a woman by the name of Nora Owens.

His last words caught me by surprise.

"I would like for you to be available to fly to New York perhaps at a moment's notice." Then, as an afterthought, he added, "And that may come sooner than later."

He ended the call and the connection was broken. I opened the sliding glass door and stepped out of the room onto an enclosed patio to breathe in the smell of salt air from the Irish Sea. Below me I could see the ferry departing the port for western Wales. I had a strange sense that this case was turning more mysterious every day. And I was the only one who knew my low tolerance for mystery.

Sam Bannion

The manor house in Rosslare struck me as a miniature version of Rosslare Park in Stony Brook. The Georgian-style edifice was monastic by comparison, but the warm and cozy interior smelled of welcome and hospitality—like a candle emitting a fresh scent. This room was peppered with family portraits, including some of Tim's grandfather, great grandfather, and Uncle Liam and Aunt Bernice. These had places of honor among the memorabilia of past generations of Cavanaghs.

These ancestors of Tim's were the major surveyors of Wexford County. That explains Tim's grandfather's venture in real estate. Whereas he uprooted and changed careers by coming to America as an

208

immigrant, his brother Liam remained a homebody and kept the family name and business profitable in the original Rosslare.

The furniture around the house was mostly period, except for the flat screen TVs, stereo system, DVD player, microwave, computers, and other conveniences that gave the house a modern touch. Other things were left untouched, such as the stately, rolling moon phase grandfather's clock, positioned in the hallway with its amazing figured mahogany case. I marveled at a sublevel wine cellar underneath the kitchen, and I chuckled at the old-fashioned trundle beds that graced all three bedrooms.

After a brief tour of the manor house, Bernice Cavanagh escorted Tim and me to the guest house, located about 30 yards away. An extended canopy built out over the two-car garage offered protection from the elements for those walking between the house and cottage. It was a modest, single-story, two-bedroom design. The centerpiece was a large common room with a stone fireplace. Vintage beach furniture, positioned around a large woven matted rug, added to the charm and warmth of the room. The decor spoke ocean motif: antique sails, well-worn boat oars, sea shells, fish netting, and even a boat anchor positioned on the wall. A sliding glass door opened onto a deck made of salt-treated wood.

Bernice opened the door onto the deck and invited us to follow. She led us down a well-worn foot path that opened up to an expansive beach. I caught a stunning view of the Irish Sea, with white caps beating against the beach.

Tim spoke first. "This is more breathtaking than the view at Stony Brook."

Lost for words, I could only nod in agreement.

"I'm afraid the water temperature has dropped a wee bit, but if you're brave swimmers, then it is the warmest just before the sun sets over the hills," Bernice said, pointing toward the west where the angle of the sun was perfectly timed with her words.

Tim kissed her on the cheek.

"Thanks for the hint, Aunt Bernice." He turned to me with a golden glow of the sun reflecting on his face and asked, "What do you say we break in our swim suits?"

"I was thinking the same thing," I answered.

When we returned to the guest cottage to don our bathing suits, we discovered our luggage had been left in just one bedroom. Tim wondered out loud if his grandmother had given those instructions and whether that was a smaller part of a larger scheme. If so, he told me, he was pleased she approved of his choice of an Irish redhead whose detective skills had so far proven to be an asset on this trip.

Five minutes later the pianist and his private female security detail were diving into the Irish Sea and colliding with waves that buoyed our spirits. We dove under the chilling waters and kissed until we needed to resurface for a new air supply.

Thirty minutes later we hurried back to the guest cottage, shivering from the approaching chill now that the sun had set. Someone had built a fire, transforming the cottage into a romantic love nest. We stepped together into the shower, where we washed away the sand and salt. We kissed for a long time under the cascading water, and then satisfied our passions with even more pleasure than the first time.

At dinnertime we returned to the main house, satisfied as only two lovers could be, but hungry just the same. Jane met us at the door.

"I was just about to say to Bernice that perhaps we should send the police to look for you, Timothy, and then I remembered that Sam is the police," she joked.

The six of us dined on Irish potato soup, salad, and stuffed pork loin garnished with a medley of fresh vegetables. We sat comfortably around a dining room table that seated ten. I admired the sparkle of the polished stemware and the richness of the Chinese-inspired wallpaper.

We enjoyed coffee and dessert in the spacious parlor that opened off the dining room. Tim's Uncle Liam shared the details of our two-day tour, which would begin tomorrow with a visit to County Cork. Lunch was planned with the Staffords at noon. Then we would go to Bantry House for afternoon tea, a prelude to checking in and spending the night in the circa 1750 mansion.

On the second day we would visit Blarney Castle and the Rock Close Gardens. Those who wished could climb the tower steps and kiss the stone before returning to Rosslare for dinner.

"If we leave early, we should have time to visit the farmer's market in Bantry," Jane said, apparently familiar with the terrain. "We can't arrive at my sister's house empty handed, can we Timothy?"

"What can I say, except everyone here knows you prefer full hands to empty hands? It's part of what makes you so lovable," he added while planting a kiss on her cheek.

By 11 p.m. everyone else had gone to bed and to sleep, except for the two of us in the guest cottage. We had caught our second wind, and our lovemaking was buoyed by the flow of Baileys Irish Crème that moved through our veins.

✑ Chapter Twenty-Six ✐

Detective Lou Perkins

After receiving an email from Sam, I began doing a police database search for one Nora Owens. No hits. She had no police record, no arrests, and no expired driver's license. I concluded she was a phantom. She was never a victim of identity theft because it appeared she had no identity.

Then I decided to enter the alias Clare O'Neill in the database and got a hit. An address matched Liffey House condo complex on East 78th and 2nd Ave.

I relayed the information to Assistant District Attorney Judith Steiner. She processed a search warrant within an hour. When the lady of the house didn't answer the doorbell, the manager unlocked the door with an expression that wouldn't win him a hospitality of the year award.

Two other police officers and I combed through the neatly but sparsely appointed apartment. It was clear Nora Owens only passed through New York. Even her walk-in closet looked like something from a convent.

As I stepped through the doorway of the master bedroom closet, my detective's eyes noticed the sight lines of the closet in comparison with the width and breadth of the bedroom. It seemed out of proportion with the rest of the room.

I stepped inside the closet again, pushed away the few clothes hanging on a metal rod, and began studying the panels along the inner wall. When I knocked on them, it was apparent there was no insulation on the other side. That meant it was a fake wall, so I started moving my fingers down the seam of the first panel until, bingo, it folded in. Then like dominos the next panel folded in, revealing a hidden chamber.

Inside was an array of wigs, hair dyes, make-up, and different styles of clothing that left me asking: *Will the real Clare O'Neill please stand up?* The only thing missing were murder weapons and a clear photo of what this woman looked like. There were no photos or pictures of anyone in the apartment, heightening the mystique around her identity.

After questioning the doorman, who said that she had left town, we decided to check all five area airports to see how far out of town she had gone. The trail went dead. If she had left town, it was under another alias.

She had to return eventually because she had one more potential victim in Bishop John Campbell, according to Sam. So the question was not if, but when would she return?

Time to set up a plan and to email Samantha with the details.

Sam Bannion

Jane had rented an SUV for our tour of southern Ireland. It comfortably seated all six of us, plus a basket of fruits and snacks, with room left over for whatever items Jane would purchase at the market as gifts for her two sisters.

We arrived at the Stafford house shortly before noon. Jane's two sisters, Bernadette and Catherine, whom they called Cassie, were at the door to greet them. I marveled how much they both resembled Jane. After the traditional hugs and kisses, Cassie showed me how to touch the Celtic cross on the door post and then make the sign of the cross as a way of blessing their home as a guest, while Bernadette escorted the others inside.

The Stafford cottage resembled something from a Charles Dickens novel. Its lines and country simplicity gave it the appearance of being a fairytale place where family stories and memories were easily accessed and shared.

This part of the Irish countryside had an unspoiled beauty that couldn't be captured on a postcard. There were no billboards along the roads, no grotesque strip malls or anything resembling the American-style sprawl. There was just an original, stunning beauty that was the heart of a national pride.

Lunch was thoroughly Irish, and in place of wine we drank a variety of Irish teas. The stories, served on the side, put Cassie and Bernadette in the role of stand-up comedians, even though they were sitting down. They kept everyone laughing—especially Tim, who delighted in this one-of-a-kind family entertainment.

One story was about his great uncle Clive, who missed shipping out on the *Titanic* because he broke his leg trying to round up a herd of sheep. At first he cursed them. But after the legendary ship struck an iceberg and sank, Clive rounded up the entire herd and gave them kisses. Only Cassie could embellish it with her lilting Irish brogue.

Before tea and dessert were served, Tim provided some unrehearsed entertainment on a spinet piano. After a medley of Irish songs, Cassie joined him for a four-handed rendition of "My Wild Irish Rose."

The Stafford sisters posed for pictures before we left for Bantry House in the afternoon. They stood in order by age: Aishling, Bernadette, and Cassie. As camera flashes went off, one of them affectionately said, "We are the A, B, C sisters!"

I leaned over and whispered in Tim's ear, "They look like the Irish version of the Golden Girls."

Tim had told me that his grandmother was quite different from her two sisters. Whereas they avoided parties and social networking for the comfort of their home and gardens, she thrived in the company of others. Her social life was as much oxygen to her as the air she breathed.

After hugs, kisses, and tears, we departed for Bantry House, arriving in time for high tea. I learned that this jewel of a bed and breakfast was still owned by descendants of the Earls of Bantry. We visitors were treated like heads of state, including our stately guest rooms overlooking Bantry Bay.

The next morning we fortified ourselves with a traditional Irish breakfast. Then Liam drove us to Blarney Castle, one of Cork's greatest treasures, where we would find the famous Blarney Stone.

Since four of our group had already kissed the stone, only Tim and I ventured up the tower steps for the kissing ritual. There was something magical about lying on my back, then arching my head backward for the kiss.

When I saw other tourists in that position, I leaned over to Tim and said, "Kissing in that position would be much more enjoyable if there were another set of lips and not a stone!"

"Shall we show them how to do it?" Tim asked innocently.

"I think not. It's probably better to honor the tradition and not risk being turned into Druids," I said, chuckling.

After we had both finished the ritual of kissing the stone, Tim said, "Can I taste what the stone tastes like on your lips?"

"You mean like Guinness beer and Listerine?"

Instead of answering me, Tim kissed me gently. Then with a smile and an Irish sparkle in his green eyes, he said, "That tastes much better than stone."

"You're spoiled."

"No, but I am growing accustomed to your lips."

When we rejoined the others, Jane Cavanagh said, "Well, was it worth going all the way up there just to kiss a stone?"

"Yes, it makes you appreciate kissing lips all the more," Tim answered her wit for wit, as he pecked her cheek with a kiss.

"I see it didn't take you long to catch the Blarney," Jane countered. Everyone broke out into a chorus of Irish laughter.

We walked leisurely through the extensive gardens and arboretum. As we strolled, Jane's and Bernice's arms were linked in Tim's, while Liam's were linked with me and Molly. I caught Jane glancing back at me, and I wondered if she was hoping, as I was, that the enchantment of this place would work its magic on Tim and me. If the thought of our being married and of Jane one day becoming a great grandmother stirred such delight in me, it must also be touching her soul.

We returned to Rosslare in time for a light supper. The four senior citizens retired early, while Tim and I stayed awake long enough to re-tap the magic of the day with hot kisses and love-making. It was much better than blarney.

The Fixer

It rained during the entire train ride from the Rosslare Euro-Port to Dublin. Every green-blooded Irishman was accustomed to this trademark climate of the Emerald Isle, where carrying an umbrella is as necessary as carrying Euros. Exiting the station, I took a taxi to the

Clarence Hotel. The reservation had been made by my contract, and a FedEx package was waiting for me.

Inside was a black clerical shirt and collar in my size. A sealed envelope contained a letter, signature, and official stamp that would give me access to the Dublin Archdiocesan Curial Offices. As per the instructions, I dressed as a priest, returned to Connolly Station to take a picture in a photo booth, then went back to my room to make a phone call, during which an official asked that I present my credentials the next day at 10 a.m.

The rain subsided during the night but left an ominous trail of grey, threatening clouds. The Curial Offices off Cathedral Street were located in a typical Dublin office building. I entered by the main door and presented my papers to the receptionist. It must have been the convincing picture of my alias and the devious smile that persuaded her to instruct me to take the elevator to the second floor. From there, I was escorted around a wide hallway that left me with the impression that the internal layout of the building resembled a labyrinth. I had a fleeting thought that I was tracing the steps of Timothy Cavanagh several days earlier.

Once I reached the archives, I was given a file on Nora Owens and read through it, noting any characteristic or unusual material or pattern. The one recurring detail was her flare for housecleaning. I wrote down a few important facts helpful in my investigation. Her picture in the file was quite dated, but her eyes were a distinctive characteristic. They were dark and troubled-looking, like someone who had lost the only person she loved and was left only with revenge.

When I returned to the hotel, I began scanning housecleaning ads in the city telephone book. None were under the name of Nora Owens, but one grabbed my attention. It was listed as "Twin Sisters Housecleaning Service."

I called the number and chatted briefly with the receptionist under the ruse that I was writing a magazine story on the subject of the art of domestic cleaning. I was told that the owner of the business lived in London and was given a number to call.

Although my subterfuge hit a brick wall when I was told the owner of the business did not do interviews, her firewall of protection was defused when I said it could mean new business in a languid economy. She asked for a call-back number. I said I would be in London tomorrow and would contact her again.

I made a reservation for a BMI flight to Heathrow. Twenty-four hours later, I was sitting in the reception area of a two-room flat overlooking Victoria Station. The girl at the desk sported a mound of thick, blond hair where, no doubt, various small insects nested, and enough make-up for every female passenger exiting the subway station across the street. The wad of chewing gum in her mouth cracked and popped like wood in a fireplace, while she simultaneously sucked on a pencil as if it were a lollypop. If not perched as a receptionist, she could have passed for a comic act at a circus. The only accessory she lacked was a plastic flower that squirted water.

Her boss came out to greet me and escorted me into the office.

"How did you hear about us?" Lisa Sheppard asked in a refined British accent.

I had memorized my lines so no flags would be raised.

"News about triple-A cleaning services travels fast. It didn't take me long in my research to find yours. "Then I decided to turn the tables and deflect attention away from me. " So tell me, how you have earned such high ratings?"

She gave me a brief history of "Twin Sisters Housecleaning Services." I fed her questions about their mission statement, work ethics, background checks on employees, etc. As we chatted, I glanced at several framed pictures on a credenza behind her desk, from which I framed my own non-threatening question. "Are these employees of the year or month?"

Having acquired a certain trust level during my thirty-minute interview, she proceeded to identify them as pictures of her family, a husband and two children. They probably lived in a two story house with a picket fence and a pet. She pointed to another picture that she identified as the owner of the company, and referred to her as Ms. Owens. I studied it intensely, uploading it into my memory like an electronic file.

Bishop John Campbell

As pre-arranged, I called the Fixer for a detailed report of his travels and an update on the information he had gathered. I couldn't help smiling when he told me he got a good look at a recent picture of Nora Owens on vacation in the Caribbean. I wrote down some details as I stood at a pay phone in the basement of the Brooklyn Marriott. No doubt this Nora Owens had several aliases, since she had killed two priests without leaving any element of a consistent description, other than that she was female. Moreover, she was a master at not leaving a trail of evidence. My contact's astute location and description of a recent photo of her features was a point in my win column.

I instructed the Fixer to return to Dublin and make sure the Cavanagh party left the airport on time for their return flight to New York.

"Wait at the Clarence Hotel until you receive another FedEx envelope. This contract will end soon."

When I heard the phone click on the other end, I knew he understood. There was no need for further conversation.

During the drive back to Islip, I began plotting a plan that would lure Nora Owens into a trap. Once it was sprung, she would be silenced forever, keeping my secrets safe and my future secure.

My plan was brilliant, except for one small snag: Timothy Cavanagh. He was a player who by now might have information that could sabotage everything. I felt the need to tread lightly; his trust fund alone was worth about fifty million. One quarter of that could be the price of the red hat of a cardinal. I would be willing to sell my soul for that opportunity; for now I could not afford to ignore the redheaded detective who could also get in the way.

One inner voice told me to be bold and daring, while another coached me to be prudent and patient. I told them both to be quiet as I calculated the pros and cons of my plan. Whatever the outcome, this chapter of deceit and murder in the Diocese of Islip would end on January 20th—the feast of St. Sebastian. I would plan a celebration at the cathedral for both a martyr and a victor, and I didn't plan on being the former.

Fr. Tim Cavanagh

The four of us returned home on November 2. Two cars sent from Rosslare Park were soon weighted down with luggage and gifts, which Granny had brought home for everyone except herself. Sam retrieved her car, packed it with her belongings, and after we had all exchanged hugs and kisses, she drove to her home in East Islip. She told me she planned to phone Lou Perkins on the way for an update and was going to see him the next day at the police precinct.

I stayed at Rosslare Park long enough to celebrate Mass there on the feast of All Souls for the departed members of the Cavanagh and Stafford Families, enjoy a light dinner with Granny and Molly, and reconcile with Bach, who no doubt felt deserted for the past ten days. Then I drove to St. Sebastian Cathedral for a good night's sleep in my own bed. It ended up being a restless night, as I sadly reached over to the empty side of my bed. I had been home only eight hours and already missed Sam.

I missed touching her soft skin and watching her eyes dance with delight during our lovemaking. I missed lying next to her and watching her sleep. I missed showering with her, lathering her with soap and then rinsing her with water cupped in my hands as if I were playing a Liszt sonata. I missed cuddling her and smelling the scent of her shampoo even long after our showers.

I pondered the meaning of this new experience, this pain of missing one special person in my life. This was different from what I had felt years ago, when I missed the piano after a sabbatical. In the wonderful grace of this experience, Sam could love me back in a way a baby grand piano could not.

I chatted quietly with God about this and was content with letting it remain a mystery. This freed my forlorn mind from having to explain the unexplainable. It allowed me to avoid focusing on the struggle to the point of losing my contentment with the assurance that God was in the mystery. Eventually I gave myself to the mystery itself, closed my eyes, and fell asleep.

It wasn't long before God intervened and revealed divine delight by entering my dreams. Together we revisited the Dublin pubs that had recharged me with a passion for human life and love; a beach on the Irish Sea; and a fairytale cottage and an elegant Irish manor house, where Sam and I had made love. I dreamed of kissing the Blarney Stone and then kissing a woman whose warm, sensual lips tasted far better than cold stone.

When I awoke eight hours later, I looked into the bathroom mirror and saw the smiling face of God reflecting back at me. My first thought was a prayer: *Please, God, may Sam see the same face in her mirror that I am contemplating right now.*

ᴄᴘ Chapter Twenty-Seven ᴄᴘ

Fr. Tim Cavanagh

The bishop wishes to see you," was Leona Helmond's own personal greeting for me after I'd been away for ten days. The virus of "all business without kindness" that pervaded the fifth floor of the Chancery had metastasized in her like cancer. I decided to call her on it.

"Good morning to you also, and yes, Leona, I missed you too."

She flashed me a look that could have punctured an artery.

After booting up my computer, I knocked on the door of the evil emperor. To my surprise, he opened it instead of barking a command to enter.

"Well, Tim, it's good to see you again. I can't wait to hear about your Ireland trip."

I faked a smile, knowing that what he really was itching to know was what I may have uncovered about his history at Holy Comforter Orphanage. I decided to play along. "What do you want to know?"

"What was the highlight of your visit to Dublin?" He was going for the jugular.

I answered him as I had mentally rehearsed it—like a tour guide without commentary. "Dublin Castle, Trinity College, and viewing the Book of Kells, in that order."

"And what about the great cathedrals? Did you tour them, especially St. Patrick's, which the Protestants stole from us?"

"We toured St. Patrick's holy well. That's as close as we came to the cathedral." Then I deflected the conversation.

"Actually, we found the pubs much more interesting than the holy sites, but come to think of it, the pubs are shrines in their own right. Lots of pilgrims meeting and drinking lots of Guinness and engaging in lively, boisterous Irish blarney. And all of it good for the soul."

I sensed his temper coming to the surface, so before he could control the conversation again, I barreled on.

"And speaking of blarney, I kissed the stone and walked through the gardens of Blarney Castle."

I could read his face; he was wondering if I had kissed a certain Irish redhead too. He left her out of the conversation, not wanting to show his card that he knew about her addition to our entourage. But since I knew that we both knew about the stalker, the rest of our chat was an exercise in mind games—mildly entertaining to me, of course, as he naively allowed his face to redden just enough for me to notice.

"I would like to have a staff meeting tomorrow at 1 p.m.," the bishop said. "I know it's unscheduled, so please inform Joe and Ted."

I nodded. He debriefed me about some matters concerning Brian Manley that had surfaced after my departure for Ireland. Before leaving the office, I alerted him to expect a call from my grandmother.

"I am sure she wants to give you her own running commentary about revisiting her homeland and would prefer to do that over wine and dinner at Rosslare Park."

He glowed like a light that had been switched on, but I knew that the glow was more for the pleasure of dining at the elegant manor house rather than for the enjoyment of Granny's company.

I returned to my office and sat at my desk, pondering what had not been said in his office more than what was said. My instincts told me he was doing the same. The mind war games had begun.

Nora Owens

After three weeks in St. Lucia, the thought of going home loomed like the shadows of the majestic volcano, Soufriere. The indicator might have been the texture of my tan. When I wasn't sunning or snorkeling, I was glued to the Internet, keeping up with the unfolding details of Fr. Brian Manley's murder investigation on the *Long Island News Day* webpage. Initially, I became alarmed when the police reported a lead for a possible female killer living in the Yorkville area of the upper east side of Manhattan.

I turned off that alarm and listened to a voice that reminded me that New York City was a large island, and that I was a skilled master of deceit who could hide anywhere in the acres of concrete caverns without being discovered. Whereas maintaining an international domestic cleaning business was my profession, creating and performing on the stage of aliases was my calling.

I still had one more name on my hit list, and I intended to keep my promise to Nan, even if it meant stepping in harm's way.

This plan had to be airtight, with no margin for errors or mistakes. It had to be executed with stealth. I had played the fox before and had always managed to catch my prey before being caught.

What I needed was an opportunity that I didn't have to create. It would take pressure off of me. Since there was no hurry, I'd wait to see if our final sexual abuser released that pressure and opened the door for me to move queen to bishop on this emotional chessboard. Then checkmate.

I would follow his schedule on the Diocese of Islip webpage. It would help me determine when to return to New York and complete the final chapter in securing my own justice for the injustice of sexual abuse—injustice for which the Catholic Church had yet to atone.

Until then, I would continue to enjoy the tropical fruits, the sun, surf, sand, and all the amenities of my five-star resort. It was what a serial killer did during intermission.

Fr. Tim Cavanagh and Sam Bannion

Tim closed the door to his office. The minutes had passed like hours up to this time when he could dial his favorite number stored in his contact list.

She answered on the first ring. "Tim!"

"How would you like to treat me to lunch?"

"Funny, I was just about to call and ask you the same thing."

He had a clear picture in his imagination of Sam wearing a devilish grin. She had turned it into an art form since enjoying an affair with a priest.

"Okay," he countered.

"Sounds like a plan. Where do I get to see you?" she asked.

"How about Buck's Diner?"

"So we're doing the greasy spoon today," Sam replied like a food critic.

"Well, every once in a while it's good to eat with the common folk. Maybe humble pie will be on the menu." The chuckle on the other end of the phone made Tim smile. This kind of freelance banter was a new form of energy for him, but given all that they had shared during the past few weeks, it had become a prelude to a deepening emotional attachment.

Three hours later, they were facing each other in a corner booth with vinyl-covered seats, patched to hide splits from age. Buck's Diner was a local landmark, a truck driver's paradise, and a place in Islip where news and gossip were served up faster than the fries. Each booth sported a miniature juke box featuring a little bit of county western and a lot of top '60s and '70s rock 'n roll. Tim dropped in a quarter and punched in a Paul Anka selection so the music would muffle their chatter. To Tim, the open booth had the feel of a confessional box that wasn't sound-proofed. Even though this was an impromptu lunch, he didn't know whether the neighbors in the next booth were spies from the Vatican Nunciature. After the experience of being followed on the streets of Dublin, he was taking no risks.

Their waitress looked like a character from a comic strip, with a rainbow of metallic colors in her straight hair. Her faux fingernails were painted with the signs of the zodiac. She stood at their booth without saying a word. Tim broke the silence by ordering a burger with onion rings, and Sam, a Cobb salad. The waitress bobbed her head and glided off.

As they waited for lunch, Tim and Sam got serious about the investigation into Brian Manley's murder. Sam spoke the obvious.

"This woman, Clare O'Neill, is a professional assassin. She managed to escape from New York, and there are no leads into her whereabouts. She's a master at aliases and probably has several fake passports so she can easily slip back into the city to murder again."

"Well, at least we know who the next victim may be," Tim said, thinking of the bishop. Did he know? "What are the police doing to protect him?"

"Since that is information known only to you and me, what kind of protection would you suggest, without giving ourselves away? If he is behind the man who stalked us in Dublin, then he suspects *us* as much as we suspect *him*."

Tim leaned forward in the booth and lowered his voice.

"There has to be a way to alert the bishop without blowing our cover."

"I'm all ears," Sam said, while cupping both ears as if she were using sign language.

As the waitress served their entrees, Tim wrestled with whether to share with Sam the information he had photocopied on Bishop Campbell from the filing cabinet in the basement of Solitude.

His thoughts were interrupted by the waitress.

"Can I get you anything else?"

"No thanks." She walked away, and Tim decided to remain silent on Bishop Campbell. "So, Sam, what's the plan?"

"My police instincts tell me the more important question is, what is Bishop Campbell's plan? He is the major player here, so I'm inclined to focus on him and not on Clare O'Neill or Nora Owens or whatever her real name is."

Tim popped an onion ring in his mouth. He wasn't satisfied with that answer. "Be assured he won't divulge any plan. He is as cautious as a CIA agent. So we may have to second guess him."

"Second guessing is not a good option for police. We have to be diligent, but patient." Sam spoke around a mouthful of salad. "It's a game of wait-and-see who makes the first move."

"That's not very consoling."

"Consolation is your business. Apprehending criminals is mine. It's better to let them unmask themselves first—then we make our move. But I am convinced the bishop is our primary concern."

Tim savored the last bite of his bleu cheese burger and changed the subject. "How would you like to be my guest at the opera?"

Sam appeared to be surprised by the question. "I have to confess I've never been to an opera."

"You're in luck. Since you're confessing to the right person, I can absolve you. For your penance, you are to join Tim Cavanagh for a performance of Puccini's opera *Tosca*. The date is Thursday, Nov. 15. I'll pick you up at 4 p.m. We can drive to Manhattan, have dinner at my grandmother's brownstone on the East Side, and then it's just a short ride to Lincoln Center for the opera at 7:30."

Sam was speechless but beaming with delight. Tim seized the moment.

"While you're pondering whether to accept, may I remind you that the opera is just the excuse you need to wear your concert evening gown and jewelry again. So don't tell me you don't have anything to wear, because then I'll have to absolve you for lying."

Breaking her silence Sam bantered back. "In that case I accept your invitation, and your penance. Are you this generous in handing out penance to all sinners?"

Tim leaned toward her and whispered, "Only to one whose name is Samantha, who has lush red hair and stands 5'10" tall, whose kissing is truly classic, and who can stop traffic in an evening gown."

"In that case, I'm glad I'm a sinner."

Tim raised his eyebrows and sported a wicked smile. "Me too."

They chatted about how they had shared details of their Ireland trip with Lou Perkins and Bishop Campbell. But beyond the light chatter was the heavy issue of not knowing how, where, or when the next murder would play out. It remained an unresolved issue, looming over them like a storm cloud that could not be controlled by either of them.

That frightened Tim, but it angered Sam. She had never liked surprises, especially when the word "murder" was in the same sentence.

Staff Meeting at the Chancery

Bishop Campbell stepped out of character and asked Tim to share stories of his trip to Ireland with Joe and Ted. Momentarily caught off guard, Tim recovered quickly. As he mentioned the pubs, Trinity College, Dublin Castle, the Book of Kells, the Blarney Stone, and County Cork, Ted and Joe nodded; they were familiar with the locations, having been there themselves. When Tim had finished, they shared fond memories of their own.

The bishop remained quiet, leaving Tim to wonder whether his thoughts were on details that Tim was leaving out, such as how much Tim now knew about the bishop's history at Holy Comforter. Or details about a certain young sexual abuse victim named Nora Owens. Or the evasive measures Tim and Sam had to take to evade a stalker who was clearly acting at someone else's direction.

Bishop Campbell interrupted the lively conversation and drew attention to himself, like a karaoke player grabbing a microphone. "Tim, your next visit must include the north. It has its own character and sights, though they are distinct from the south. Much like the differences between the north and south here in the States."

Tim nodded, and the bishop continued in an officious tone of voice. "The diocese has been through a nightmare with two priest murders. Everybody, including me, is still affected by the fallout. I have decided to preside at a Mass of Hope and Healing at the cathedral on the feast of St. Sebastian, which this year happens to fall on a Sunday. I have spoken with Msgr. Quinn, who has reserved January 20th for this diocesan event. I plan to preach at all five weekend Masses and to preside at the 11 a.m. Solemn Mass. I thought the afternoon would be a good time for hearing confessions. I will make myself available before the 5 p.m. evening Mass.

"We don't have much time, so I'm delegating Ted and Tim to work with the cathedral staff and diocesan worship office in planning this feast day like a diocesan pilgrimage."

The three clergy discussed ways to help this idea ignite a new spark and defuse the cloud of fear and sadness over the clergy and the laity. Tim sat back and enjoyed their creative chatter, occasionally contributing some input to give them the impression that he was still engaged in planning the event.

Tim's right brain was churning with ideas, while his left brain raced like a computer program running a check trying to unravel the true motivations for the bishop's idea. Thirty minutes later, he left the bishop's office obsessed with determining the significance of what the bishop had left unsaid. Since he had never known the bishop to be this pastoral, he struggled to find the hidden motivation for this out-of-character behavior. Not knowing what that motivation could be released a haunting presence in him.

Keeping with his usual ritual following a staff meeting, the bishop cracked the window behind his leather swivel chair, opened the humidor atop the mahogany executive desk, and slowly inhaled the aroma of the Havana cigar he held in his hand like a precious relic.

After striking a match, he slowly guided the flame to the tip. Simultaneously he extinguished the match with one swipe of his right hand, while inhaling the addictive charm of the Cuban tobacco. As it began to release its intoxicating effects into his system, he took pleasure in the plan he had just initiated.

The countdown had begun. The bishop's three confidential consulters would innocently become conspirators in laying a trap. It would be sprung in nine weeks—plenty of time for him to put the missing pieces in place.

The bishop always considered it a venial sin not to finish a Cuban cigar. Forty minutes later, he extinguished the stub, composed a letter on the computer, printed it, affixed a FedEx label to its envelope, and placed it in the inside pocket of his suit coat.

Within a week, the remaining pieces of the plot would be set in place.

ᨀ Chapter Twenty-Eight ᨀ

Tim & Samantha

The two weeks before the dinner and opera date with Sam was pure torture for Tim. He occupied himself with detailed plans, which were all in place by November 15th. He left the office at 3 p.m. and retrieved a piece of luggage at the cathedral rectory.

At 4 p.m. he rang the doorbell at Sam's house. She looked wonderful, even in jeans and a jacket. He had asked her to dress casually for the drive to Manhattan. They would both change into evening clothes at the brownstone on East 75th St.

Sam spoke as she slid into the passenger seat. "I went online and read an article about *Tosca*. It sounds tragic."

Tim kept his eyes on the road while processing a response.

"That's because Puccini is the master of tragic operas. I hope you brought some Kleenex, because there will be tears."

"They're in my handbag, but you should know it takes a lot to make an Islip police officer cry. If I should shed one or two, I hope it will be dark enough in Lincoln Center to spare me embarrassment. By the way, where are our seats?"

Keeping his focus on driving through heavy traffic, Tim answered half of her question.

"Yes, it will be dark enough for you to wipe your tears, and we are in the mezzanine."

At the brownstone, Sam craned her neck to view the entire four-story structure. The police officer in her viewed the thick, rusticated bars on the two street-level windows as deterrents against break-ins. Sam had no idea she was about to step into a four million dollar piece of real estate until Tim unlocked the door and motioned her inside.

The granite floor hallway was designed with an inlaid checkerboard pattern. A marble staircase curved at the landing and with a bronze railing led the way to the living quarters on the upper three levels. Sam caught a glimpse of luxurious appointments that echoed all she knew of Jane Cavanagh.

Tim led Sam upstairs to the third floor, opened the door to a guest bedroom with a private bath, and gently laid out her evening gown on the bed like a valet who knew how to handle precious clothing.

"My room is on the top floor. I'll meet you downstairs at 6 for dinner. The clock is running to see if you make that deadline, so keep your make-up time modest. If you spend more than fifteen minutes in front of the mirror, it will turn you into Medusa."

"Do I want to know who that is?" Sam called as Tim made his way up the stairs two at a time.

The answer echoed back to her from the top floor: "Trust me, NO."

Sam made it to the kitchen on time—just as Tim popped the cork on a bottle of French chardonnay. He poured her a glass and then offered a toast.

"Here's to the chardonnay that came in out of the cold." Then he added his trademark wine toast line, "May your life always be good again before and after an opera."

Sam clinked Tim's glass. "I'll drink to that." She added, "I sense a story with that line."

"Some other time," he said. "Dinner awaits."

With that he opened the doors into a dining room that appeared to have been plucked from a Victorian castle. The walls were covered in elegant damask fabric, and a working gas fireplace wrapped in pink marble was located on the outer wall. A full-length portrait of Tim's grandparents dominated the opposite wall. A table and eight chairs were neatly positioned on a Kashmiri rug. An arrangement of freshly cut flowers cascaded over an ornate brass container at the table's center.

Tim sat opposite Sam so his eyes could feast on her beauty. "The menu is Chicken cordon bleu with a white wine sauce, rice pilaf, and a green salad with Gorgonzola cheese," he announced.

Sam raised both hands in a gesture of amazement. "When did you have time to prepare this?"

"It took me five minutes yesterday to call Yorkville Caterers. They delivered it while you were applying your lipstick. Your timing was perfect!"

They enjoyed the meal and fine wine, both savoring the moments of moving from liking to loving each other. "Love" was a word both harbored in their hearts but was as yet unspoken. A transition in their unconventional relationship had begun.

Sam had already experienced and lived the transition with her brief marriage to Todd. Tim was discovering the difference, truly experiencing for the first time the life-giving emotions that love for a woman released in him. He already knew he wanted more, and he wanted it with Sam.

She completed him in a way that neither a piano nor the priesthood could. She could push buttons directly to his soul and open new doors to his inner creativity, both of which he welcomed. She could say things that awakened in him the gift of repartee, leaving him high on laughter. She could wear denim and be the envy of every wife at a policeman's party. And she could wear a Carolina Herrera designer gown and make him the envy of every man.

What have I done to deserve her, God and what must I do to keep her?

Sam attempted to break his prayerful trance.

"Hello, is anybody there?" Then she added, "A penny for your thoughts."

"Never put a price tag on anyone's thoughts," he chuckled. "You might end up bankrupt."

"In that case, I will expect you to bail me out."

With that one comeback, she had confirmed his thoughts about healthy bantering. Then he heard the grandfather clock chime 6:45.

"How about a little entertainment before we leave?" With that he escorted her to a living room that spanned the entire length of the front of the brownstone. In the corner was a Steinway baby grand piano. As Sam got comfortable in a silk-upholstered wing chair, Tim played the overture to the second act of *Tosca*.

Five minutes later, they heard a knock at the front door.

Tim jumped up from the piano seat and extended his hand to Sam. "Time to keep our date with Mr. Puccini."

Grabbing her wrap and handbag, they walked down the marble staircase to find their town car and driver waiting.

"No one goes to the opera in a taxi," Tim said, wearing the grin only she could paint on his face. When the limo driver pulled up to the entrance of the Lincoln Square Cinema, Sam's excitement turned to bewilderment.

"What's this? I thought we were going to the opera?" she asked.

"We *are* going to the opera," Tim assured her while gesturing toward the marquee, where the title *Tosca* shone in neon lights, along with the names of other newly released films.

Sam tried to comprehend the breadth of the joke Tim had played on her.

"When I think of opera, I think of Lincoln Center and not a movie theater."

"Well, your operatic horizons are going to be stretched this evening."

She exited the limo like Cinderella gracefully leaving her horse-drawn carriage.

Tim had already purchased their tickets, so they bypassed the ticket booth and ascended the escalator, heading for their theater. In front of them were a couple in jeans, hoodies, and sneakers.

She couldn't resist taking a swipe at her date. "I feel like I'm overdressed."

Tim was ready with his comeback. "True, but you'll be the hottest over-dressed female at the opera. And your date is the only one dressed in an Armani tuxedo with a silk scarf, onyx stick pins, and a killer smile. So let's have fun with everybody guessing who we are and wondering if they'll see us on a morning news show tomorrow."

Sam responded with a mournful thought. "And what would your boss say if he saw us on TV tomorrow morning?"

"Have no fear," quipped Tim. "When it comes to TV, he doesn't know his ABCs from his NBCs."

They both erupted in laughter, leaving everyone around them even more suspicious about their identities.

232

Sam found the laughter therapeutic. She began to soften from the effects of Tim's humor and mischievous planning. If anyone other than Tim Cavanagh had seduced her into this charade, her inner child would have thrown a temper tantrum.

They were seated in the middle of the front row in the Mezzanine section. By the time the lights dimmed, over 600 opera lovers had powered down their cell phones and settled in to enjoy Puccini's tragic three-act opera without any interruptions.

Two-and-a-half hours later, Sam had used her last tissue wiping away tears evoked by the tragic end to the love between Floria Tosca and Mario Cavaradossi. The penultimate scene of the heroine holding her beloved Mario's body released emotions in Sam that she had dammed up for a long time.

Tim put his arm around her and drew her closer as a gesture of leaning on each other for comfort. He secretly hoped they would continue to comfort each other in this manner, as neither of them yet knew how the third act of the priests' murders in Islip might turn out.

They remained in the theater until the last credit reeled off the screen. Tim hummed part of the score, causing Sam to smile.

"I'm probably the only one here with a classical pianist as a date who can serenade me with the music on perfect pitch."

Tim kissed her cheek and whispered, "Thanks for the complement, and yes, I have perfect pitch, just like my taste in perfect dates."

Sam needled him with a punch to his ribs.

The limo was waiting for them as they exited the theater. The driver kept the car running so the interior was warm. On the bar in the back seat was a thermos of hot cinnamon tea. Tim poured a cup for Sam, then one for himself. He offered a toast.

"Here's to Puccini and his art of awakening the long-lost lover in us all."

After they each took a sip, Tim asked, "So what are you thinking after your first night at the opera?"

Her face revealed someone who was in a state of deep pondering. "I am thinking about what Carolina Herrera would say if she knew I dropped buttered popcorn on her designer gown."

The roar of their laughter caused the limo driver to deflect his eyes from the road to the rear-view mirror, perhaps hoping some of their happiness would infect him.

When they arrived back at the brownstone, Tim tipped the driver and opened the door. He flung his arms around Sam to rescue her from the biting wind blowing off the East River. Once they were in the warmth of the brownstone, Tim loosened his black tie as they went to the kitchen.

Tim poured Baileys Irish Crème in two brandy snifters, handed one to Sam, and walked with her to the living room. They got comfortable on the sofa, kicking off their shoes and stretching their legs on the two matching footstools. Tim then stroked Sam's left arm like he was playing the piano and looked pleasantly into her eyes. He knew them like the sheet music he didn't need to look at while playing. Her eyes remained in his soul when Sam wasn't around. She blinked her enjoyment of his gaze, an audience of one.

The grandfather's clock in the entranceway of the foyer chimed 11 p.m. Tim waited for the last chime to strike on the hour before breaking the silence. He kept his green eyes focused on Sam's blue ones.

"I have an hour to get you home before my Honda turns into a pumpkin."

"In that case, let's move, since my shoe size is not petite."

They kissed deeply, not caring about the clock ticking but enjoying the intimacy of the moment and the taste of Irish crème on each other's lips.

As the clock chimed the quarter hour, they were out the door, in the car, and heading east. Each was lost in the new memories of this night. How they would savor them—like the Baileys they continued to taste on their palates, made all the more delicious by their passionate kissing.

❧ Chapter Twenty-Nine ❧

The Fixer

Half of the six-hour international flight from Dublin to New York City was uncomfortable due to turbulence over the North Atlantic. But the Fixer shrugged it off like a stubborn Irishman. He had weathered worse storms in his life, and the few bumps and bounces at 35,000 feet was equivalent to an amusement ride at Euro-Disney.

It helped that he was in first class. He could afford those comforts, one of which was a bulkhead seat to accommodate his 6'3" stature. The reclined seat allowed him to stretch both his legs and his mind.

While most of the passengers occupied themselves watching movies on the sophisticated, in-seat video system, others snoozed with earphones attached to their iPods. The few workaholics had connected to the onboard Wi-Fi and were browsing the Internet or obsessing over work.

The Fixer pretended to nap after a lunch of beef tips in a red wine sauce and two bottles of Guinness. While navigating the caverns of his mind with all the details awaiting him after his arrival at JFK Airport, he pondered how his business required him to be methodical and precise. He had a perfect score fixing other people's problems, and he didn't intend for this contract to ruin that record. His propensity for exactness, timing, and subterfuge had earned him a lifestyle he didn't wish to exchange for anything. He had studied the pictures and history of his target. Those were two advantages he had over her.

"No Northern Irishman is going to be outwitted by a southern Irish woman," he thought to himself. Stealth and patience was the preferred cocktail whenever he wore the hat of the Fixer.

The flight arrived on time, and after breezing through Customs and retrieving his luggage, he hailed a taxi. His destination was the Port Authority in Manhattan. His mission was not to catch a bus, but to open a locker and empty it of a package he needed for the next chapter in his contract.

Jane Cavanagh

Twenty years ago I started a new tradition at Rosslare Park. The Cavanaghs opened their home to the homeless and served them Thanksgiving dinner. Everyone in the family and the staff pitched in, sharing in the bounty of reasons to be thankful. Eventually a few neighbors joined the small army of volunteers, thereby turning the holiday into a neighborhood event. We accomplished this every year without an act of Congress.

Molly and I did the planning weeks in advance. We had it down to such a science that it was now the fall social event of Stony Brook. Wealthy mingling with the poor, those who worked on Wall Street chatting with those who lived on the streets, the clean and the dirty, those donning designer clothes and others in discarded clothes, those who were warmly sheltered in Tudor mansions and those who sought warmth in shelters.

The homeless were our guests. We give door prizes—mostly new, warm coats and gloves for an impending cold winter. The coats were my late husband's idea. The gloves were my idea. The neighbors would start contributing to the coat collection in early October.

For the past four years, Timothy had elevated the dinner to a classical level by playing holiday music on the Knabe grand piano. This annual holiday of joy transformed the hearts of those on the receiving end, as well as those on the giving end.

After all the guests had left and all was cleaned up, the family and neighbors would sit around the living room fireplace, feasting on Molly's Irish soda bread and hot apple cider. We shared how listening to and interacting with the poor gave us a new reason to be thankful. We shared tears and laughter. Both were reverenced with an easy, prayerful silence.

On Black Friday the Cavanaghs escaped to the city. It was Long Island's version of the biblical Exodus. The suburbanites marched due west with their wallets to the Promised Land of Manhattan to worship at the retail shrines of Macy's, Bergdorf-Goodman, and the fashion boutiques along 5th Ave. On this pilgrimage, the exiles purchased whatever they needed to make new covenants with family and friends for Christmas.

While on our march, we window shopped and began to make our lists of Christmas gifts for the family, including those who were both naughty and nice. I gave everyone $1,000, along with strict instructions that the total budget for everyone's gifts was not to exceed $500. The balance must be given to a charity or special-needs project that benefited others.

On Christmas Day, each person would open their wrapped package while telling the others about their Christmas charity gift. Only after that ritual did we exchange and open gifts with each other. It was the best thing Dermot and I could have done to teach the children how putting others first would make their hearts grow larger.

Samantha Bannion was now an extended member of the Cavanagh family. The naughty me thought it was time to invite her to both gatherings. The nice me would make it sound so enticing that she couldn't say no.

My heart blossomed into a wide smile, knowing that since she now talked to Timothy more than I did, I wouldn't have to play the naughty grandmother and leave them to unravel the meanings of my devious matchmaking. Scratching that activity off my job description should add years to my life. I could think of so many things to do with that new supply of energy.

An inner voice coached me: "No time like the present."

"Yes, yes, I hear you," my brain replied, as it commanded me to reach for the phone and dial a certain redhead who had catapulted to the top of my list of most favorite people.

"Hello, Jane," she answered, sounding more like a network broadcaster than a uniformed police officer.

I thought being apologetic would be a good start. "I hope I'm not interrupting you as you foil a break-in or chase bank robbers."

"There are days when I wish my work was that exciting. To tell you the truth, I am at my desk typing reports on the computer. These reports are every police officer's curse."

Discerning that it was time to come to the point, I took the initiative.

"I'm calling to invite you to join the family, staff, and neighbors for Thanksgiving. We feed the homeless at Rosslare Park and let them select new coats and gloves for winter. Your pleasant face and helping hands would be welcome."

There was a pregnant pause as she seemed to calculate her response. "I am touched by your thinking of me, but my divorced brother and niece and nephew would feel abandoned if I didn't have Thanksgiving dinner with them."

Prepared for that excuse, I barreled on. "Consider them invited too. The more the merrier."

She hesitated, like someone walking a high wire without a balance rod. "Let me think about how best to present this to them, and I promise to get back to you."

Wanting to affirm her sensitive style and putting a hopeful spin on the idea, I replied, "That sounds like a plan, as my secretary would say. I will wait to hear back from you."

Without a surveillance camera linking the house with the precinct, I couldn't see her troubled features. All I could do was imagine her having second thoughts about entangling an angry brother and a bitter sister-in-law in the loving circle of the Cavanagh family.

Nora Owens

A notice on the Diocese of Islip website caught my attention like a weather alert flashing across a TV screen. It read:

Bishop John Campbell invites the faithful of the diocese to join him in a pilgrimage of healing and hope following the murder of two diocesan priests. Catholics are asked to journey to St. Sebastian Cathedral in Islip on Sunday, January 20. The pilgrimage coincides with the feast day of the cathedral. Bishop Campbell will preach at all five weekend Masses, preside at the 11 a.m. Pontifical Mass and be available for confessions beginning at 4 p.m. prior to the 5 p.m. evening Mass. Plenary indulgences will be granted to those who make the pilgrimage and participate in the graces of the sacraments.

This was a miracle handed to me on a platter, like Salome receiving the head of John the Baptist. I couldn't have planned this better myself.

My mind kicked into overdrive, imagining how the plan would unfold. I jumped up from my laptop and began dancing around the suite. I poured a fresh glass of Chablis and began drinking it like a new elixir. I swayed onto the balcony, breathing in the cool evening breeze of the Caribbean like someone revitalized with an electric charge to the heart. The sun had long set, but the moon spoke to me like a forgotten mistress.

I pretended to hear her speak.

"This final darkness in your life will soon be lifted. Be brave and stalwart as the day of your inner freedom nears."

I tipped my wine glass to the moon shining with eye-catching brilliance in the darkened sky. Then I pirouetted back inside, sat at the table, and with a yellow pad began making a list of things to do in the next sixty days.

At the top of the list was booking a round trip from St. Lucia to London. There I would collect everything I would need for this last mission.

Fr. Tim Cavanagh

A heavy rain did not dampen the spirits of those who had assembled in the morning hours to parade in front of the Chancery Office. They had abandoned umbrellas, submitting to the frisky wind rather than fighting it. About fifty people were picketing Bishop Campbell's announcement of the pilgrimage for the two murdered priests.

One of them carried a sign that read, "When did I miss the announcement about a pilgrimage for sex abuse victims?"

Another contained the message, "Sex abuse is murder without a bullet."

Another sign stated, "Whatever happened to healing and hope for clergy sex abuse victims?"

The nastiest one, written in brilliant red paint, caused heads to turn: "Bishops are the real criminals."

Most of the protesters braved the elements and ignored the stormy weather. Their spirits were buoyed by the arrival of two local television stations.

A reporter for station WNLI jumped out of her satellite van and pushed a microphone in the face of a demonstrator, like a commander leading a battlefield charge.

"Could you tell me why you are here today?" she inquired, like a vulture scooping a story.

"We're here to let Bishop Campbell know that the pilgrimage for hope and healing after the murder of two priests is insensitive to victims of clergy sex abuse. There are hundreds in the Diocese of Islip whose need for healing has never been acknowledged, let alone invited to be part of a pilgrimage to restore their loss of hope."

The reporter moved on to another demonstrator and queried in the same manner. "What message are you trying to send here today?"

The man stepped out of the circle and engaged her, looking directly into the camera.

"I was sexually abused as a teenager for three years by Fr. Nikko Sardis. My family settled with the diocese out of court. This is a chance for me to have my day in court, to face everyone out there in the TV audience and ask them to stay away from this pilgrimage. Why are priest sexual abusers entitled to a pilgrimage when their victims are not even prayed for in their own churches?"

He started to get emotional, but quickly recovered. "I want to remind everyone that Christianity is founded on Jesus Christ as a victim. But when it comes to the Catholic Church, it seems to me they have the characters in this scandalous story backwards. I am here to say that is wrong, and the main character in the Passion story backs me up."

An equally aggressive reporter from WNAU snagged a demonstrator on the other side of the circle. He said, "I would like to hear why you are demonstrating here today."

His victim, a woman in her mid-fifties welcomed his question. She appeared to be drawn to the camera like a magnet to metal.

"I am here to call on Bishop Campbell to include some atonement for victims of clergy sex abuse in the pilgrimage on January 20th. That day would have been the 51st birthday of my youngest brother, Sebastian. My parents gave him that name because he was born on the feast of St. Sebastian. But he committed suicide at age eighteen after being raped and sodomized by Msgr. Joshua Carruthers for four years."

The reporter asked, more gently, "So you are your brother's voice today?"

The demonstrator didn't miss a beat. "His voice, and the voice of any other victims who lost their voices to sexual abuse by sick priests who have been protected and shielded by arrogant bishops."

This scene did not go unnoticed by the eyes peeking out of the fifth-floor windows of the Chancery Office. Bishop Campbell lost his temper, erupting like an active volcano.

"Tim, I want you to call the police and have these people removed. And while you're at it, confiscate and destroy those damn TV cameras." He spoke like someone without a shred of gospel compassion behind his Roman collar.

Tim was not destabilized by his boss's commands or threats. On the contrary, he left the bishop in shock, like a deer in headlights.

"They have a valid permit from the city to demonstrate. I for one think their cause is justified, and if you will excuse me, I am going down to meet with them."

As he turned toward the elevator, Bishop Campbell shouted one last plea: "You getting entangled in that mess down there will not help the situation. It will cast a grave light on the chancery and make us all look bad!"

His misguided attempt to change his secretary's mind with the guilt factor was about to backfire. As Tim waited for the elevator door to open, he turned and faced his boss square in the eyes and said calmly, "You're welcome to join me.'"

The bishop's face, filled with Irish fury, looked on the verge of exploding. "And what will happen to the pilgrimage if this is the kind of press we get?"

Tim held his hand in the seam of the elevator to keep the door from closing. Breathing in a new supply of courage, he kept his cool. "In the words of Rhett Butler, 'frankly bishop, I don't give a damn.'"

He stepped in, and the elevator doors closed.

Bishop Campbell and Leona Helmond stood speechless, as if their mouths had been glued shut. Msgr. Barnes cracked a subtle smile, as if he was thinking, "Way to go Tim!"

A few minutes later, Fr. Tim Cavanagh, personal secretary to Bishop John Campbell and grandson of the Long Island philanthropist Aishling Jane Cavanagh, walked out the front doors of the Chancery Office. His Roman collar attracted the cameras like vultures circling a deer carcass. He stood patiently to see what would happen.

Several of the demonstrators stopped walking and gathered around him. At that moment, he had a clear sense of what it was like for Daniel to step into the lions' den. But like the prophet, he leaned on the higher power that offered the spiritual antidote to fear. In the freedom of that choice, Tim gave his heart to trust and waited for Jesus, divine victim and healer, to place words on his lips that would be comforting and consoling to this flock of wounded and hurting people.

Part of him wanted to begin with the words of the prophet, "Thus says the Lord..." But he followed his heart, smiled warmly, and said, "Teach me how to walk with you in a way that will be healing."

Several caught the double entendre of the word "walk." They broke out into smiles. Some cheered. Others looked skeptical. Tim scanned the crowd and caught a glimpse of the many faces of the faithful, knowing in that moment that he had made the right decision to affirm their dignity just by standing among them.

☙ Chapter Thirty ❧

Fr. Tim Cavanagh

Tim decided to watch the evening news at Rosslare Park. The last thing he needed was to be alone. There was too much of the demon of that emotion in the files he had copied at Solitude. He watched with his grandmother, who could calm his inner demons with tea and an Irish smile. Before he turned off the TV news, Jane Cavanagh rose from her chair, walked over to him, and kissed him on the cheek.

"I'm going to recommend you for one of President Bush's Thousand Points of Light awards."

He smiled at her with the warmth of family love. "Thanks, but those stopped when he left office. Your kiss is better than any presidential award."

"In that case give me the other cheek."

Tim's cell phone rang. Jane must have suspected who the caller was, because she quickly excused herself.

"I'm calling to see if you need a media agent," Sam said, "or a new job recommendation, or police protection."

Tim adored how Sam could defuse his inner struggles with humor therapy. He was instantly lightened by her unique brand of caregiving and compassion.

"Actually, I was hoping to find someone who wears all three hats."

"Good luck."

He shared with Sam some details about his confrontation with the bishop that had taken place before he left and met with the demonstrators outside. He got deep and personal about stories they shared with him. He was already familiar with some of the names of the clergy abusers, but kept those details out of his conversation with Sam. He promised to meet with them as a group, and his grandmother had said the doors of her home were open to them.

"That's a wonderful thing for her to do," Sam said.

"Yes, that takes the pressure off asking Msgr. Quinn about using a room at the cathedral, thus not putting him in an embarrassing position. He called earlier to express his admiration for my prime time appearance. But I can't compromise his twenty year record at the cathedral."

"Can Bishop Campbell forbid you to follow through with meeting with them?"

Tim got quiet to ponder her question. "At this point my obedience is to Jesus Christ, who gave me the courage today to stand with victims, survivors, and their loved ones. I am now called to trust where He leads me on this new path."

Sam responded in kind, sharing in her own words an understanding of the pain that the demonstrators had shown earlier that day. However, she did not name her younger deceased brother, who could have been among the group if he were living.

"I'll walk with you and the victims any way I can. This might be a wake-up call from God for me to get out of the pew and practice the true meaning of Mass. I must confess, I haven't been so good at translating the worship piece into action."

Tim decided to defuse the serious tone with some levity "If you're confessing over the phone, is this call 'Dial a Penance?'"

"Only if some of your courage and compassion rubs off on me."

They chatted some more before Sam changed the subject.

"Your grandmother invited me and my dysfunctional family to her house for Thanksgiving dinner. I need to decline and I was hoping you would deliver that message for me."

Tim was ready to bargain with a counter-proposal.

"I'll be happy to, but for your penance you have to join me for a day of Christmas shopping in Manhattan the first week of December."

"I accept your penance. Maybe I should go to confession to you more often."

"Well, you know my cell number."

The mischievous Sam decided to pry before hanging up. "Are you spending the night there or going back to the cathedral?"

"I don't know. Are those my only two options?"

He knew she was grinning from ear to ear. She equaled his art of innuendo.

"Well, if you think of another one, stop by and tell me what it is."

"You can count on it."

They hung up, beaming like two children waiting to un-wrap, later, a surprise hidden in a gift box.

The Fixer

As per my instructions, compliments of FedEx in Dublin, I checked in at the New York Hilton Hotel on the Avenue of the Americas. So far, my contract has met all my conditions requiring first-class travel and accommodations.

After I unpacked and had a "wee bit of nap," as the Irish say, I took a taxi to the Port Authority building on the east side. The place reminded me of an indoor city under the constant glare of lights. Travelers were moving at different paces by clocks, timetables, and destinations. Everyone seemed to be multitasking with cell phones, iPads, tablet PCs, and a host of other electronic gadgets. Several distracted commuters walked into me, the result of texting and walking, and doing neither very safely. I pulled one guy back by his coat collar.

"Excuse me, but did I hear an 'I'm sorry' from you?"

He grunted some words that sounded like Russian. I released him, not knowing if he had apologized or cursed me.

I made my way to the locker area and found #118. It was not particularly large. The key that I had received turned easily. Inside was a medium-sized tote bag. I pulled it out and walked away, leaving the key in the lock.

I hailed a taxi and returned to my room at the Hilton. Once inside, I unzipped the bag and removed a garment that obviously hadn't been selected to accommodate my height—when I tried it on, it was at least six inches too long. Two other matching pieces completed the outfit. Wrapped inside was a .44 Magnum with a silencer attached, no doubt purchased on the black market.

I went online and found a tailor. When I called from the hotel phone, he assured me he could tailor my garment within 24 hours. Less than thirty minutes later I had gone in for my fitting and was back out on the street.

When I returned to my hotel room, I reviewed the instructions in the tote bag. I bristled at the requirement that I attend Mass at St. Sebastian Cathedral on the next three Sundays. I was a Catholic in name only and didn't frequent the company of hypocritical people who practiced piety one day of the week, then pissed people off the rest of the week.

My instructions included specific travel directions, along with a short list and description of certain noteworthy features inside the cathedral that were integral to setting and releasing the trap. After this early phase of the plan, I would be free to do whatever I wanted from Christmas to January 20th. I started pondering my options and decided that the warmth of Florida would be preferable to the cold of New York City.

Fr. Tim Cavanagh

I had trained and worked in spiritual direction long enough to know how to have a listening heart with this particular survivor group. Sr. Mary Louise Carberry had listened to the outpouring of my heart regularly, following the death of my parents and most recently with the inner turmoil the clergy sex abuse scandal had released in me. She had directed it on a path that had kept me internally free and centered on Jesus.

That was enough, but vital, for listening to and directing people whose hearts had been broken by institutional scorn and who were aching for some comfort and healing. My desire was to help them invite Jesus the victim into their experience as sexual abuse victim, then walk with Him to the place inside, where He would become their healer. Once there, I hoped we could celebrate the redemptive meaning in their suffering as Jesus did in the Resurrection. From there, I hoped they would discover how to live as survivors.

Granny was magnanimous in welcoming the group of survivors to Rosslare Park. She had Molly prepare snacks and beverages. Bach was secured in the kitchen to avoid interruptions. We assembled in the family room for appetizers, wine, and cheese, and time to get acquainted. As the group of sixteen engaged the traditional ice breakers, I quietly sat at the Knabe piano and started playing Marty Haugen's haunting song, "Healer of Our Every Ill."

As I began to sing the words softly, each began to find a seat as if on cue. When the song had worked its magic, a sacred sound of silence infused the room. I turned from the piano bench and addressed the group.

"Two days ago, on a rainy street outside the chancery, I asked you to teach me how to walk with you so that I can help bring some healing to your hurting lives. All I have to offer is a listening ear and a caring heart."

They reverenced my pauses as my heart formed the words on my lips.

"This isn't an AA meeting where everybody begins with 'Hi, I'm Tim, and I am an alcoholic.' This is my grandmother's home. And tonight you honor her and me by your presence. You have something in common that I don't share. You are all victims of clergy sexual abuse. I am sorry it has taken me so long to say, 'I am sorry about that.' Having said that, I wish to move on and say, 'Talk to me so that together we can find out how to move to a place on your path that will help you become a survivor.'"

A long silence hung in the air. It took a few minutes for the first person to speak up. Once she had become a storyteller of her experiences, then others followed. Some confined themselves to describing how the Catholic Church had exacerbated the hurt of the abuse by not offering any spiritual antidote; they drew a poignant analogy to the medical profession that so unquestioningly offered chemotherapy for people suffering from cancer.

As a result of being neglected and having their freedom to speak openly about their ordeal taken away by contract or otherwise, their spiritual tumors had metastasized into new lesions caused by years or decades of anger, disgust, intimidation, insensitivity and dehumanization. In near unison, they expressed that they had been treated like lepers by those who were charged with spiritual healing of their flocks.

All of our visitors agreed that sexual abuse had morphed into institutional abuse, and each had his or her own story of the insidious ways that had been carried out. Several commented that the bishops were better abusers than they were evangelizers. That might explain why church attendance was at an all-time low.

Others shared how the legal settlements had been masked as a new form of victimization. Several got specific and shared horrific details about their abuse. Some were paid to let priests perform oral sex, or to perform it on their abusers. Others were raped and had anal intercourse without protection. Two women shared how they were raped, then forced to shower with the priest, performing fellatio on their knees. All of them were told that if they squealed to parents, teachers, or authorities, nobody would believe them and they would only be hurting themselves. One victim said the priest threatened to strangle him if he ever said anything.

Tears flowed like rivers. I had removed all tissues from the room. It was a professional tool I had learned from Sr. Mary Louise when I began years of spiritual direction after my parents were killed.

The first time I cried with her, I asked for a tissue. Instead, she said, "I want you to reverence your tears, not dry them. I want you to let them flow. I want you to let them drop in your hands and feel them. I want you to taste the salt in your tears. Tell me where they're coming from inside."

The deeper I went to the source of my tears, the more I found liberation, freedom, and purification from anger and hurt. I had found God in the tears, and that intimacy eventually led to being awakened to a new call to help others do the same as a priest. It was a mystery how all that had been wiped out by my involvement in this current scandal.

Now, struggling with my love for Sam, and sitting in a room with victims who were hungry for human compassion and spiritual wholeness, I found myself at a different place on life's path. I had feelings for Sam that I could no longer deny. I had respect for victims I could no longer ignore. It was time to once again stand up on the side of where my new values were and stop hiding behind the security of a religious institution whose values I now questioned more than accepted.

I had become a conflicted Catholic, and the undercurrent of restlessness was something I wouldn't deny or cover-up. Doing that was the DNA of the power-hungry hierarchy, and something I was grateful the creator God did not weave into my genetic code.

I was in awe of the vulnerability of our visitors' wounded hearts. I was respectful of the depth of their anger. I said little so they could say more. I was learning something profoundly new about relating to them as a caregiver.

Ninety minutes later, we agreed to meet at Rosslare Park again in two weeks.

"There is something spiritually healing about this place; something mystical," one member of the group said. Many of the others nodded in agreement.

"Then I invite you to make your trip here a pilgrimage; not just an outward journey to my grandmother's house, but also an inner journey where you can recapture some lost hope."

I greeted each of them as they left, some with hugs, others with handshakes, and a few with what I hoped were healing smiles.

After I closed the front door, I leaned against it and pondered this initiating experience of God breaking into my life. I also considered its spiritual meaning, with the beginning of the season of Advent in one week.

Msgr. Joe McInnes

Msgr. McInnes knew what to expect on the other side of the office door before he knocked and entered. He smelled the remnants of a Cuban cigar. Then he noticed the unctuous look on the bishop's face. It was as ugly as a gargoyle perched on the side of a weathered medieval cathedral. As usual, Bishop Campbell dispensed with the usual pleasantries.

"Please tell me you saw yesterday's evening news."

The vicar general nodded yes.

"So, play the critic and give me your review of my secretary's media appearance."

"Is that why I am here?" Joe McInnes asked like a diplomat.

Bishop Campbell didn't appear amused. "You're here because I want your advice about whether to fire him as my secretary."

The vicar general pondered his response, carefully measuring his words. "Are you open to other options?"

"I am so damn angry that I can only see 'You're fired!' in my option column right now."

Msgr. McInnes paused to collect his thoughts so he could express them in a way that would somehow soothe his boss's bruised ego. The bishop gave him space to ponder before speaking.

"My instincts tell me, if you give Tim some distance between you and this crisis, he might present an option that would be a win-win for everyone."

"And what might *that* be?" the bishop asked with jackhammer speed.

Msgr. McInnes replied slowly. "He might resign."

Bishop Campbell sprang from his desk chair "I'll be damned if I give him the courtesy of resigning. He needs to apologize for his insubordination."

"And how will that help keep the Cavanagh money flowing through the diocesan pipelines?"

"I can't make a decision in this matter based on Jane Cavanagh's wealth and whether or not she continues to share it with the diocese. She is not going to hold me hostage."

"I am only suggesting that you be open to Tim's initiatives. If he offers to resign, and then negotiate the terms so that everybody wins."

The bishop didn't seem placated. He barreled on like a runaway train. "There is also the issue of his questionable relationship with that redheaded detective. I wouldn't be surprised if they're sleeping together. If that's true, it could be the end of his vocation."

Joe McInnes's thought was that a love affair would not be nearly as deadly to a priestly vocation as smoking Cuban cigars. Knowing better than to cross that boundary, he practiced strict silence, like a cloistered monk. Instead, he opined about Tim's private life.

"That's pure speculation, and even if it were true, and I for one don't want to know, then I credit Tim for choosing a woman over a man. The gay sexual preference has gotten too many priests in the diocese in hot water and left me having to clean up too many messes."

He made it sound like he resented being a clean-up man, but Joe McInnes was the rare one who was better at damage control than at causing the clergy messes in the first place. His temperament was more suited for resolving conflicts than initiating them.

"My sixth sense tells me he knows more than he's letting on," the bishop said.

The vicar general raised his eyebrows when he heard that statement. "What do you mean by that?"

"I mean he is noticeably quiet when we discuss the clergy's checkered sexual histories. It leaves me feeling likes he's been spying and hiding what he really knows."

The vicar general offered another perspective. "My sense is that Tim is unhappy with an office job, which is why we need to tread lightly with how we respond. It would be to our advantage to give him enough room to find a way out rather than trap him."

The bishop nodded in agreement. His forced smile betrayed sincerity while at the same time keeping details of Plan B to himself.

❦ Chapter Thirty-One ❧

Nora Owens

The climate change from the Caribbean tropics to the cold caverns of London made Nora bristle. Following a seven-hour flight from paradise to the chilly concrete world of the British capital triggered a body temperature change that she welcomed.

Nora loved the pulse of this city, glittering in a pre-Christmas mode. There was no other place she would rather be than holiday shopping at Harrods. The city and the store breathed with life.

She liked seeing the warmth of her breath collide with the cold air. She liked wearing designer coats, scarves, gloves, and full-length boots. They belonged to winter like blizzards at the North Pole. She liked maneuvering around dirty piles of snow on streets, like obstacle courses at the winter Olympics. Winter was not a disruption for Nora; it was necessary to the cycle of Mother Nature.

Winter triggered nostalgia in Nora that other seasons did not. It awakened her to memories of Nanette that warmed her inner life: the snowball fights at the orphanage, the taste of hot cocoa after coming in from outside, the noise of heat travelling through cold radiators, the feel of flannel pajamas and the piles of extra blankets for staying warm through the chilly nights.

Nora fondly remembered that something about Nanette's face and attitude had always made her sister glow in winter. Maybe it was because the sexual abuse tempered during the cold nights and days. What she remembered most was having more of Nanette to herself during winter than during any other season.

Nan's suicide in the spring of 1975 had robbed Nora of the most precious thing she loved. When that was taken from her, all she was left with was memories and revenge. Since then she had stopped drinking cocoa, stopped wearing flannel pajamas, and her inner child still bristled at the thought of snowball fights. It was no fun doing those things without your twin sister.

Within a day of arriving at her flat one block off Kensington Gardens, she began to make a list of things she needed in order to dispose of the last name on her list. They would be necessary for a new alias and for a plan that would be air-tight.

The Christmas shopping list would have to wait. She would become a Grinch first and set on a path to get what she needed in order to steal a life for a life.

Tim & Samantha in NYC

It was two weeks before Christmas. Scores of tourists were descending on New York City to view the elaborate holiday decorations and window displays and squeeze into the department stores and boutiques for their door-busting sales. Native New Yorkers Sam and Tim knew how to practice crowd control. Instead of shopping along the famed Fifth Avenue, they opted for the holiday markets as a festive alternative to the mega-stores and designer boutiques.

Tim and Sam started their hunt at Union Square. After browsing through a dozen kiosks, they took a break and stopped by the Gluhwein booth for a glass of warm, mulled wine, a staple at German markets.

Tim reminisced, "I tasted my first glass of warm mulled wine when I performed a concert in Munich about ten years ago. It actually tastes better here in the Big Apple."

Sam countered, "Doesn't everything taste better here in the Big Apple?"

Tim raised his eyebrows in a mischievous look. He grabbed her hand, and they walked leisurely over to Seventh Street to catch the train to Columbus Circle.

After stepping back onto the sidewalk of the city's Upper West Side, they blended into the army of shoppers. Sam stopped at a stall displaying screen-printed shirts. She pulled one off a rack to study it more closely. It was colorfully decorated with florals, sparkling crystal accents, and the word "Chocolate."

"My niece is a chocoholic," she said. "This has her name written all over it."

Tim searched inside the shirt to check the label. "It says, 'Made in Hershey, PA.'"

"The next thing you'll tell me is it comes with Hershey Kisses." She punched him playfully in the arm.

"Better than that, it comes with Cavanagh Kisses."

Sam paid for the shirt while Tim blew kisses to her just inches away from her ear. They walked on to another gift stall, where Sam picked up a zipper hoodie with a sundial embossed on the front in shades of brown, beige, turquoise, and deep reds. She looked at the price tag and sighed before placing it back on the rack.

Tim sensed her inner conflict. As she walked away he remained standing there. "This hoodie is saying it wants you as an owner."

Sam faked an excuse. "Tell it I'm sorry, but it's made in Nepal."

Tim stood his ground. "This may be the closest you get to Nepal."

"Now is not the time to discuss global consciousness," Sam retorted as she continued walking away.

He made a mental note to return and get the hoodie for her. He would have it wrapped and left under the Christmas tree with her name on it. He knew she would look as good wearing it as a model walking down a runway.

They stopped at an Italian cucina in the Village for dinner and enjoyed a bottle of wine while chatting about their shopping adventures. Tim decided to open up about his conflict and, at the same time, pop an important question.

He reached for her hand. "Sam, if I should resign from the priesthood and return to the piano as a career, would you marry me?"

The look on Sam's face spoke volumes. Tim didn't know how to read it.

"Help me out, Sam—is your look a yes or a no, or do you need a tiramisu to help you decide?"

Sam recovered and surprised Tim with her response. "How long have you been thinking about resigning from the priesthood?"

"Let's see, how long have I known you?" He started moving his fingers like a calculator. "Over a year."

"It's been that long for me, too."

Tim remained quiet, sensing she was going to say more.

"But, I wouldn't marry you because you decided to return to the piano," she said. "I *would* marry you because I was sure I loved you."

He reached out to lock her other hand in his. "Is that a declarative statement? Because if it is, you're the best thing that has happened to me, and from where I am sitting, marrying you will make best even better."

She curled his hands tighter into hers. "I'm open to talking about this some more," she said. Then hesitating, she changed her tone of voice. "No, make that 'I will be thrilled to talk about this.' But could we get through the holidays first?"

"Yes," Tim agreed. "I'll make it a New Year's resolution, and I'll even provide the champagne."

It was nearly 9 p.m. when they returned to Sam's house. Tim walked her to the door and opened it with his own key, since her hands were shaking from the cold.

"Come in for some coffee?" Sam asked with her unique smile that always disarmed him.

Faking an Irish lilt, he responded, "Make that coffee, tea, or me, and the answer is yes."

She grabbed his hand, drew him inside the warm house, and closed the door with her foot. They undressed each other with the speed of a wildfire and made love on the area rug in the hallway. Words were unnecessary; they spoke a blissful, silent language that only they could decipher.

It was nearly midnight when Tim returned to the cathedral rectory. His hope for a restful night's sleep was hijacked by restlessness about how to proceed with the next chapter in his life. Make that *their lives.*

Christmas holidays at Rosslare Park

Jane Cavanagh never celebrated Christmas during Advent. She preferred to host family and friends for her own version of the Twelve days of Christmas, starting on Christmas Day.

On Christmas Day, the family exchanged gifts and decorated the tree. It took an entire afternoon to turn a 15-foot blue spruce into an eye-catching and prize-winning holiday spectacle. It would remain the centerpiece of the grand hallway for three weeks.

The second day was spent hosting the children of the estate workers. Jane hired a magician and storyteller to entertain them and dressed up and played Mrs. Claus, giving each child a gift. This was her way of babysitting so parents could have some downtime on the day after Christmas.

On the third day Jane hosted her adult employees for lunch. At each place setting was an envelope containing a generous bonus.

On the fourth day of Christmas, she hosted young people from the neighborhood who were home from college for the holidays. Over lunch in the grand dining room and dessert in the family room, she sparkled, listening to their stories of college life and how they colored their hopes and dreams.

On the fifth day, she invited her neighbors for a happy hour. Wine and mixed drinks, cheese, crackers, fruit, and hors d'oeuvres flowed and mingled among guests dressed in traditional Christmas colors and new clothes fresh out of gift boxes.

Unlike the Creator, Jane Cavanagh did not rest on the seventh day. Rather, she hosted a New Year's Eve party by invitation only. The rules were clear to everyone: arrive by 8 p.m. sharp for drinks and appetizers, followed by dinner at 9, dancing from 10:30 until midnight, with departure at 12:05 a.m. drinking modestly was expected, with no one needing a designated driver to get home.

Jane was the happiest during the Christmas holidays. Her party animal instincts made her the envy of neighbors and an icon of respect to their children. Her activities fueled a new year's supply of happiness and contentment among her employees.

The entertaining came to a resounding musical end on the twelfth day. She hired a string quartet and four vocalists to lead her guests in caroling and wassailing as many Christmas songs as they could sing and play in 90 minutes. It always ended with the musicians and vocalists performing the Halleluiah Chorus from Handel's *Messiah*. No one left without tasting Molly's homemade eggnog and assortment of homemade Christmas cookies.

This year, Tim and his beloved date hung around after everyone else left. They relaxed in a small parlor on the second floor while workers cleaned downstairs.

Jane kicked off her Prada platform pumps, perched her feet on a foot stool, and stretched out in a Queen Anne chair. Tim and Sam sat comfortably on a love seat. Their bodies snuggled into each other like matching gloves. Sam was beaming, wearing Tim's gift of the zipper hoodie with a sundial for the first time.

Tim leaned forward and reached over to take his grandmother's hand.

"Well, Mrs. Claus, you've pulled off another memorable twelve days of Christmas. Who's going to carry on this tradition after you?"

Jane wove her flare for innuendo into her soft tone of voice.

"Well, I am hoping you and Sam can answer that question."

"Thanks for making this easy," he said, with a noticeable sigh and a wink. "Here's the plan you've been waiting to hear. I'm going to resign from the priesthood at the end of this month, return to the piano, and hopefully within a year, Sam and I will be married."

Jane shifted her focus to make eye-to-eye contact with Sam. Her grandson's future wife was aglow with happiness. She decided to cash in on that capital.

"And how much longer after a year will I have to wait for my first great grandchild?"

Tim decided to slow her down and bring her back into the moment. "First things first, Granny. We want to make sure you're okay with this."

"Not only am I okay with this, but I give you a hundred Irish blessings." Pausing briefly, Jane added, "Make that fifty, since a hundred Irish blessings could be dangerous."

Laughter led to hugs and tears. Jane walked to the wall behind her and pulled a bell cord. Ten minutes later, Molly appeared with pints of Guinness for all. Tim and Sam relived their evening in the Dublin pubs and the first night they made love in the Merrion Hotel. They had lost count of the rest of the nights of lovemaking since then.

Tim's date of transition would be Sunday, January 20, the feast day of St. Sebastian. After the diocesan pilgrimage to the cathedral, he would begin a new journey in his own life.

Basking in the delight of this company, he had no idea just how new that pilgrimage would be.

ᛒ Chapter Thirty-Two ᛒ

Fr. Tim Cavanagh

I always trusted my instincts more than I trusted playing by a game plan or a script, when it came to discussing serious matters. Submitting a letter of resignation from the priesthood to Bishop Campbell was a serious matter. Although I had just recently broached the subject with Samantha and Granny, I had certainly been wrestling with it for some time, with the help of my spiritual director.

Getting to a point where my interior life was becoming free to discuss it with the two most important women in my life was a prelude to breaking the ice with the bishop. It seemed like an apt metaphor to act on today, as a coating of ice had developed on buildings, sidewalks and cars—the residual effect of overnight rain that turned to ice as the temperatures plummeted. Our offices were closed due to the weather and hazardous driving conditions, so I buzzed him in his house next to the chancery.

I decided to take a comedic approach. "Since there is no ice indoors, but only a cathedral between us, I was wondering if I could see you."

He surprised me with an unexpectedly cordial reply.

"By all means, please come over. I have a few details to discuss with you about the upcoming pilgrimage of healing."

I took the back stairs down to the ground level of the rectory, opened the hallway door that led to the cathedral sacristy, knelt briefly at the foot of the Blessed Sacrament Chapel in the interior of the eerily quiet church, and opened my heart in prayer for courage. I then headed west through the choir room, opened a door, and walked down a long hallway. This passage was the "escape route" the bishop took when he wanted to avoid certain people or the press after Mass. I rang the bell before opening the door into the bishop's house.

He was dressed leisurely, though none of his secular clothing would make fashion news. He invited me upstairs to his suite. The live-in housekeeper, Sadie Breslin, appeared shortly after with refreshments.

John Campbell lived a modest lifestyle. He had never redecorated the bishop's house since occupying it for the past six years. Rather, he had spent his energy sending money to Rome and networking regularly with influential archbishops.

The furniture had not been replaced or changed for the past 20 years. We sat opposite each other in wooden chairs with faded and thinning cushions that could have been plucked from a 1950s movie set.

"What's on your mind?" he said.

I handed him my letter of resignation. He read it without revealing any emotion. Typically, John Campbell used sixty-two muscles in his face to frown, rather than the mere twenty-six it took to smile. He methodically folded the letter and returned it to the envelope.

"I am not totally surprised, since you have not been yourself lately."

I was taken aback by his uncharacteristic attempt at being caring, but I did not mellow. "I am not here to discuss not being myself lately. My resignation is final. I will stay on until the January 20th feast day and pilgrimage. At this point, the planning committee's work is complete. You can count on me to be there for the day. But after the 5:00 Mass, I will vacate my rooms at the cathedral rectory and live at Rosslare Park. I plan to take Msgr. Quinn to dinner sometime before leaving and explain everything to him then. I respect him too much not to tell him the story myself."

To my surprise, he kept the flow of the conversation going.

"And just what is the story?"

I took time to capture an image that would speak for me and hopefully turn a light on for him.

"My short life has only had two major chapters. The first was a brief career as a concert pianist. It ended with the premature deaths of my parents."

He respected my need to pause and gather words to express my thoughts.

"The second chapter has been a brief vocation as an ordained priest. It is ending because I can no longer square the double standards staring me in the face about the scandal. Within two months of seeing two priests murdered, we have planned a pilgrimage of hope. But after eight years we have done nothing to offer healing to the survivors."

I spoke my thoughts in a slow syncopation, not wanting to divulge the information to which I was privy regarding the two murdered priests' history of sexually abusing girls at Holy Comforter Orphanage. Nor could I disclose the bishop's own direct connection with the whole sordid mess.

"Also within two months of two priests being killed, we are planning a pilgrimage to honor them. And we're not including Terry Engals in that event. It leaves me asking, why are we hiding the obvious? Death is death, whether it is self-inflicted or murder."

I took a deep breath before speaking again. "The next chapter in my life will include a woman who has taught me things about love that never found their way into the first two chapters. I want more of what she has awakened in me and what she so unconditionally offers me in terms of happiness and fulfillment."

The bishop allowed me to pause and ponder how much more I wanted to say.

"Samantha Bannion has helped me discover new inner reservoirs of love that I never knew I had. She is a soul mate who I never found as a pianist or a priest. I have discerned she is worth giving it up because there is more for me to gain by making room in my life for her. And since the Catholic Church has made priesthood and marriage an 'either/or' choice, I now choose the 'or.'"

It was the bishop's turn to ponder. He took a deep breath before speaking.

"Would you consider a year's leave of absence first? A resignation is so final. A sabbatical or leave would give you some space for more discernment without closing the door to perhaps reversing things later."

I only needed a few seconds to formulate a reply. "I appreciate your offer, but I don't need a leave of absence because I don't need any more discernment. I am sure that God brought Samantha into my life. I need to trust God's calling me to discover a life that includes more of the two of them."

Sensing that his option was not persuasive, he emitted a deep sigh before speaking. "Very well, I am sad for you and for the diocese. But if this is of God, as you seem certain, then I can't stand in God's way."

He paused as if he wanted to say more.

"I appreciate your staying on for the pilgrimage in two weeks. I also appreciate your confiding your decision to Msgr. Quinn. That shows great respect. I will inform Ted Barnes and Joe McInnes at the staff meeting on January 21st. If there is anything else I can do to make things smooth for you, please let me know."

With that he stood and ushered me to the door. We shook hands in silence before I turned, walked down the stairs, and retraced my steps through the cathedral and back to my quarters in the rectory.

My departure seemed so sterile. The bishop was not one who warmed to hugs or other displays of affection. He was a church bureaucrat who satisfied the hunger for intimacy in his soul with the food of greater prestige and power. He would never reveal the truth that that hunger never went away. He simply continued to choose the wrong food to satisfy it.

Back in my room, I collapsed on my knees, repeating the prayer, "Thank you God," about fifty times. As I replayed the thirty-minute meeting in my mind, I admitted that I had just experienced a bishop who was a total stranger to me. His care for me seemed genuine, leaving me to ask, "Will the real John Campbell please stand up?"

I reached for my cell phone and called the person through whom God had helped me find new meaning in the words "thank you."

When Sam answered, the sound of her voice quickened my pulse. She melted my heart like the warm sun outside melting sheets of frozen ice.

"How did it go?" she asked with a concern for me that only she could show. Her voice pulsed with care, affection, and love.

I told her about the meeting and the image of a new chapter in my life with her in it. Since I couldn't get enough of her, we talked with words and pauses that left me feeling guilty for being so happy. She had recharged in me a desire to return to the piano as much as she had opened a new door for discovering the joys of love and intimacy. I never would have known these pleasures, had I not found them with her. The last year had been like living a second adolescence as a thirty-something.

I decided to pop another question and surprise her. "Is it too early to ask what you would like for a wedding gift?"

It was actually Sam who surprised me with her reply. "No, it's not too early, and promise me you won't laugh at my answer?"

I went through the whole "cross my heart and hope to die" thing until she was satisfied.

"I want you to write a song just for me, for our wedding, for our life as a married couple and for the intoxicating love that will keep us as two becoming one. You play other composers' music and sing other artists' songs. But I want a song we can sing when we dance alone, when we are high after making love, a song after making babies. When we teach it to our children, it will become a song they can sing for becoming part of the circle of our lives."

Her request left me speechless.

"Has the cat got your tongue, or are you beginning to write it in the quiet?"

"Maybe a little of each," I said, caught between her poignant request and the sense of pure awe she had released in me.

What have I done to deserve this woman? This was a question I kept to myself, but often pondered.

I said, "I love you and I can't wait to say that to you every night before we go to sleep and every morning when we wake up."

She repeated it to me before we hung up.

By noon the sun had melted the ice, while the fire of creativity in me was at a boiling point. I jumped in my car and headed to Rosslare Park. By the time I arrived, the lyrics to the song were in my head. I sat at the Knabe grand piano and let my heart set them to music.

Nora Owens

I breezed through customs following my arrival in Toronto. I decided to fly in coach class. It was one less flag to draw attention to myself.

The immigration agent never gave a second look at the picture of my new alias, professionally doctored in my passport. I decided to stay in the largest city in Canada for a week to give the U. S. intelligence network time to drop me from their radar screens. Their vigilance in tracking terrorists and assassins since 9/11 had raised the bar for counter-vigilance. But I was up for the game and succeeded at playing it by their rules.

I decided that my port of entry would be Philadelphia. The city of brotherly love was far enough away from the Big Apple to allow me to remain anonymous, yet close enough to get to NYC quickly via Amtrak. Knowing they already had a surveillance team casing my apartment house, I would stay overnight in a hotel before taking a Long Island train to Islip. Once there, it was just a short walk to St. Sebastian Cathedral where, hopefully, my mission would end with the murder of the fourth and final priest who had sexually abused my sister and me.

Once that was complete, I would retrace my steps and return to London within thirty-six hours. Then I would take the cremated remains of Nanette for a proper burial and hopefully begin to rest in peace myself. I needed to bury with her my history of the abused becoming an abuser—the abused becoming a murderer. I didn't feel at all guilty for putting four of them to death, considering how they stole my youth from me, how my sister was brought to her death, and how many other abuse victims might be spared. Knowing my actions would disqualify me for canonization by the Catholic Church, I could only say, "Shame on you for creating this scandal in the first place."

I carried some sense of closure, knowing I only had to account for ending four lives, compared with the longer list of sins that so many Catholic bishops had to account for in light of the thousands of innocent lives stolen. By protecting and shielding priest sexual abusers, then working overtime to cover it all up, they had lived a long line of sins, the seriousness and repercussions of which we could never fully measure.

I had come to believe that when that time of ultimate justice arrived, God would be on the side of the victims and would be merciful to me, as one of them.

The Fixer

I picked up the robe once the tailor was finished with it. He had worked a miracle, for after trying it on, I found it fit like a glove. I paid in cash, careful not to leave a paper trail.

I took one final stroll around Times Square before returning to my hotel room. Then I reviewed the instructions from my contract for the last time. Once I had memorized them, I shredded the two-page document with a pair of scissors. Not even a NYC forensic technician could reassemble what I could destroy without the help of a shredder. I dropped the shreds in different dumpsters as I walked the ten blocks to Penn Station.

I decided to order room service for my final night in midtown. Tomorrow was a travel day, then Sunday was D-day. In less than forty-eight hours, I would be back home in Ireland. By the time I set foot again in Belfast, my bank account would have quadrupled, my arsenal of guns would have diminished by one, and retirement would be within reach.

As I lay on the hotel bed listening to the weather report, I started to ponder a new title to replace "The Fixer." Maybe I would go back to using my real name. It might be a better fit for someone who would have earned the respect of being the newest millionaire in Belfast.

ᴄᴀﾉᴼ Chapter Thirty-Three ᴄᴍᴼ

Bishop John Campbell

The weather report was accurate. Snow started falling on Islip during the night. By 6 a.m., ten inches of it had turned the city into a giant white blanket. Bishop Campbell was not amused by this display of divine comedy.

How dare God cancel my pilgrimage. He kept his thoughts quiet.

Fr. Tim Cavanagh

The weather forecast was for clearing about noon, with sunshine and melting in the afternoon.

Morning Masses at the cathedral were cancelled. When Tim reached for his cell phone and saw the number flashing on the screen, he knew the bishop had other plans.

"I want you to get a press release out announcing a streamlined pilgrimage today with confessions at 3 p.m. and Mass at 5. People are welcome but should use caution about traveling."

Tim decided to acquiesce and not argue, sensing a bit of desperation in the bishop's voice about salvaging the pilgrimage.

"I will take care of that now."

"Please inform Msgr. Quinn of those plans. I will be there for the last hour of confessions and to preside and preach at the Mass. Obviously, I will be in my house if you should need me for anything."

Tim exchanged pleasantries before ending the call.

After typing a press release on his laptop and emailing it to five TV networks and ten radio stations, he called Samantha to alert her to a change in plans.

"God didn't change the bishop's mind. He has decided to salvage part of the pilgrimage with confessions at 3 pm and Mass at 5."

Sam seemed partially relieved. "The snow won't be cleared by then for a large attendance, so we'll only need a small police presence. I will make sure they dress in plainclothes."

"That will help in not drawing attention to ourselves. Because of the weather, Nora Owens may not show up. Has anyone seen her on their radar screens yet?"

"No, but she could be in Islip as we speak and so disguised that no one would recognize her." Sam sounded wary. "Has your schedule changed because of the weather?"

"I'm going to hear confessions at 3. Msgr. Quinn and the bishop are scheduled for 4 p.m., and then I'm free to be a watchman to make sure no one is murdered. I thought I would sit at the grand piano and play some soft, prayerful, sacred classical music."

"Alarm bells are sounding in my head, Tim. Make sure you do nothing but watch while playing the piano, and don't take any risks."

"I just plan to be another pair of eyes. I won't get in the way of anyone or anything, especially of any bullets if they start flying around."

"Okay, good." Sam sounded relieved. "I will be close by, though not clearly visible."

They chatted about how both of them wanted this to end today and hopefully without bloodshed. They both said "I love you" before hanging up.

Nora Owens

At the MacArthur Airport Hilton Hotel, Nora Owens sat glued to the television. Her initial gloomy expression turned to excitement when she heard the local news reporter announce that the Pilgrimage of Hope and Healing would take place today at St. Sebastian Cathedral, with confessions at 3 p.m. and Bishop John Campbell presiding and preaching at 5 p.m. Mass. The reporter urged caution for people traveling to Islip and assured everyone that the cathedral parking lot and sidewalks would be cleared of all snow.

Nora looked at the alarm clock next to her bed. It was 10:30 a.m. That left her a little over four hours to have breakfast, transform into her new alias, and get to the cathedral by 3 p.m.. She sprang out of bed and began her morning routine of physical exercises, followed by thirty minutes of yoga. She wanted to be physically and mentally fit for her final victory and her last confession.

Two hours later, she was laying out her clothes and applying the delicate facial features for her new alias. If they were looking for Nora Owens today, they wouldn't find her—not when she was wearing this face and these clothes.

The Fixer

At the Ramada Hotel in downtown Islip, the Fixer also cracked a smile about the media announcement for the pilgrimage.

"Let's get this over with so I can get the hell out of this sleepy town and back to Belfast," he murmured as he shaved his face.

Two hours later, he gathered his duffle bag, checked out at the front desk, and began walking the four blocks to St. Sebastian Cathedral. To avoid crews of people clearing snow, he had to shift from the sidewalk to the street and zigzag around the city snow plows.

As he approached the Chancery Office, he turned left into the parking lot and walked parallel to the cathedral. From there he made two right turns that brought him into a narrow alley and a nondescript door. He knocked on the door three times instead of ringing the doorbell. That was the signal for the occupant inside to let him in. He was escorted to another door that opened up on the hallway to the cathedral sacristy. He opened the duffle bag and changed into the clothes that would camouflage his appearance and his identity. In a calm and methodical manner, he applied the silencer to his gun and waited for the cathedral bells to strike 4 p.m.

The Pilgrimage

St. Sebastian Cathedral has three confessionals. The two on the east side were Reconciliation Rooms. They offered a penitent the option of either making a confession face-to-face or remaining anonymous behind a grille. Ten years ago Msgr. Quinn had ordered the traditional confessional boxes demolished and replaced with rooms that were tastefully decorated. The warmth and appointments spoke welcome and healing. They included a see-through glass panel as a security measure for both priest and penitent. That meant neither could accuse the other of any unjust indiscretion.

Thirty yards away on the west side was a traditional confessional recessed into the stone wall. Two long, grey, velvet drapes hung inside the entrances to the small cubicles designated for the penitent. In between was a slightly larger area for the confessor, enclosed with a full-length wooden door. Small acoustical tiles were hammered inside the door to help with sound insulation. The exterior had a traditional Pre-Vatican II appearance, built with expensive mahogany in a classic Revival style.

But this confessional had a unique feature unlike the others. A tunnel five feet wide and 20 feet long extended from the back and ran along the inside wall, from the priest's box to the Shrine of St. Sebastian. A thin wooden pocket door was camouflaged to resemble the faux marble in the shrine. This tunnel had been carved fifty years earlier by the rector at the time, who suffered from a serious bladder problem. He would escape from the confessional, use the rest room close by inside the sacristy, then return. Parishioners, especially the elderly, were very understanding while he relieved himself. The rector always thanked them profusely for their patience.

As the bells in the tower chimed at 4 p.m., Fr. Timothy Cavanagh exited the Reconciliation Room while holding the door open for Msgr. Quinn to replace him. By this time, a crowd of about four hundred people had gathered inside the cathedral. As Tim walked up the aisle to cross over at the cruciform, his eyes caught the shadow of a figure walking toward the confessional on the west side.

He recognized the back of the tall, erect bishop entering the tunnel, wearing a long black cassock with a shoulder cape etched in purple, a pectoral cross and chain dangling around his neck, and a scarlet skull cap. Two minutes later the confessional light was turned on from the inside.

Tim walked confidently toward the grand piano positioned outside the sanctuary, about fifteen feet from the Shrine of St. Sebastian.

As he opened the lid of the keyboard, he glanced over the congregation until he finally recognized Samantha. Her red hair was bundled inside a knitted wool cap that was pulled over her ears. It hid the ear buds that she and several other undercover police officers were using. She was sitting at the far end of a pew in a section to Tim's immediate right. In the event of any suspicious motions or sounds, she could sprint to the bishop's confessional in two seconds.

Sam's police skills kicked in as she scanned her zone with hawkish eyes. She was unaware of another set of eyes honing in on the confessional behind a vertical grille that separated the sanctuary from the sacristy. They were not police eyes, but were just as deliberately focused on the target as hers. This figure was partially obscured behind a life-sized statue of the Blessed Virgin.

Tim played Bizet's haunting "Agnus Dei" prayerfully, and for five minutes no one moved toward the confessional. Then a petite woman stepped out of a pew behind Sam. The detective eyed the short woman, who had cropped dark hair and was dressed in denim jeans, a white turtleneck shirt, a red Fordham University sweatshirt, a wool scarf around her neck, and snow boots. As she walked toward the confessional she reached inside a small knitted shoulder bag with her right hand. The figure standing behind the Blessed Virgin Mary statue noticed this gesture with radar eyes and quickly dialed a cell phone. She didn't know it vibrated inside the confessional. The penitent slowly knelt on a small raised kneeler.

"Bless me, Bishop, for I am a sinner. I'm going to commit murder today."

"No you're not, I am."

With that, the man on the other side of the grille, who was not the bishop, raised his .44 Magnum with a silencer and shot Nora Owens between the eyes. Part of her brain matter splattered against the back wall of the confessional as she fell against the thick, grey curtain, tearing it from its moorings. Her body tumbled out onto the terrazzo floor.

Chaos erupted inside the cathedral. Some people hid underneath pews while others rushed to the nearest door. Msgr. Quinn stepped out of the Reconciliation Room to check on the commotion.

Tim pushed back the piano bench and rushed to the aid of Nora Owens. Sam sprang forward to the Shrine of St. Sebastian. She pointed her gun toward the tunnel's pocket door and waited. Ten seconds later, it slowly opened. The figure backed out and just as slowly closed it. Then he faced forward. Sam's memory bank quickly computed that she was staring at the face of the Dublin stalker.

"Police!" Sam shouted. "Put down your weapon and get on the floor."

He hesitated, causing her to scream, "Do it now!"

He slowly bent over, as if to place the gun on the floor.

At that moment Tim raced up to Sam and said, "She's dead."

In the time it took to blink an eye, Sam deflected her attention toward Tim. It was enough time for the stranger to raise his gun with the precision of an assassin and fire two shots into Tim Cavanagh's chest. The priest dropped to the floor, bleeding profusely.

Without hesitation, her training kicking into gear, Sam fired four bullets into the assailant's chest. The bullets hit with such force they propelled him five feet back against the wall of the shrine. He collapsed with a loud thump, while his gun dropped from his hand.

Sam holstered her weapon and ran to help Tim. She pulled him tight into her arms, knowing that he was gravely wounded. Msgr. Quinn removed the shoulder cape from his cassock and applied it to Tim's chest, pressing hard to slow the bleeding.

"Oh God, no! Oh God, no," was all Sam could shout. It echoed through the vaulted church like a beggar's plea. She screamed into her radio, "Get the emergency medical crew here now!"

She rocked Tim in her arms, her tears flowing and her clothing bloody. She was living the final act of *Tosca,* holding her beloved in her arms.

Msgr. Quinn made the sign of the cross on Tim's forehead, spoke the words of absolution, and began praying Psalm 46.

Tim looked into Sam's eyes. He coughed blood and struggled to breathe, but managed to whisper the words, "You're the one." Then he went limp in her arms.

Sam held tight to his body and wailed in mourning. Inside the now empty cathedral, with sirens screaming outside, Sam and Msgr.

Quinn shed tears in the torment of the moment. Two police officers stood over them, feeling helpless.

Twenty feet away the assassin regained consciousness. With everyone's back to him, he gradually recovered his bearings and reached for his gun. A size-ten wet boot stomped on it. Detective Lou Perkins put the barrel of his weapon to the assassin's head and quoted his favorite movie hero: "Go ahead, make my day."

Two other police officers stood the assassin on his feet and put him against the stone wall. They tore open the black cassock fastened by Velcro. Underneath was a bulletproof vest. None of the four bullets Sam fired had penetrated his flesh. They cuffed him while Lou Perkins read him his rights, and he was led away to a police car.

Within minutes, St. Sebastian Cathedral had become a bloody crime scene. Within an hour, the medical examiner had removed Tim's lifeless body. Sam's coat, soaked in Tim's blood, was removed, bagged, and tagged as evidence.

Sam leaned against the wall of the shrine, painfully stranded between coherency and shock. Nothing anyone said could comfort her.

Msgr. Quinn sat on the piano bench, dazed and speechless. His bloody cassock cape was now evidence. Lou Perkins tapped him on the shoulder.

"Monsignor, have you recovered enough to drive with me to Rosslare Park? I am going to need your help in explaining this heartbreaking news to Mrs. Cavanagh."

Lou Perkins knew that a tragedy like this didn't call ahead. It wasn't in anyone's day-planner or neatly entered on the schedule in a cell phone calendar.

"Please give me a few minutes to freshen up in the rectory and get into warmer clothes," Msgr. Quinn said. "I also need to grab an envelope that belongs to her."

The medical examiner gave Sam a sedative. When it began to take effect, two police officers walked her to their car to drive her home. Investigators would defer questioning her until tomorrow, when, they hoped, she would be more coherent and able to speak about what she had witnessed.

Ten minutes later Detective Perkins and Msgr. Quinn were headed north. The cold night air and the dirty snow piles reflected the inner landscapes they both felt. Neither relished the mission of bearing eternally sad news to a loving and devoted grandmother.

Chapter Thirty-Four

The Funeral

Jane Cavanagh put her sorrows on hold as best she could in order to plan and orchestrate her grandson's funeral. She was all too familiar with the many details, as she had done this before for two sons, a daughter-in-law, and a husband. The poise and dignity she displayed would be talked about in Islip long after this tragedy.

She insisted on several conditions, including the cathedral as the funeral venue, the exclusion of Bishop John Campbell from the funeral, and the selection of Msgr. Ambrose Quinn as presider and Msgr. Ted Barnes as homilist. Her musical selections, the vocalists and a string quartet, were all carefully chosen in her grandson's honor.

An all-night vigil at St. Sebastian Cathedral brought a constant stream of parishioners, friends, acquaintances, family members, and strangers to pay respects during the wake for Fr. Timothy Cavanagh. When the church closed at 10 a.m. the next day to prepare for the noon funeral Mass, some four thousand mourners had signed condolence books.

In attendance at the funeral were the vice president of the United States, the mayor of New York City, scores of local politicians, and artists and musicians related to Tim through their musical bloodlines with Bach, Mozart, Verdi, and other classical giants. Responding to a personal request, a famous New York Metropolitan Opera soprano sang Andrew Lloyd Webber's stirring lament, "Pie Jesu."

Seated among the other mourners were dozens of common people whom Fr. Timothy Cavanagh had befriended and helped to heal as a priest and caregiver to the church's victims of abuse and neglect. Seated among them were young people in the Be-Sharp scholarship program funded by the Cavanaghs for musically gifted students. They wept without shame.

Noticeably absent was a redheaded Islip police detective. After days of speaking with her in an effort to share their need for comfort, Jane Cavanagh could not convince Samantha Bannion to attend. Even a visit to her home was not persuasive.

When Jane personally visited two days before the vigil and funeral, she found Sam a physical and emotional wreck. Her eyes were red and swollen from endless crying. Empty tissue boxes were strewn haphazardly around the living room. Pictures of their trip to Dublin lay scattered on the floor. A flattened pillow and crumpled wool blanket half on the floor indicated that Sam's life for the past week had been confined to an area no larger than a space on the couch. Empty coffee mugs were evidence of a liquid diet that had left her thinning if not emaciated.

Her inability to communicate coherently told Jane Cavanagh that Samantha's trauma was teetering on chronic clinical depression. Shortly after leaving, she called the police commissioner to personally ask for a professional mental health intervention.

Tim's private burial ceremony took place at the family plot at All Hallows Cemetery. In attendance were family, Msgrs. Quinn and Barnes, employees of Rosslare Park, and several police and emergency responders who had attended to Tim on the day of his murder. Jane invited them all back to her home for a late lunch.

While the mourners quietly dined in Jane's living and dining rooms, sharing stories of their encounters with Tim, Bach lay still at the foot of his master's piano bench. He periodically raised his head, only to sadly replace it onto his front paws. His floppy ears had fallen lifelessly against his furry head. He was slowly beginning to understand that the music had stopped.

In the early evening, when the house was once again empty and quiet, Jane turned on the gas in the family room fireplace. Almost instantly it warmed away a chill that had followed her like a ghost all day. Molly brought her a tray of hot tea and biscuits. She stayed a while and shared a reverent silence with her grieving but beloved Lady Jane. Then she kissed Jane on the forehead and left her alone to cherish her memories and stories.

Jane walked around the room and looked at every picture of Timothy, as if she were drinking a large glass of pride. She reached down to pat Bach on the head, then she sat on the piano bench and allowed her fingers to skip over the keys, hoping she could feel his touch and hear him speak to her through the ivories. Her eyes settled on two pieces of handwritten music resting on the lyre. At the top right was "Composed by Timothy Cavanagh." She read his name out loud as the composer. Then she read out loud the one to whom it was dedicated. She tried to hum the music in sync with the lyrics.

Her emotions opened up, and new tears began to flow. But this time she was crying tears of joy. Her beloved Timothy had left something behind for a very special person. This was the beautiful work of the grandson she cherished. She would call and share the good news tomorrow. As she collected the two sheets, she discovered underneath a CD in a white disc envelope.

She walked to the fireplace to turn off the gas. Her eyes caught a large white envelope that she had placed on the top of a small desk a few days earlier. She recalled that Msgr. Quinn had handed it to her the night he came to Rosslare with the shocking news about Timothy's death. That was six days ago. In the sorrow and hurry of planning the funeral, she had forgotten to open it.

The message on the envelope, written in her grandson's hand, said, "Msgr. Quinn – Please give this to my grandmother when the time comes."

Retrieving a letter opener, she slashed open the envelope and began reading its contents. In less than ten minutes she knew she would make a second call tomorrow to the district attorney's office.

᎒ᏗᎤ Chapter Thirty-Five ᎒ᏗᎤ

Assistant D.A. Judith Steiner

Judith Steiner was not accustomed to being interrupted in her office when she had no appointments. Her agitation was palpable through the intercom line when her administrative assistant buzzed.

"This better be good."

Keeping her cool, the secretary was not intimidated.

"Miss Steiner, Mrs. Jane Cavanagh is here to see you."

The assistant D.A. changed her tone of voice when she heard that name:

"*The* Jane Cavanagh?"

"Yes," the secretary replied, keeping her part of the dialogue brief.

Judith Steiner knew that Jane Cavanagh was in a league of her own and was entitled to being personally greeted. She was not the typical client to be treated with the usual protocol of "send her in."

"I'll be right there."

Placing her coffee mug on the credenza behind her executive desk, she swiveled her chair and headed toward the door, straightening out the wrinkles in her suit and instinctively smoothing her hair as she approached her visitor.

"Mrs. Cavanagh, I am Judith Steiner, please come in."

She invited Mrs. Cavanagh to sit at a chair at a small conference table, offered her a glass of water or coffee—which Jane Cavanagh declined—and waited a moment before she spoke.

"I would like to express to you my deepest sympathies for the death of your grandson. I was honored to attend his funeral Mass, which was a wonderful tribute to his many priestly and musical gifts. This part of Long Island has lost a great treasure."

277

Gracious as ever, Jane Cavanagh replied, "Thank you for your kind words, but I have something very urgent and important to share with you. I am only sorry I did not bring it to you sooner."

Intrigued, Judith Steiner watched as Jane Cavanagh retrieved a large, white envelope from her designer handbag. She placed the envelope on the table.

"On Sunday evening, the 20th of January, Detective Perkins and Msgr. Quinn came to my house to inform me of Timothy's murder. Before they left, Msgr. Quinn handed me this envelope, which my grandson had entrusted to him months ago. I put it aside to deal with my grief and plan his funeral. It wasn't until last evening that I opened it. It contains a cover letter from Timothy with specific instructions. I read some of the documents and understood why he directed me to deliver it to you. It is now for you and law enforcement to deal with these matters."

Jane paused, as if to re-group her thoughts. Judith Steiner remained quiet.

"On an unrelated subject, I would like to enter a confidential arrangement with you to pay for Nora Owens's funeral expenses. When the time comes, please call me at Rosslare Park to discuss the details."

The two women talked softly and respectfully for a few moments before Jane Cavanagh stood as a sign of her readiness to leave. Judith Steiner took the bereaved woman's hand and pressed it warmly.

"Thank you for coming to see me, Mrs. Cavanagh. I will be in touch soon," Judith said. She opened the door and told her visitor goodbye.

The assistant D.A. returned to her chair at the conference table, removed the rubber band fastening the envelope, and began reading. Less than an hour later she was on the phone with the district attorney, asking to see him about an urgent matter.

Sam Bannion

Detective Lou Perkins was questioning the Fixer in an interrogation room inside the county jail while Judith Steiner and Sam Bannion watched from the other side of a mirrored window.

Sam was still on leave, but the invitation to witness the interrogation was exactly what she needed. It would help to bring her closure and pull her out of a ten-day mourning period that had morphed into depression. Earlier in the morning, she had visited with her doctor concerning some unusual symptoms that alarmed her. A series of tests had confirmed the diagnosis. She needed to talk about this with a trusted friend, but deferred making the call until after witnessing the interrogation.

The Fixer sat in a metal chair wearing the standard issue orange cotton inmate overalls. His hands were cuffed and his posture was as stiff as a marble statue. His facial expression read, "Drop dead."

Detective Perkins sat across from him with a file in his hand. "Your real name is Fergus Craig," he said, watching the prisoner, whose hardened face never twitched a muscle. "You were born in Belfast on November 3, 1942, and lived on York Street with your parents and an older brother, Colum. You were baptized on December 1, 1942, at St. Aidan's Church. Your brother was killed by British forces occupying Northern Ireland during a raid on June 10, 1965. When you turned twenty-three you signed up as an undercover agent for the IRA and crossed paths with Sean Campbell, also known as Bishop John Campbell."

As the detective rattled off this information, placed in a brown file with the county seal embossed on it, the prisoner continued to appear like he was in an induced coma.

"Sean Campbell was ordained a priest in 1968, and from 1970 to 1972 he served as chaplain at Holy Comforter Orphanage in Dublin. During those years he sexually abused twin sisters, Nanette and Nora Owens. In 1978 he legally changed his name to John Campbell to help camouflage his past as he was promoted up the ladder within the Vatican City diplomatic corps.

"He ended up at the embassy in the United States in 1986 and became Bishop of Islip in 2002. When he made a choice to offer protection to Fr. Dennis Flaherty and Fr. Brian Manley within his diocese, both of whom had served as chaplains and were also sexual abusers at Holy Comforter, Nora Owens tracked them down—along with Fr. Michael Mulgrew—with the intention of murdering them all. You became the paid assassin of Nora Owens, and your contract was initiated by none other than Bishop John Campbell, her intended fourth victim."

Detective Perkins took a breath before uttering his final words.

"You have been charged with the murders of Nora Owens and Fr. Timothy Cavanagh. Both of these charges carry a sentence of the death penalty, and I wouldn't count on your boyhood friend coming to your aid. He has his own murder charge to deal with."

That last sentence prompted Fergus Craig to swivel his head and look up Lou Perkins.

"This is all bull," Craig said with a heavy Belfast accent.

Lou Perkins slid his chair back, stood, and looked the prisoner in the eye.

"If so, then it's going to be part of your daily diet until you get a lethal injection." With that he left the room, leaving Fergus to ponder changing his mind about a plea deal.

Judith Steiner and Sam Bannion joined Lou Perkins in the hall outside the interrogation room.

"Ready for act two," the assistant D.A. said, like a legal advisor on a movie set.

The three officers of the law drove ten minutes to the Chancery Office of the Diocese of Islip.

The Arrest

Leona Helmond intercepted the three as they stepped off the elevator, attempting to block their way toward the hall to the bishop's office.

"I don't know who you are, but if you don't leave, I am going to call security," she said with a nervous vibrato.

With her trademark calmness, Judith Steiner stepped within one foot of her and flashed her badge.

"I'm the assistant district attorney. This is Detective Sergeant Samantha Bannion and Detective Lou Perkins of the Islip Police Department. We have a warrant. I'm going to count to three, and if you are still in the way, I will have them arrest you for obstruction of justice."

Judith Steiner only counted to one before the Gestapo-style secretary turned into a timid kitten and stepped aside. They proceeded down the hall, and Judith Steiner opened the door without knocking.

Bishop Campbell was seated behind his elegant desk with Msgr. Ted Barnes seated in a chair to his left. The chancellor reacted to this surprising interruption by rising from his chair. The bishop remained seated, gazing at the intruders coolly.

Judith Steiner matched every ounce of his fake composure.

"Bishop Campbell, you are under arrest for the murder of Elena Garza."

Msgr. Barnes could not contain himself.

"Who the hell is Elena Garza?"

"Do you want to tell him, or should I?" Judith Steiner spoke directly to the bishop.

He deferred, seeming somewhat amused, gesturing toward her with his hand.

"This is your show."

The assistant D.A. spoke her lines as if she were in a courtroom.

"Elena Garza was a domestic worker at the Vatican Embassy, where John Campbell worked as a canonical advisor from 1986 to 1996."

Turning to face him directly, she continued speaking like a first-class prosecutor she was.

"You had a sexual affair with her and got her pregnant. She refused an abortion, so you murdered her and the child. It has been a cold case for twenty years, until we retrieved evidence you left behind—the remains of a Cuban cigar, which matches the brand you smoke. Thank you for disposing of your ashes here in the chancery. Once they became garbage, they became evidence to shed new light on this cold case. And I am sure that once we swipe your mouth, your DNA will be matched to the fetus."

Judith Steiner stood over Bishop Campbell, staring directly into his face. "You are also under arrest as an accomplice to the murder of Nora Owens."

Once again, Msgr. Barnes erupted in shock.

"God Almighty, who is Nora Owens?"

Judith Steiner continued her monologue with relish. She was enjoying putting the fear of Almighty God in this ungodly man.

"Nora Owens and her twin sister, Nanette, were raised at Holy Comforter Orphanage in Dublin, where Fr. Sean Campbell, Fr. Dennis Flaherty, and Fr. Brian Manley served successively as chaplains, and where they each took turns at being habitual sexual abusers of the Owens twins and countless others.

"After Nanette committed suicide, Nora made a pledge to take her revenge on the three of you, as well as Fr. Michael Mulgrew in Boston.

"You were going to be her fourth victim, and she would have succeeded if you hadn't paid Fergus Craig to impersonate you and kill her. Once you figured out that Nora Owens was the killer of Mulgrew, Flaherty, and Manley, the pilgrimage was all a ruse, a trap designed to lure her to you, and where you hired someone else do your killing."

Msgr. Barnes had to visibly restrain himself.

"Good Lord, I don't want to know who this Fergus guy is." Then turning toward the bishop, he said harshly, "For that matter, who the hell are *you*?"

Bishop Campbell barked at his chancellor like a bulldog, "Shut up Ted."

Judith Steiner then changed her focus as if turning a page in a law book.

"You will also be charged with orchestrating a criminal cover-up of a sexual abuse scandal in the diocese. We have Fr. Timothy Cavanagh to thank for that evidence, as well as your connection with Holy Comforter Orphanage. He was very selective in the documents he copied from inside the filing cabinets hidden deep in the basement of Solitude, as well as the information he secured in Dublin."

When faced with that revelation, Bishop Campbell released his full fury on her. "These stories are bull without much evidence. As for Fr. Cavanagh, he was disappointing as a secretary and a man whose emotions got in the way of his being a protector of the church."

Sam bristled at the bishop's critique of Tim. "I believe what you mean to say, John, is that Tim was the protector and you are the criminal."

The bishop became visibly agitated at being addressed by his first name. Ignoring her indicting words, he continued to assail Judith Steiner while pointing to Sam.

"As for Fergus Craig, since *this* detective shot and killed him on January 20th, your prosecution case has no witness."

Samantha stepped forward and stood elbow to elbow with Judith Steiner, who nodded. It was now Sam's turn to enlighten the bishop.

"You left the cathedral too soon, Bishop, from your hiding place behind the statue of the Virgin Mary. Fergus Craig was wearing a bulletproof vest underneath the robes you left for him in a locker in the Port Authority, along with a .22 magnum obtained on the black market. You underestimated his resourcefulness. Yes, I did shoot him, but I did not kill him. He is in the county jail blabbering about you like a biographer. The thought of a gurney and a lethal injection has a way of turning killers into chatterboxes, regardless of their terrorist training."

With that, all color drained from the bishop's face, leaving him looking like a corpse.

Judith Steiner had the last word. "Detective Bannion read him his rights and cuff him."

In desperation, Bishop Campbell said to Msgr. Barnes, "Call the diocesan attorney now."

Ted Barnes marshaled all the courage he could. "You're entitled to one call when you get to jail. Call him yourself, since I don't even know who you are."

Barnes swiftly left the office as if fleeing an advancing fire. His friend had betrayed him beyond belief. His handcuffed boss and the three law enforcement officers followed behind.

Sam Bannion

Sam's call to Jane Cavanagh was long overdue. It had been three weeks since Tim's murder, since Sam's withdrawal from life. Her trauma, her grieving, her depression, her guilt over not being able to protect him, her struggles with once again being alone and having no one to help her fight the demons—she found herself emotionally overwhelmed.

Tim was her demon-slayer who had selflessly brought the power of his lovemaking, his humor, and his healing to her inner wounds. Now he was gone, leaving inside of her a black empty hole that she stared at with nothing reflecting back at her. It was time to ask another Cavanagh to help her fill that hole.

On a surprisingly mild February day, she dialed the number in her call log.

"What a nice surprise to see your name on my cell phone," Jane answered.

Jane Cavanagh always shared an unconventional way of saying "hello" to Sam. This time, her voice was like wireless therapy, and her words cast a magic spell over Sam.

Sam responded in a mellow and apologetic voice. "I'm sorry I behaved badly and dropped off everyone's radar screen."

"Well, welcome back." Jane steered the conversation in a different direction. "When can we meet? I have something to give you from Timothy."

Hearing his name sent chills through Sam's body. She pulled the cell phone away from her mouth to muffle her tears. At that moment, she hesitated, thinking her timing was wrong for this call with Jane. Two seconds from hanging up, she took a deep breath and harnessed new strength to stay on the line.

"And I have something to give you," she said softly, almost a whisper.

"Can you join me for lunch at Rosslare tomorrow?" Jane asked. "Food, company, and Guinness are good for grieving Irish women. That is one of the wisdom sayings I learned from my late husband."

Sam chuckled softly and felt the effects of her humor like a rainbow after a storm. "Yes, I accept your invitation, but only if I can bring something."

Jane's reply left her in total wonder.

"All right, but also bring a large capacity for surprise."

Only after they hung up did Sam realize that those words also applied to the surprise she had to share with Jane.

The next day Sam arrived for lunch fifteen minutes early. During the drive she had listened to a classic Billy Joel CD. As she entered Rosslare's circular driveway, she ejected it and replaced it with Brahms' *Piano Concerto #2 in B-flat major,* her favorite piano concerto Tim had played for her. As she enjoyed the magical sounds of the first movement, she sat in her car surveying the grand house. She let the music quietly speak to her of all the memories linked with Tim.

She remembered her first visit and her last visit as if they both were yesterday. She remembered the clothes he wore, his dark hair, his classical swagger, his captivating green eyes, and the mesmerizing music he played on the piano. She remembered his affection for Bach and his humorous interplay with Molly. She remembered their first kiss upstairs at the pre-concert party and his glow during the Twelve Days of Christmas gatherings. She breathed in the memories like new oxygen for her recovery.

Jane had the door open as Sam walked up the front steps. Instead of greeting her with a brief hug, she held Sam for a long time. No words were spoken. Their arms wrapped around each other and the flowing tears said all they needed to say and released what they needed to release.

Instead of escorting Sam to the dining room, Jane diverted into the family room.

"I asked you to bring a large capacity for surprise, and I can't wait to give it to you."

She walked toward the grand piano and lifted two pieces of sheet music from the lyre.

She sat across from Sam and spoke to her with a gleaming sparkle in her eyes. "One week after Timothy's death, I found this on the piano. It is a song he composed and dedicated to you. I can only assume you know the rest of the story."

When Sam saw the title of the song, she began to sob. Jane put her arms around her, pulled her into an embrace, and gave her all the time she needed to weep.

After she composed herself and dried her tears, Sam spoke in pauses.

"The last words he spoke to me before he died in my arms were the title of the song—'You're the One.'" She caught her breath and struggled to continue. "He spoke the words with such love in his eyes, but I didn't know what they meant until now."

Again, she paused to dig deeper for courage. "On the day he asked me to marry him, he also asked what I wanted as a wedding gift. I said I wanted my own song that we could sing as a couple."

Sam gazed at the music, blinking to clear the tears from her eyes. "I wonder what it sounds like," she whispered.

Jane Cavanagh walked back to the piano, picked up a CD, and brought it to Sam.

"He made it easy for you, Dear. He recorded it in his own voice."

Jane's revelation brought more tears, but this time they were mixed with laughter.

"He thought of everything," Sam said softly.

"I know you are eager to listen to it," Jane said, "so let's have lunch first, and then you can be alone with the song in your car when you leave."

"I can't wait that long," Sam said as she reached over to touch Jane's arm. "This would be a special moment if we listened to it together."

Jane's smile spoke approval. She went to the stereo and inserted the CD. Moments later she was sitting next to Samantha on the sofa, listening to the music and following the lyrics. They both cried softly as they heard Tim's voice serenading them with a gift they would treasure forever.

When it ended, they hugged without words. Tim had said all that needed to be said in his song.

Jane turned the stereo off and ejected the CD. "Samantha dear, would you like to go to the dining room now?"

Sam rose, but she took Jane's hand and led her back to the couch.

"You'd better sit down. I can't wait to share some news with you."

With that, Sam reached into her shoulder bag and handed Jane a large envelope preprinted with the name and address of the Suffolk County Medical Center.

Jane removed the glossy diagnostic imaging inside, and asked, "What is this?"

Sam turned the obstetric sonogram counter-clockwise and pointed to the figure hiding in it.

"This, Jane, is your new great grandson, Timothy Stafford Cavanagh."

Jane's eyes widened with glee, and she shouted, "Oh my!"

The two women hugged and cried and laughed over the two precious gifts bequeathed to them by the man who was so precious to both of them.

Their mood over lunch was joyful. When they had finished, and before Jane waved goodbye to Sam, she handed her a key to the front door. Sam and her child, Tim's baby—Jane's great-grandson—would come and go through it for years to come.

Sam shivered in the cold and got into her car quickly, turned on the ignition, then placed the CD in her sound system. Her heart soared and fresh tears flowed as she listened again to Tim's voice:

"I dedicate this song, 'You're the One,' Opus 1, to the love of my life—Samantha Bannion."

She dried her tears, driving and listening to the soft opening chords, hearing Tim's sweet voice singing the lyrics. She smiled through her grief when she detected a mixture of both Brahms and Bruce in the chords and rhythm.

As she left Stony Brook and headed south, Sam sang it with him, as together they taught it to the child growing within her. The song was working a miracle in her heart as she felt Tim say to her, "May your life be good again."

She patted her belly, stroking the new life growing in her womb, and said softly, "Someday, Tim, we will both drink to that."

❧ The End ❧

❧ You're the One ☙

Words by: Paul Mast
Music by: Alex Marthaler
October 1, 2011

1. True love, like a precious stone is hard to find,
    Until I found it with you for the first time,
    Kissing and hugging,
    Holding and cuddling.
    Once words I only spoke,
    But in your eyes I see new hope,
    That with you, true love can be mine.
    Refrain:
    You're the one who brings a smile when I am sad.
    You're the one who heals my hurt when I get mad.
    You're the one who teaches me to sing,
    When things go wrong.
    To remind me,
    You're the one.

2. I like the new me you've helped me to become,
    More tender and soft like a symphony of one,
    One movement in your arms with ease and grace, then,
    Moving closer, dancing face to face,
    Find a new me, a new us, in your warm embrace.
    Refrain:
    You're the one who brings a smile when I am sad.
    You're the one who heals my hurt when I get mad.
    You're the one who teaches me to sing,
    When things go wrong.
    To remind me,
    You're the one.

To listen to a recording of the song, please go to the website:

www.gospelsoftretreats.org

and click on the link for "You're the One."

Author photo by http://bechetphoto.com/

ᴄᴀ⅋ About the Author ᴀ⅋ᴄ

I am humming the tune to the song *"Getting to know you"* from the award-winning musical *The Sound of Music* as I share some pieces of my life story as the author.

I was born in Dover, (Kent County) Delaware in 1946 and raised in Clayton. It was our version of Mayberry where the sheriff walked the streets, without Barney Fife, and chatted with citizens on their front porches. Radar wasn't on the screen then. My four siblings and I helped each other with homework, passed down our clothes, which miraculously seemed to fit, went on family vacations in a Plymouth station wagon without car seats, rode our bikes and played with friends around town without the threat of child predators. It was an idyllic time when bullying was not part of our vocabulary. We were raised to look after the elderly, mow their lawns, ran errands and shovel snow from the churches, pharmacy and doctor's office as gestures of community service.

Our parents were modest people, and not celebrities. My father was a truck driver who worked hard and steadfast to care for the needs of our family. He lived his 91 years of life, fully. My mother was a high school graduate who lived her entire 87 years in her hometown. Being from what Tom Brokaw named, *The Greatest Generation,* they lived frugally in a pre-credit card era. They both had adventurous spirits. We all inherited their DNA for being travel bugs.

Back then Sundays were special days in our home. We went to Church, ate dinner at the dining room table, or traveled to visit family in Maryland, Pennsylvania or Virginia. Ferry boat rides and crossing long bridges, made getting-to-know aunts, uncles and cousins, an adventure long before Travelocity.com was born.

Strong religious practices and attending Catholic high school sowed the seeds of a vocation to the priesthood. Following ordination in 1972, I began to network with many new friends I had met in different parish assignments. In 1979, I suffered a bad case of *Burnout.* Thanks to an understanding bishop, I treated it with a return to graduate school. Sixteen months at Fordham University was wonderful conversion therapy. Studying the stage theories of human development, alongside the RCIA, *(Rites for the Christian Initiation of Adults),* opened new interior doors for me, to the stages of my own faith development.

Back then I was an avid tennis player and a fan of baseball. During my two summers in the Bronx I occasionally enjoyed a Yankee's game at the famous house that Ruth built. I began to harbor a dream of someday having a candy bar named after me.

After graduation at Fordham, I thought my school days were over. That's when I began to find enjoyment in reading novels. I credit Mary Higgins Clark, a fellow Fordham graduate, with unleashing that passion in me. I have her entire collection of novels signed and proudly occupying the top bookshelf in my home.

In 1983, I returned to graduate school at The Catholic University of America. This heavily academic program helped me develop skills as a critical theological thinker. One of my course papers was published, opening new doors that I found exciting.

In 1990, I began doctoral studies at the University of St. Mary of the Lake in Mundelein, IL. Learning from a biblical master like Eugene LaVerdiere and a storyteller-mystic like Jack Shea was a life-changing chapter in my personal and professional life. Doors were opened to the world of spiritual direction. During these three years it was a special grace to cross paths and be inspired by the prophetic leadership of Cardinal Joseph Bernardin. I will always cherish the memories of our encounters.

In 1996, I returned home to my diocese with three graduate degrees. In 1999, I completed a Certificate in Spiritual Direction at Neumann University in Aston, PA. Little did I know then how all that theological learning and ongoing spiritual growth would impact a new ministry of serving as spiritual director with victims of the clergy sex abuse scandal unfolding in our diocese in mid-2002. Companioning with them through their emotional trauma was the equivalent to a spiritual trauma for me. It was my own version of *"the dark night of the soul;"* a spiritual metaphor of interior growth, beautifully captured as a canticle by the 16th century Spanish Carmelite mystic, St. John of the Cross.

I had to dig into a deep inner well to help their healing while keeping myself from spiraling into darkness and despair. Having my ears and heart opened wider than ever, I began to confront some interior struggles with the human dimensions of a flawed religious institution. The thing that saved me was falling in love with Jesus Christ as victim. This was the new spiritual piece I offered the victims as Jesus offered it me.

Two things complemented my journey of interior freedom. First, it certainly helped around that time that television had moved into the "reality TV" genre. That's when I unplugged the TV and fed the right side of my brain by re-visiting the Victorian novels of Jane Austen, the Bronte sisters and Charles Dickens. I also fed a hungry soul by re-reading the spiritual masters of the Carmelite, Jesuit and Benedictine traditions. Second, for the past nine years I have served as Chaplain at St. Gertrude Monastery and the attached Benedictine School for Exceptional Children. Located on 500 acres in the rural area of the Eastern Shore of Maryland, this pastoral setting offered the kind of quiet environment where God could be encountered as a divine caregiver. The Benedictine

Sisters and the special needs children were 200 good shepherds nurturing my wounded soul back to health. I sing the praises of these women religious and specially gifted children for so freely sharing their love that became channels of grace.

From 2008-2010, I wrote and published four articles, in major Catholic periodicals, reflecting on my experience as a spiritual director with clergy abuse victims. I found a voice to weave the fruits of my spiritual conversions into preaching, workshops and major addresses with different church groups.

Many of those who I have inspired, with my own spiritual story around the scandal, encouraged me to write a novel. I began seriously doing so two years ago. It was a leap of faith as I was unfamiliar with the world of fiction. But, I have learned over the years how to clear out the voice of fear whenever it triggers static with the nurturing voice of confidence. Once I did, new doors opened interiorly. I leaned on trust that the combination of years of education, along with growing a creative religious imagination, made it a challenge I was ready to accept.

The most exciting thing about writing *Fatal Absolution* was creating the characters and weaving a plot that gave their personalities and flaws, their behaviors and choices, authenticity. I hope you befriend them, and engage them, in such a way, that a story about love, romance, scandal, conspiracy, murder, injustice and justice, threaded together with a gentle interplay of classical and rock music, becomes a parable about the threads of redemption woven into your own lives.

It will be a special grace, if someday, our paths cross so I can rejoice in your stories of redemption as, I hope, you rejoice in the story of redemption hidden in *Fatal Absolution.*

I considerate it a blessing to let you *"get to know me"* through some of the major chapters and verses of my life story I just shared.

Now that you have come to *The End,* I hope you will find new energy to embrace life with the kind of hope and courage that helps you reconstitute the story of "you" as an autobiography of *New Beginnings.*

For more information about Paul G. Mast, please visit:

www.gospelsoftretreats.org